Claire McGowan grew up in a small village in Northern Ireland. After a degree in English and French from Oxford University she moved to London and worked in the charity sector. She is currently the Director of the Crime Writers' Association.

After spells in exciting places like France, Oxford, China, and Kentish Town, she now lives in Tunbridge Wells where she tries to pretend she's not midde-class by laughing at the middle-class things she overhears and putting them on Twitter @inkstainsclaire.

Visit her website at: www.clairemcgowan.net

THE LOST

When two teenage girls go missing along the Irish border, forensic psychologist Paula Maguire has to return to the home town she left years before. Swirling with rumours and secrets, the town is gripped with the fear of a serial killer. But the truth could be even darker. Surrounded by people and places she tried to forget, Paula digs into the cases as the truth twists further away. What's the link with two other disappearances from 1985? And why does everything lead back to the town's dark past — including the reasons her own mother went missing years before? As the shocking truth is revealed, Paula learns that sometimes it's better not to find what you've lost.

CLAIRE McGOWAN

THE LOST

Complete and Unabridged

CHARNWOOD
Leicester

First published in Great Britain in 2013 by
Headline Publishing Group
An Hachette UK Company
London

First Charnwood Edition
published 2014
by arrangement with
Hachette UK
London

The moral right of the author has been asserted

A catalogue record for this book is available
from the British Library.

ISBN 978–1–4448–1841–3

Published by
F. A. Thorpe (Publishing)
Anstey, Leicestershire

Set by Words & Graphics Ltd.
Anstey, Leicestershire
Printed and bound in Great Britain by
T. J. International Ltd., Padstow, Cornwall

This book is printed on acid-free paper

For Oliver

Prologue

'Imagine all of you went missing.'

She waited until they were all listening, putting down their pens on top of blank paper pads, sitting up straight. Light filtered in through the dusty blinds of the room.

'Every two minutes in this country, someone disappears — that's over 200,000 a year.' She paused so they could take in the numbers. They were listening now; attentive. Mostly middle-aged men, a few women dotted here and there. Nobody younger than her.

She clicked the next slide. 'Research shows we can divide the missing into four main groups. If we take a hypothetical one hundred people — all of you here — statistically, sixty-four will have gone missing voluntarily. Money trouble, family breakdown . . . many reasons.' *I can't go on. I just can't bear it any more.* 'Around nineteen in the hundred will drift away. People in this category typically have weak societal bonds, addiction problems — drugs, alcohol.' *Envelopes piling up in a hallway*, Return to Sender *scrawled across the name.* 'Many in these groups will come home again, or be found safe years later.'

She clicked again, and in the dark they scribbled down her words. 'And some people

1

don't mean to go missing. They just get lost somehow, on the way to the shops or the bingo hall. They may not remember who they are, where they're meant to be.' *Something slipping out of your pocket, a loss you don't even feel until it's too late.* 'This group makes up sixteen out of the hundred.'

Some in the audience had begun to count, and she could see they knew what she'd say next.

'This leaves the one per cent. Among the missing, this is the one who didn't want to go. Who knew exactly where they were going, and remembered their own name. The reason this person disappeared is what keeps me awake at night. Who took them? What happened? *Where are they?*'

She could see them nod, taking notes, and she stopped and put down her laser-pointer, and didn't say the rest, what was really on her mind when she ran these numbers and figures. *When I think about her — which I try not to do — I hope she wasn't in the one per cent. But sometimes, I must admit, I hope she was — because otherwise, it means she wanted to go.*

1

Berkshire, September

There was no point in running.

Everyone knew that. The response team knew, crouching in the early dawn. It was the first morning it had felt really cold, and a wintry sun tinted the windows of the vans where they huddled. The reporters half a mile off in the village, doing hushed live broadcasts, they knew. *'As police move in to search for missing Kaylee Morris, hope is fading fast . . . '* Even the girl's parents, staring at blank walls back in the police station, squeezing the blood from each other's hands, they knew too, deep down. After a month gone, taken on her way home from school, the police weren't likely to find her alive. A body, maybe, for the parents to bury. Better than not knowing. Gentle lies that she hadn't suffered.

No, there was no point in running up the damp field to the ramshackle cottage on the hill. But when the lead officer silently lifted his Hi-Vis arm, she was out and moving too, over the wet ground. Her feet squelched, red hair tangled in her face. Ragged breaths tore her lungs. She reached the trees and crashed through, branches ripping at her face, and only stopped when strong arms pinned her.

A voice in her ear. 'Where the *hell* are you going? I told you to stay put!'

She struggled. 'Please. I have to!'

The policeman's face was kind between his helmet and bright jacket. 'Let it go, Paula. You've done your bit.' Ahead of them, dark figures took up silent positions round the cottage. Paula sagged and gave up. The sky was streaking pink with dawn. Overhead, the trails of planes to Heathrow, oblivious. And up in the house, a single light was burning.

★　★　★

At times like this, Paula liked to focus her eyes on a jokey plaque someone had pinned up behind the boss's bald head. *You don't have to be mad to work here, but it helps.* Was it possible he'd put it there? Could there be a spark of humour somewhere inside the red-faced man who was currently reading her the riot act? She tuned in from time to time, just to keep the thread of what it was she'd done.

' . . . don't know how many times I've told you come to me first, don't go haring off to the middle of nowhere, somewhere not even in our JURISDICTION . . . '

The rhythm was almost soothing. Blah blah blah blah blah BLAH blah.

' . . . once again taking it upon yourself to enter a crime scene, when, if I may remind you, you are *not* a police officer, Miss Maguire — and yes, I am calling you Miss on purpose, you can put that in your employment tribunal and smoke it, because let me tell you, you'll get short shrift . . . '

4

Paula sucked on the nail she'd split running into the bushes. The fount of adrenaline was still pumping under her ribcage, and outside she could hear muffled cheers and pops as her uniformed colleagues celebrated. Because unlike her, they were actually supposed to go to crime scenes where convicted rapists were holding abducted girls hostage.

' . . . all very well to sit here with your little theories, look at the messages on Facebooker or whatever it is — well, let me tell you, that's not how we work here.'

Paula lowered her hand. There'd be no time to grow the nail back for the weekend. 'Look,' she broke in. 'I know I'm not supposed to go to crime scenes. But I had to see her. I had to see her come out.'

He gave a grunt of irritation. 'I don't make these things up to try you, Miss Maguire. There's a reason we have rules and regulations. You're supposed to have a desk job. What would I tell your family, if you were injured?'

Paula stared at her shoes until the pricking in her eyes subsided. If she cried in front of him, she'd never forgive herself. 'But we found her, didn't we? We found her safe.'

The boss had run himself down, like a wind-up toy. 'Yes. We did find her.'

'So.' She glanced at her watch. 'Official warning, full report, that sort of thing?'

He grimaced. 'Full report by eight a.m., with your deductive reasoning set out. But the warning . . . ' He gripped his pen as if it gave him actual pain to speak. 'The parents are very

5

pleased, of course. Very positive PR for the force. So in the circumstances . . . '

'Right.' She was getting up. 'So in conclusion, you don't want me to go to crime scenes?'

'No, Miss Maguire, you must not go to crime scenes, ever, ever, EVER. Unless for some reason I tell you to. Which I won't, after today.'

'If you say so.' She moved to the door.

'*I'm not finished.*' She turned round. 'Please — sit down.'

When Paula reluctantly sat, he fixed her with his flinty eyes, exasperated. 'This has to stop, Paula.'

'I know.'

'You have a consultant post, yes? Forensic psychologist? We aren't covered to have you in dangerous situations. I believe we've been over this. And over.'

'I *know.*'

He seemed to think for a moment, then sighed and slid a letter across the desk, neatly squaring it off. 'That came for me today.'

She glanced at it, scanning the text. 'About time, I suppose. They want your help?' As one of the country's most advanced missing persons departments, they were often asked to consult for other forces.

'They want you.' *God knows why*, his raised eyebrows said. 'Seems you've made quite the impression. What was that paper you gave at the York policing conference — 'The Psychobabble of the Lost' or something? Earlier this year, if I recall.'

She didn't react. ''Psychopathology: A Case

6

Review in London's Largest Missing Persons' Unit'.' Or 'this shithole here', as it was also known by most of its occupants.

'Hmm. Well, it must have worked — they want you to help set up a cold case review team.' He threw a folder over; making a breeze that ruffled her hair. 'Given that you haven't entirely . . . *meshed* here, I wonder if perhaps a move sideways — '

She didn't look at it. 'I'm not going back.'

'I thought you'd jump at the chance. It is your home town, isn't it?'

'I live here now.'

'It's a good opportunity. I hear there's reams of old unsolveds over there. Not to mention however many thousands vanishing each year.'

'Six,' she said. Her blue eyes held his bloodshot ones. 'Six thousand missing every year in Ireland. Sixteen a day, on average.'

He gave a grunt of something that might have been satisfaction. 'And a little bird tells me your father's not been well.'

She shifted restlessly, hating that he knew things about her. 'He broke his leg, but he's OK. He doesn't need me.'

He spoke as if he'd planned the words carefully. 'I'd have thought you'd be quite keen on this kind of work, Miss Maguire. With your family history.'

Her face clenched. 'If you think that, Inspector, you've another think coming.'

'Just take the damn file. At least consider it. I feel it would be a good outcome for you. And for me, if I'm perfectly honest.'

She took it, but her eyes didn't leave his face. 'Is that all?'

His pen was getting mangled. 'I just have to ask, Paula — '

'Yes?'

'How did you know? How did you guess, that she wanted to go with him? That he didn't take her at all?'

Paula thought about it. 'Inspector — have you any idea what it's like to be a teenage girl?'

'Is that supposed to be funny?'

'No. Well, I don't think I can explain it, then. See you later.'

'I prefer *sir*, Miss Maguire.'

She called over her shoulder, making her red hair bounce. 'I prefer *Doctor*.'

Behind her she heard the snap as the boss's pen broke in two.

★ ★ ★

Outside, Paula was washed in the glow of a happy incident room, sleeves rolled up and discreet cups of corner-shop fizz circulating under desks. Not really allowed, but it wasn't every day a girl was abducted by a sex offender and brought home safe and sound. Beyond the tinted windows of the Rotherhithe station, even the Thames was lit with sharp autumn light, as if joining in the celebrations. Photos of Kaylee smiled down from every wall. Paula had been picturing her all this time as a cheerful girl: the pink scrunchie, the frizzy dark curls. Not the snarling young woman they'd found in the cottage, hair bobbed and bleached out of recognition.

'Not even a scratch on the girl!' It came out *gurrrl*, as relief sharpened DS McDonald's Edinburgh accent. He squeezed Paula round the shoulder. It was McDonald who'd brought her to the scene, when she came to him with her theory, waving the internet history Computer Crime had got off Kaylee's pink netbook, saying they had to go now, they had to rescue her. Paula knew she was supposed to go to the boss first, but there hadn't been time. There was never time, not when you had to find someone at all costs.

'It was this one here,' McDonald called to the team. 'When she said, How do we know Kaylee's even *been* abducted, it just clicked. We were going at it all the wrong way. And then you said, Go back to the girl's computer, see what she searched for, and there's the cottage in her history, and she's in it, right as rain. Which is more than can be said for my DC.'

'Is he OK?'

'Bit of a shiner. It's not often your rescuee belts you one.'

That was true. The girl hadn't been restrained when they brought her in; why would she be, poor, kidnapped Kaylee Morris? She'd lunged across the station at the officer handcuffed to her 'fiancé': paedophile, rapist, and suspected murderer Mickey Jones, forty-three — AKA *hotmickey18*, as he'd posed on the site where they'd met. Kaylee was fifteen and two stone overweight, but before anyone could reach her she'd given the DC a black eye, screaming, 'Let him go! He loves me! He's the only one who cares about me. I hate you all!'

Which was nice, after the month-long, multi-million-pound investigation, posters in every shop in London, TV appeals, all trying to find the supposedly missing girl who wasn't even lost.

In the incident room, the DS slapped Paula's back. Never a touchy-feely man, he seemed almost giddy with success. All that time looking for the girl. Hoping she was alive; sure she was dead. 'Tell them how you worked it out.'

'Ah, no — '

'Tell them! It's brilliant.'

Reluctantly, Paula looked around at the team. 'It was all in your reports, really. I just did the analysis. That friend of hers who said Kaylee was desperate to 'lose it' . . . you know. The Pill prescription you found in her room.'

'And the rest — tell them!'

'The offender profile. Mickey Jones. His previous record — he'd always approached the women first. Tried to talk to them, then lost his temper when they weren't interested. He doesn't look to hurt, this one — not at first. He looks for *love*.' She suppressed a small shiver. 'You see?'

They looked blank, all except one of the new Community Liaison Officers, WPC Singh. Her voice was soft. 'They were planning it.'

Paula nodded. 'There you go. It made me think — maybe she was *planning* to go off with him. Maybe he didn't abduct her at all. So if we checked her internet searches . . . '

10

The DS was shaking his head. 'And we found her safe and sound. Never thought I'd see the day. Bloody great work — proud of you all today.' He pointed at the file in Paula's hands. 'See you got the Ireland offer then.'

She shrugged. 'Allen just wants rid of me.'

McDonald didn't deny it. 'Well, have a drink, lass, you deserve it.'

'He wants his report.'

'Ach, let him wait. Take a moment, for God's sake.'

'I can't — too much work.' That wasn't the real reason Paula couldn't celebrate with cheap wine and cheer, but it would do. She retreated to her own glass cubicle and closed the door, took a deep breath. Tried to clear her mind of how the girl had shrieked as they tore her from Mickey Jones's arms, and the man's crazy, jittering eyes as they locked him away.

Paula jumped as her door swung open again, bringing in a babble of happy voices.

'McDonald says drink this.' One of the PCs was putting a plastic cup on her desk. 'Amazing, isn't it? Everyone's dead chuffed.'

The officer — what was his name again? — leant against the wall, and she watched his long legs stretch out. Andy, was that it? 'Yeah. It's great.'

Andy, if that was his name, had lovely eyes, blue as police sirens and blatantly checking her out. 'Hey, eh, Paula? You fancy a drink after work, maybe? Celebrate?'

How old was he? Twenty-seven, twenty-eight? A few years younger than her, she was sure. She

11

looked down at her broken nail. 'I don't think so. I'm a bit manic here. Maybe another time.'

He was too open. He was thinking, Is she saying no, or is she really busy? She watched confusion slide over his face. He said, 'All right. Catch you later.'

'Bye.' As he went out, her expression changed. Really, she hadn't time for all this. Kaylee Morris was found, but the in-tray groaned with those who were still lost. She placed Kaylee's file on her right, under OUT, and lifted the next case off from her left. Picking up the flimsy cup, she took a swig of the cheap sour wine, and set to work.

★ ★ ★

The next day's dawn was colder, mist leaching in from the Thames and creeping up to the windows of Paula's Docklands flat. She watched it from the sofa, her tea grown cold. It was only seven but she'd been awake for hours. Papers were scattered all around her towelling dressing-gown.

A male noise came from the bedroom, a throat-clearing nose-blowing sort of noise, and out came PC Andy, wrapped in a very small towel. He ducked his head, shy. Despite his good looks and strapping frame, she'd realised last night he didn't do this very often. That was a shame. It made things easier if they did.

'Up already? Didn't hear you stir.' He ambled over.

She swirled the grey tea round her cup, embarrassed at how she'd peeled herself out

12

from his heavy arm and escaped to the living room. He was a cuddler — who'd have guessed? 'I'm not a great sleeper, sometimes.'

'No? My mum takes these tablets. All herbal, so it's healthy, like.'

Paula sighed. Could she get him out without making breakfast? The pale light of dawn highlighted his ribbed stomach, the strong arms grasping the towel. Muscles shifted in his shoulders and she sighed again. 'Sorry, Andy. I've got paperwork.'

He peered over her shoulder. 'That the Ireland thing? What is it, cold cases and that?'

'Yeah. There's a big problem with it over there — lots never got solved, with the border and everything.'

'Sounds like a wicked opportunity.'

'Does it? I think sometimes the past is better left alone.'

He looked surprised for a moment. 'But I thought — '

She shut the file. 'Anyway, I'm not going.'

'Well.' He held the towel awkwardly. 'Can't say I want you disappearing anyway.'

She stood up. 'Sorry. I've got to get some work done.'

'Ah, fair enough.' He looked about him. 'Do you know where my — ?'

'Here.' She pushed his jeans across to him with her foot. 'Your T-shirt's in the kitchen.'

'Right.' The backs of the policeman's clean ears were turning pink. God, he was nice. He bumbled into her small strip of kitchen with his towel, knocking into the fridge and dislodging one of the magnets. A photo fluttered down like a dead leaf. 'Crap, sorry. Clumsy.' He picked the photo up. 'That's your mum, is it? She looks just like you.'

Paula was already moving towards him, but she steeled herself not to snatch it back. 'Just put it on the side, would you?' When he did, she slid her hand over the smooth surface of the photo, covering it.

He cleared his throat. 'Right, I best — '

'Yeah. You know the way out, don't you.'

When she heard the door shut she placed the picture back on the fridge, adding an extra magnet in the shape of a strawberry. She wiped his prints off with the sleeve of her dressing-gown. Paula looked at the picture for a long time. Another girl found safe, that was good. But once again she was realising it would never be enough.

2

Two Weeks Later
Northern Ireland, October

'Shit!' Paula's foot slipped on the clutch of the rented Ford Focus. When agreeing to drive herself from the airport, she'd forgotten she hadn't been behind the wheel in nearly ten years. But in a way it was good to think about the terror of accelerating, rather than dwell on the rest of her circumstances — stuck in a long queue of traffic from Belfast International Airport (a somewhat grand name for the building set low and squat among green, fertile fields), heading south, south to the border town among the hills that she'd left years before. She was drumming her fingers on the steering wheel and wishing she smoked just for something to do. Growing her nails had been futile. She'd bitten them to the quick again, unable to stop once she knew she'd be coming here. Coming home.

It was raining, of course. It was only October, but it was Northern Ireland, and the chill mist crept up to the car and under her skin, making her shiver. She finally got on the motorway, luckily quiet at this time of day, and tuned the radio to local news. Voices filled the car, rich and heavy like clods of soil. That made her shiver too, the memories returning like ghosts.

15

She'd never wanted to come back again, but here she was following signs to the border, to Ballyterrin. Twenty miles. The radio voices were arguing about the new policing Bill, devolving final powers to the Police Service of Northern Ireland — a different name to paint over the murky past. Politics saturated daily life here, just like the insidious rain. Acned teens on the side of the road, they'd be able to tell you the names of all the local politicians and exactly what was wrong with most of them. Old men in pubs, mums pushing buggies, schoolgirls. Everyone watched the news here, fierce and avid, ready to pounce.

Here already were the hills around her home town, the rolling mountains veiled in rain. It must be a beautiful place, people always said — people who didn't have to live there — and she always shrugged. Scenery was one thing, twisted hatred another. And the past was still everywhere, creaking with spectral life.

As Paula inched into the town, the traffic heavy as always, she saw her first sectarian graffiti. *Sinn Féin*, it said, in bold green. *We deliver*. Underneath someone had scrawled Pizza. Funny, unless of course they got their knees shattered for it. As she watched, a council employee was painting it out with thick white emulsion, slapping on layer after layer until the green was wiped out.

She'd never wanted to come back again. But somehow, here she was.

★ ★ ★

'Jesus, Mary, and St Joseph. Is that wee Paula Maguire I see before me?'

'It is. Hello, Pat.' Not so wee now, Paula was nearly a foot taller than the small woman hugging her to an acrylic-covered bosom.

Paula manoeuvred her bags into the front door of her childhood home. It was exactly the same dark poky space, walls lined with family pictures, going as far as 1995 and then stopping dead. The same smell of Pledge and cooking. By rights the family should have moved far and often, designated legitimate targets by the local IRA, but they'd stayed — just in case *she* came back and they weren't there. It was common, in families with one member permanently lost. The hope that kept you rooted to the spot.

'Now let me see you.' Pat shepherded her into the also poky but slightly less dark kitchen, its brown seventies fittings unchanged. It overlooked a small passage that ran from the front of the semi to the strip of lawn at the back. That was where Paula had seen the man, all those years ago. On what had been the last day, though of course she didn't know it — you never do. If she closed her eyes she would find the layout of this house etched there: downstairs the kitchen and front room, upstairs the bathroom and two small bedrooms. And that was even without the police diagrams they'd made her study over and over.

Pat was nodding at her. 'A wee bit peaked from that dirty city, but you're looking well, pet. That's a lovely jersey you've on you, is it M&S?' She stroked the soft cashmere.

'Eh — no.' Paula wasn't about to tell Pat how

much the jumper had cost. 'How is he?'

'Like you'd expect. Not used to taking it easy. On you go, I've a pot of tea waiting.'

She was suddenly nervous. It was far too long since she'd seen him, a few strained visits to London and one failed holiday together in the Lake District. Why hadn't she seen him more? He was stretched out on the sofa in the parlour, which still had its plastic head-cover on from when it had been bought in 1980. The year of Paula's birth. A cabinet was lined with china kittens, gifts from Irish seaside towns, cut-glass statues of the Virgin Mary.

'Hello, Daddy. Are you well?'

'I've been better.' The man on the sofa was approaching sixty, still tough and rangy but for the cruel metal cage pinning one strong leg.

'God, it's bad, isn't it.' She winced at the metal cutting into her father's flesh.

Pat hovered in the doorway. 'They said he twisted the bone right round like a corkscrew. Three months he's to wear it.'

'Ow. You'll be off your feet a while, then.'

'I'll be bored out of my mind, Paula.' His arms were folded, eyes fixed on the muted TV, which played the early evening news. A boring affair now the almost-daily shootings, bombings, and kneecappings were in the past. Mostly.

'How did you even break it this time, Daddy? You never said.'

'It was my fault,' said Pat.

'It was not indeed, Patricia. It was me fell like an eejit. Patricia wanted some old boxes out of the attic — '

18

' — for my project, Paula — you know, the town history.'

'So I go up the ladder — and doesn't it break clean under me. Came down on me leg like a ton of bricks.'

Pat clucked. 'You were never right anyway since that first accident, PJ.'

Paula remembered the circumstances, the way her father had first hurt his leg, and pushed it away. She couldn't think about that now.

PJ made a grumpy noise. 'Well, I'm still in the land of the living, thank God. I'll just have to sit and wait.'

'And here's Paula back to mind you! It was lucky you got that job too, pet. Sure didn't it all work out for the best.'

'Lucky' wasn't the word Paula would use. She had made her mind up to say no to the job — though she took the file out every night for two weeks to look at it — when the call came in. *If you can come now, we need you. Something's happened.* And something had. Big enough to draw her back, send her to Gatwick for a budget flight, on the way home to the town she'd promised never to set foot in again. The excuse was she'd be looking after her father — if, in fact, anyone could look after the hulking ex-policeman, who was 'PJ' because in the old Royal Ulster Constabulary it hadn't been wise to advertise your Catholic name of Patrick Joseph.

Pat was still fishing. 'How long are you back for, pet?'

'Not long,' she said quickly. 'It's a consultancy gig, is all. I'm just over for this one case.'

19

Pat grew sombre. 'Those poor wee girls. Please God you can help find them.'

Paula said nothing. She hoped so too.

'I'll be on my way, so.' Pat was fussing round for her sensible navy coat.

'Ah, stay,' said Paula and her father, almost in unison.

'I'll leave you to catch up, and I've to make Aidan's tea. He's coming round to programme the Sky yoke for me.'

'Oh. How is Aidan?' Paula felt she had to ask, though really she wasn't sure if she wanted to know.

'Ah, he's grand. You know he got the Editor's job last year? Well, he knocked the drinking on the head after that.' Did Paula imagine it, or had her father made a 'humph' noise? 'I'll tell him you were asking for him, pet. Bye now.'

Great. Now Aidan O'Hara would think she gave a damn what he was up to. Paula had known Pat O'Hara all her life, since the day she was born, in fact, and wouldn't hurt her for the world. Pat and John O'Hara had been her parents' friends, their only friends really, and when they came round for dinner they sometimes brought their annoying son, Aidan, who pulled the heads off Paula's My Little Ponies. But that was a long time ago, before what happened to John O'Hara and — all the rest. Now it was just Pat and PJ left, living in the same town, popping in on each other, and Aidan had grown up even more annoying than he'd been at seven, in a variety of new, adult ways.

When Pat left, the house seemed to sag, silent

and damp. PJ stared at the TV.

Paula cleared her throat. 'Will I pour the tea, Daddy?'

'Aye, good girl. I'll take a wee bun too, if Pat left some.'

Tea. Would Ireland have ground to a halt without it?

* * *

As Paula went to bed that night at the shocking time of 9.30 p.m. — she'd completely run out of things to say — she saw the leg-breaking boxes lined up along the narrow landing, old and mildewed. She knew what was in them. They hadn't been opened in nearly eighteen years.

'You're all right up there?' Her father, who'd refused all help to get up the stairs, called to her. 'You want a hot-water bottle?'

It was freezing — PJ didn't believe in central heating until at least November — but she said, 'I'll get it myself, if I'm cold. You rest yourself.' Back in her single bed. Back with her chipboard desk, her Anglepoise lamp. The walls still marked in Blu-Tack from where she'd had her posters — Take That, first time around. Early Boyzone. Then later Nirvana, Pearl Jam.

Paula rooted in the lower drawer of the desk — set squares, dried-out pens — and it was still there. The framed picture showed a teenage Paula, sulky in Adidas sports clothes, with the same red-haired woman from the photo in her London kitchen. It was the last picture ever taken of her. At least, as far as they knew.

Every time Paula came home she felt it again. It was stupid. Of course *she* wouldn't be here — hadn't been here in years. But somehow it was always a loss just the same.

3

' . . . co-ordinate our strategy with other cross-border units, and work together to improve outcomes on missing persons . . . '

Voices were already coming from the conference room as Paula rounded the corner, feet tripping on the thin grey carpet. Bollocks, they'd started without her. First day and late already.

'God! Sorry!' She burst into the room in the small building that housed her new team. 'That Market Street traffic's got a whole lot worse, hasn't it?'

Blank faces round the table. Four, five people. 'Dr Maguire?' The man standing at the whiteboard was tall, fair-haired, a laser-pointer in one hand. 'Please, join us. I'm Guy Brooking. I'm with the Met Police, but acting as consultant here for a year.'

Her new boss; the Englishman abroad. Paula sank into a plastic chair as the faces stared at her. 'Sorry to be late. It's just . . . the traffic's worse than I'm used to.'

Guy Brooking spoke smoothly. Paula stared at her bitten nails, shy of all the new people.

'Now you're here, Dr Maguire, I can introduce the team.' He gestured fluidly round him. 'The Missing Persons' Review Unit was set up several months ago — you've read the files?' She nodded, hoping there wouldn't be questions. 'Then you'll know it came from a report into

23

Ireland's very high number of unsolved missing persons' cases, and a recommendation from both sides of the border for an all-island response to the situation.' Around her Paula felt a subtle slump in the other team members; clearly they'd heard this many times before. 'Our role is to examine the old unsolveds, and where applicable advise the relevant local police force on reinvestigation, with the aim of successfully reducing our statistics for outstanding cases.' The man talked like an official report. He went round the table with his laser-pointer, indicating an older man stuffed uncomfortably into a nylon suit. 'This is my deputy, Sergeant Robert Hamilton. He'll be taking over the operation once we're up and running.' The sergeant had the air of a man who'd worn uniform all his life; Paula recognised it from her father.

'Avril Wright's our intelligence analyst, shared with the regular Police Service of Northern Ireland.' Guy pointed to a scrubbed-looking girl. 'She'll be helping us out with research and data management. DC Gerard Monaghan is attached to the local PSNI station.' Young, scowly, clearly Catholic from his name. 'And joining us from the *Garda Síochána*, Fiacra Quinn. I'm sorry, is that right this time? *Fay-kra?* Fiacra's our liaison on all cases south of the border.' Also young, pink-faced, the only one to risk a small smile at her.

Paula quickly worked it out from the names, an unfortunate but unavoidable habit ingrained in you when you grew up along the border. They were being led by an Englishman and a

Northern Ireland Protestant, probably ex-RUC. The rest consisted of a female civilian analyst (Protestant) and a male detective (Catholic), plus one from south of the border. She wondered how long it had taken someone to come up with that balance of religion, nationality, and gender. The two young men wore shirts and ties, Fiacra's askew, un-ironed, Gerard's in razor-cut creases over powerful arms. Avril Wright was in a neat skirt and lilac cardigan. Paula wished she'd bothered to iron her own outfit of white shirt and black trousers, what she normally wore to the office.

'And everyone, this is Paula Maguire — do you prefer Doctor?'

'Er . . . Paula is fine,' she said, floored.

'Paula is a chartered forensic psychologist. She's made quite a name for herself in a London Missing Persons' Unit, and she'll be working alongside us on strategy and analysis for our current caseload.'

'Paperwork, you mean.' This muttered from Gerard Monaghan. Paula gave him a look; he'd be trouble, this one.

'Yes, but also some direct interviews and assessment. We've specifically brought Paula in for her expertise on missing teenagers — you may have seen the coverage of the Kaylee Morris case in London a few weeks ago. Paula's insight was directly responsible for recovering that girl alive.'

Paula smiled nervously round the table, wondering if she should say that Kaylee's life probably hadn't been in danger. Not then, anyway. She said nothing.

'So.' Guy Brooking clicked his pointer and the white wall glowed with colour. 'I'll cut to the chase. Paula, as you know, we've brought you in because we've got an unprecedented situation. Given the gravity, this unit has been asked to help with a current investigation.' The face of a girl appeared; smiling, straightened dark hair, a cluster of spots on one cheek. 'Cathy Carr's been missing for a week now.' He clicked again. Another girl, a different school uniform, her chestnut hair longer and wilder. 'Majella Ward's been missing for three.'

'Wait,' Paula interrupted. 'That wasn't in the files. She's been gone *three weeks* and you're calling me in now?'

Guy shuffled his notes. 'She was part of the travelling community, I understand. Majella's school said her attendance had always been poor, and the family failed to report her missing for some time.' He saw Paula's face. 'Perhaps a ball was dropped — but we're on the case now. There's been a terrific response from the town. We've had volunteers out every day, searching the fields and woods, and the local diving club even offered to drag the bay for us.'

'But nothing?'

'Nothing so far. Both girls have gone, and as far as we can see there's no connection between them. They'd never even met.'

Paula nodded; she'd made it that far in her reading. 'The original job offer was to review old cases. I need to ask — what's changed now? Why is the unit leading on this?'

Glances went round the team. Guy answered quickly. 'There's a few reasons. They're short-staffed at the main station right now — the DCI's off with some family issues.' From the corner of her eye, Paula thought she saw Gerard Monaghan frown, and wondered what the story was there. Guy went on: 'And as I said, in such a serious case it was felt we were well-placed to co-ordinate, make sure the right organisations talk to each other from all over Ireland. You'd be surprised how much information got lost before.'

She probably wouldn't be, Paula thought, but she let him explain.

'There's something else as well. Part of our task is to create a complete database of every missing person in Ireland, North and South, which we've now assembled, thanks to Avril's hard work.' The girl gave a tight little smile. 'Well, to be frank — when we ran these new cases through it, we discovered it wasn't the first time two girls have disappeared from Ballyterrin.'

Paula stared. 'What?'

Guy moved his pointer again. The rest of the team looked glum. This was for Paula's benefit, clearly, and they'd already had whatever bad news it contained. 'This is a map of all the cases we're currently considering, going back forty years. The dots represent one case each.' On the screen was a map of Ireland, bisected by the border, and red dots covering it like the start of some pernicious disease. 'Now if we look at 1985 . . . you wouldn't remember it, but you might have heard.' Two more faces had appeared on the

27

screen. These girls were also pretty, also smiling, but their haircuts belonged to a different decade.

Paula breathed. 'Yes. God. I do remember now.' She'd been very young, but the shadow of those disappearances had hung over the town for a long time, even in the middle of bombs and shootings and all the rest those years had brought.

Guy pointed at the screen. 'These two girls, Rachel Reilly and Alice Dunne, went missing within months of each other, and they never found a trace of either.'

Paula was thinking hard. 'Wasn't there another case — a third one?' She had a vague memory of fear, of everyone talking over and over and sending her out of the room when it came up.

Guy fielded this question too; he clearly knew his stuff. 'There was a third girl, but she was eventually found hanged in woodland, so the RUC concluded it was an isolated case. Suicide.'

'And is there any link between then and now?' She was very aware of her heart, a sort of fuzzy whir like the noise of someone's iPod through headphones. 'Anything to say they're connected?'

'Not that we've found,' said Guy reluctantly. 'The ages of the girls, where they were last seen, there are similarities, but everything else is just circumstantial for now. Nevertheless we're involved, and we're taking it very seriously. As of now we have no other leads at all.' He clicked one last time through the pictures, Rachel Reilly and Alice Dunne, Majella Ward and Cathy Carr, nothing in common except they were all from the same town, and they were all missing.

Guy Brooking wasted no time; she liked that. She liked his clean, efficient movements as he passed them their assignments. Gerard, who was leading on the new cases for the local PSNI, would focus on the north, with Fiacra working south of the border. Avril would analyse the data, look for patterns. Check out the families. Look again for any connection between Cathy and Majella — they went to different schools, but did they have any friends in common? Belong to any clubs, do any hobbies? Anything that might lead to running away — problems at home, exams, boyfriends?

Guy leaned on the back of a chair and Paula saw the glint of a wedding ring. 'This is a safe town. There's a good chance, as Paula's research has shown, that Cathy and Majella went missing voluntarily, independent of each other, and we'll find them safe. But the clock is ticking, and the second disappearance does increase the likelihood of some foul play.'

The room fell silent for a moment. Paula felt it again, the pulse in her blood, the need to track and find. *Where are you?* They hadn't just vanished into thin air. That was the thing, it always was. They had to be somewhere — but where?

Guy Brooking raised his hands, dismissing them. 'OK, everyone. Let's meet later and debrief.' He had very nice hands, strong and clean, and Paula realised she was staring at them as the team filed out, the dark man and the girl ignoring her, the Irish guy giving a small nod, the sergeant hurrying past as if he couldn't even look at her.

'Paula?' Guy was watching.

She blinked. 'Sorry. What did you want me to do?'

'Come with me a minute.'

★ ★ ★

The unit was housed in the town's old police station, where the former RUC had been based before they were burned out during the '96 Drumcree riots. It had been spruced up with new paint and some second-hand, mismatched office furniture. Paula understood. The idea would be to give the unit a different location, an identity apart from the regular police on the hill above town, where the PSNI were based in a nice modern building but still behind their high security fence. New name, but everything else the same.

Guy's office was small but neat, a framed picture of two children on the desk. Boy, girl. Paula scanned the room for insight. West Ham calendar. Books on Ballyterrin. Every inch the hardworking career policeman. He was following her eyes so she stopped nosying and snapped on a smile. 'So here I am.'

His hands were steepled on the tidy desktop. 'Do sit down, Paula. I'm sorry you didn't get much time to prepare before you came. Things rather escalated when Cathy went missing and we realised Majella had too, so we needed you here as soon as possible. How is your father?'

'Ah, he'll do. Not used to being dependent.' That morning, PJ had fallen over in the bathroom and not been able to get up — it was this rather than traffic which had really delayed her.

'There was something I needed to discuss with you, actually, about your family.'

Not already. She should have been ready for this.

'Your father. He was an RUC officer, I understand.'

'Oh, *that*. Yes. Why?' Maybe he didn't know the rest. How nice would that be, to meet someone with no preconceptions. *Oh, she's that Maguire girl.*

'I'm new to the area, of course, but as I understand it the Catholic officers had a hard time of it. They were seen as traitors, almost, by the locals?'

'Stooges, scabs, legitimate targets, yes.' Bricks in the window, bullets in the post, graffiti on the door. She said, 'But that's in the past now.'

'Hmm. The past seems quite . . . present round here, I must say.'

'It does.' She was thinking of the slogans she'd seen the day before.

'Do you know why you're here, Paula?'

'To make up the Catholic numbers?' She saw his face and backtracked. 'You can tell from the names. Irish thing. Bad joke, sorry. I'm here because you've got two missing girls, I suppose. That's my main research background.'

He moved some papers aside and laid his

hands on the desk. He had a small scar on his upper lip, she noticed, drawing the eyes to his strong mouth. 'I saw you speak at that conference in York, you know. '*Psychopathology of the Lost*.'

'You did?' She could feel herself redden.

'Very impressive. I asked for you on the strength of that — and your background, of course.' Which made her even surer he knew very little about her 'background'. 'You did very well on that Morris case. You seem to have something of an affinity with teenage girls.'

She stopped herself from making a flip remark about boy-band crushes. 'Most likely group to go missing,' she said, looking at his lapels to avoid his face. 'Girls aged thirteen to seventeen, and men aged twenty-four to forty.'

'I didn't know that. See, you'll be an asset.' Again the neat compliment, and the snap into business. He was a sharp customer, this Guy Brooking, with the wedding ring and no picture of his wife. 'We're under pressure for funding here already — I had to work quite hard to get you in. We need to prove we can function cross-border — it's never been tried before — and we need some quick wins. I don't know if you've followed it,' he lowered his voice, 'but since Cathy Carr went missing, there's been a lot in the media. Her father's Eamonn Carr — you know, he's a town councillor, and a very prominent local businessman.'

But no outcry for the Ward girl, the traveller. Paula said. 'I notice you didn't spell it out in the briefing, but you must be thinking about a connection between the old and new cases — some kind of forced abduction, a serial offender?'

Guy winced. 'We're doing our best to stop that speculation. Panic won't do any good. But I must admit, when we realised the pattern it was very worrying. For two girls to go missing is unheard of here — and for it to happen twice . . . '

'OK. I assume you want victim analysis, risk assessments on all of them. Is that why I'm here?'

'Yes. But today I'd like you to come with me. We'll set off in ten, if you're ready.' He stood up and held out his hand for her to shake, and when she took it, it was strong and warm, just as she'd imagined.

4

Ballyterrin meant 'Border Town' in Irish, the place names mangled and anglicised from long centuries of colonisation. The border ran a mile outside the town, an invisible line cut through fields and farms and EU-financed roads. Sunk for years under the weight of violence, the town had ridden high on the peace dividend and Celtic Tiger economy. But then the recession had come, and now many of the tawdry pound shops and casinos stood empty.

Paula looked out of the window of Guy's car — his own, very clean, BMW — as they drove down through the town, cradled in the hollow between sea and hills; the docks, the terraced houses, the shuttered-up shops and graffiti. It was all as familiar as the palm of her own hand. She clenched her fingers shut.

Guy was filling her in on the diverse business interests of Eamonn Carr, father of the second missing girl; he was also deputy leader of the local council. 'But I'm sure you know this?' He glanced at her as he waited correctly at the Market Street box junction, ignoring the hoots of the locals, who interpreted traffic law as loosely as they saw fit.

She shook her head. 'I've been away twelve years. I don't follow local news.'

'No?' He was surprised. Well, he didn't know she had her reasons.

★ ★ ★

The family of Cathy Carr lived on the hill above town, in a street where each house spread itself out for room and the driveways jostled with cars. If Cathy was found, if she came home safe, Paula had no doubt she'd get her own car for her seventeenth birthday.

Guy slid her in past the camera crew from a local TV station, which was doing a broadcast on the street outside the house. The blonde reporter flicked her hair at him. 'Any progress, Inspector?'

Guy was charming with them. 'We're proceeding. We'd like to thank all the press — especially you, Alison — for your sensitivity at this difficult time. Excuse me.'

Paula cringed behind him. It was a side-effect of the job, sometimes, but she hated seeing herself on TV or in the paper. It brought back too many memories. Guy was leading her up the crushed-gravel path to the front door. Neat lawn, children's shoes lined up in a rack on the porch. The windows seemed to have been recently cleaned, and through the frosted glass of the door Paula saw the dark shape of a man approach. She smoothed down her shirt as the lock clicked open.

'Inspector.' Eamonn Carr wore jeans and a golfing jumper, an expensive watch on his wrist. He was going grey at the temples — a handsome man.

Guy was shaking hands. 'Good morning, Eamonn. This is Ms Maguire, the psychologist I told you about. Can we have a quick word?'

35

He shook her hand in a powerful grip, and gave her a slightly doubtful look. Paula was used to this, and met his gaze full on. 'Mr Carr. I'm very sorry for what you're going through.' She could hear that her accent had already compressed, flattened back to its Ballyterrin tones, shaping itself unconsciously to the landscape.

He nodded, still watching her. 'Will you have a cup of tea?'

'Lovely, thanks.'

A ginger cat shot past them as they went in, heading for the safety of upstairs. Despite the damp weather of the past few days, the hardwood floor bore no trace of muddy childish footprints. It reeked of newness — the furniture gleaming, the walls white, even a fresh smell of paint. Paula heard noise from the living room, and as they were led in saw that the huge TV was on, blaring out a daytime programme where people sold stuff from their attics.

'Angela,' said Eamonn gently. 'The police are here, love, will we put that off?'

It took the woman on the sofa a few seconds to react. 'Oh! I just had it on for the news, in case . . . ' She looked vaguely round for the remote control, until her husband found it and switched off the TV. Silence poured into the room. Irrationally, Paula thought of the playground rhyme: *Silence in the courtroom, silence in the street, the biggest mouth in Ireland is just about to speak . . .*

'Tea then? Sugar, milk?' Eamonn Carr took charge as his wife stayed seated, twisting the gold

36

rings on her thin hands. She had on a silk top, expensive jeans, very heavy makeup for a weekday. She looked to be younger than her husband, in her thirties, slim and dark-haired. Paula watched her closely.

Guy smiled at the woman as they sat down on the stiff leather sofa. 'The kids at school?'

'Oh.' Angela Carr seemed to think about this. 'Yes. Yes, the weans are out.' Over the fireplace was a large family portrait, Angela sitting with Eamonn behind, and around them five children. An upwardly mobile Catholic clan, nothing strange there.

'This is Cathy?' Paula got up and examined the face of the eldest child — a dark-haired girl, neatly dressed in a maroon school uniform. Bright smile, concealer caked on a few pimples. 'She's at St Bridget's?' You had to be tactful, with missing persons. Always use the present tense unless you knew otherwise.

'Yes.' Angela Carr looked out of the window.

'I was, too. It's a good school. And Cathy was last seen leaving there, is that right? Her friend saw her walking away from the gates, at hometime?' It had been a Friday, when everything changed. Only a week before.

Angela frowned. 'I never liked that Anne-Marie. A bad influence, hanging out with boys down the town. Cathy's a good girl — she's never been any trouble.'

'But you've said you think she might have run away?'

Angela's face convulsed. 'I — maybe. She might have.'

37

'Here we go.' Eamonn Carr was coming in with tea on a tray, and what looked like home-made biscuits. Paula took her drink gratefully, but saw that Guy just sipped his and put it down on a well-placed coaster.

She leaned forward. 'Can I ask — is there a reason you think she could have run away?' This was strange. Most families were convinced something awful had happened to their loved one, sure they would never leave of their own accord; although as Paula's research showed, most did.

'You know girls,' Eamonn Carr said. He sat down beside his wife and took her limp hand. 'She might have fallen out with one of her pals.'

'I'm sorry, I'm sure you've been asked these questions already, but I just need to run through them again, if that's OK. Did she take anything with her, any clothes or money?'

Eamonn glanced at his wife, who was staring at the floor. 'We weren't sure. She could have bought her own clothes, couldn't she? I mean, what do we really know about what they get up to?'

Paula made herself look him in the eyes. His dark hair was swept back, and his eyes were dark too, unreadable behind heavy shadows. Cathy's eyes were green, the file said. Did that come from the mother? She couldn't see Angela's face. 'Did you give her much pocket-money?'

Eamonn shook his head, his eyes on Angela.

'Was she having trouble at school? Bullying or anything like that?'

She noticed he looked at his wife again before

38

answering. His voice was forced. 'Cathy's very popular, isn't she, love? Always the centre of attention.'

'Maybe — a boyfriend, even?'

Angela Carr sat stiffly forward and finally spoke, in a high, almost childish voice. 'Cathy didn't have boyfriends. She was a good girl, far too young for all that carry-on.'

Cathy Carr was fifteen, old enough in most people's book to at least be interested in boys. 'Yes, I'm sure she is. It's just there's often an emotional reason for going missing — some kind of pressure . . . '

'She would never do anything dirty.'

'I'm sure, but — '

Guy caught her eye and Paula fell silent as he took them through Cathy's last movements, her day at school, who her friends were, and her state of mind over the previous few weeks.

'Normal,' said her father, rubbing his hands over his face. He looked exhausted. 'She's been studying for her GCSEs. She's very driven.'

'She's a good girl,' said her mother again. 'Works hard and then she's busy with after-school classes.'

'Tell me about them.'

Her father looked blank, but Mrs Carr reeled off: judo, choir, first aid, volunteering. 'And she does church youth group, of course. Never misses Mass.'

'And you, Mrs Carr, do you work?' Paula was sure she didn't, but asked anyway.

Angela Carr's eyes wandered to the window again. Her husband squeezed her hand. 'Angie's job is with the wee ones. She's a Eucharistic minister too, and she does the church flowers and collects for the handicapped children.'

'And Mr Carr, what time do you typically get home?'

'Me?' He looked surprised. 'Maybe eight, nine. Why?'

'Oh, it's just girls are often closer to their dads at that age.' She smiled. So Eamonn Carr probably never saw his daughter.

He was frowning. 'You don't think it's something to do with my work on the council, do you — something political?'

Paula glanced at Guy. 'Statistically, the most likely thing is she's run away. I'm trying to work out why that might have been. Did you come home late that day?'

Eamonn cleared his throat. 'Angie rang me when Cathy didn't come back, and I went straight home. Five o'clock. Then I drove round the streets to see could I find her.'

'OK. Just one last thing — does Cathy have her own computer?'

'No, indeed. Load of filth on that internet.' Angela Carr looked disgusted. 'She's no phone, either. No need for it. It's crazy what some of these young ones have nowadays.'

'I see. Did she keep a diary?'

Angela frowned. 'No. Cathy had no secrets. Why would she?'

'Her room's been searched,' said Guy quietly. 'There were no diaries, nothing like that.'

'See? She was a good girl.' Angela's eyes flicked between them.

40

'And I suppose she had her schoolbag with her when — Well, that's OK. If you don't mind, I'll take a look at her bedroom before we head off. Thank you, Mr Carr, Mrs Carr. Sorry to take up your time.' Paula stood up. 'Lovely biscuits, by the way.'

Eamonn Carr smiled distractedly. 'Oh yes, Angie's a great cook.'

The woman did not smile. Her gaze swept over to the blank TV screen, and Paula saw that her thin fingers were twisting pleats into the fringed edge of the sofa.

★　★　★

A quick glance in Cathy's bedroom was as expected. Painfully neat, like the rest of the house, the pink duvet pulled tight over the single bed. The only pictures were framed shots of dogs and kittens. No posters, no stickers, no mess. A brush sat on the scalloped dressing-table, long dark hairs caught in the bristles. That had been the only trace the girl was ever there.

Outside, Paula felt she had to breathe deeply. Guy held the car door for her.

'Your thoughts?'

'God, where do I start?' Paula ticked off on her fingers. 'One, she used the past tense twice, talking about Cathy.'

'Mm, I noticed that.'

'Two, who the hell makes biscuits when their daughter's missing? And watches *Cash in the Attic*?'

41

'People deal with grief in different ways.' He started the engine.

'Of course, but there's usually a pattern. And in Ireland, there's a lot of judgement. You'd never watch TV when someone was dead and not buried, for example. And also — they've redecorated that house recently. Have you had Forensics in?'

He was frowning. 'Cathy disappeared on her way home from school. She never reached the house.'

'Maybe.'

He was quiet for a while. 'I can see you know what you're talking about, Paula. But you don't — forgive me — you don't have children, do you? Maybe we need to let people cope however they know best, without jumping to conclusions.'

Paula opened her mouth and shut it again. 'Fine. But you could still check the house out.' She might not have children, but she did know about loss. Far more than she'd ever wanted to, in fact. 'Inspector?'

'Oh, call me Guy. We're such a small team.'

'OK. You don't have to take the tea, you know. You don't drink it, do you?'

He looked surprised, then laughed. 'Can't stand the stuff, but I take it to ease them in. You're good, aren't you.'

5

The next stop for Paula and Guy was St Bridget's Grammar School — the girls-only convent that sat high on the hill over the town. 'This is your old school, I gather?' Guy looked over again. His fair hair had recently been cut at the back, revealing a pale line along the neck.

'That's right. Wore the maroon outfit for seven years. It's hideous.'

'I know, my daughter's there.'

That was surprising. 'But you're not Catholic?'

'No — but we couldn't find a secular school that was any good.'

That made sense. The religious orders still had the school system pretty much sewn up in Northern Ireland. 'You brought your whole family over?'

'More or less.' A look crossed his face. 'Katie transferred to St Bridget's when I took the job. In London you'd pay a fortune for that kind of education.'

'How old is she?'

'Fifteen.' He flicked the indicator to turn into the drive.

'So she's in the same year as — '

'She doesn't know Cathy, they're in different classes. Katie's not been here long enough.'

She risked, 'And what does your wife make of Ballyterrin?'

He was silent for a while as he manoeuvred

into the teachers' car park. 'Well, Tess has gone back to London for a while. She — there were a few things to sort out.'

Did that mean they were separated? Paula wished it wasn't so rude to ask.

He turned off the engine. 'We're meeting with the Principal now. She's called Sister Attracta, can you believe it?'

She undid her belt. 'When it comes to nuns, that's the least of your worries. Well, here we go. I feel like I should be in uniform again.'

It was a small joke, but when she said it she had the feeling he was picturing her as a schoolgirl. She turned away abruptly as a faint blush spread over his fair skin. 'Let's go then.'

* * *

Entering her old school foyer was like stepping back in time. Paula felt an urge to roll down her socks and undo the top buttons of her shirt. Girls seemed to appear from every door and window, aware by some strange telepathy that a man had entered the premises. The air was heavy with Impulse and mild hysteria. It was strange, she thought, watching Guy's strong back go up the stairs. At that age she'd have considered him desperately old — someone's dad. But at some point, everything had changed.

The Principal's office was also the same, that smell of dust and glue. Paula swallowed down her memories of being summoned there when they found the first body — the way her knees had wobbled as she walked down the corridor, trying to put one foot in front of the other, until she had to hold onto the wall to stay up. But that was then. It had been Sister Magdalena in Paula's day, a dragon in a wimple. She blinked and saw a different nun coming to let them in.

Sister Attracta had a soft Southern accent. 'Good morning, Inspector.' With such a shortage of nuns, the Order often sent them round the country.

'Sister.' His tone was respectful. 'This is Ms Maguire, a former pupil.'

'Yes, 1992 to 1999, wasn't it.' The nun's hand was cool and soft. So she'd checked — that must mean she knew all of it. 'You did very well here, Paula,' she smiled, and Paula gulped. They could read minds! Under the brown veil, the nun was younger than she'd thought.

'I'm afraid we've nothing more to say about Cathy.' The Sister folded her hands. 'A popular girl, and clever — although lately, her work had gone off a wee bit. Nothing to worry about.'

'No trouble?' Paula sat down on a hard school chair.

'One of the teachers, Miss Kenny, she told me she saw Cathy crying in the cloakroom last week — but then she is fifteen. The girls, they're so sensitive to everything; any criticism, a row with a friend — they take it all to heart.'

'Boys?'

The nun smiled. 'Ah, I'm sure you know the way of it, Miss Maguire. Most of them are crazy over boys. You'll maybe want to ask her friends again, but as far as we know there was no actual boyfriend in the picture.'

'How are the girls taking it?' Guy leaned in.

'You'd know as well as we do.' She fixed him with her brown eyes. 'Katie seemed quite upset about it. Is she all right?'

He frowned. 'She doesn't really know Cathy,' she said.'

'But in these situations, the atmosphere spreads very quickly. There's been a lot of tears. And coming after the poor child in the summer . . . '

Paula flicked a glance at Guy. 'Another missing girl?'

'No, no.' The nun shook her head. 'Very sad. She died — well, the coroner said he wasn't sure, but it looked as if she'd taken her life, God rest her. Louise McCourt was the name. She was sixteen, the year above Cathy. These things, they don't happen in Ballyterrin. At least we thought they didn't.'

Guy had been staring at his feet and now stood up abruptly. 'We ought to go, Sister. Thank you. Ms Maguire will talk to Cathy's friends, if she may.'

'Certainly, it's all set up in the Chapel. I thought you might like to see Miss Kenny first though — she's Cathy's form teacher. You'll find her downstairs.'

Outside, Paula looked at Guy curiously. 'Everything all right?'

'It gets to you, when you have a child,' he said shortly.

'Did you look into the suicide?'

'It wasn't ruled a suicide.'

'Hmm. You said there was a suicide in 1985, didn't you?'

'Yes, but that's all it was. No connection.'

'But there could be a link — '

'The girls didn't know each other, Paula. None of them did. What kind of link could it be?'

'Well. I don't know.' Paula fell silent, her mind churning through all this information.

As they walked downstairs, Guy stiffened. 'Katie!'

Across the main lobby, Paula saw a teenage girl, hunched and scowling, walking in the same direction as them. The girl looked away as if she was going to pretend not to hear.

'Katie, it's Dad!'

Paula winced for the girl as she slunk over. 'Da-ad, stop coming here, it's so embarrassing.'

'I have to, it's my job. Have you got your lunch? I made it last night.'

'Ye-ah.' Katie Brooking was as dark as her father was fair, with thick curly hair pulled back in a plait. She must take after her mother.

'This is Ms Maguire, she's helping us look for Cathy. Where are you going anyway? Isn't this classtime?'

'Nowhere. Just the toilet.' Though she had her schoolbag with her, fiddling with its strap on her shoulder.

'Well, see you at home.'

The girl said nothing, just swept Paula with dark suspicious eyes. Paula did an awkward adult smile.

'That's my daughter,' Guy said needlessly, as Katie stalked off in the opposite direction from where she'd been going. Paula wondered again what had happened to his wife, and why he still hadn't mentioned the other child in the desktop photograph.

*　*　*

'Come in! Come on in! Welcome to the English room.'

Sarah Kenny was one of those people who shake your hand with both of theirs, a clammy grasp that says, *I have never been more pleased to meet anyone in my life.* Her fair curls were escaping from the headband she'd placed on them, and though she couldn't have been far into her thirties, her pale Irish skin was already lined and freckled. 'Ms Maguire, isn't it? An old pupil!'

Paula gently disengaged her hand. 'That's right. You're Cathy's form tutor?'

The smile dropped. 'We're so worried. I keep telling myself, if only I'd talked to her — but sure you never know, do you? I saw her that day — break time on the Friday. I was on cloakroom duty. They're not meant to hang around in there, but she was on her own, and she'd been crying.'

Paula took a few steps away, looking round the classroom, which was cheerfully upholstered in green and yellow crepe paper, poems and posters stapled up for the edification of the girls. Ten chairs had been arranged in a horseshoe in the middle of the room, desks pushed back. 'Did you speak to Cathy, when she was crying?'

'Och, I could see she didn't want to talk. The girls know I'm always here for them. We have a problems box.' She proudly patted a shoebox

48

which had been covered in hand-written question marks and a small sign that said *Ask Anything!* 'I read them out anonymously in form class and we have a wee chat.'

'So you've nothing to add on where Cathy might have gone, nothing that might help?'

'If only I did. She's a lovely girl, hard-working, bright, popular — all that. I mean, she was crying, yes — but they always are! If so-and-so sits with the wrong person at lunch, or so-and-so sees a boy the other likes — well, I'm sure you remember. It's non-stop drama at that age.'

Paula looked at the chairs. 'Are you having a meeting?'

'Oh yes, I'm getting ready for lunchtime — my little discussion group. I set it up at the start of the year, after — well . . . ' The teacher lowered her voice. 'We had a pupil kill herself over the summer. Terrible thing.' She mouthed the word. '*Hanging.* So I'm trying to be there for the girls more, support them. Anyone can come. We have little chats, discuss anything that's on their minds, do some role-play and things. It helps them to deal with the issues they're facing.'

Paula considered the empty chairs. 'Did Cathy come?'

'Oh yes — yes, she did.' As if it had only just occurred to her.

And you didn't think to tell us sooner? 'But not last Friday?'

'No, no. She didn't come that day. I suppose that must have been when she disappeared.'

★ ★ ★

49

Paula had thought it odd that the Principal arranged meetings in the Chapel, but she understood why when, with Guy gone back to the station, she slipped into the quiet room, which contained only a stained-glass cross over a simple wooden table. It was peaceful, intimate — the kind of place where you'd want to whisper out your secrets.

A girl sat in the front row, eyes closed, hands pressed together.

'Anne-Marie?' Paula kept her voice low.

The girl looked up. She had bad skin which she'd caked in makeup, and ratty blonde hair done up in elaborate clips. 'You're the police lady?'

'Sort of. My name's Paula. Were you praying for her? Cathy?'

The girl nodded.

Paula sat. 'So, what class are you out of?'

'Maths.'

'Miss Connolly, is it? Does she still have that old red jacket?'

The girl smiled faintly and looked at her bitten nails. So much for trying to connect.

'Anne-Marie, I need to ask you a few things, just to check what you remember. When did you last see Cathy?'

The girl took a deep breath. 'Last Friday, just at the gates out there. After school. Mammy picked me up, but Cathy said she was going down the town.'

'Was that strange?'

'A bit. Normally she's not allowed. Some of us go on a Friday but she wasn't meant to. Then

50

later I tried texting her, like, but she never replied.'

Paula frowned. 'She had a phone?'

Anne-Marie gave an *are-you-daft* look. 'Yeah. Course.'

'Right. And did Cathy have a boyfriend, Anne-Marie?'

She saw the girl think and shake her head. 'She never met boys. I go to the disco sometimes, but — '

'She wasn't allowed?'

Anne-Marie lapsed into silence.

'Was it hard for Cathy to meet boys, then?'

She mumbled, 'That's why she was on at me to go down the Mission. She said we'd meet boys, but there weren't any nice ones. They were all rotten, except for the leaders.' She stopped herself, as if surprised at the three full sentences she'd uttered.

'The Mission? What's that?'

'It's on Friday nights. We sing songs and that. Like a church.' She shrugged. 'They're nice. It's like they really listen.'

'Where is it, the Mission?' She didn't want to confuse the girl by asking more about what it was.

'Down on Flood Street, you know?'

'I do.' Paula digested this. 'Were you meant to go that Friday?'

'Yeah, but, like — Cathy, she'd already gone before then. Before the time we'd normally go.'

'Did Cathy seem OK to you before she went — not sad, or weird?'

Another shrug. 'Dunno. She was OK.'

51

'Right. Just another question, Anne-Marie — did you or Cathy ever meet Majella Ward?'

'The traveller girl?' She shook her head firmly. 'No.'

'Did you know Louise McCourt?'

The girl looked confused. 'Course, we had an assembly for her.'

'But did you know her to talk to, like as a friend?'

'No.'

Paula tried to recall the list of Cathy's hobbies, provided by her mother. 'Louise didn't do choir, or first aid, or — did she go to the Mission?'

'Oh yeah,' said Anne-Marie, surprised again. 'Course she did. Loads of people go to the Mission. Their mums don't mind, 'cos it's like Mass.'

6

After several hours with a succession of tight-lipped teenagers, Paula wasn't finding out any more about Cathy Carr, or indeed Louise McCourt. It was frustrating, when she was sure these same shy teens would be hollering their heads off at the bus stop in just a few hours. She wandered down to the office to hand back her visitor's pass, texting Guy to say she'd finished. Was that allowed, texting in school? No one even had mobiles when she'd been there.

In her day the office ladies had been scary gatekeepers who'd interrogate you about sick leave, but as an adult Paula received a smile from the curly-haired woman at the counter. 'Please God you can find the wee one. It's a crying shame.'

Paula still quailed, as if in possession of a forged exeat note. Catching sight of framed class pictures on the wall, she gestured at them. 'Could you show me Cathy's class?'

'Aye, of course, come on in.' The woman lifted the barrier and Paula went under, still with a small surge of fear. 'Top right there. Lovely wee girl.'

Paula's eyes were scanning quickly over the other photographs, in search of someone else. She found the name in tiny letters on the brass plaque. There she was, in the picture below. A bigger girl than Cathy Carr, reddish curls, big warm smile.

'When were these done?'

'It's usually summer, end of the year.'

So just weeks after this, something had prompted smiling Louise McCourt to end her own life.

★ ★ ★

The gates of St Bridget's closing behind her gave Paula a welcome feeling of release. She was far too old to be back there, remembering all those tears and resentments, the whole place reeking of periods and cheap perfume. As she turned back to look at it, Paula heard a voice up close in her ear. A warm breath of Polos.

'Back to school then, Maguire?'

She didn't turn. 'You know you're not meant to hang out at the school gates.'

'Funny. Last schoolgirl I went for was you, as I recall.'

'Lucky me. What d'you want, Aidan?' She faced him, and found familiar dark eyes level with hers. Aidan O'Hara hadn't shaved in days, and looked as if he'd slept in his blue shirt, but still she stepped back, away from the flood of feeling that hit her in the chest.

'Any word on the girl?' he asked casually, jingling change in his jeans.

'Ah, here we go. Got a tape-recorder in your pocket?'

'No, just pleased to see you.' A smile was spreading over his lean face, and she flicked her hair, cross.

'I hear you're the Editor now — why don't

54

you find out things for yourself?'

He laughed. 'I will surely. Nothing gets past the mighty *Ballyterrin Gazette*.'

She saw Guy's car coming up the road. 'There's my lift, will you move yourself.' With some satisfaction, she noticed Aidan's old Clio was parked nearby, same car he'd had at eighteen. But that brought back memories of its own.

'We'll be running an interesting article this week,' he said, moving aside to let her pass. He leaned against the Clio with his hands in his pockets. 'Can the English Inspector get to the heart of Ballyterrin's secrets?'

'He's doing his best.' She waved Guy over.

'Especially with his history — can he cope?'

'What are you on about, for God's sake?'

'Have to read the paper to find out.'

Paula made herself turn, walk to the car without letting him see he'd riled her.

'Who was that?' Guy pulled away, and she let herself look back. Aidan was still leaning against the car, watching her.

She turned away. 'Just some eejit.'

★   ★   ★

'You all right going in here?'

'I'll be fine.' She said it confidently, but in truth she'd never been into the traveller camp before. For years it had sat on the outskirts of Ballyterrin, down by the silty mudflats of the dock area — a place of fear, of lore. She belted up her trench-coat against the thin rain falling.

Guy parked his BMW near the entrance to the camp, on a barren stretch of wasteland outside town. 'Sometimes they throw bricks,' he shrugged. 'OK to walk?'

Paula was always OK to walk, because she didn't wear heels. Female officers didn't, and she'd learned that everyone took you more seriously if you could race after them when needed.

The camp consisted of about sixty caravans — some huge and plush, some ramshackle — the 'travelling' community who now sat, unmoving, dipping in and out of the town as they pleased, drawing prejudice like a lightning-rod and providing employment for the place's social workers, doctors, and dole officers.

Guy walked with long strides, and even in her flat boots she struggled to keep up. Rain was collecting in dank puddles on the muddy ground; there was a smell of sewage and neglect. He said, 'I'm sure you'll be aware of the sensitivities here. The PSNI have been carrying out interviews since we realised Majella was gone, but there's a huge backlog to get through, and we're behind on time.'

'They didn't report her for two weeks, I see.'

'The parents didn't, and the school didn't want to interfere, they said.' She could hear the anger in Guy's voice and liked him more for it. No one had worried about interfering when middle-class Cathy Carr went missing. 'It was Majella's sister called it in, in fact — when the news broke about Cathy. She's only twelve. The school thought Majella might have gone to get

56

married, but Theresa said no way. Said there'd have been a huge ceremony. They've got money, the family, though you'd not think it.'

'Yeah, that sounds right. So you think she's really missing?'

'Seems like it.' He ushered her up to the first caravan, large and white, surrounded by a neat fence, and she noticed he was shielding her with his body, as crowds of men in tracksuits began to gather several yards away. The gesture seemed instinctive, and she had time to wonder dimly if Guy had been in the Army. A vicious black dog was tied up outside the caravan, snapping at her heels. Paula made herself stand up tall, show no fear.

'Here we are. The Wards. Actually, they're all called Ward.' Guy sounded embarrassed. 'Majella's family are the Paddy Wards — he's one of the community leaders. They won't tell us much, I'm afraid.'

Paula nodded; they wouldn't have much use for the police round here. Then the door of the white caravan flew open and a wrinkled woman shouted out, 'Yis are too fecking late, she's gone now.'

'Mrs Ward?' Paula took in the woman's missing teeth and gilt earrings, skin avalanching out of a vest top and pedal-pushers.

'No fecking point coming round here now — me daughter's gone.' Letting the door swing shut, Majella's mother ducked back inside. Paula had a fleeting glimpse of a clean-scrubbed floor where a baby sat nappyless, pushing a broken Barbie round in circles. She held the door open.

57

'Mrs Ward? I'm new, how are you? Paula's my name. I just wanted to ask a few questions about Majella.'

'She won't talk to yis.' Paula and Guy turned to see a skinny girl in a navy school uniform, high ponytail, hoop earrings. 'You'll have to talk to me. Theresa.' She pronounced it *Treeza*. Theresa led them around the side of the caravan, where plastic patio furniture stood collecting rain. 'Yis are back for more, then.'

'This is Ms Maguire — Paula. She's going to help us find your sister.'

'Not doing a good job so far, are yis.'

Feeling thoroughly steeped in teenage girls, Paula let herself be sized up by the twelve year old. 'Where did you last see your sister, Theresa?'

'Told yis, she went off to school on Friday, never come home. Da went mental, sent me brothers down the town to get her. But she wasn't there, she wasn't nowhere.'

'You're at the same school as her?'

'Aye.' She should have been there now, Paula thought.

'She normally came home straight away?'

'She did them after-school courses and that. Da didn't mind them. Computers and that shite.'

'But no one called the police when you couldn't find her?'

Theresa shrugged; the police didn't count for much in the camp. She was grasping her phone and Paula glimpsed the screensaver, wet with drops of rain — a girl with a mane of chestnut

58

hair, braces on her teeth.

'That's Majella? Can you tell me — how was she, before she went?'

Theresa looked down at her sister's picture. 'Same as always. She's a right moody cow, our Maj.' She shrugged again; at just twelve she had that teenage insouciance thing nailed.

'So it was a Friday, the last time you saw her. Where was she meant to be, do you know? Is there an after-school course that day?'

Theresa thought about it, fiddling with the phone in its pink diamanté case. 'Dunno. Typing, maybe.' She scowled up at them. 'The peelers reckon Da took her off to get hitched.'

'But you don't think so?'

'Naw.' She was scornful. 'Hit the fecking roof, so he did. He's not, what's his name, Robert de Niro, y'know?'

Guy looked puzzled but Paula tried to decipher this. 'You mean, he's not much of an actor? So he must not have known where she was? I see. What about your mum?'

'He says jump, she says how high.' Theresa was going to have a really excellent sneer in a few years. 'All me uncles are off looking for her round the country now.'

'Did Majella have any boyfriends, anything like that?'

The girl's tight ponytail swung as she shook her head. 'No way, José. Mammy'd have skinned her alive if she went with fellas.'

'Well, tell me more about her after-school courses — you said computers?'

'Aye. Like when they reckon you're too thick

59

to get a job.' Majella had gone to the high school in town, a non-denominational institute for those who didn't make the grammar schools, so Paula was afraid there might be some truth in what the girl said.

'Did she ever mention something about a mission?'

Theresa gave her a suspicious look. 'You been doing your snooping, missus. Aye, she went there a few times. Mammy'd not have let her, so she never said.'

'Have you been?' Paula was aware of Guy's warning looks, but ignored them.

'Jaysus, no — load of Holy Joes clapping and singing about God and shite. Haveta be fourteen anyhow.'

Guy was frowning, so Paula smiled at the girl. 'Thank you, Theresa. We're going to do our best to find your sister, I promise.'

Theresa nodded as if she didn't quite believe this. 'Missus? You reckon some pervert took her? Her and that other wee girl?'

'Most people who go missing come back safe and sound,' said Paula truthfully, and the girl relaxed a bit.

'Mammy'll feckin' skin her when she's back.'

Well, there was an incentive to return.

They were on their way to the car when a banging broke out and Paula flinched. '*Peeler peeler peeler, out out out!*' From between the caravans came the slam of fists on sheet metal; the men were punching the sides.

'What are they saying?' Guy called out over the din.

60

'That we should get out! We're the peelers, apparently.'

'OK. Well, let's go then.' His hand gripped her elbow, secure.

'Aye, yis useless fecks, when you gonna find my Majella?' The man who wobbled over had a dark moustache and ponytail. A tall man, and powerfully built, but his face seemed to be crumpling in on itself. You could smell the booze at ten paces.

'Paddy Ward,' said Guy quietly. 'Jesus, he's gone downhill.' He raised his voice. 'Mr Ward, we understand it's a very upsetting time, but we are doing all we can.'

'You don't give a shite about a traveller girl.' He swayed slightly.

'I assure you we are taking it very seriously — '

'Racist, that's what you are,' a woman in white jeans was shouting. 'None of you care unless we're after robbing your roof tiles.'

There was a chorus of assent, but Paula was looking at the man's eyes. Glazed as they were with drink, he was in real pain. When she spoke, it was to him. 'Mr Ward — I know you miss her. I know you've been looking yourself, yes? We'll help. We'll do what we can. There's every chance she's safe somewhere.'

He swayed, the hand with the bottle of Buckfast dropping to his side. 'My wee girl. You don't give a shite.'

People were patting Paddy Ward, leading him away and casting angry looks at Paula and Guy. She felt a small tug on her jacket and Theresa was there. 'Sorry about me da. His head's wrecked over Maj. Thinks yis won't bother, now this posh girl's gone and all.'

'I promise we will.' But even as she said it, Paula's heart sank. Could she promise that?

'Jesus,' said Guy as they reached the safety of the car. 'Didn't see that coming.'

Paula shut the door gratefully on the dry interior. 'You know how for years we'd no ethnic minorities? 'Cos who'd want to come here, with all that violence? Well, the travellers were our only minority, the ones that got all our racism, and it turned out we had a *lot* stored up.'

He looked at her keenly again. His eyes were grey, she noticed; unreadable. 'Why did you ask about the Mission?'

'Just something Cathy's friend said. It must be some kind of church group, meets on Fridays. A youth ministry.'

'Cathy went there too?'

'Her friend said so. It was all she was allowed to do, pretty much.'

He started the engine, looking out at the sleeting rain. 'If that's true, you know what it means?'

She did, but she said, 'What?'

'It's the first link we've found between the girls.'

7

'As you can see, my analysis of Cathy suggests she has a very restrictive home life, with no room for transgression. At fifteen that often leads to rebellion — self-harm, drinking, early sex. This would support the hypothesis of voluntary absence, or running away. But if she didn't take any clothes or money, that's a negative indicator. I think there's a good chance she will have had a boyfriend — perhaps an older man. She has a phone her parents don't know about, so we can check the records for that.'

It was the next day, and following another night of rubbish TV (PJ refused to get more than four channels), Paula had woken up early and with a sense of purpose. A few hours in the office had given her time to prepare full risk assessments on each of the girls, which she was now outlining in the meeting room.

Avril Wright was looking disgusted again. Her blonde bob was neatly combed, ankles crossed in unladdered tights. 'Cathy seems a lovely girl. You can't assume things about her.'

'Well, you're right that so far we've seen no evidence — except for the fact she's gone. On the balance of probability, I also think we should be looking more closely at the family, specifically her father.'

Bob Hamilton was apoplectic. 'Eamonn Carr is a pillar of the community!'

'Sure — and they never abuse kids, right?' Everyone fell silent. She ploughed on. 'Majella Ward has on the surface more vulnerability indicators than Cathy; she's one of ten children, and no one reported her disappearance for several weeks. Her school is equally out of touch. I'd say it would have been very easy for Majella's life to fall apart and no one to notice.'

Guy was watching her across the table, his expression impassive. 'Have you found anything to suggest the disappearances are linked?'

Paula scrunched up her face. 'The most likely thing is they're not, that both girls ran away. But in a town this size, two random cases — well, it's not very common.' There was a sort of shift round the table; no one wanted to think what it meant if they weren't random. 'Given that the only link we've found between the girls is this Mission, I'd recommend starting enquiries there.'

'OK,' Guy said, again betraying nothing. 'You say two cases — you won't have had time to look into the 1985 ones?'

'Not much, yet. Were there any similarities with what I've outlined?'

'Some. It's tenuous — Bob's going to bring us up to speed.' He nodded to his deputy.

Bob Hamilton stood up, buttoning the jacket of his straining suit, and started clicking through a PowerPoint to get past the slides they'd had the first day. White-haired, solid, Paula could practically see the Orange sash round his chest. Be nice, she chided herself as the screen warmed

64

into colour. Just because he was probably an Orangeman didn't mean he wasn't also perfectly pleasant.

Bob spoke to Guy — conspicuously not to Paula. 'Alice Dunne and Rachel Reilly both went missing round about the end of summer, 1985. Alice lived just over the border, so her case was handled by the *Gar-da Síoch-án-a*.' He pronounced the words carefully, with a small glance at Fiacra Quinn. 'Rachel lived outside town, on a farm. She went for a night out to the disco — never got home.'

Paula was making notes. 'And she was seventeen?'

'Aye. And Alice, she was nineteen. Away at university in Dublin.'

'Hmm.' That was a big difference, psychologically. A fifteen-year-old schoolgirl, and a university student. 'I'll need to look at all the case details. How did Alice disappear?'

Bob clicked again, getting stuck on the same screen. 'Er — can't get this yoke to work.'

Guy said, 'She went out for the evening to see friends. They found her car by the side of the road, abandoned.' Paula thought she could hear a hint of irritation in his voice. Just the tiniest hint, like a ripple on water, but nevertheless there.

'And they never found anything?'

'Nothing. No trace of either girl, no leads. It doesn't give us much to work with. There were also some . . . er . . . cross-community tensions in both cases.'

Paula looked at him enquiringly. 'You mean

65

because Rachel was a Catholic, with the RUC? And Alice — '

'Alice was Protestant, living in Éire,' Guy finished. Nothing marked him out as an outsider more than the fact he called it 'Éire'.

'Sergeant?' Paula put her question to Bob Hamilton. 'You know that map of cases we had the other day — can you cluster it according to demographic criteria?'

He looked surprised. 'Religion, you mean?'

'Not really. I was thinking more of age.'

'Oh aye.' But he looked helplessly at the machine until Paula jumped up.

'Mind if I . . . ? OK.' She fiddled with it for a moment, pressing buttons on the Excel sheet until a bar chart was generated. 'So, this is the data from around Ballyterrin, see? We have just four teenage girls missing over the past ten years, and all found again quite quickly. So two in a month — that's a big spike. And it's happened twice now. That's doubly unusual.'

Gerard Monaghan was sceptical. 'But surely girls go missing all the time — it's the most common group, you said.'

'That's right. But for this area,' she pointed to the screen, where red dots represented each case, 'it's a lot, you know?' Risking more cold looks, she took a deep breath and said, 'Any chance we can get the same data on suicides?'

'Lord help us,' muttered Hamilton, and Paula saw the girl, Avril Wright, look horrified.

'Er, why?' Guy asked quietly.

'Well, there was a suspicious death over the summer, another girl from Cathy's school called

66

Louise McCourt. Louise also went to the Mission, it seems. So if we can find out more on her — '

Bob's face was red with outrage. 'That child's hardly cold in her grave!'

'But they might be connected, maybe. There's a lot of new research coming out that suicide and self-harm can function almost as a trend among teenagers — so if Louise *did* kill herself, perhaps it would give us some insight into Cathy and Majella, their state of mind . . . ' There was a pause where she felt just how far out of line she'd stepped. 'What about the suicide from 1985 — do we have her name?'

Silence. 'We'll get it,' said Guy, shooting a glance at Bob.

Paula nodded. 'We should. I think it could be quite significant. We should pull all the data we've got on suicides and suspicious deaths, back to and including 1985.'

Bob Hamilton coughed. 'Suicides aren't in our remit, God rest them.'

But Guy said, 'If it can be done quickly. Avril, have you got time to do that?'

Avril pressed her pretty lips together. 'Well, sir, I am very busy, but — '

'Excellent, I'm sure you'll manage. Now, we're under a lot of pressure, as Bob says. Not only in finding the missing girls, but also, I suppose, in justifying our existence as a unit.'

A strange kind of sigh went round the table. Avril Wright looked at her neat cuticles; Gerard Monaghan pushed back his chair, and Fiacra Quinn thumbed his eyes. Bob held his laser

67

pointer, crestfallen. Paula looked up enquiringly.

Guy said, 'There's been some — criticism. Some people think the money would be better allocated elsewhere — they don't see missing persons as a priority. And there's been comment in some sections of the media about the balance of cases we've re-opened. Whether it might be . . . weighted more towards one side of the community than the other.'

Paula wasn't surprised; it was a standard Northern Ireland response. 'So the funding's not secure.'

Gerard gave a bitter laugh. 'When's it ever? I s'pose you're used to London. There's no money round here.'

She decided not to retort that her car had been tail to tail in Jeeps that morning. 'Well, we'd better get results then.' No one responded to this peppy statement.

Guy moved on. 'So Avril and Fiacra, you're looking into the older cases — make lists, identify areas for review. Lots of the documents are on microfilm, I'm afraid, but we need a complete record. You can call in Paula if you want her input.' He smiled at her briefly. 'Gerard's leading on Cathy and Majella for the local PSNI, and we'll help where we're needed. Let's look at Paula's finding about the Mission, but we also need to focus on getting through the interviews on the traveller site. We're looking at a lot of people there, and a lot of criminal records — not necessarily the kind we're after, of course.' He cleared his throat to mark a change in tone. 'Now. I thought it might be nice to welcome Paula with an after-work drink — anyone?'

Avril said primly, 'I don't drink, sir.'

Gerard shook his head. 'I've a football match.'

Fiacra looked as if he might be convinced, but seeing the expressions of the others, he said, 'Better get home for me dinner.'

'Well — Sergeant?'

Bob looked shocked. 'I have my church duties, sir.'

'Oh well.' Deflated, Guy turned to Paula as the others filed out.

'I'd love to, really — but maybe some other time?' she said. 'It's just my dad, I don't like to leave him . . . '

'Oh, of course.' Guy looked disappointed. Paula thought fleetingly of the children in the picture on his desk, the wedding ring. There was nothing she could offer him. Better to say no. She turned to go with an apologetic smile.

★ ★ ★

Paula was set up on a very old computer in the corner, listening to the younger team members settle in around her. Avril and Fiacra had a hushed, slightly stilted discussion about a TV programme from the night before, and Gerard coughed at one point and asked Fiacra did he follow the football. None of them spoke to Paula. She'd do her reports, but she wanted to look into this Mission herself too. Anne-Marie had said it was on Flood Street, near the hospital. Who would know about it? She lifted the receiver of her desk phone.

It rang a few times, and when she picked it up Pat was breathless, music in the background. 'Ballyterrin 44520!'

Paula had a jolt; her mother had drummed it into her to answer the phone this way. It was rude to say 'hello', apparently. 'Pat, it's Paula.'

'Ah, hello, pet. Just doing my aerobics. On my own today, what with your daddy's leg.'

'He does *aerobics* with you?'

'Oh aye. We like that Davina McCall best.'

'OK. Eh . . . right. Just wanted to ask, since you're doing that history project, do you by any chance know about some youth mission that's in town?'

'The Mission? Of course, pet. It opened up in the summer, Flood Street, and all the young ones are off to it. You know wee Sarah that lives next door, she went down a few times and — '

'Eh, Pat? Do you know where on Flood Street? A big building, I'd have thought.'

'It's in the old home, pet.'

Bingo. 'A children's home?'

'No, no. You'd call it a Magdalene home, I suppose.' Pat lowered her voice fastidiously. 'For girls that got in trouble, you know. They had their weans and gave them up for adoption. Safe Harbour was the name, there was a whole chain of them.'

'And when did it close — I suppose years back?'

'No no, it was open till the eighties.'

'No way!' How had she never heard of this before?

'It'll all be in my project. It's very interesting. You see . . . ' Oh dear. Once started on the topic of local history, Pat couldn't be stopped.

'Sorry, Pat, you'll have to tell me all about it one time. I need to run now.'

'When are you calling in for your tea? Aidan said he saw you at the school.'

'Yeah, he did.' What expurgated version of the meeting had he told his mammy? 'Bye so, Pat. Take care!'

The website took forever to load on the clunky computer. She sighed and tapped her pen as it came through. THE MISSION, it said, in big letters. There were stock photos of smiling teens, and a large image of a cross. The few other pages had waffle about spreading God's word to the community through song and prayer. It was hard to work out who was behind the parent company. They had offices everywhere: London, America, red dots all over the map of the globe marking the Mission offices. Paula couldn't help thinking of her own red spots, representing missing people. One dot hovered over Ballyterrin, so she clicked it. Just the address on Flood Street, nothing else. Site of the old fallen-girls home. Who would run a place called Safe Harbour?

But this wasn't her job. Recalling the bollocking she'd got for investigating Kaylee Morris, she went to Guy's office, glass-fronted with slatted blinds.

'Inspector.' Guy was sitting at his desk staring at some papers in front of him. 'Quick question?'

He seemed dazed. 'Oh . . . sorry.'

71

'About this Mission thing, for whoever looks into it.' She showed him the printed-out screen. 'I found out a few more things about it.'

He nodded slowly. 'I'll pass it on to Gerard. They're very stretched up there though, with the DCI being off.'

'Are you OK?' Because he didn't look it. His skin was the colour of the plasterboard walls.

'Yes.' He sighed. 'Just got a package.'

She looked at his desk and saw it was covered in photos, slipping and sliding all over — all of the boy from the desk picture, the one with gap teeth.

'My wife sent it. My soon-to-be ex-wife, I gather.'

'Oh. You mean — '

'She wants a divorce, or so she tells me.'

'I'm sorry.'

He ran his hands through his hair. He was still wearing his wedding ring. 'I'm sorry too, Paula. Just struggling a bit. You can see we're under a lot of pressure. And this town — God, does it ever stop raining?'

'Not really. You know what they say: if the cows are lying down, it's raining. If they're standing up, it's about to rain.'

He didn't smile. 'We're not popular here, are we? The Brits. The police.'

'Don't worry, it's all in the past,' she lied. He didn't look any happier. The words were out almost before she knew. 'Listen — if you're still on for that drink after work, I think I could actually make it.'

He looked up. 'Really? Could we do it later?

Katie has a sleepover, so that way I can drop her off first.'

An evening drink was different — more like a date, not like an after-work thing. And he was her boss, and still married. But he looked so lost she hadn't the heart to say no. 'OK. See you later — um, the Square Peg, maybe? It's pretty central.' An old man's pub might reduce the danger.

'Great.' He looked better already. Giving herself a stern talking-to, Paula went to write reports. For the rest of the day she read through what they knew on Rachel and Alice (not very much), and highlighted avenues for investigation on Cathy and Majella — possible boyfriends, running away to Belfast or Dublin, accidents. The prospect of forced abduction seemed so unlikely, especially in a town like Ballyterrin, but they'd have to look at that too. She mapped them out, these girls, from their totally different homes and backgrounds. *Where were they?* The unanswered question that drove her on, every time. Again and again she found her eyes straying to the computer screen, where the minimised site of the Mission remained in view.

As she left on the dot of five, copying everyone else's dash to the door, Bob Hamilton fell into step with her. 'You're PJ's girl, then, I hear. I worked with him.'

'Did you?' She wondered was he one of the officers who'd driven her father out.

'He was a good man, a very good man.'

'I'll be sure to tell him that. He still is a good man, I think.'

'Oh aye, oh aye.'

She gave him a tight smile and started up the Ford Focus.

★ ★ ★

What to wear, that was a good question. Perhaps in denial about how long she'd be in Ballyterrin, Paula had brought hardly any clothes, and mainly jeans and jumpers, anticipating the chill nights of Ireland. Nothing for a drink with Guy Brooking. In her dressing-gown after dinner with PJ — her speciality of beans on toast — she stuck her head round the door of her small bedroom. 'Dad?'

'Aye?' He had the football on, sound down low.

'Can I look in the boxes for a dress?'

Silence. She thought he hadn't heard, but then he said, 'Aye, you may as well. They're only fit for the poor box, otherwise.' The unspoken words were there: *and it's not like she's coming back to get them.*

'You don't mind?'

'Tear away.'

The boxes were on the landing, taped up, smelling of damp. She touched the top one gently, but what was the point? It was only possessions. They didn't mean much when the person was gone. She had a vague idea what she wanted, and after rooting around among books, photos and shoes, there it was — a rust-red raw silk dress with a Chinese neck. Her mother had worn it that last Christmas, to a dinner-dance with PJ, and Paula remembered her going down the stairs in it, clouded in Anais-Anais, her red hair done up in some kind of knot.

She rubbed the fabric; it was lovely stuff, thick and cool. Her mother must have bought it in Dublin, on one of her Brown Thomas shopping trips. Was it weird to wear one of your mum's old dresses? Of course not, it was probably trendy now. But maybe not when you hadn't seen her in seventeen years.

A ghost of talc rose up as she pulled it on. The dress was tight on Paula's larger frame, and came to halfway up her thighs, but she got into it. She ringed her eyes in liner and attempted something with her hair, pulling it into a plait. She hadn't her mother's skill with hair, who had often sent Paula off to school with elaborate French dos that were the envy of her friends. God, it was too dressy for the Square Peg. Maybe boots would tone it down, and her ordinary wool coat. For a moment she considered taking it all off, going in jeans, but something stopped her. She wasn't sure what. Her other clothes were so plain, and for some reason, she wanted to look nice.

She clumped downstairs, self-conscious, and PJ was wobbling in from the kitchen on his crutches. He'd developed a way of holding a flask of tea under one arm.

'I'd have made the tea, Daddy.'

'I'm grand by myself.' He looked up at her on the stairs. A silence. 'Jesus. You're the spit of her.'

'Ah, no.' Margaret Maguire had been — was? — a smaller woman, slim, fragile-looking, whereas Paula had her father's height and strength. There was nothing fragile about her — not to see, anyway. 'I'm away now.'

PJ looked at his daughter. 'You be careful.'

'I always am! Dad, I've been living in London.'

'But you never know who's about.' The same warning he'd given her every day when she lived at home. Somehow it was comforting, like speaking a charm of protection.

'I will. You rest yourself, Daddy.'

★　★　★

Guy stood up when she walked in. He was watching her, but so were the dozen or so old men hiding in the recesses of the dark, sticky pub. It was raining again, and she flicked beads of it off her grey wool coat as she crossed the floor to him, horribly self-conscious.

'Is this OK?' she started babbling. 'I just thought, the others'll have kids in them tonight, and you might have to bust some for being under-age, and that'd be a bit of a downer, and — '

'No chance of being under-age here,' he muttered, looking round at the clientele. 'And I definitely heard someone say 'Brits Out'.'

'Ah, ignore them.' She slid into the booth; he looked her over, slowly. She bit down the urge to start babbling again.

'Horrible weather, isn't it,' he said. 'So dark already.'

'True, there's a quare shrink in the nights.' She caught his baffled look. 'It just means 'very'. Do the Irish expressions get to you?'

'I'm still lost. My first month here, I couldn't make out a word anyone was saying.'

'You'll be OK with me. Everyone says I'm as English as the Queen now.'

He laughed, a deep, generous sound. 'Sorry, but you really aren't. You're still Irish to me.' Finally, he looked at her in the eyes. 'You look very smart.'

'Smart?'

'Well, nice. I'm sorry, there are rules on paying compliments to staff.' He hurried on. 'Would you like a glass of wine or something?'

'Here? God, no. It'll be something the barman brewed up in his garden. I'll have a Guinness.'

He raised his eyebrows at that, but got up and went to get it. She watched his back as he waited at the bar. Then he was back with a pint. 'He said would the lady like a glass not a pint. I said she wouldn't.'

'She would not indeed.' She gulped the creamy foam. Guy was still watching her. 'So, your daughter's at a sleepover?'

'Yes. I was worried about her at first, when we moved, but she seems to have made this group of friends. They stay at someone's house every Friday.'

'Yours too?'

'Not yet. I think maybe she's embarrassed — you know, just having me and not her mum.'

Paula was thinking of the scene earlier in his office, and he must have been too, because he said, 'I'm sorry about today. I shouldn't have told you all that. It wasn't professional.'

It wasn't professional to be out for a drink

either, but she said, 'It's fine.'

'I suppose I don't have many people to talk to. Katie's settled in better than I have.'

'It's Ballyterrin. Not so open to strangers.'

'You still know many people?'

She shook her head, thinking of Aidan. 'Not really. Some schoolfriends are about, probably, but when I left for uni — well, it was hard to keep in touch.' Especially when you'd promised yourself you'd never go back.

'Well, cheers.' He forced a smile. 'I'm sure now you're here the team will gel better.'

'Cheers.' She swallowed the heavy stout, feeling it calm her, weigh her down. 'Sergeant Hamilton didn't seem too keen on the idea of a drink.'

'No, he doesn't really fit the Irish stereotype.'

'Now that's a mistake. Don't call him Irish, that's a lot more offensive than saying I look nice. British, please.'

'Oh, dear. I'm a bit clueless, aren't I? You'll have to be my guide.'

'What, like a leprechaun or something?'

He was about to answer, a genuine smile for once stretched on his face, but his phone started to ring. As he dug it from his jeans pocket he was laughing, his face open. From the way it closed so quickly, she could tell something very bad had happened.

★ ★ ★

'Can I come?'

He was already marching out of the pub,

78

phone clamped to his ear. A thin light rain was falling, catching in her hair. Into his phone he was saying, 'No, I've got my car. Only a few sips of beer so far, that's lucky. Hmm?' Whoever was on the end had asked him something and he turned to her, thoughtful. 'Yes. I'll call for Paula on the way.' So he didn't want Hamilton — she assumed that was the caller — to know he was with her.

He hung up and they stood on the high street, looking at each other. A chill wind was blowing in from the docks, and the smokers outside the strip of bars had turned up their collars. Music drifted on the breeze. He said, 'Sorry, I just didn't want to — '

'It's OK. Can I come, then? I mean, it might be helpful, if I can see it.'

He looked at her. 'You've seen this kind of thing before?'

She thought of the first body, and then the second, back in the nineties; each time someone else dead, not the person they were looking for. 'I have.'

'All right then.' He started walking again. 'It won't be pleasant, Paula, I'm warning you now.'

She got in. 'It never is.'

8

Though Ballyterrin was a small town, on a bad day it could take you an hour to drive through all the traffic. But on that damp Friday night, with everyone either at home or ensconced in warm pubs, they reached the canal in ten minutes. Here the old flax mill, once the foundation of the town, stood empty by the sluggish waterway. In summer it would bloom poison-green with algae, but now it flowed thick as treacle in the dark. The wind blew hard here, and Paula shivered into her coat as they picked their way from the car over muddy grass, to where blinding lights illuminated the scene of the crime.

Bob Hamilton was directing operations, a blue anorak pulled up round his red face. 'Evening, Inspector. Miss.'

'When was she found?'

'Round an hour back. These two clowns were smoking drugs on the towpath, saw something in the water, they said.' He jerked his head to where two teenage boys in tracksuits sat in a police car, looking dazed. They'd probably get away with a caution, but what they'd found in the canal might put them off drugs for life.

'Where is it — she?'

'The SOCOs are in now. The wee tent.' Hamilton hesitated. 'It's not what you'd want to see, Miss — Paula.'

She raised her chin, although her stomach was

already churning. 'I need to. I need to know how.' Because she was going to find whoever had done this. She had to.

He led them further along the old towpath, to where Forensics had set up their white tent against the gale. 'The boys pulled her out. I think they thought maybe she was still . . . well, they got a wee bit of a shock, anyway.'

A disturbed crime scene caused many headaches, and she heard Guy sigh, but this soon faded at the sight of a small figure marching towards them, clipboard in hand. The person drew closer, pulling off a protective white cap and mask to reveal a short woman with glasses, dark hair held back in a metal clip. Her eyes moved over Paula with no sign of recognition and she thrust the clipboard at Guy. 'You need to sign this.'

Paula stepped back, heart hammering. Guy blinked. 'Sorry, I don't think we've — '

The woman removed her gloves with a snap. 'I'm the on-call FMO. Saoirse McLoughlin. Will you sign it so I can get out of here?'

Guy scribbled on the paper, which was rapidly growing soggy in the drizzle. 'So what are we looking at? Is it a drowning, do you think?'

Dr McLoughlin wrinkled her small nose. 'You'll need to wait for the autopsy. If you're lucky, they'll do it over the weekend.'

'There's no way to speed it up?'

The doctor eyed him. 'You're the one who's over from London? Yes, well, we've a different system here. Bodies all get sent to Belfast. They'll do it as fast as they can.'

81

Paula cleared her throat and spoke. 'That's new, is it?'

The doctor stared at her for a moment. Guy paused and said, 'Sorry, this is Ms Maguire — Dr Maguire, our forensic psychologist consultant. She's from here, in fact.'

'Is she, indeed.' The eyes were dark. Paula looked away first.

Guy was still pushing. 'You couldn't possibly let me have some early thoughts? If we even knew probable cause of death — '

The woman's small face twisted. 'Have a look for yourself, Inspector. It'll be fairly obvious. Anyway, the coroner's been notified and she'll likely be moved to the mortuary later. You'll want to get the family in for an ID.'

She held out her hand and Guy hesitated for a second, perhaps thinking of what she'd been touching, before shaking it. 'Thank you, Doctor. I'm sorry for getting you out in this rain.'

She sighed. 'I wish to God I could have done something for her. Goodnight, Inspector.' She turned to go, hunched against the rain in her black jacket, without a backward glance.

Bob Hamilton took the cue and crossed the muddy ground to the area marked off by yellow police tape. He spoke to one of the officers inside, who stood up, pulling aside the tent flap with a gloved hand.

Guy got there first. Paula saw his reaction, and for a second she didn't want to look, but then it was too late.

Don't cry don't cry. It was like being punched in the stomach, every time. You couldn't control

82

the reaction — the nausea, then the tears in your nose — but you could learn to hide it. She thought Guy Brooking was doing the same, as he stared down. Of course, his daughter was the same age.

He spoke. 'She was found like this?'

The white-masked SOCO (identifiable as male only by his voice), said, 'We're not sure, sir. The plastic's come off a bit — but that could have been when the boys pulled her out.'

The body had been wrapped in green tarpaulin, tucked around with cords like you might use to fix bikes to a roof-rack. In the water they had begun to swell and loosen, so the head now emerged from the plastic, the feet poking out in their woollen knee socks. Underneath, you could see the maroon school uniform, drowned and sodden. The face and hands were white, bloated with water, awful. But from the dark hair and the small pierced ears, the body was just about recognisable as Cathy Carr.

★ ★ ★

The unit worked all night, summoned from home. Gerard came racing in, still in his Gaelic football jersey, coated in either sweat or rain or both. Avril drove up in her tidy little Corsa, her face pale above her black polo-neck. Paula was wearing her mother's dress under her coat, and kept forgetting, wondering why everyone was staring at her. A while later, Fiacra arrived from Dundalk in his rusting Toyota. Glancing at each other in silence, the team gathered their papers and laptops and decamped to the main station on the other side of town, where the case would now officially be launched as a murder enquiry.

The station was a brand-new monolith of bullet-proof glass, erected with PFI money and in another effort to bulldoze the past. Everything smelled new and unboxed, like the inside of a fresh pair of trainers. It was strange that night, full of buzzing phones and unfamiliar officers in rolled-up sleeves, constantly walking in and out with bits of paper in their hands. In a country so long inured to death, to horror, it was frightening how safe you could feel. The terrorists had never targeted children, not deliberately. The streets had always felt safe to walk in — but now this. A fifteen-year-old girl snatched on her way home from school, killed, dumped in the dark waters of the canal, until the twisting weeds and shopping trolleys had yielded her body back again.

Guy and Bob Hamilton had been closeted in a briefing with station detectives, grim faces behind tinted glass. No one else was quite sure where to put themselves, except Gerard, who as lead officer on the missing person's case had already pinned a large map of Ballyterrin to the wall. Cathy's way from school to home would have taken her through town, past the old mill where she'd been found. Paula watched Gerard across the room instructing uniformed officers.

'Let's get CCTV from every business she'd have passed.' He pointed on the map. 'There's a garage on that corner, chip shop; car showroom

84

— and get door-to-doors on all the residents. We can also run licence recognition on any cars passing through.'

Avril was struggling to find somewhere to put her laptop, settling finally for the end of a long open-plan desk, where she had to perch on a stool looking less than pleased. Paula wasn't sure what to do. Her work wasn't in the awful blurred aftermath of a crime, it was in clear-headed analysis, piecing together reports, trying to get a picture of what had been going on inside Cathy's head, what steps had led her to that dark canal, and who might have put her there. She made notes on what she'd seen — the careful wrapping of the body, the knots in the ropes, the glitter polish still visible on Cathy's muddy hand — but her thoughts wouldn't settle, as swirling with sediment as that dark water itself.

At some point, everyone in the room seemed to stiffen; voices came in from the desk. *The family were here*. Everyone seemed to know it. Through the glass you could see a dark-haired man, shouting at the desk officer: ' . . . tell us nothing! Where the bloody hell is she? Where is the wean?' He had a look of Eamonn Carr about him — one of the brothers? — and then the man himself came into view. By contrast, Cathy's father was pale and composed.

'Come on, Jarlath, they're doing their best.'

The door to the conference room snapped open and Guy strode out, buttoning his suit. He shot Paula a quick look as he passed; his face was set in sharp angles. She knew where he was going — to the mortuary at the hospital above town, where Cathy was waiting in a body bag. Taking the family to identify the body was the worst, the absolute worst, worse than crime scenes or arrests or autopsies. It was the moment you saw the final bit of hope drain away like blood down a sink.

The remaining team worked frantically, as if activity could stop them thinking of the dead child. Around midnight Paula went into the ladies' to breathe for a minute, and heard loud sobbing. Since there was currently only one other woman in the place, she called, 'Avril?'

Avril came out, flushing the toilet. Her eyes were red. Defensively, she said, 'She was so young. It's tragic.'

'I know.' Paula leaned against the hand-dryer as Avril splashed her face with water.

She looked at Paula in the mirror. 'You've done this lots, have you? I just did traffic analysis before. How come you don't cry?'

Paula thought of all the bodies she'd seen, starting with the ones back in her teens, the ones they'd made her look at because they didn't entirely trust her father. She shrugged. 'Sometimes I think I've no tears left.' As she went out, she knew the younger woman was staring after her with narrowed eyes, but she didn't care. She was sick of trying to explain how it was. How she'd learned there were worse things than finding a body.

Not finding one, for a start.

★   ★   ★

Finally, around midnight, Guy came back to the station, walking stiffly as if his back hurt. He went to Avril, Paula, and Fiacra, who were huddling together on one end of a desk, hardly daring to make eye-contact with the regular station officers.

'Let's call it a day, everyone,' he said. 'The autopsy will tell us more. There's nothing we can do tonight.'

Gratefully, Avril went, sniffling as she shut down her computer. Gerard hovered, still holding a magic marker, shirtsleeves rolled up. 'They'll get onto those checks first thing?'

'I'll make sure of it.' Guy spoke to him gently. 'You go home too, Gerard.' Bob said he'd better get home to the wife — he looked exhausted — and Fiacra said goodnight pleasantly, though more quietly than usual. Their first murder had left no one untouched.

Paula packed up her shoulder bag more slowly, allowing the others to get to their cars, and then she and Guy walked down the carpeted corridor to the reception. Outside, the cool air hit them with a kiss of rain, and she risked looking at him. 'How was it? With the identification?'

He just shook his head. 'Hardest part of the job by far. God, I wouldn't wish it on my worst enemy. That poor kid. I went back to the house after — to pay my respects, you know. The brothers and sisters were all sobbing, though I don't think the little ones really understood why.'

'And the parents?'

'The mother's in some kind of shock, I think. The father's functioning, making tea and so on.

87

Like we saw. But people's grief is different. He seemed to feel it very keenly that we can't release her body for the funeral.'

'Yes. More than two days is a lot, here. I suppose we need the rituals.'

He said nothing for a moment, clutching his keys in the dark of the car park, the security lights glowing orange on his face. 'I phoned Katie to tell her,' he said. 'She was upset. Said all the girls at the sleepover were in tears. It's made the news already.'

Paula recalled girls at school crying over what had happened to her, even though they hadn't really known her, or her mother. 'Are you picking her up?'

'She's in her pyjamas. May as well let her spend the night, I won't be much use to her.' Guy looked Paula full in the face. 'Sometimes I wonder if I'm cut out for this job any more. That poor kid. Same age as Katie. Christ.'

She nodded, brushing stray hairs from her face. There was nothing to say.

'I'm sorry about our drink,' he said.

'Not your fault.'

'I can offer you a gin and tonic of my own making, instead?'

'You mean — at your house?'

'Unless you need to get back.'

She looked at her boots. 'Well — no. I'm a bit too wired to sleep.'

'All right.' He held the car door open, his manner casual — nothing wrong with colleagues sharing a drink after a hard night. But the more he acted this way, the more nervous she got.

Guy's house was close to the Carrs'; a large spacious home on the hill — doctors, lawyers for his neighbours. 'I'm renting it from a solicitor,' he said, opening the front door. 'People are defaulting all over the place in the recession. Luckily for us, crime doesn't go away.'

'No, but the budget does.' She laid her coat over an armchair, upholstered in deep purple. This room didn't seem a man's taste at all; all floral prints and bowls of pot-pourri.

Guy winced at her last remark. 'You're right. Christ, and we've lost one already. The papers'll have a field day.'

'She was already dead.' Paula shook her head. 'We couldn't have helped Cathy. She was long gone, probably by the time you even started looking.'

'I suppose.' He sighed again — heavily.

'So, that gin?'

'Right.' He gathered himself. When he came back in from the kitchen, he had forced on cheerfulness like a comedy hat. 'Well, this was meant to be your welcome drink. What can we toast?'

It seemed wrong with Cathy stiff and cold in the mortuary. Paula took the smeary glass. No ice or lemon, but it was alcoholic. 'To catching the bastards.' Somehow she didn't think he'd mind the swearing at this point.

'The bastards,' echoed Guy, and swigged the pure liquid.

Later, Paula woke up with her cheek on scratchy fabric — a cushion. She must have fallen asleep. Guy was sitting on the floor, leaning against the sofa she lay on. He nodded along to the CD he'd put on — Pink Floyd. Before her time. Aidan's favourite, too. 'What time's it?'

He started. 'Oh — about three.'

'Bollocks,' she muttered. Her mother's lovely dress was creased. 'I'd better — oh.' She tried to sit up and sank down again. 'Why am I so tired? We only had, what, three drinks?'

He looked exhausted too, head falling back. 'Shock. First time you see the body, it gets me every time. God, it was bad. And who was that stroppy doctor with the weird name — *Seersha*?'

'Saoirse. It's Irish for 'freedom'.' Paula swilled round the remnants of her drink.

'I can never pronounce them.' He pulled himself together, with effort. 'You'd better stay here, Paula.'

She smoothed at her dress, not looking at him. 'I can get a taxi, if you want.'

He passed a hand over his face. 'It's late for taxis. I'd worry about you.'

'I suppose it is late, yeah.'

'There's plenty of room — let me show you.'

For a moment, she paused again. It felt like the edge of some tiny slippage, the roll of the pebble that starts the avalanche.

Guy stood in the doorway, face drawn with tiredness. 'Coming?'

She picked up her bag. 'OK.'

The upstairs, shrouded in gloom, was empty.

It was as if no one lived here. Paula saw a closed door, the sign in pink curly writing — *Katie's Room*.

'Here you go.' Stumbling a bit, Guy switched on the lights in a neat, anonymous guest room. No way had a man selected this flowered cover, put ornaments on the windowsill. It must have been recent, the departure of his wife.

'Anything you need, I'm just along here.' He was turning to go.

'Wait.' She held out her hand. 'You're leaving me?'

His face when he looked at her was tired, hopeless. 'I'm sorry, Paula. I shouldn't have brought you here. I'm struggling, I won't lie to you. The town, it's so — like I'll never understand all the history, the past. And at home, with Tess — it's knocked me for six. I never thought it would be us, you know? Katie — I don't know how to reach her. I can't be father and mother to a teenage girl. I don't know how. I don't know what went wrong.'

Paula remembered her own father saying the same, all those years ago when everything had happened. She held out her hand again and Guy sat down heavily on the bed.

'You shouldn't have to hear all this — you're young, you've got time. Not all this mess, this — failure.' He looked down at the blue carpet.

Paula was close enough now to smell his aftershave, the sweat of his tired body. His hair grew pale at the temples, almost grey. He'd look good grey. She realised she was staring at his mouth again. 'You think I don't know about mess?'

'You're so young. It's all ahead, your life.'

She reached for his hand, strong and warm. 'You'd be surprised, what I know.'

Around them the house was quiet, the hum of a fridge, distant traffic. The town huddled below, lights burning orange, a young girl's body at the heart of it. She put her hand up to his face, tracing the outline of his mouth, the small notch of the scar. 'How did you get this?'

'It's nothing. Accident.' He took her hand away. 'I want to say — maybe I shouldn't, but — how much I think of you, Paula. Already, I mean. You're — '

'Sssh.' She moved her hand up to the vulnerable back of his neck, which she'd been wanting to touch all day. 'Come on,' she whispered close to his ear. 'Stay here. Stay with me.'

9

The light was so harsh. God, the light! Her eyes were breaking, surely. The time — her heart turned over and calmed as she remembered it was Saturday. But when she opened one eye to see where the assault of light had come from, Guy was standing there fully dressed, in a sober black suit and grey tie. She sat up, her voice croaky. 'Working at the weekend?'

Gently, he sat on the bed. 'I have to attend the autopsy in Belfast. And there'll be a press conference later. The Superintendent's still on his golfing holiday, and as the DCI's off, I have to do it.'

'Could I go — to the conference, I mean?'

'If you like.' He looked awkward. 'Er, Paula, last night?'

Her mouth felt dry and sour. 'What about it?'

He was blushing to the roots of his hair. Paula had trained herself not to do this, as it wasn't a good look on a redhead. 'I'm so sorry. I can't believe I let that happen.'

Paula stared fixedly at the duvet. She was naked underneath, and her mum's silk dress lay crumpled on the floor. No. She wasn't going to blush, even if she'd just slept with her boss and he was now clearly drowning in regret.

He stood up, the suit shifting over his muscles. 'What's wrong?' He caught her looking.

She blinked. 'Nothing. Just — the suit.'

'You don't like it?'

'No. I do. Really.' She looked at the long lines of his body.

He rubbed his face. 'I'm sorry, Paula. I never should have — it was extremely unprofessional. There are protocols for this sort of thing. If you wanted to make a complaint, I'd completely understand.'

'Complaint?' She pulled the duvet round her naked chest.

'Sexual harassment.' He lowered his eyes.

She stared at him. 'I asked you to stay, didn't I?'

'Well, yes, but I never should have let this happen.'

'I see.' She pulled the cover tighter. 'Any other morning-after classics you want to trot out? It's not you, it's me, and so on?' He looked even more stricken, and she sighed. 'For God's sake, Guy, you're not really my boss. I'm not on the force. And you know as well as I do that officers are always at it with each other. So stop torturing yourself — you're not even Catholic.'

'I'll try.' Awkwardly, he leaned over and kissed her forehead. 'I have to go. But do have a shower, help yourself to food. I'll call you later.' He went, and soon afterwards she heard the front door close.

★ ★ ★

Paula felt like a thief sneaking down the corridor to the bathroom. Done up in yet more florals, it was another room where his wife — ex-wife?

94

— was all too present. However, the shampoo bottle she tried to use was nearly empty, and the bath showed signs of limescale. So all wasn't as immaculate as it seemed.

Scrubbed clean of mascara and with her hair heavy and dripping, she got back into her creased dress and crept downstairs. No sign of any teenagers. She opened cupboards at random, finding most bare, eventually locating one tea-bag and a mug. As the kettle boiled, she peered round her. A cork noticeboard was covered in shiny photos — someone had selected these with care. There were none of Guy, but lots of Katie and another child, the boy she'd seen in Guy's office. She smiled at his gap-toothed grin and sticking-up hair. And in a few pictures there was a tall dark woman, black curls falling round her face. This must be Tess Brooking. Had she taken her son back to England with her?

'My mum's really beautiful, you know.' Paula jumped as the kettle snapped off. In the doorway stood Katie Brooking. She looked awful — skin grey and pasty, hair greasy, a baggy tracksuit covering all of her except bare feet with chipped red nails.

'Oh, hi, Katie. It's Paula — we met the other day?' No point in making up an excuse for why she was there. The girl was fifteen, and not a Ballyterrin fifteen either. 'You're back from your sleepover already?'

'Felt sick.' Katie opened the fridge.

'I'm sorry. You heard about Cathy — did you know her well?'

She shook her head.

95

'Well, I'm sorry anyway. It's very sad.'

The fridge closed loudly and Katie emerged with some ham, peeling slimy slices from the packet and eating them from her fingers.

'I think I used the last tea bag.'

'I don't drink tea. Anyway, Dad forgot the milk again. He always does.' The girl stared at Paula, chewing with her mouth open.

'Never mind. That's your brother, is it, in the picture with your mum?' Paula had thought it a neutral question, but the effect was bizarre. Katie's face contorted, turning an even worse shade of grey, and she bolted from the room. Paula heard her feet pounding up the stairs and then the sound of a toilet seat banging up and violent retching. She called, 'Are you OK, Katie?'

A groan. 'Just go away, for fuck's sake! Why are you even here?'

A good question. Could there be anything more embarrassing than getting caught by your one-night-stand's child? Maybe walking through your hometown in last night's clothes. Paula saw at least ten people she knew on her way down from Guy's, into town and up the hill where PJ Maguire lived, in the same terraced house as years ago. Old schoolmates, her former dentist, the man who drove the school bus. Everywhere changes — a Starbucks, a new nightclub — but everything so much the same too. The lonely car park down by the weed-choked canal, where she used to go with Aidan. The bus station where they'd hung out after school. The traffic-light where she'd failed her first driving test, back when she was seventeen. A lifetime ago. The town even smelled the same, the salt ozone tang of the mudflats, the meaty reek of the dog-food factory on the outskirts. This was home, and like it or not, the map of it seemed to be etched into her skin, indelible.

★ ★ ★

PJ was at the table when she went in, and she saw it flare in his eyes for a second — a red-haired woman coming in the door. Even after so long you couldn't stop your heart lifting up. Even when you knew it couldn't be her.

Suddenly she was flooded with shame. Why hadn't she called to say she was safe? Didn't he deserve that much? 'Sorry, Dad, it was a late one.' She tried not to blush — it wasn't easy to lie to a policeman father. 'We found the Carr girl.'

He swallowed his toast. 'Aye, it was on the news. Poor wean. Have they any leads?' It didn't go away, the instinct to seek, to find. To punish.

Paula sat at the table, weighed down by the knowledge of what had happened to Cathy. No more hope now. No way to bring her back alive. 'Not sure. What do you reckon to this Eamonn Carr character? There wasn't much in the file, but he's the one built all those housing estates, is he?'

PJ swept the crumbs from his *Irish News*. 'He's a slippery one. A cute hoor, as they say in South Armagh. He's got the council all sewn up, anyhow. Deputy leader indeed! It's well seen no one remembers his da ran all the operations round the border for years.'

'Hang on, is he *Patsy* Carr's son?'

'The very same.' Patsy Carr had been a major IRA commander in the border areas, until the day someone rang his doorbell, posing as a collector for St Vincent de Paul. When Patsy came into his glass-sided porch and opened the door, the man had shot him dead right there beside the potted fern. All eight of his children had been in the house at the time.

PJ gulped his tar-like tea. 'So you've your eye on him, have you?'

She yawned. 'I just have a sense it's close to home, somehow. Course, Bob Hamilton won't hear of it. Pillar of the community, blah-blah.'

Her dad gave a dry chuckle. 'You're never working with old Sideshow Bob? Well, well. If he gets up off his knees long enough to catch anyone, it'll be a miracle indeed.'

She laughed, and then fell silent, rubbing her tired eyes. The kid was dead. That was it. She'd never get moved to the found pile.

PJ went on. 'Thing about yon Eamonn Carr is, he's got the Prods and the Taigs eating out of his greasy hand. And on the Ballyterrin council, there's not much else to stop him.'

'Where'd he make his cash? Not off Patsy, surely.'

'Patsy hadn't 2d when he died. No, Eamonn's built most of the new houses in this town, and now there's this development they want down where the travellers are.'

'They're building something down there?' Her ears pricked up.

'Oh aye, it's been all over the papers. They want to put in luxury flats and shops and that. 'Waterside regeneration' me arse. Eamonn persuaded the council to give the travellers the boot, but they put in a High Court appeal, so he's not had his way yet. But he will, the same fine fella.' PJ looked at Paula over his paper. 'You don't follow the news over here, then.'

'No.' Silence.

'Will you take a cup of tea?' PJ fumbled for his crutches.

'You're not really letting me look after you, are you.'

'I'm not decrepit yet, Paula.'

It was nice, sitting in the kitchen. A typical father-daughter chat about tea, the IRA, and dead bodies. For some reason, this was how she felt closest to him. 'I'm heading out again in a bit, anyway. Remind me I need petrol for the Ford.'

He handed her a mug of tea. 'I wish to God you'd take the Volvo, Paula. Shocking waste of money, that hire car.'

She shook her head. 'It's grand.' As long as she had the hire car, she could get out of here any-time she wanted. Get behind the wheel, drive to the airport, and hop right off this flat green island, where the past still gripped like bindweed.

* * *

A few hours later, freshly dressed in jeans and a warm jumper, Paula was parking very badly at Ballyterrin General Hospital, a big square

99

building which had been the town's workhouse until the early 1900s. She got into the space, missing a doctor's Mercedes by millimetres, and struggled out. She was going to be late, and wasn't entirely sure what had made her take this stop on the way to the press conference.

God, she hated hospitals. Nothing good ever came of them, least of all this one. As she jogged down the squeaking corridor, following signs for A&E, she tried to suppress the reaction that came with the smell of bleach. Memories, buried somewhere inside her. The first body, coming down here in her school uniform, running and slipping on the plastic floor. PJ sitting outside the mortuary with his head bowed.

'*Da — duh —* ' She'd lost the ability to speak.

'*It isn't her. It isn't her, Paula.*'

Vomiting into a bin right there and then. With relief, or maybe disappointment, because at least then they'd have known.

She pulled herself together and went through the reception desk to ask for Dr McLoughlin. When she was shown in to a small consulting room, the short doctor from the crime scene was ostentatiously tidying papers on her desk. 'If you're here for more, I can't tell you anything, like I said to the Inspector. You'll have to wait.'

Paula ignored this. 'It's still McLoughlin, is it, not Garvin?'

'You did read the wedding invite, then. Shame you didn't reply.' Saoirse turned, slamming a drawer shut.

Paula said nothing for a moment. Sometimes, there was so much to apologise for, it was easier

100

not to start. 'I didn't know how to explain.'

'Explain why you couldn't be bothered coming to your best friend's wedding?'

'No, explain that I just couldn't do it. I couldn't come back.' She spoke quietly. 'I'm sorry, Saoirse. I heard it was a lovely day.'

Dr Saoirse McLoughlin looked at the discreet gold band held on a chain round her neck. 'You've never even met Dave.'

'I know.' Paula waited.

Saoirse sighed deeply. 'I knew you were back. I saw Pat in Tile World and she told me.'

'There was this job. And Dad broke his leg again.'

'Yeah, Pat said. He's OK?'

Paula shrugged. 'He asks after you.'

'Hmm.' Saoirse stared at the yellow bio-waste bin. 'Mammy's always asking after you, too.'

'Well.' Paula shifted on her feet in their flat leather boots. 'I better get to the station. Listen — I hope . . . well.' It was all there between them, the twelve years Paula had been gone, the silence, the husband she'd never even met. 'I hope we can catch up sometime.'

The doctor stood stiffly, not looking up, and after a moment Paula went out, closing the heavy door behind her.

10

The first person Paula saw as she pulled into the new station car park was Aidan O'Hara, lounging by the entrance, cigarette cupped against the chill breeze. The collar of his wool coat was pulled up against the wind, fine beads of rain caught in the fabric. Gesturing at her car, he called out, 'If you go back and try again, you might actually clip that Beemer. You're so close!'

She ignored him, squeezing out of the admittedly very small gap she'd left between her car and Guy's BMW. 'Must be a big week for you,' she said, smoothing down her hair. 'An actual murder to fit in between the Ballyterrin Farm Show and the classic car ads. You won't know what to do with yourself.'

He ground his cigarette butt under his vintage Adidas. 'You'll see, next week's edition is a cracker. Never mind your *Times* or your *Guardian*. The *Ballyterrin Gazette*'ll be breaking the story.'

'Ah, move, would you?' She pushed past him and through the glass doors of the big modern building. She could already see the thick black of cables, the incandescent flash of TV lights, and the desk set up for the press conference.

Aidan called after her, 'You saw Saoirse then?'

She stopped short. Bloody Ballyterrin. She'd forgotten news could move four times round the town in the time it took to draw breath. 'That's your so-called investigative skill there, is it?'

'Nah, Saoirse's after texting me.' He smiled, tucking a pen behind his ear. 'I go round for a drink the odd time, with her and Dave. He's a good lad.'

Not that Paula would know. 'Piss off, Aidan,' she said pleasantly, letting the door swing in his face. They'd all been friends, hadn't they, so Saoirse had every right to still see Aidan, even after what he'd done. Did she? Probably.

Guy caught her eye as she went into the crowded room, and gave her a grim little nod. He looked steady and confident at last, whereas beside him at the desk Bob Hamilton was clearly queasy with nerves.

She heard footsteps behind her and there was Avril Wright, neatly turned out in grey trousers and a white blouse. Paula felt scruffy as hell with her jeans and hungover eyes. Avril was placing papers on the fold-up seats that had been placed through the room; already reporters had gathered in protective knots about them.

Paula indicated to Hamilton. 'He looks like he's ready to puke.'

The girl swung her straightened bob. 'Oh aye, he always gets nervous. It's why he never went into the Church in the end.' Seeing Paula's blank face, she said, 'You never knew he was my uncle? He's my mammy's brother.'

'Oh.' That explained a lot.

'He didn't choose me for this,' said Avril quickly. 'I mean, I had the interview and all. Gerard — DC Monaghan, I mean — he's always giving me stick for it, but if anything, Uncle

103

Bob'll go harder on me 'cos I'm his niece.'

Paula believed her. 'So what do your parents do, then?' She'd already guessed.

The girl licked her finger and sorted through the remaining flyers. 'Daddy's a minister. Mammy stays at home.'

'I see.'

'Your dad, he worked with the force?' Avril asked.

'Yep. He's retired now, since decommissioning.'

Avril nodded, and Paula saw she didn't want to ask any further. There were lots of reasons police officers had been put out when the PSNI came into being. You didn't want to enquire too deeply.

'Did you see that fella outside, smoking away?' the girl went on. 'Isn't he the one whose dad was the Editor?'

'Aidan? Yeah, that's him. He's taken over the paper himself now.'

'He gave me an awful cheeky look. I hear he's a terrible drinker, too.' Her tone was one of thundering disapproval.

Paula looked out of the plate-glass window, to where Aidan could still be seen pacing, collar up. He seemed to be on the phone — who to, she wondered. 'It fu — It messed him up, what happened to his dad.'

Avril was nodding. 'That's right. He was shot, wasn't he?'

'Aidan was there, you see. He saw — he was only seven.' Paula had only been six herself, at primary school, but she remembered it well. The

104

phone call coming in when she'd just gone to bed, and young as she was already knowing that phone calls meant something bad, someone else dead. From downstairs she'd heard her father answer it ('*Ballyterrin 94362*') and then there was a long silence, during which she'd held her breath, upstairs beneath her My Little Pony duvet. And then her father had made a noise she'd never heard before. '*Ah Jesus God, not John. Not John, for Christ's sake.*' And she'd known, even at six she'd known that nothing would ever be the same after that.

'Paula,' said Avril quietly, as movement up ahead suggested they were about to get started. 'I wanted to say to you, I remember when your mum — well, I just wanted to say I'm sorry. It must have been awful.'

Paula stared fixedly at the front. Of course everyone knew. Who'd she been kidding? The whole town knew, with the possible exception of Guy Brooking. 'You remember that? You must have been at primary school.'

'Yeah, I'd've been seven or so,' said Avril, and then she pointed to the front of the room. 'Look, they're starting.'

* * *

Guy faced the cameras solemnly, not a hint of nerves. Paula saw again how the role suited him, made him more assured. This wasn't the same broken man who'd sat on her bed the night before.

Light exploded round his head. 'Welcome,

105

everyone. I'm Detective Inspector Guy Brooking of the Metropolitan Police, on secondment here in Ballyterrin, and today I'm filling in for my colleague DCI Helen Corry, who can't be with us.' At that, murmurs went up from the journalists, and Paula wondered again what the story was with this Corry. A woman DCI was unusual enough, and for her to be AWOL on a major investigation was very strange indeed.

'Today we are launching a murder inquiry,' Guy continued. 'Last night, the body of Catherine Carr, aged fifteen, was recovered from a stretch of the Ballyterrin Canal. I can reveal that Cathy's body was wrapped in tarpaulin. First indications are that she had been there for up to a week.' He looked round. His hands were folded on the desk, his expression serious. 'The PSNI and the Missing Persons' Review Unit are making this case our highest priority. A child has lost her life, and a local family have been robbed of their young daughter.'

'Not bad, is he?' whispered a voice by Paula's ear.

'Just can't stay away?'

'Not when there's your man to go after.' Hands in his pockets, Aidan nodded to Guy.

'What's your problem with him?'

'I don't like the Brits sending their washed-up coppers over here, that's all. We deserve better — so do those missing people.' He looked at her steadily, and she waited, but thank God he didn't say he thought she would have understood that. Of course she bloody understood.

She spoke from the side of her mouth, as up

106

ahead Guy was praising the PSNI officers who'd conducted such an effective investigation. 'I don't know what you're on about. I looked him up, he's top brass.'

'Maybe he was before.' Aidan leaned forward to listen to Guy.

'Before what?'

He didn't reply, just gave an annoying smile and stepped forward with his hand raised. 'Excuse me, Inspector Brooking?'

Guy stopped mid-flow. 'We'll take questions after, if that's all right.'

'Just a wee one.' Aidan didn't even have a notebook, and was sucking on his pen like a cigarette. 'You really call this an effective investigation, when the girl's just turned up dead?'

Guy frowned, then forcibly cleared his brow. 'Sadly, it appears Cathy was killed before the start of our search for her. This is now a murder investigation, so from next week it will be handled by the Serious Crime Branch of the PSNI.' His tone said that was that, but Aidan waved his hand again.

'So what's the point of this Missing Persons' Unit, if you can't find people? Majella Ward, for example?'

All the reporters were watching now. Guy's face was a professional mask. 'I can't comment on another investigation, but we're working closely with Majella's community leaders, and police North and South of the border.'

'So just 'cos she's a traveller, it's not important.'

Guy sat back. 'I'm sorry, I didn't hear a question — Mr O'Hara, is it? So as I was saying — '

'Can you comment on reports that Cathy was stabbed?' Perhaps taking a cue from Aidan, a woman from a national paper had called out the question.

'Are the two cases linked at all?'

'Are you increasing efforts to find Majella?'

Aidan shouted over the din. 'Why's this unit even involved? Is there a link to an old case, is that it?'

Guy and Bob Hamilton exchanged looks, and Bob cleared his throat. 'There is no evidence at the current time that Majella Ward's case is linked in any way, though we're continuing to look for her, with the cooperation of the *Gar-da Sío-ch-ána*. We can also reveal that Catherine's cause of death was indeed assault with a sharp object, likely with a long, slim type of blade.'

'However . . . ' Guy looked round at the room, and Paula saw the reporters held rapt. He was good at this. He had them. 'I can now reveal that the unit is involved because we're investigating a possible link to several older missing persons' cases, which we may now reopen.'

He was drowned out by a crescendo of voices in the room.

Paula looked at Aidan, who'd been thoroughly upstaged, but he was smiling, tapping the pen off his teeth. 'Aye, he's got the right idea. Give them a wee show.' Sure enough, the reporters were feverishly snapping and scribbling, desperately trying to work out which cases Guy meant. The

108

story would make the front cover of every paper in the country the next day. In Ireland, that was. The British press wouldn't care enough to put a dead Irish girl on the cover, even when she'd been murdered.

Paula glared at Aidan. 'You should head off now. Those farm shows aren't going to cover themselves, you know.'

He laughed, the deep dry chuckle she remembered. 'Catch you later, Maguire. Look out for Monday's paper.'

'I'll use it to line the bin,' she muttered, deliberately not watching him go. But despite herself she could feel it when he'd left the building, as if an itch had stopped in the middle of her shoulders.

* * *

After the press conference, Guy shot out to his car, phone clamped to his ear. Had she expected anything else? Of course he'd pretend last night hadn't happened. She could hardly complain, since that was her own favoured approach to the morning after. But she was unlocking the Focus when he pulled up beside her, looking round furtively.

'Paula. I'm sorry I'm not — well, I'm just worried about this scrutiny we're under. I'd hate to damage your career. Or even if there's a conviction, affect the investigation — you know.'

She nodded, with her back to him.

'Please believe me, last night meant a great deal. Maybe after — '

'It's fine.' She refused to look at him. 'Let's get on with the case. That needs to be our focus now.'

'I'm still sorry. It was very unprofessional.'

She wished he would stop saying that. If anything, it just made the idea more appealing. She watched him drive off, hands rigid on the wheel, and went home herself through the evening traffic.

Saturday night was early to bed again, after an evening of PJ, endless cups of tea, and a film with sex scenes that made her father mutter, scandalised, and fiddle with the TV guide. In spite of how tired she was, she couldn't sleep. It was too cold in the room, her nose frozen above the covers. The photo stared down at her in the dark, the red-haired woman, until eventually she got up and turned it to the wall. She couldn't think about that now on top of everything. Finally she fell asleep with a head full of knives, and the stockinged feet of a dead girl. *Her shoes. Where were her shoes?* But the thought slid from her head as she fell asleep, slippery as the mud in the canal.

11

'Paula! Paula, up you get, it's time for Mass.'

Christ! She sat bolt upright, stricken with terror that she was fifteen again. But no, it was worse, she was thirty and just living the life of a fifteen year old. In a single bed, wearing flannel pyjamas, and her dad knocking on the door to get her up.

She shuffled downstairs in her old dressing-gown, which had teddies on the pocket. 'Mass is at ten now?'

'Aye, I like to go to the early one these days. It's easier to get a seat, the eleven's always bunged.' Any church in England would love to have this problem; here, everyone just moaned about parking and finding a good seat.

PJ was getting stuck into a plate of bacon, eggs, black pudding, white pudding, and soda farl, while Paula winced and nibbled at toast. She was still queasy from Friday night's booze, and all the rest. She coloured at the memory. Perhaps going to Mass would make her feel less awful for sleeping with her boss, her *married* boss, in the first week on the job.

She'd have thought God would allow PJ a few weeks off Mass, since he could barely walk, but as her dad hobbled up the aisle, she saw him smile and nod at neighbours, and she was glad she'd gone.

'And there's Paula,' people greeted her, no

111

doubt storing away how she looked and what she did in order to tell their mammies or husbands or second cousins once removed.

'Come on, Dad.' She escorted him near the front, crutches propped up against the old painted radiator, paint chipping off. The church was always freezing, women in good wool coats huddling to the ends of rows, suited-up thugs bowing their shaved heads to pray. It looked the same as it had last time she'd been in — for the service of memorial. Not a funeral, as such, since there was nothing to bury. There'd been prayers for the safe return of her mother, prayers that even then Paula had been sure would come to nothing. She'd sat breathing in the smell of polish and damp, watching the statue of Mary with her face full of mercy. Wondered how Jesus would have turned out if Mary had vanished when he was thirteen. After that, she hadn't been able to go back. It wasn't a conscious decision, to never go to Mass again. It was just that she couldn't bear it, and then she'd moved to London, hiding herself in that pulsing crowd, and no one gave two hoots if she went to church or temple or mosque or nowhere at all.

The priest came out in his ornate green surplice, white-clad altar boys following, their robes kicked up to show the latest trainers underneath. He raised his hands and everyone stood.

Paula saw her father struggle up with everyone else, and she put out her arm. 'Would you ever sit down, Daddy,' she whispered. She felt him bristle and then give in, and sink down. Instead she did the standing and kneeling for both of them, rising and falling along with the crowd, muttering the words that came back to her like breathing, as if she'd never been away. *Christ have mercy. Lord have mercy. Christ have mercy. Forgive us our trespasses, as we forgive those who trespass against us.*

⋆ ⋆ ⋆

Afterwards, there was Pat, bustling over in her good Sunday trouser-suit, navy-blue. 'It does my heart good to see you with your daddy, Paula. And here's Aidan with me.'

Oh God, there he was, dressed up in a blue shirt and tie, shaved for once.

PJ grunted. 'Don't see you here often, Aidan.'

Paula smirked to herself. Trust her dad to puncture Aidan's Holy-Joe act. But Aidan just smiled widely. 'Sure didn't Our Lord Himself welcome back the lost sheep, PJ?'

'He did,' said PJ coldly. He wasn't a fan of using Scripture in this flippant way, and Paula was sure he'd prefer Aidan to call him *Mr Maguire.*

Pat was smiling between them all, kind and oblivious as Mary herself. 'That was nice, wasn't it, the prayers for wee Cathy? She'll be at peace now, poor wean. Normally you'd see the Carrs all there, in the front row, all the wee ones washed and pressed. God rest her. Will we get our coffee, PJ? Your daddy comes round for a wee cup after Mass most weeks,' she explained to Paula. 'You'll come too, pet?'

Coffee with Aidan and his mum and her dad, in Pat's polished house with doilies under the cups? 'I've a bit of work to do, actually, if you could get up the road with Pat, Dad?'

'Don't work too hard, love.' Pat looked disappointed as she helped PJ to the door. Aidan turned and shot Paula a mocking backwards glance, dropping a pious genuflection as he reached the end of the aisle.

'Fuck off,' she muttered, then remembering where she was, crossed herself in some strange throwback gesture, and headed out to the car.

★ ★ ★

Ballyterrin was quiet on Sundays. Many shops were shut, everyone at home for their Sunday dinner, GAA on the TV. Paula drove the Ford down quiet streets, through the heart of town, past the Meadows shopping centre and the new cinema, past the identical housing developments which had made Eamonn Carr his fortune, up by the old swimming baths, near the hospital. There was the bus stop where she'd once waited for Aidan after school. There was the fast-food joint where Saoirse had gone on a terrible date with a meat-handed boy called Darren. The weight of memory, it almost seemed to crush her.

The Mission was on a deserted street near the bus station. A shuttered bookies, a hairdresser's called To Dye For, a sign swinging to and fro in the salted wind. Not a place with much life, it seemed.

114

But by contrast the Mission building, when Paula drew near, was glowing with light and music. Parking the car in the street, she crept round the side of the old pebble-dashed walls. It looked like a prison — *had* been a sort of prison, in fact — but now the high barred windows were lit up and song poured out. It sounded like normal rock music until you listened to the words — *let's crush Satan, underneath our feet! Yeah!* People were singing, clapping. She could hear the high squeal of electric guitars.

'Welcome!'

Paula tried not to look shifty as a man appeared in the porch. He was young — mid-twenties, she guessed — and had fair hair bound back in a ponytail. 'Oh, hi, sorry. I just wondered what was going on.'

'Would you like to come in? We're open to all.' He had an English accent; you didn't get many of those in Ballyterrin. The Midlands, she thought.

'OK. I, er, I've got a teenage niece. I heard this was a youth club or something?'

'Yes, it's something.' He smiled, ushering her in. 'I'm Ed, the leader here.'

'Paula.' The only other name that came to mind was Petunia, for some reason. She didn't think he'd believe that.

'Welcome.' She felt a light touch on her arm as he closed the door behind them, and she jumped back, shoving her hands in the pockets of her raincoat. 'How old is your niece, Paula?'

'Fifteen? Yes, she's fifteen.' Crap, what was the imaginary niece called? Paula was an only child,

115

so how old would her imaginary brother or sister be, then, to have a teenage child? 'I'm sorry?' Ed was speaking.

'I just asked if you were a family of faith.'

'Oh, yes, yes, we are.'

'And your niece — what makes you think she needs a youth club?'

She was looking all around her. The walls of the corridor were lined in photos and posters; she tried to glance at them all but there wasn't time. Several doors led off it, with its church-hall smell of paint and rubber. An office, door ajar. 'You know how it is, she's gone to a new school, a bit lonely, needs some friends.'

His smile grew even wider. 'We're very friendly here, Paula.'

'That's lovely.' She ducked her head to peer into the open office. Cables, files, nothing sinister.

He was holding open a glass door for her. 'Do come into the main hall.'

The noise grew louder as they went in, and she saw that a rock group were tuning up at one end of the room. There were guitars, drums, even a girl with a tambourine.

'One, two, three,' said the singer into the mike, and they launched into another song. This one also seemed to be about Satan.

'Don't mind the din, I hope? It's part of what we do here. We're practising for the Friday session.'

The rest of the room was filled with sofas, a pool table, a drinks machine. Like a real youth club, until you saw the posters. *Crush evil. Let*

God into your life. 'What sort of club is it?'

Ed rolled up the sleeves of the ethnic tunic he wore. His eyes were very green, friendship bracelets twisted round his sinewy wrists. A sharp face, handsome but somehow not attractive. A line of spots marked his jaw. 'We have a mission to bring God's love to all young people, especially those most vulnerable to abuse and self-harm. Our programmes combat drug-taking, teen sex, and drinking, and give the young folk something to feel pride in. We communicate God's message through song and drama.' He reeled it off smoothly. 'We're not denominational Christians, we're a cross-community venture. Equal opportunities.'

She nodded along. It reminded her of the old joke that wasn't really a joke — *I don't mind Muslims so long as they're Catholic Muslims.* Or Protestant Muslims, depending on your point of view.

'What's your niece's name?'

'Oh, it's eh . . . ' She'd been about to say Katie, since Katie Brooking had been on her mind — a teenager who really *had* just moved to a new school — but then the hall door opened and the girl herself came in. A look of horror crossed Katie's face as she saw Paula, and the girl rapidly shot back out again. Ed was watching closely; Paula saw him frown.

She tried to gather her thoughts. 'Oh, sorry, my niece's name is, eh, Mary. So she could just come along, meet some people her age?'

He moved forward to fix a poster that was drooping at one corner, something about making

117

Godly choices. 'We always leave it up to the young person themselves. To really join us they have to be willing to say no to drink, to sex, to all those evils, and engage with our community here.'

'Oh, of course. She'd never do any of that.' In Paula's head the imaginary Mary was turning into a right goody two-shoes.

'You might be surprised. They're under so many pressures now.' He looked sad. 'Mary's welcome to come to our Friday-night open sessions — it's sort of a taster. Or if not, we're having a big concert in a few weeks, in the centre of town. All welcome.' The smile didn't quite reach his eyes.

'Lovely.' She pointed to the rock group. 'Locals, are they?'

'We're from all over — Ireland, England, even the States. We get sent out as part of our training, to start missions in new places.'

'Training?' It sounded like the Mormons.

'That's right. We set up in new towns, and the young people come to us. Then we're able to train more leaders, and in a few months there's a functioning Mission here. We plant the seed, and it grows, and then we move on. This is our first one in Ireland.'

'I see. You don't mind being far from home? You're English, aren't you?'

'I don't mind at all. It's very joyful,' he said, his face revealing nothing. 'Isn't it joyful, Maddy?' This was addressed to the tambourine player on stage, a tall dark-haired girl in a long print dress. She looked also to be in her mid-twenties, and stopped beating along when Ed spoke.

'Training? It's awesome. It's, like, the most totally spiritual experience, you know?' Maddy seemed to be American. Her voice rose up at the end of her sentences and there was not a trace of irony in her words. Her eyebrows were heavy; her face not entirely pretty, but striking.

Ed introduced them. 'This is Maddy Goldberg, one of our missionaries. Paula might be sending her niece along to us.'

'Awe-some!' Maddy high-fived Ed, who returned it with alacrity.

Paula tucked both hands under her armpits in case they tried to engage her in this frankly unnatural behaviour. 'That's great, great. I best be going.' In the corridor, where Ed followed her out, she tried to buy time to search the photographs on the wall. 'These are nice, aren't they?'

Ed said nothing. She felt him watching her, a certain tension vibrating from his muscles. 'If there's nothing else . . . '

Paula was scanning the pictures. She couldn't spot Cathy or Majella in any of them, but there was a face she recognised at the end, shaking hands with Ed and holding up a sign that said *St Bridget's Mission Group* — Sarah Kenny, Cathy's form teacher, a huge beatific smile on her face. Paula tried to give no sign of recognition.

'Shocking, wasn't it,' she said conversationally, as Ed led her out. 'The girl who died. Did you see it on the news?'

119

He looked blank, then nodded. 'Oh yes. Terrible. That's why we're here, of course, to help the young people before it comes to that.' They were outside now, in the chill afternoon, and Paula hadn't managed to spot where Katie Brooking had gone. Something told her Guy didn't know his daughter was here.

'How do you mean?'

The man hesitated just for a second. 'I assume she ran away. I think that's what they said on the news.' Ed was firmly directing Paula to her car — seeing her out politely, or making sure she was gone? 'I hope we'll see Mary soon, then.'

'Mary?' She'd forgotten, and she saw from his eyes he knew she was lying. 'Oh yes, thanks very much. Did she come here, by the way?' Paula said it casually, as she unlocked the car. 'Cathy Carr, I mean. The girl who died.'

'I don't know. We get so many young people.' Bland. Uninterested.

She was glad to get into the warm car and drive away.

12

On Monday the team gathered back in their own unit, which bore a stale fug from a weekend of work: sweat, old coffee, lost hope. Paula still felt exhausted, as if experiencing some strange kind of jet lag between the two parts of the same country. Avril was neat as usual but pale and quiet, Gerard scowling at the table with a fierce intensity, his body coiled, and Bob Hamilton was popping indigestion pills like Smarties. Fiacra hadn't even turned up yet.

Everyone was silent, reading the photocopied pages of the autopsy report Guy had given them. It was all there in stark detail, how this girl had met her end. Not the why, or the who, just the aftermath, a fraction of the puzzle. Guy stood watching them in a grey suit, his shoulders held rigid.

'The pathologist estimates Cathy had been dead a week,' he told them. 'It's harder to be sure because of the water being cold, but it's likely she was dead when we started looking for her. She'd been stabbed in the neck. At the moment we're looking for a sharp knife, with a long, slim blade.'

Bob Hamilton coughed. 'The divers never found anything in the canal, so that's a priority, locating the weapon.'

Guy went on, 'Aside from the wound, there were no other signs of violence, and no ligature

121

marks except post-mortem.'

So it looked as if she'd been killed right away, not held somewhere, not tied up and made to suffer. In cases like these you could find comfort in the strangest things.

Guy glanced at Paula and she started, a trill of embarrassment making her hands shake. 'Paula, when you talked to Cathy's friends, none of them mentioned a boyfriend, anything like that?'

She spoke to his lapels. 'They said no, but I got the feeling it might not be true.'

'You might have been on to something.' He tapped the next sheet of paper. 'Cathy was two months' pregnant.'

It was as if he'd dropped a bomb into the room. Bob Hamilton's face flushed red and he muttered, 'Ah, God have mercy.'

Gerard's brow furrowed. 'That's a motive, then,' he said heavily. Avril dropped her eyes, suddenly glassy. Paula met Guy's gaze until they both looked away. She'd been sure there was a boyfriend — or if not quite a boyfriend, something else going on. Once again, it wasn't pleasant to be right.

She forced herself to ask the question of Guy. 'Did you tell her parents? That she was pregnant?'

'Yes. I visited the father this morning. With the mother, I thought — I wasn't sure she could handle it.'

'And did *he*?'

Guy seemed surprised at her vehemence. 'It was a shock, as you'd imagine. I'm not sure he took it in either.'

'Hmm.'

'What made you think she had a boyfriend, Paula?' He held her eyes for a second, looking away again. Was this how it was going to be now?

She spoke as neutrally as she could, in the wake of this revelation. 'Cathy had glitter nail polish on — I noticed that at the scene, and it's photographed here. I'm fairly sure that's not allowed at St Bridget's. And this underwear in the report — that's not typical school stuff.'

'What are you saying?'

'Maybe she went to meet someone. It says they didn't find her shoes?'

'No. The diver found nothing, and they weren't at the scene either.'

'I wonder which ones she had on.'

'Shoes.' Gerard looked at Paula with barely concealed contempt. 'You want to ask about shoes.'

Paula tried not to react. 'The school is strict about footwear — so if she had nice ones on, high heels maybe, it's a good sign again that she was planning to see someone after school.'

Gerard sneered, 'Or maybe she liked the colour. Where'd they go, that's the important thing.' He leaned back in his chair. 'I mean, did he take the shoes as some kind of trophy, or — '

'You're trying to say there's a ritualistic element?' She glared at him. 'There's no evidence of that. And she wasn't sexually assaulted, which is very significant.'

Guy held up his hands. 'I should stress there's no assumptions here. We don't know who killed Cathy, or why. It could even have been an

123

accident, and then the killer panicked, hid her body. We don't know anything yet, except what we don't know.'

Paula and Gerard subsided, him scowling again, her keeping a carefully blank expression. Guy said nothing for a moment. 'Right. What about mobile records, Avril? Did you check out the number Paula got from Cathy's friend?'

The younger woman blinked for a second, then snapped into business. 'It looks as if Cathy did have a phone after all, though the parents said she hadn't. It hasn't been found, and wherever it is, it's either switched off or disabled. The last triangulated point was on her way home.' She tapped the town map they had spread out in front of them, Cathy's usual route home inked in red. 'Earlier on the Friday she rang the same number a few times. The last call she made was to that again, no answer. There's no record of this number and it's now also disabled.'

Guy nodded. 'OK. So that's about all that's useful. Can you do anything with it, Paula?' When he spoke to her his voice betrayed nothing; only the fact he couldn't look at her showed how he felt.

She tried to focus, be equally cold and professional. 'Maybe. They mention fibres in the wound — did they say what they were?'

'It's with the lab. Cotton, probably.'

'So maybe someone tried to stop the bleeding. Maybe it *was* an accident.'

'Perhaps. Let's wait and see. They'll send the other results when they come. The tarpaulin is also with Forensics, and the ropes it was tied with. It wasn't weighted.'

'Amateur,' Bob muttered. An inexperienced killer wouldn't always realise that, filled with decomposition gases, dead bodies tended to float.

'Possibly. These are all the leads we have. They can get DNA from the foetus, of course, but unless the father's on the database it won't be much use at first.' He spoke tonelessly; Guy wasn't spending much time on 'team building' this morning. 'That's all then. We're under a lot of pressure as you know, not just on this current case, but on Majella's too. We need to get officers on the streets — sweeping fields, divers in the rest of the canal and any lakes nearby, door-to-doors . . . '

'What's the progress on those?'

'They're busy with Cathy's neighbours,' said Gerard. 'There's an old lady on one side, so maybe she saw something. Single fella on the other, he was out at work, he says.'

'OK. Did you get the CCTV from last Friday?'

'Some. A few businesses aren't keen to hand it over.'

'Well, remind them who's asking, and if needs be, pull up some dirt on them. They probably won't have any older footage, but get them to look back three weeks as well, to when Majella went.'

'Will do. Sir, did — did they say how it'll work, with us here and Serious Crime at the station?' Gerard, as a detective attached to the

125

main Ballyterrin station, was going to be uncomfortably torn in this case. You can't ride two horses with one arse, as Paula's father used to say.

Guy winced. 'We're still wrangling over it. Corry being out's putting a real strain on things, so the Super wants us to carry on some of the work. I'm saying we're not a murder team and we've still got forty years of unsolved cases to go through. I think we'll end up with a bit of both in the end. Try to get the footage, anyway. We want to know did anyone see Cathy leaving school, how far did she get down that road — was she taken somewhere else before she was killed?'

'What about Majella? Are we doing anything else?' Paula spoke up.

Avril agreed. 'People'll be asking, after your man and his carry-on at the press day. There was a piece in the *Irish Times* yesterday. Will Majella end up dead too, they were saying.'

Guy was frowning at the mention of Aidan O'Hara. 'We still don't know if there's any connection. We will, of course, be carrying on the search, along with the station officers. There will be posters, maybe another TV appeal, and more interviews of people living on the traveller site. Let's get those local volunteers back on the case, dragging the canal and so on. We'll have to be seen to take action, but I'd really prefer we didn't entertain the notion of an associated case at this point.'

'People'll only worry,' said Bob. 'No sense, when we don't know they're linked, is there.'

Paula didn't say that people were probably already worried, seeing as a dead teenager had just been pulled out of the canal, and another one had been missing for nearly a month. 'And what about the older cases?' she asked Guy. 'You mentioned them at the conference. Why?'

He looked at her. 'People need to understand why this unit is involved, and see that we're earning our keep.'

'You don't think we should tell the families, the Reillys and the Dunnes? It's not very fair on them. They'll be wondering which cases you mean — whether you have new information on their daughter, maybe, or their sister . . . ' She stopped. Everyone was watching them.

Guy drummed his fingers on the table. 'I take your point, Paula, but it's too early to tell them. It may be nothing, after all. That's what I want you on — reviewing the cases for any similarities.'

She tried to keep her voice steady. 'Did you find the name of the third girl back then — the one who killed herself?'

He didn't even need to check this time. 'Annie Miller, that was her name. We also need to go through the files of the Gardaí — where's Fiacra, by the way?' No one knew. Guy tutted. 'He should be here by now. I'll call him.'

But as Guy took out his phone, the glass door buzzed and a dishevelled Fiacra Quinn almost fell in, weighed down by the stack of something in his arms.

'Fiacra, what — ?'

'Sorry, boss, sorry.' He pushed into the room

127

and dumped his burden on the table, looking round at them. 'Sorry I'm late and all, but have any of yous seen the paper this morning?'

* * *

For the next ten minutes, eyes were glued to the paper and lips were moving, as the team digested what Aidan had written in the hot-off-the-press *Ballyterrin Gazette*.

'The gurrier,' Bob kept growling, as he leafed through the pages. 'The wee gurrier.'

For once Paula concurred with him. It was all there — a big smiling photo of Majella Ward on the front page, captioned *Why aren't they looking for this girl?* He'd interviewed Majella's father, who'd given a long tirade against the 'institutional racism' of the unit. There was a smaller photo of Guy, looking like a shifty politician in his smart wool coat — *Why English 'consultant' got fired from London force*. Inside, Aidan had gone after Bob — *washed-up RUC man linked to bullying of Catholic officers* — and the team itself — *failed unit costs thousands a day to run*. He'd also used the Editorial to thunder about 'taxpayers'' money wasted on paper-pushing cross-border projects', pointing out that the unit had so far only opened cases of supposed IRA victims: was there a sectarian bias at work? He even slyly blamed them for Cathy: *Team bungled for a week while girl lay dead*. Page after page of it. Speculation about what 'old cases' Guy could have meant when he spoke to the press. *Is there a serial killer*

128

in our midst? The rest of the team hadn't been named — typical Aidan, only going after management — but Paula had featured as *forensic psychologist brought in from London at taxpayers' expense.*

She lowered the paper. 'Well, those car rallies don't seem too bad now, I must say.'

Guy seemed to come back to himself. She'd watched him read, betraying nothing — just a tightening round his mouth. 'This is unfortunate, but it's just one opinion.'

'A lot of people read this now,' said Avril despairingly. 'What's he got against us?'

'He's a gobshite,' growled Gerard. 'Er — sorry, Sergeant.'

But Bob didn't seem to mind this time. He was shaking his head, sucking his teeth. 'They'll be going mad, the press lads.'

The Northern Ireland Police were so concerned about public opinion they'd even started a new force to escape the past. They weren't going to like this.

'It doesn't matter,' said Guy firmly. 'We have to get to work. Fiacra, there's a briefing for you to check with the Gardaí. Paula, I'd love to see your findings, when you're ready.'

In other words, *get on with it.* Paula watched as he strode into his office, a copy of the paper under his arm. The blinds went down.

Gerard swore again as Bob also barrelled out of the room. Avril gave him an offended look. 'Sorry, sorry. But he's a wee fecker, this O'Hara fella.' Avril tutted, but did not disagree.

Fiacra spoke. 'Isn't he the one whose da was

129

the Editor before, aye?'

They all thought for a moment about what had happened to John O'Hara.

'It's no excuse,' Avril declared. 'He's no right to say all this.'

Fiacra scratched his head, his open smiling face downcast. 'It's bad craic, this. Well, I'm away to Dundalk. Catch yous later.' He went out, inserting white headphones into his ears from the pocket of his suit.

Paula quickly re-read the bit about Guy. *Inspector Brooking was formerly working on London counter-terrorism, in the wake of the 7/7 bombings. But he was removed from this post in 2008 after two men died in dawn raids by his team. The police Complaints Commission ruled that 'unacceptable force' had been used by Brooking's officers. Don't we deserve better than a washed-up English bobby on the beat?*

She knocked softly on his door. After a while, he said, 'Come in.' He was sitting at his desk with his head in his hands, the paper in front of him. She saw how hard he'd been holding it together in front of the team; he looked awful.

'Are you all right, Inspector?'

He frowned at the use of his title. 'You don't have to call me that.'

She sat down. 'Just ignore it. Aidan's, he's — well, he has issues. Especially with the police.'

'You're close then. The two of you.'

'I wouldn't say that. His parents were friends with mine.' The moment she said it, she could have kicked herself. What was she thinking, bringing up her family? Hastily she added,

130

'Aidan's dad was killed in the Troubles. The IRA shot him in his office, and Aidan was there at the time. It's sort of messed him up a bit.'

Guy rubbed his eyes. 'Everyone has something, don't they?'

'That's what happens in a war.'

He looked up. 'It isn't true, you know. What he wrote.'

'I didn't think it was.'

'Well — I mean, some of it is technically true. The men did die; it seemed like one of them had explosives, so an officer fired some shots and . . . well, it turned out he hadn't. It was awful, of course, but an accident. Everyone was so jumpy then. Mistakes happened. But that's not why I left. He got that wrong.'

She watched him. 'Why did you?'

Guy shuddered, pressing his palms over his face. 'I left because my son was killed.'

13

For a while she said nothing, listening to him breathe hard, as if he might cry. 'Is that your son?' He followed her gaze to the photo on the desk.

'That's him. Jamie.'

'How did he — '

'After the terrorism job, they moved me onto gangs. I was a sort of czar, as they call it in the media. I wanted out of anti-terror anyway. To be honest, I thought we were doing more harm than good. Repeating all the mistakes made here.' He gestured out the window. 'And also — a lot of people had died in terrorist attacks, yes — but where we lived, in East London, a child was being stabbed nearly every day. Every bloody day you'd wake up and find some other skinny kid lying dead in the gutter.'

Like the early nineties in Northern Ireland, when you listened to every bulletin tensed, waiting to hear who else was killed. Her mother gone too during that time, lost through the cracks somehow.

'We did well for a while — knife armistices, education in schools, helping girls get out. You know what they do to the girls?'

She knew; she'd worked on gang cases at Missing Persons. 'They rape them.'

'The boys take turns,' said Guy. 'Girls younger than Katie. Initiation, they call it.'

She waited.

'I think it was getting to them, the gang leaders. So they found out where I lived, which was easy enough. I'd made a big deal of living locally, being part of the community. They drove round one Sunday. Quiet day, sunny. Jamie was playing football in the garden. I'd fallen asleep in front of the TV. Tess — she'd gone to work. She's a midwife, and someone was having a breech birth or something.' He paused. 'Katie heard the shots. She was in her room doing homework. She woke me, and then — and then we found him, and I did CPR, but ... ' His face convulsed. 'I think they only meant to shoot at the house, just to scare me. But it got him right here.' He touched a hand to the breast of his suit, over the heart. His eyes were fixed on the photograph of Jamie, gap-toothed, smiling. 'It's one of the reasons I took this job. I thought maybe, if I was lucky, I'd never have to see a dead child again. If everything's already happened, if it's in the past, then it can't hurt. That's what I thought, anyway.'

'I'm so sorry,' she said quietly. For all of it, she meant — his son and his job and the paper, and having to see Cathy Carr's poor broken body.

'Did they catch the killers?'

'Yeah. Seventeen year olds.' He shook his head. 'They got two years each.'

'And Tess — she's really gone, then?'

'She came with me here. We thought, a new start ... But she was lonely and cold and I suppose she felt we'd left Jamie behind. As if we'd forgotten him. She's selling the house in

133

London now. Can't stand living there any more, with the memories.'

All Paula could think of to say was to offer her own story, the thing she carried round on her own back like a hod full of stones. But she'd spent too many years trying not to, and anyway, he'd find out soon enough. 'That's awful for Katie,' she said instead. 'She's been through so much, and now this with her schoolmate too.'

'Yes. She seems very shaken up about Cathy. They didn't really know each other that well, she said, but I think it just reminds her. Of Jamie.'

'You said she'd made some friends?'

'She went to Siobhan's again yesterday. I think they're planning a memorial for Cathy.'

Funny, then, that Paula had seen her in the Mission. It wasn't her place to say anything though, was it? Guy's shoulders were hunched, his face haggard. She wanted to touch his hand, kiss him — anything to make it better. 'How old was Jamie?' she asked.

He said nothing for a long time. Then: 'He'd have been ten the week after.'

Paula stood up. 'I need to go out, is that OK? I've something to do.'

'Fine.' He was still staring at the photo as she left. If she couldn't kiss him, she decided, she was damn well going to do the next best thing.

★ ★ ★

'There you are, Maguire. Looking good. Always liked you in — well, black, and more black.'

'What the fuck's this?' Paula slammed down the newspaper on Aidan's desk.

She had pushed her way into the empty open-plan office on the first floor of the paper's HQ. The ground floor had once been smart, glass-fronted, but now the paint peeled and the window was smeared with handprints from many years of passing schoolchildren. There seemed to be no other staff in the building.

Aidan squinted at the paper. 'Oh, you bought it? Thanks for supporting us!'

'Aidan. *Fuck off.*'

'Jesus, don't let my mammy hear you talk like that.'

'Tell me what the hell this is.' She rattled the paper in his face.

'It's a serious investigation into a public body that's not fit for purpose.'

'We're looking for two missing children, how's that not fit?'

'And what have you found? One of them's dead, and as far as I can see, no one gives a flying fuck what happened to the traveller girl.'

She opened her mouth and shut it again. 'Guy Brooking's a good man. He's doing his best.'

'Maybe that's not good enough. Ballyterrin needs better.' Aidan tapped at his computer, pencil held in his teeth.

'Well, you got a fact wrong.'

'Always happy to correct errata.'

'The reason he left London — he wasn't asked to. He wanted to go. You know why?'

'Felt a wee bit guilty, did he?'

'Yes. But because his son died, not because of what you think.'

Aidan's fingers stopped.

'You didn't find that out in your, what was it, *exclusive in-depth investigation*? I mean, Christ, Aidan, it's not the *New York Times*.' She turned to go. 'Look it up. Jamie Brooking. I'm sure a top-notch journalist like yourself can easily find out.'

He looked at her. 'Is that true?'

'Of course it is. You'd have found it if you'd the slightest modicum of journalistic impartiality.'

'Those are some big words, Maguire.'

She sucked in her breath. 'You haven't changed a bit, have you.'

'Listen, I . . . ' He fell silent and she rounded on him.

'If this is all to get at me, it's a bloody spineless way of doing it.'

'What? No, it's not about you. Christ, I'm just trying to make this place something real. A proper paper, not just, you know . . . pictures of people holding up those stupid big cheques.'

'By running a hatchet-job?'

'No, it's not — Ah, Maguire, you know what I'm about.'

'I used to.' It was all there between them, the sharp edges of the past, unblunted by time.

'I'm sorry,' he muttered. 'Just trying to make it — you know. Like the old days. When Da was alive.'

She sighed and stopped in the doorway, mid-dramatic exit. Even after everything, she owed him more than that. 'I know. I get it, OK? It just seemed a bit pointed, with me starting the job.'

'It wasn't about you.'

'You swear?' She forced herself to look him in the eye.

'Cross my heart, Maguire. I'm just trying to run a paper.'

She sighed and looked around her. 'Some paper. Where's the staff, for God's sake?'

'You're looking at it, Maguire. There's a few old-timers doing the ads and classifieds still, and the odd local column, but, well, times are hard.'

'You don't mind working in here?'

Aidan shrugged. 'He's here with me.' It was a strange thing for a self-professed atheist to say, but she knew what he meant. John O'Hara's typewriter still stood on the desk, his sharpened HB pencils in a jar, even his hat where he'd hung it up the last night he came into the office, never to leave alive. The problem was, bits of his blood were also probably still in the floorboards behind where Aidan sat.

'You don't . . . think about it?'

Aidan turned on her, eyes very dark. 'You think about your mammy every time you're in your kitchen?'

Paula swallowed. 'Yes. Every time.'

'Well then.' He paused. 'I was sitting under there when they came in.' He pointed to a heavy wood table against the wall, stacked with back issues of the paper. 'Playing with my soldiers, which is sort of funny 'cos at first I thought the men were soldiers too. The guns, that's why.'

They'd never know if the IRA gunmen who came for his father had just missed Aidan (balaclavas not offering much in the way of peripheral vision), or if a seven year old wasn't seen as a 'legitimate target'. Either way, he'd been there for two hours before anyone found him, his father's shattered head leaking blood all over the floor. When asked why he hadn't moved, all Aidan could say was that Daddy had told him to *sssh*. *When the men did the bangs*, Aidan said, *he did shh*. And the little boy had put his finger to his lips, as a dying man might when his only thought was to save the son he thought he'd never have.

'He always had Polos, your dad,' Paula said after a moment. 'That's what I always think of.'

Aidan's face twisted. 'You'd hardly remember him, Maguire.'

She'd been six. Just the hat, the smell of mint, and the voice saying, *There's a good wee girl, Paula*. She shook herself to clear the mist of the past. 'So you're taking the paper back to the investigative style.'

'My dad got shot for what he wrote. Seems the least I can do.' He stared fiercely at his screen.

'Mmm. Sort of a shame though. I mean, who's going to cover the golf dances and car rallies now?' She was relieved to see him laugh, finally, and that in itself brought a gush of memory to her chest, the sound, thinking, *It'll be OK, he's laughing, I made him happy. It'll be OK.*

Aidan gave her a strange smile, one she couldn't quite fathom. 'No bother, Maguire. We'll do those too.'

138

14

Guy was in his office on the phone as Paula hurried back in. She was so behind on her work, but she'd barely turned the computer on when he opened his door, indicating to the rest of them that they should listen as he talked into the receiver. 'I appreciate your saying so. Thanks. Good to speak to you.' He hung up and smiled. 'Well! That was unexpected. The *Ballyterrin Gazette* wants to do a profile on us — our side of the story. I want to let them know exactly what we're doing to find Majella, put the word out.'

Round the room there were looks of surprise, and from Gerard Monaghan a deep scowl. 'We should tell him where to go,' he said.

'Well, I think it's good,' said Avril decisively. 'He'll see we really do care about the cases, and he'll write something nicer.'

'Sure. You believe that if you want,' Gerard sneered.

'Not everyone's out to get us!' she shot back.

'Aye, and what would you know. You think you can solve crime with spreadsheets.'

'Come on, everyone.' Guy had his public face back on. 'Let's help him.'

'So long as he keeps a civil tongue in his head,' said Bob Hamilton, who had glared at his niece for her outburst. 'He's always effing and blinding, that O'Hara lad.'

'Will there be photos?' asked Fiacra, wide-eyed.

'Only I need to get me hair cut.'

Guy laughed, then quickly stopped when he saw that Fiacra was serious.

'Will there?' Emerging from her sulk, Avril bit her lip.

'It's about policing, not vanity,' said Bob the killjoy.

'I don't want that fella taking pictures of me,' said Gerard, folding his arms. Suddenly he gave Paula a dark look. 'Bet you wouldn't mind. Thick as thieves with him, you are, I hear.'

Guy held up his hands. '*Please*, everyone, be professional.'

'What's that supposed to mean?' Ignoring Guy, Paula glowered back at the dark-haired detective.

'I heard you and him go way back. Getting the ride off him, weren't you?'

'*Were* you?' Avril gaped.

Paula snarled at Gerard. 'I know him, yes. It's a small town, everyone knows each other.'

'*Can we stop this, please!*' Guy's tone made them all look up, quarrels subsiding. She'd never heard him speak that way before: it made your spine spring to attention. 'I don't want to hear these kinds of personal comments in my team, OK? Now get back to work.'

But as she went out she saw him cast her a look, and his face wasn't happy.

★ ★ ★

An hour later, Guy and Aidan were holed up in Guy's office, doing another *in-depth exclusive interview*. Paula was supposed to be writing reports, but kept looking up, wondering with irrational panic if they were talking about her. She did her best to ignore them and get under the skin of the 1985 cases.

To all appearances, the two girls who went missing twenty-five years ago had nothing in common either, just like Cathy and Majella. Rachel Reilly was a tall healthy girl with strawberry-blonde hair and freckles on her nose, who'd left school at fifteen and worked for her parents on the family farm, as well as part-time in a petrol station. She'd been going to discos since she was old enough to use her tractor licence as ID. Reading through the files, it struck Paula that Rachel's parents hadn't seemed all that surprised she was missing, or even especially upset. There were hints at rows, late nights, a wayward girl who'd likely run away. The RUC seemed to have the same assessment, based on the avenues they'd explored. Paula stared at the old typed pages, wishing she could interrogate the girl's family. *Did Rachel take anything with her? Did she seem strange before she went?*

Alice Dunne, on the other hand, had been small, fragile, fair-haired. According to her parents, who'd clearly been frantic when her car was found abandoned beside a nearby river, Alice had never even had a drink, let alone a boyfriend. And yet the Gardaí seemed to have come to the same conclusions as the RUC had about Rachel — there must have been a boyfriend. Paula wondered why. Was there something in the files she hadn't been able to interpret?

As for the third girl, who may not have been the third girl at all, she was little more than a name: Annie Miller. There was nothing online and the files had long since been archived away, the case dismissed as a straightforward teen suicide, if there was such a thing. All Paula could discover was that Annie had been sixteen, an only child whose father died when she was five and whose mother didn't last much after Annie was found hanging in woods outside Ballyterrin. Only the fact that the girl hadn't been discovered for a week had led her into this case at all.

Paula struggled to come up with ideas. How could she, when she didn't even know if these cases were linked? If there was a killer, it would be someone in at least their mid-forties. A man. Nearly always a man. Someone with a car, to pick the girls up as they made their way to school or home or out for the night. How to explain the gap of twenty-five years? It could be someone who'd moved around a lot, who'd maybe left Ireland for a while, leaving a trail of missing girls behind him wherever he went. It happened.

She sighed and tried to remember what she knew about 1985. A bad year, a year of killings, riots, blood on both sides, Margaret Thatcher in Downing Street, and by the end of it the Anglo-Irish Agreement, allowing the South a formal say in the future of the North. Everything fracturing into deep fissures. No surprise if people fell through them.

Unable to settle, she got up. 'Tea, Avril?' The

142

younger woman was now the only person left in the office, the others having been dispatched to their various tasks.

'You can't.'

'I'm sorry?'

Avril looked up from her terminal, her nails clacking without pause on the keys. 'If you turn the kettle on, the electrics in here short out.'

'You're joking me.'

'No. If you wait till I've finished with this here scanner, I'll have one. Thank you.'

Avril had been busy, filling the table in the centre of the office with stacks of paper: all the open cases from the past forty years, North and South of the border. Earlier than 1997, most weren't computerised. The team were trying to establish some kind of order so cases could be re-investigated. In reality all they could do was ask for new evidence, examine DNA in some cases. It wasn't likely many of these lost could be found.

'Ow!' Prowling about, Paula had stubbed her toe on something round and heavy.

'Microfilm reels,' said Avril darkly. 'It was somebody's genius idea to put a load of the files on there. And do we have a single microfilm reader in the whole of E region? We do not.' She stretched her neck and pushed back her wheely chair, walking over to where Paula was. 'It's a mess, is what it is.'

'So many,' Paula murmured. It was almost overwhelming when you looked at it like this — hundreds of people just vanished. Like a conjuring trick, you opened the box and they'd

143

gone. *Where are you? Where are you?* The questions came back, empty echoes.

'Look at this,' said Avril, holding up one file. 'This wee boy, Johnny Burke. He was six when he disappeared out of his own birthday party.' She frowned at the paper. 'Where could he have got to? It says his mum just turned her back to look for matches for the candles, and he was away.'

Paula was rifling through the stacks. 'It'd be a family member, usually. Murder, or accident. Or sometimes kids are stuck somewhere and can't get out, like a bog or a ditch. Even a cellar, I've seen.'

Avril looked stricken. 'You've done a lot of these? Wee kids and all?'

'Yep. Kids, teenagers, old folk — a lot of people go missing in London.'

'And you don't — you don't feel upset, like?'

Paula pushed her hair behind her ears. 'I did at first. You get used to it.'

'I wouldn't want to get used to things like this.' Avril pulled out another paper. 'Mum with four wee ones, disappeared on the way to the shops, 1976. Someone must have taken her. I mean, she wouldn't just leave her kids, would she? It's awful.'

Avril clearly didn't remember who she was saying this to, so Paula kept her face neutral. 'I don't mean to sound horrible, but you sort of have to get over it. Or else it's just too much, every time.'

The girl sorted in silence for a while, her blonde hair falling over her cheek. 'Paula, is it

144

true what Gerard — I mean DC Monaghan — said, about you and that reporter?'

'It was a long time ago,' said Paula carefully. 'We were at school and we went out for a while. I mean, not the same school. I was at St Bridget's actually.' Just in case Avril wasn't sure how to broach the religion issue. Best to get it out of the way. 'What about you?'

'I went to Down Upper.' That was it done. 'So it was true about you and him.' Avril sounded disappointed. 'Gerard was on about it and I said I didn't think you'd go with the likes of him.'

'He's not the worst.' Paula lifted another file. 'He's been through a lot.'

Avril seemed uncomfortable. 'I know. We prayed for him in chapel.'

It was always there between you, when you spoke to someone from the other side. How many of ours have you killed? And us yours? Although in this case Aidan's father had been gunned down by his own 'side', for the truths he'd dared to write in his paper.

Avril was fiddling with her hair. 'You think he'll take our photo, for the paper?'

'Maybe.'

'Oh. I didn't want to say in front of Uncle Bob, but I put a wee colour in my hair sometimes. Wouldn't mind a touch-up, if there'll be pictures.'

Paula smiled to herself. 'I won't tell. There's a salon down on Flood Street, I hear. I might check it out sometime.' It was the one beside the Mission, and for a moment it flashed in her mind again, that building on the forlorn end of town, its walls steeped in so many years of misery, now ringing with laughter and light and fervent joy.

★ ★ ★

Some more time later, the door to Guy's office opened and Aidan came out. The two men were laughing forcedly, shaking hands. 'Great to see the dedication of the team,' said Aidan. 'I'll be sure to give it a big write-up next week.'

'Always happy to help the press.' Guy's smile was stretched.

Aidan took a good gawk round the office, running his eyes over Avril, who blushed and bent her head to the files. He spotted Paula. 'Ah, there's yourself, Maguire. Hoping to get a wee word with you too for the paper — local girl back from London, blahdey blah.'

Paula looked at Guy, who nodded. 'That's a good idea.'

'Grand, grand, will we go for a jar so, Maguire?'

She looked pointedly at the clock. 'It's only lunchtime.'

'Fair enough. A sandwich, then?'

'I suppose so,' she said reluctantly. 'Is this OK?' she asked Guy quickly, putting her jacket on as Aidan ambled out to the front and lit a cigarette.

Guy's eyes narrowed. 'Maybe you can get him to help. He seems to know a lot about the town.'

She sighed. 'He does — it sort of runs in the family. Shame it's buried under all that

146

gobshitery.' Whoops. She had to stop swearing in front of the boss.

Guy just blinked. 'I don't trust him, not one bit. But see what you can get out of him. Maybe it'll encourage more witnesses to come forward for our old cases.'

'OK.'

'Listen, Paula — '

'Yes?' She turned on her way out.

'If you're free tomorrow lunchtime, it's the funeral.'

For a moment she didn't understand. 'Oh. Cathy's funeral? They released the body?'

'Yes. I should go, to pay my respects. Would you come with me, maybe? It's just I don't know the area, and — '

She'd have to be his native guide. 'Of course. See you later.'

★   ★   ★

'What do you be taking now, Maguire? Some manner of macchiato or crackiato or whatever you call them in the Big Smoke?' They were queuing at the counter in a small coffee shop over the road. When Paula was younger there'd been not a single one in Ballyterrin; now there were dozens.

'Just tea'll do.'

'Fair enough, staying true to your roots. I'll get this.'

She sat down and he brought over a pot of tea and a ham baguette, with a slice of carrot cake for her. 'I know you'll get weak in the head if you

147

don't have your feed of sugar.'

'Thanks.' Grudgingly, she nibbled at the food. Aidan had a black coffee, and she pointed at it. 'They teach you that habit in Dublin?'

'Even the mammy does be drinking coffee now. With your da, as it happens.' He winked and she looked away, irritated.

'What do you really want? It's not like you to make amends.'

He fiddled with the spoon in his coffee, holding it like a cigarette. 'Had a wee look into some of the things you said, and you were right about your man's son and all that. I'm not one to kick the fella when he's down. Not that I trust him as far as I could throw him.'

She blew on her tea, realising the two men were more alike than you'd think. 'So you got a fit of conscience, then. Was it called Pat?'

He laughed. 'She might have had a few sharp words. But I think we could get our heads together and find out some more about all these cases.'

'That's all we'll be getting together,' she said. 'Anyway, what do you know about this Mission down in Flood Street?'

'The one the kids are all off to? Let's see, they came to town round about July time, I think. Part of some big American church, all that hand-clapping and guitar-playing and Jesus saves. I mean, Christian rock, Maguire — Kurt Cobain'd turn over in his grave. They were in England before, picked Ballyterrin 'cos it's near the border, I s'pose. They set up in the schools and do plays and that, get the kids to swear off

148

drugs, sex — all the fun stuff.'

She refused to meet his eye. 'What would you say to digging a bit of dirt on them? Religion stories are big sellers, aren't they?'

He considered it. 'It'd have to be more than your regular sex abuse. Sad to say, but we're up to our eyes in that in Ireland.'

She told him that the only thing they could find linking Majella Ward and Cathy Carr was that both girls had gone to the Mission, and she described her encounter with the creepy Ed. Aidan looked interested. 'Now then. I wonder what they get up to down there?'

'Here's something else — another girl who went there may have killed herself a few months back.'

'Would that be Louise McCourt?'

'Yes, poor kid. But no one wants to look at a link.' Suddenly she saw he had one hand in the pocket of his coat, and she lunged her arm across the table at him. 'You better not be fecking taping this.'

'Jesus, Maguire, it's the Creamery we're in, not Watergate. I'm after my pen.' He produced the blue ballpoint in evidence and began jotting down notes on napkin. 'Anything else you want dug up?'

'Well.' She looked round her, but the café was quiet for a weekday, just one young girl behind the counter, with striped hair extensions and head-phones in. 'Eamonn Carr. You know anything?'

'Aha. The plot thickens.' He held his hand about a foot above the table. 'That's the height of the stuff I could give you on him. He's a whole ton of companies and not a few of them steer close to the wind. Lending money; waiting till people default then seizing their houses to sell on; this new development down at the docks — you know about it?'

Paula's mind was whirring. 'Dad mentioned it. And seeing as the traveller camp's taking up a fair portion of the land, he'd be wanting rid of them?'

'Oh yes. The travellers have a High Court appeal in, but Eamonn Carr's got the council in his pocket, even the Prods — ever since he waved a bit of money in their faces. So he'll get his luxury waterside homes in the end, and the travellers'll be out on their arses. But the thing is, Maguire,' he leaned forward, 'his wee girl's dead, isn't she? And as you and I know, Eamonn Carr's not the only crook in this town who's driving around in a Merc. Doesn't mean he had anything to do with the poor wean ending up in the canal.'

She shook her head slowly. 'I know. I can't even say what I think, I'd be lynched. But there was just something weird about the family. It didn't ring true, somehow.'

'I'll look into it. Thing is though, he's got lawyers from here to Dublin who'll shut the *Gazette* down faster than you can say 'injunction'. And I can't afford to fight them.'

'Finances not too good, then?'

'Let's just say we're about one stapler away from disaster.'

'I see. So this Mission, you've looked into them before?'

'Yeah, same problem. Lawyers all over them like a rash. They might look nice and happy-clappy, but there's some serious American muscle behind these fellas. I tried to do a story about them setting up here and they weren't one bit pleased about it.'

'Maybe you can see if there's been allegations against them. Cult stuff, extorting money, abuse.'

Aidan drained his coffee. 'They've a big prayer concert coming up. All the schools are involved; it's supposed to be good for cross-community relations.'

'Yes — he said. The leader guy, I mean — Ed something.'

'Ed Lazarus, he calls himself. Blond fella, ponytail?'

'That's him. Lazarus — surely to God that's a fake name. We should find out the real one.'

He looked at her quizzically. 'Am I to gather from all this that you've already been snooping round?'

'Not snooping. Just looking for a youth club for Mary — you know, my niece.'

He laughed out loud. 'And you an only child. Well, well, it's Paula 'Miss Marple' Maguire.'

'I do my best.'

He twiddled the pen in his fingers. 'You're not going to tell me what old cases your man Brooking's investigating, are you?'

'I can't. It's too soon, he says — might upset the families. So far there's nothing to really link them, anyway. It's not very responsible of you to print it, causing panic like that. Making people think we've some kind of serial killer in town. I

151

mean, there's no evidence for it.'

'Hmm.' She could see he'd caught the scent of a story, like a dog sniffing the air. 'You're not a very good liar, Maguire. Never were.'

She ate the last bite of carrot cake. 'I can't say any more. I better shoot. Thanks for the cake, I suppose.'

'No bother. Am I forgiven my trespasses?'

She looked at him for a long time across the table, until he smiled, sheepish, and said, 'Only a joke, Maguire. Say hello to the wee blonde girl for me.'

'Ha! Avril wouldn't give the time of day to a boozy Taig like yourself.'

'Let me guess — Protestant schoolgirl, runs a Sunday school, teetotal?'

'She's Bob Hamilton's niece,' said Paula, and heard him laugh again, and made herself go. She had to be clear about one thing. He might be a useful person to dig up dirt, but that didn't mean for one moment that she forgave him. Their banter was fragile as ice, a layer spread over the fathoms between them. She leaned over close to him as she stood up. 'Aidan, are you going to your mum's for dinner?'

'Suppose so — I normally do. Why so?'

She sniffed. 'You better get a shower before you go. I can smell the JD from here.'

★ ★ ★

Back in the office, Paula saw that Avril had arranged the old cases into piles, adding Post-its to each to identify them. One was marked

152

Women aged 31–50. Paula rested her hand on it, knowing the name she didn't want to see would be buried there in all that paper, under the layers of dust, and time. 'Have you looked at these yet?' she asked innocently.

Avril was in the small kitchen annexe off the main office. 'Not yet. I was doing younger girls first, like you said.'

'Right.' Maybe Guy wouldn't make the link. After all, Maguire was a common enough name. She leafed idly through the pile that said *Women aged 15–30*, then slowed down. She fanned the papers out into a row and looked over the details again. 'Avril?'

The girl poked her head round the door. 'I'm making a cup of tea, since I finally finished the scanning. Want one?'

'I'm grand — what are you doing with these papers?'

'Oh! I just put them in order, like. Was it not right?'

'No, no, it's fine. Did you notice anything?'

Avril came forward, puzzled, a carton of milk in her hands. 'No.'

Paula held up a sheaf of paper. 'These are all girls, right? Under twenty?'

'Yes.' Avril peered at the papers.

'Look.' Paula snatched up a yellow highlighter from Avril's desk — she was the kind of person who always had a full set of stationery — and traced out a phrase.

Avril read over her shoulder. '*Church group.*'

'And this one too — the same phrase.'

'They both went to church groups, and then

153

they disappeared.' Avril set down the milk and shuffled through the papers. She frowned. 'Here's another. A coincidence?'

'I don't know.' Paula's heart was beating hard. 'The cases are all from different areas — Galway, Cavan, Limerick — all in the South.' Her mind was whirring. The link might not always have been noticed right away — not over so many years, cases from all over the country . . .

'Paula?' Avril's blue eyes were anxious. She wore no makeup on her clear pale skin. 'You think there's a reason for it? They're all linked?'

'I don't know.' She tried to slow her thoughts, her heart-rate. It could be nothing. 'People go missing for all sorts of reasons. But I wonder. Avril? Are you any good at Excel?'

'Of course. I passed top in my analyst training.'

'Reckon you could knock this up into some kind of chart? See if there's any more cases in the database with this keyword — 'church', or maybe 'mission'?'

Avril raised her chin. 'Only if you'll be sure and tell Gerard you can too fight crime with spreadsheets.'

'I will. That other girl too — Annie Miller. The suicide, from 1985. What's the best way to find out about her?'

Avril glanced at their other colleague's desk, on which stood no fewer than four dirty coffee mugs and a screwed-up paper bag that had contained a pasty. 'We could get Fiacra on it. Annie lived near the border, if I remember from the file.'

'OK. And if you can maybe pull the suicide stats too for this age group . . . ' Paula fell silent as Guy burst from his office, phone in hand and a strange wild expression on his face.

'They've had a hit from the CCTV — Cathy got into a car on her way home. They ran the plates.'

'And?' She could feel the tension course through the three of them.

'It's her next-door neighbour.'

15

Gerard Monaghan was already scowling when Paula met him at the PSNI station. Did he have any other expression? He'd be all right if he smiled, she decided. He had nice white teeth and a sort of brooding darkness that could be attractive.

'What took you so long?' he demanded.

'Er, I practically had to leave my kidney with your desk sergeant out there, that's what.'

'Security's tight.'

Paula had been astonished by just how tight it was, used to England where anyone could walk straight into the station reception. Here it was still bombproof glass, barbed wire, ID in triplicate. 'I've seen prisons that are laxer.'

He glared at her. 'I suppose you're here to tell me how to do my job. I know how to run interviews.'

'I'm not here for that,' she lied. 'But maybe we could talk it through first?'

Gerard sighed. 'We got the CCTV off the garage she passed on her way home. They weren't keen, but luckily we'd a tip-off they were selling illegal diesel, so they caved in, in the end. You can see Cathy on it, getting into a car. So we ran the number and got a hit.'

'Could I have a look at the footage?'

He hesitated and then shrugged. 'If you want.' He indicated she should follow him down the grey-carpeted hallway, lit by small bulletproof windows. 'Anyway, the plate belonged to Cathy's neighbour. Odd fella, lives by himself.'

'Hmm. Well, let's keep an open mind.'

Gerard shot her an irritated look, but said nothing except: 'I'll show you the footage.'

He'd led her into the main control room in the new station, and the noise and hubbub made her blink. It hadn't been so full the other night. Officers sat at new high-tech desks, with built-in phones and monitors; everywhere was the noise of voices and buzz of electronics. 'It's a bit fancier than our place, isn't it?'

'All style and no bloody substance. See those terminals, right? They're rented off the company who built the place. You plug in so much as a mobile phone to charge, and you've gone over your limit — costs a fortune. They even took the kitchens out so we had to get our coffee in the canteen. Two fucking pounds a go. Sorry.'

'It's OK.' She found his anger strangely appealing, a sort of raw energy source.

'Anyway, look at that. I need to get on.'

He sat her at a desk, in an arched metal chair, and pressed his mouse. As he leaned over her she could smell his aftershave, his eagerness to get on and nail this case. She tapped the screen. 'That's Cathy?'

'Tech reckon so.' On the fuzzy CCTV footage, a figure in a maroon uniform could be seen passing the garage forecourt. Dark hair, around Cathy's height. As Paula watched, a blue hatchback car drew up at the kerb, and after a short chat through the window, the figure got

157

into it. Paula squinted. There was a bag, definitely, but she couldn't make out what type of shoes the girl had on. 'What car does the neighbour drive?'

Gerard snapped off the footage. 'Kia Picanto, gunmetal blue. That's — '

'Yeah, I know what it is, thanks.'

'All right, all right.' He said something under his breath. 'Suppose you want to watch the interview. Come on then.'

As they got up, a woman was clacking across the floor. Dressed in a smart black business suit, she was around forty, fair hair tucked up in a neat bun. She stopped her progress sharply and stared at them. 'DC Monaghan. Is this the famous Dr Maguire, then?'

Gerard was suddenly standing straighter. 'It is. This is — '

The woman held out her hand. Her nails were polished ovals, and Paula wanted to hide her own bitten ones. 'DCI Helen Corry. I run Serious Crime up here. We're in a bit of a state, what with Inspector Brooking taking all our constables.'

'I thought you were — '

'Yes, I'm back off leave now, so I'll be taking over the murder case. How are things on the other missing girl? You're hanging on to that one. For now.'

Paula answered cautiously, thrown. 'Well — we're working on it.'

'Hmm. Tell Brooking we do have a few other deaths and the like to solve up here. And the travelling community isn't very happy about all

158

the scrutiny he's sending their way. We'll have trouble on our hands, I'd bet.'

It was impossible to tell if she was joking or not. Paula felt the woman's keen scrutiny, and saw that even angry Gerard was discomfited by her presence. Then Corry smiled, unexpectedly. 'I'll let you go then. I could use you up here sometime, Dr Maguire, if you ever get bored.'

'Er — OK. Thanks.'

Not much chance of that, she thought.

⋆　⋆　⋆

The Carr's neighbour, Ken Crawford, was the sort of man who had sweated all through his workshirt every day by lunchtime. He was in his late fifties, Paula judged, and had an unhealthy corned-beef complexion. She watched him through the two-way mirror.

'State your name and occupation for the tape.' Gerard favoured the 'bad cop' approach, clearly.

'You never said what it's about?' The man was sweating.

'Your name, please.'

'Eh, it's Ken, Kenneth Raymond Crawford. I work in the bank.' He mopped his head with the sleeve of his shirt, pespiration glistening in his greying walrus moustache. 'This is about wee Cathy, is that it?'

'Since you bring it up, Mr Crawford, tell me how you knew Cathy.'

'I've lived over the fence from her all her life, God rest her.'

'How often did you see her?'

159

He looked bewildered. 'Well, I saw her every day, heading off to school, that big ould bag on her shoulder.'

'Did you see her the day she disappeared? Last Friday, that was.'

The man shook his head slowly. 'Don't know, rightly. I see her most days, so I do.'

Gerard said, 'Mr Crawford. We've got you on the traffic cam leaving the bank at three. Any reason for that? You normally work till six, don't you?'

'Aye, aye — I took an early day, so I did.'

'Why?'

He was sweating even more. 'Eh — I'd a friend coming to visit. I wanted to get the house ready.'

'Mr Crawford?' Gerard leaned in. The man wiped his brow with a sleeve. 'Mr Crawford, are you listening?'

'Aye, sorry, son.' He took a shaky breath. 'It's just — I don't know what this is about.'

'You saw her, didn't you? That day?'

His face screwed up. 'I — I see her most days . . . '

'What time did you see her?' Gerard's voice was a growl.

'After school,' the man said reluctantly. 'Just saw her after school, like. Seeing as I was back early . . . you know.'

'You saw her in the street where you live? Or before that?'

Paula saw the fear on the man's face, now swimming in sweat. Gerard insisted. 'Did you pick her up, Ken?'

He started. 'I — no. I never.'

'We've got you on CCTV.' Gerard had his arms folded, staring up into the corner of the room. 'When you passed the garage forecourt, you picked up a passenger.'

Ken Crawford's eyes darted round, the wall, the floor, the window where Paula was watching, though he couldn't know it. No escape.

Gerard said quietly, 'Did you give her a lift home, Ken? We've got your car, you know. We'll be able to tell if she was in it.'

He started to talk all in a rush. 'I just seen her walking up the road, and it's a long way up that ould hill, what's the harm in giving the child a run up the road, I swear to God, I just gave her a lift, she was right as rain when I left her — '

Gerard slammed his hand down on the table and the man jumped, silenced. '*What did you do to her?*'

'I dropped her off in the street.' Ken Crawford was gasping for air. 'She asked me to let her out at the end of the road. I thought — maybe she'd be ashamed to be seen with an ould codger like me, so I let her out and I went on home, no harm done. She'd her phone with her in her hand, so maybe she wanted to ring someone, like.'

'Cathy never got home, as you know fine well. Isn't that right?'

The man was staring at the table, as if puzzling out some fiendish crossword.

'Mr Crawford? Do you understand what I'm asking you?'

'Aye, sorry. I just can't fathom it, son. Where

161

else could she have gone? I left her at the end of our street. Just gave her a lift 'cos I saw her walking, like. Normally I'd never be home that early, but . . . you know.'

'Why didn't you tell us you'd seen her? You must have known we were looking for information, but she was actually *in your car* and you never said. Why wouldn't you tell us something like that, Ken?'

The man opened his mouth, like a drowning fish, but nothing came out.

Gerard spoke almost gently. 'You left her at the end of the road.'

'Yes. On the main road, like, just before our street. She said, 'Would you let me out here, Mr Crawford', so I did. I did.'

'And Majella?' Gerard asked casually.

'Who?'

'Majella Ward. She went missing four weeks ago. What do you know about her, Ken? Did you give her a *lift* too?'

The man gaped. 'I never met the girl in my life. She's the traveller? I only saw her on the telly. Swear to God. Only Cathy. That's all.'

Gerard tipped his chair forward with a bang. 'Wait here, Mr Crawford.' He stood up calmly, but as soon as he was out he was rigid with excitement. 'I'm calling Corry.'

Paula was still watching the man through the window — he was shaking with fear. 'Now, hang on — maybe he did drop her on the street. Is there any CCTV round there?'

'Ah, for God's sake. She never got home! He's lying through his teeth.'

'But do we know that for sure — that she didn't get home?'

Gerard gave her a disgusted look. 'Her mammy and daddy said it, didn't they?'

'Yes.' Paula looked at the closed door, the fire escape symbol. Something about this just didn't seem right. It was too easy, the odd-ball neighbour who lived alone, caught on camera giving the girl a lift. Paula thought again about how frightened Angela Carr had seemed.

Gerard was still talking. 'I'm getting a search warrant. We need to get into his house — there's bound to be blood traces — and look at the age of him; he'd be in the frame for 1985 too, if we can link them.'

'Wait. Did anyone talk to Cathy's siblings yet?'

He was already walking off and wheeled round on his heel. 'What? Why?'

'Just to check if she really didn't come home that day.'

But he was gone, shaking his head in irritation. Nobody seriously thought to doubt the word of Cathy's grieving parents. Because what kind of person would do that?

16

Half of Ballyterrin seemed to have turned out for Cathy Carr's funeral, on a chill grey afternoon the following day. The rain fell in shards, piercing through to the skin with damp. Under the lowering skies, a stream of girls in maroon walked behind the coffin, keening, clutching each other. Almost like professional mourners from days gone by, bringing all the grief a teenage girl can muster. Before them marched Cathy's many uncles, aunts, and cousins.

'God, it's endless.' Paula and Guy were shivering in his car by the side of the road by the church, waiting for the cortège to reach them.

'Eamonn Carr's the eldest of eight kids,' she told him, clearing a patch of the misted-up window. 'And they've all gone forth and multiplied.'

'Like good Catholics.'

'Mmm. There was nothing in the file about the mother though, Angela Carr.' As she said it, the family themselves came into view getting out of the hearse, the parents with the four remaining children strung out like pearls between them. The older brother and sister had faces cold and frozen; the younger two were stumbling along, crying but probably not understanding how their sister Cathy could be in that box, in that car, in the sea of flowers. Angela Carr wore a smart black coat and hat, and was moving forward with

164

jerky, robotic steps. 'She's an orphan from Dublin, apparently. I wonder how they met.'

Inside the hearse, someone had spelled out Cathy's name in chrysanthemums. It was the usual bloom of choice for floral funeral lettering, and made Paula shiver even more as she thought of other burials she'd seen.

'Jamie's was the same,' said Guy, as if reading her mind. 'When a kid's murdered, it's always a huge turnout.'

'Yes.' She didn't really know what to say to Guy about his dead son. For the first time she was having some understanding of all those people who'd ignored her for years after her mother — sometimes, you just hadn't the words. And it was his child. How could you even carry on?

'Let's go.' The crowd was thinning, finally, so Guy undid his belt. They were about to get out when a bang on the window made Paula jump out of her skin. 'Jesus!'

A dark-haired man, running to bald. She recognised him vaguely as one of Cathy's uncles, the one who'd been at the station when Cathy was found.

Guy wound down the window. 'Is this OK to park — '

'Yous aren't wanted here.'

Guy blinked. 'I'm sorry?'

'We don't want no peelers here. Keeping her wee body in that morgue!'

'We just want to pay our respects,' said Paula, inching away from the open window. She wished Guy would put it up again.

'Aye, you can shove your respects. Never shifted your arses to find her in time, did you. The bloody next-door neighbour you've arrested, and you never even checked the whole time she was missing! You could have got her back safe! Wee Cathy!'

A woman in straining black was pulling him off — *leave it, Jarlath, would you* — but not before a gob of spit landed on the window. Hastily, Guy slid it up and they watched the man be dragged away in the rain, shouting words they couldn't hear.

'Well,' he said heavily. 'Perhaps we should just have sent a wreath.'

She tried to explain. 'I'm sorry — people here still don't trust us. And the Carrs — they're an old IRA family, going way back. They've no love for the police.'

'It's fine. I've seen it before. Gangs don't like us much either.' But as they drove away she felt he was hurt all the same — another rejection from the people of Ballyterrin. 'Shall I take you back to the station?'

'Er — no. If you could leave me back to my car, I've something to follow up on.'

He flashed her a curious look, but didn't enquire further, as they drove through the lunchtime traffic and the rain continued to fall, light and soaking.

★ ★ ★

Suicides were the worst. She had always thought it was the murders she couldn't stand, the

166

bereaved families, the horror, the wait, the child snatched off the street. But no, this was worse. The shock in the parents' eyes. Not some monster who did this, but their own child. It wasn't uncommon for parents to follow their children on in those circumstances. It wasn't the kind of thing everyone could survive.

God, the rain in this place! How could she have forgotten the everlasting, relentless, icy rain? It knifed down from a bruised sky, pooling in the gutters of the small semi Paula had come to, dripping thickly down the drainpipes and into the road. The family of Louise McCourt lived in a semi-detached house in one of the villages near Ballyterrin. Paula had driven the car out on the long dual carriageway, past the scrappy dock area of the town, with its shipping containers and warehouses, rounding the muddy curve of the bay. She got there in twenty minutes and did some very bad parallel parking in the cul-de-sac. Taking deep breaths, she did up her trench-coat against the autumn chill. It was OK, wasn't it? Guy had said she could look into the suicides. And where else to start but with the most recent?

Breathing hard, holding her bag over her head against the downpour, she went up the gravel path. Behind the house were the dark shapes of the hills, shrouded in mist. Not a large house. Lower middle-class, a garage on the side and a small pocket of lawn. She leaned on the chiming doorbell and waited. Nothing for a while, then a slow tread.

The door opened to a buzz of radio and the smell of stew. The woman wore a tracksuit and her face was lined. 'Yeah?'

'Mrs McCourt?'

She just inclined her head.

'My name is Paula. I'm working with a new unit based in Ballyterrin — we're looking into missing persons.'

The door hadn't budged.

'I'm investigating a possible link with St Bridget's, so I wondered if I could talk to you about — well, about Louise.'

It was like a shutter coming down. The woman stepped forward a pace, eyeing Paula. 'You didn't pick her over enough, then?'

'I'm sorry. I just — '

'My daughter's dead. You tell me what good it'll do us to rake it all up.' And when Paula grasped for words, the door slammed shut. She blinked at the pebbled glass. So. They didn't want to talk about Louise.

'Sorry about the wife.' She turned; the garage door had swung open and a small bald man stood there, wiping a wrench on a cloth. He wore an oil-stained T-shirt and jerked his head into the dark cool of the garage. 'Come on in. I'll hear you out.'

★ ★ ★

Stephen McCourt, Louise's father, was restoring a very old Jaguar in his garage. Every space being littered in tools, oil, and rags, Paula perched against a workbench, paranoid about dirt seeping into her good trousers. The radio was on low, playing a tinny pop song.

168

'Our Lou used to give me a hand out here. She was a handy wee mechanic. Never minded getting her hands dirty.'

Paula recalled the photo, the pretty smiling girl with coppery curls. 'You were close?'

He just nodded, peering into the engine. What could you say?

'Mr McCourt — I'm working on the murder of Cathy Carr.'

'Terrible thing.' He picked out some unidentifiable bit of metal and examined it. 'Don't know what's worse. Knowing someone came and took her, or knowing she done it herself, like.'

Paula didn't know either; she never had. She spoke carefully. 'It wasn't ruled a suicide, as I understand it.'

'No. There was some doubt, they said — could've been an accident. But sure I don't see how. The wife, it gives her comfort to think it was.'

'At the time, was there any reason . . . was Louise unhappy? I know this must be hard.'

He scratched his ear with the screwdriver, leaving clumps of oil. 'Our Lou, she was always a happy wee girl. Never any trouble. But then just before — she wasn't smiling so much. Fighting with her mammy. And she was out all hours, whenever we'd let her. We'd to say no a few times, though I didn't like to do it.'

'Was she — do you know where she went?'

He frowned at the car. 'Ah, sure how would you know. They do be up to all sorts, weans nowadays.'

'Did she ever go to the church group?' Paula risked.

'The Mission thing, you mean? Aye, all the weans go there now, I think. Her mammy didn't mind that, but how'd you know if she was there or not?'

It was a good point, Paula conceded. 'Did Louise keep a diary or anything?'

'She'd hardly tell her ould da. You'd have to ask the wife, but she's all cut up about it. Thinks that if we admit Lou done it herself, we'll never see her again on account of the mortal sin. But I don't know. What kind of God would He be, if a poor wee girl was punished for all eternity?' He looked at Paula.

'I don't know, either.'

He glanced behind him, to where a large metal beam bisected the garage. 'That's where she was. She used the tow-rope for the car. Climbed up on the bonnet.'

'I'm sorry.' The newspaper reports had been muted, not mentioning the details. There was a good deal of evidence that too much detail could spark copycat suicides, especially in teens.

'I mean, how could that be an accident? She knew not to mess about out here. Where do they learn these things, miss? Does it be off the TV or films or something like that?' He shook his bald head. 'It has me beat. Sometimes I think I'd ask her, 'What was it, love? Did you not think you could tell me?' But I don't know if we're meant to know.'

Paula felt tears burn in her throat. 'Sometimes, it's the only way to make it stop. Whatever you're feeling inside, you have to make it stop, so you try it. But you maybe

170

don't realise it's forever.'

He didn't ask her how she knew this, just took the screwdriver out from his belt. 'Well, that's about the lot of it. Any use to you?'

'Oh yes. Thank you. And I'm so sorry, for intruding, and for — for Louise.'

He just nodded. 'You know what, miss? She's out here with me still. Some people says, How can you go out there after what happened, but that's the way of it. Don't be thinking I'm away with the fairies or anything, and I couldn't tell you how, but I know she's still here.'

Paula felt a breeze steal through the damp garage, and looking at the strong beam, suppressed a shiver.

★ ★ ★

'Where've you been?'

Coming back into the unit, flushed from the chill, Paula was stopped short by Guy's irritated tones as he stood in the door of his office.

'I've been making enquiries,' she said. 'You said I could.'

He ran his hands through his hair. His shirtsleeves were rolled up. 'OK. Sorry. I need you back on Cathy again. We'll have to do some urgent assessments of the siblings.'

'But what about the neighbour?' Paula hung her coat over her chair. The atmosphere in the office had changed from the excitement of earlier. Gerard and Fiacra were round the big table labelling plastic bags. 'How come everyone's back?'

171

'Alibi-ed,' barked Gerard.

Guy winced. 'It seems Mr Crawford really did have a friend coming to stay — or rather, an escort hired from a certain unnamed agency in Belfast.'

'And did she — '

'*He.*'

'Oh. Oh, I see.'

'Yes. Look at these.'

She peered at the table and saw that the bags were full of DVDs, magazines, videos. *Sailor Love. Hot Studs. Young Dumb and Full of* . . . Oh. 'Well, that explains why he looked so guilty.'

Guy shook his head. 'From the way he cried, you'd have thought he didn't realise the alibi at least cleared him of murder. The 'visitor', who's about twenty, said Ken came home at around half three, alone. He was waiting round the back of the house and saw no Cathy in the car.'

'If we can trust him,' said Gerard, savagely sticking a label on a bag. 'I'm sure some of this stuff is illegal.'

'Well, Corry got her constables to redo the door-to-doors, and the woman at number five said she saw Cathy getting out of Crawford's car on the main road, like he claimed. Apparently Cathy was on her mobile, and she *may* — emphasis on may — have got into another car shortly after. Which was possibly, but not definitely, a silver colour. 'One of those small wee cars', and I quote. Thank God for busybodies, eh?' Guy grimaced. 'Though why she didn't think to mention it before is beyond me. It seems no one wants to help the police unless we actually ask them a direct question.'

'Poor man,' said Paula, examining the buff torso of one cover model. 'Probably kept this a secret all his life.'

Guy looked frustrated. 'I've never met anyone who'd rather go down for murder than say they were gay.'

'Welcome to Northern Ireland.'

He frowned — another thing he didn't understand — and called, 'Avril, can you sort out the evidence papers, please? It'll all have to go back to him.'

Avril was pale when she came in from the kitchen, eyes firmly averted from the table.

'You OK?' asked Paula.

'Yes.' She licked her lips. 'I just never knew there was stuff like this about.'

'Get your preacher to explain,' said Gerard, stretching out his arms. 'I'm sure he knows all about it.'

Avril flushed but said nothing, giving a furious look at his departing back.

'What was that about?' asked Paula curiously.

'Oh, he teases me because I'm, well . . . the youth pastor at church, he's my friend.'

'Your boyfriend?'

She flushed harder. 'We see each other sometimes. Alan's very good at what he does, very moral.'

Paula was distracted by the sound of the glass doors swinging open and a muttering in the corridor. Bob Hamilton was talking in Guy's ear. Both men were staring straight through the door — at her.

* * *

'You want to explain what you've been up to?'
Guy spoke quietly, but she could hear the anger
in his voice, a low vibration.

Paula leaned against the window of his office.
She didn't like this tag-teaming, Guy at the desk
with his hands folded, Sideshow Bob rocking
from one solid foot to the other. Hopping mad,
in fact.

She bridled. 'I told you. I've been doing some
enquiries.'

'That's not all you've been at!' Bob burst out.
'Louise McCourt's mother is after ringing up the
main station, and she's raging, so she is.'

'I didn't mean to upset — '

Guy said carefully, 'The death was ruled an
accident, I believe. I can't see why you felt the
need to intrude on a bereaved family. Look into
the *files*, if you must, was what I meant.'

She opened her mouth and shut it again. How
could she talk to him openly with Bob there, his
chest swelled out like he was wearing his Orange
sash? 'I can't determine her state of mind from
looking at files. She was dead when they were
opened — I need to know about when she was
alive.' Bob sucked in his breath, and she tried
again. 'Look. There's this Mission, yes?'

'And what's that got to do with — '

She spoke over Bob's apoplectic tones.
'Louise, Majella, and Cathy. Majella's missing,
Cathy and Louise are dead. Louise's father
thinks she killed herself. And all the girls went to
the Mission.'

174

She saw that Guy was struggling to speak calmly. 'So did a lot of children. What if I told you all three girls went to, I don't know, McDonald's? My point is, Ms Maguire, it's probably just coincidence. I can't allocate all my resources on the basis of coincidence.'

'I know, but . . . ' She breathed out hard through her nose. 'Sergeant Hamilton. Do we get many murders, suicides, or missing children in Ballyterrin?'

'No. It's a safe town,' he said stiffly.

'There you go. And this Mission's been here how long — three months — and in that time we've had all these things? I just think it's worth looking into.'

Guy wasn't convinced. 'We also have a million leads, a mysterious car to track down, a knife to find, Forensics to come back, and a whole town full of suspects to interview. Corry's back from leave, and all of a sudden I have to let her run the show — except when it suits for us to do her grunt work. We're up to our eyeballs interviewing the traveller camp — ten appeals already under the Human Rights Act! They won't tell us a thing. And Cathy was nowhere near the Mission when she went missing, we know that. We've also checked with the staff there, as I said we would, and they have alibis. There was a full team meeting on Friday afternoon, and they were all at it.'

'Oh, really?' She frowned.

'Really. I don't just ignore major leads like that, but it's a non-starter. So it would be very helpful, Paula, if you stuck to your brief. I

175

brought you in to help us find these girls, and establish whether there's any possible link to the cases twenty-five years ago. Cathy is dead — now I need you to help me find who killed her. So can you do your job? Please?'

'I will. Sir.' He didn't react to the 'sir', and as she went out, she saw he wouldn't meet her eyes.

★ ★ ★

Back at her desk in the corner, Paula sat down with a sigh. Avril was labelling the bags of porn, eyes averted, back turned on Gerard, who was at his own desk typing so hard the keystrokes sounded like cracks. Fiacra met Paula's eyes as she went in, with a small shrug: bad times.

She looked around in her heap of papers and took out the newspaper clipping of Louise McCourt, teeth crooked in a pretty face, smiling. The picture of Cathy Carr, dark, some mystery in her eyes. And lastly Majella, with her shock of hair and hoop earrings. All of them lost, in their own ways.

17

The Family Liaison Officer was cut from the same cloth Paula had seen a thousand times. Any age from thirty to fifty, running to plump, a sensible haircut. A woman, always a woman. She was having trouble remembering this one's name. Mairead, something like that? Another new Catholic recruit.

'It's just that they're very upset,' said Mairead, if that was her name. She was standing in the Carrs' porch, almost barring Paula's way. Behind her the house looked shrouded, Venetian blinds drawn.

'Of course, I understand that. I just need a word with the siblings.'

'And you're trained with child witnesses?'

Paula made herself smile and said as she had many times before, 'I'm older than I look, Officer.'

The woman eyed her dubiously, chunky shoes still firmly planted on the doorstep. 'The parents can't cope with more intrusion in the house.' And again the implication — *you don't have children, do you?*

Paula looked around her. It was a bright autumn day, the rain had finally let up, and it was not too cold for Ballyterrin. 'I can talk to them in the garden, if that's easier. Out of the house, in nature . . . '

The FLO put on an expression of *what-is-this-carry-on*. 'I suppose if the Inspector sent you . . . '

'He did. He wants the children assessed.'

The woman was wavering, Paula could tell. Her hand was on the doorknob. 'Just the two oldest, was that it?'

Angela and Eamonn Carr had spaced their children neatly. Two years after Cathy there was Sean, and after another two, Anna. Then a gap of four years, and two smaller children aged seven and five. Paula wondered how she'd even go about talking to those kids who'd lost so much. It was true. She didn't have any of her own.

Cathy's nearest sister was coming towards her now, hesitantly crossing the lawn to where Paula sat on the garden bench, Mairead hovering disapprovingly nearby. Even the lawn was neat, the toys tasteful and wooden, the grass mown. Paula didn't know much about grass — had they done this since Cathy was found?

The girl was joined by her brother, a gangly boy of thirteen in the school uniform of the local boys' grammar. Where Aidan had gone, in fact. Constellations of spots marred his cheeks. Paula arranged her face into a smile as they came over in a nervous clump, knocking their limbs off each other.

'Hello, Sean, Anna.'

Neither spoke, pressed closer together than she'd bet they'd been in years. Kids never got on at that age, or so Paula had heard. Because as well as no kids, she also had no siblings of her own.

'How are you both feeling?'

They looked away, Sean flexing his bony knuckles, Anna biting a chapped lip. At eleven

178

she was still child-like, legs coltish, face chubby. Her St Bridget's uniform was also too big for her. 'Are you in first year, Anna?'

A brief nod.

'I'm not a police person, but I work with them. My name is Paula. My job is to find out as much as I can about Cathy and how she was feeling, to see if I can understand who . . . hurt her.' She was picking her words very carefully. 'Can you try to help me with that?' More faint nods.

'Nobody knows who did it,' Sean muttered, gnawing his finger.

'That's true. But we're looking.' She smiled, trying to find a rapport with them. 'Sean, I hear you're into computer games, is that right? Which ones?'

His sister elbowed him sharply. 'He doesn't have any. Da doesn't let him.'

'Shut up, Anna Onion. I play them at school.' They scuffled briefly and Paula wondered if she would have to physically separate them.

'So you're not allowed games at home?'

'Mammy says they rot his brain,' said Anna, in tell-tale fashion.

Sean just rubbed at his eyes, as if they were irritated. Paula tried to pull the conversation back. 'So your mammy and daddy, are they sort of strict compared to your friends' ones?' A few metres away, she saw Mairead shift uncomfortably on the lawn.

She'd expected a resounding yes to that, but the two exchanged a quick glance.

'Dunno,' Sean said, quietly.

'They let you go out with your friends, or hang out downtown?'

No answer.

'Do you do things after school, yes? What days?'

'Every day,' said Anna, in a 'duh' tone of voice, twirling a bit of hair. 'Judo, band, Irish dancing . . . '

'What about Cathy? Did she ever go out with her friends?'

'I don't like her friends,' declared Anna. 'They're mean. Sometimes they hide my things and then I hear them all laughing their heads off.'

'Did you ever go into Cathy's room?'

'She said she'd skin me.' Anna bit her lip again, as if remembering her lost sister.

'You, Sean?'

He hesitated.

'You can tell me. It's OK.'

'One time. Just to read her diary. She was pissing me off. I didn't mean to upset her.' He stared at his shoes.

Paula's heart beat faster. 'What did it say?' There'd been no diary, according to the parents.

He shrugged. 'She liked a fella but some other girl was after him, blah blah, her friends were being bitches — being bad to her, all that.'

'And where is it now, the diary?'

He shrugged again. Anna wasn't even listening, just picking at the skin on her fingers. Paula tried another tack. 'Do you know if Cathy had a phone?'

Another glance between them, quick as a bird

skimming water. 'She's not allowed a phone,' said Anna uncertainly.

'OK. Listen, guys — did you see Cathy that day? The day she went missing, I mean.'

'Some bad man took her.' Another look went between the two. 'Daddy said we don't know who.'

'I meant — did you usually walk home from school with her, Anna?'

'No, she doesn't let me. Anyway, we always have activities.' They still used the present tense, though their sister was dead and buried.

'Cathy didn't have anything after school on Fridays, is that right?' Nods. 'What about you two?'

'I go to speech and drama, he goes to chess.'

Sean made a deep noise of irritation as his sister spoke. He rubbed at his eyes again, clenching his hands into fists.

'Your mum picks you up?'

Anna shook her head so the ponytail flew. 'Not on Fridays. We get lifts home, 'cos Mammy's here with the wee ones.'

'And what time do you get home?' Shrugs. 'What's on TV when you come in?'

'We're not allowed TV.'

Sean volunteered, in a small voice, 'Mammy has the news on sometimes.'

'So if you can remember back to that Friday, you came in about six, and Cathy wasn't back?' Paula had re-checked the interviews with the parents. Angela Carr said she'd been expecting Cathy back around four, but the girl had never arrived. Eamonn had come back at five and gone

181

out in the car to look for her.

'S'pose so. Dunno. She just never came back. She wasn't there.' The boy was blinking hard. 'Miss, can we go now?'

'Well, OK. Thanks very much for your help.'

Mairead stirred. 'Come on, pets, let's go inside and get a sandwich.'

'Miss?' Sean stomped off, but Anna lingered. 'Does Cathy know I'm sorry?'

'Hmm?'

'I didn't show love to her like the priest said. I pulled out her hair one time and called her a bitch. Does she know, like, that I didn't mean it?' Her eyes were huge and dark, shadows marking the young skin underneath.

What to say to that? 'I'm sure she does, Anna.'

The girl nodded, clearly unconvinced, and was gone, like a gawky bird. Paula was about to get up when she realised that two new pairs of eyes were watching her. 'Hello.'

The children flitted away at her voice, but soon popped their heads back round the shed. Of course Eamonn Carr would have a capacious shed.

'You must be Ciara and Niamh?' All the Carr children had good Irish names. These would be the youngest two.

Ciara came out first. In jeans and a pink sweatshirt, she was a bouncy little girl. 'Are you the questions lady?'

'Hmm?'

'The lady who does be asking all the questions.'

'I suppose I am, yes. You're seven, is that

182

right?' Ciara nodded, but like her sister Anna, watched Paula with a dark gaze. Cathy seemed to have been the only one with those sharp green eyes, which must have come from her mother. 'What's that you're doing?'

The girl had a piece of paper in her hand, an orange blur crayoned onto it and *lost catt* written across the top. 'Daddy told me to go out and play with Niamh, but she doesn't know the rules — she's a baby.'

Niamh was five, Paula knew. As the youngest Carr emerged from behind the shed Paula saw she still had a toddler plumpness to her cheeks, and was dressed identically to her sister. Same jeans, same sweatshirt, same Clark's shoes. Did Angela Carr like order even in her children? 'Where's your mummy?'

'She's sleeping,' said the youngest, then retreated with an embarrassed giggle.

'She sleeps in the day?'

Ciara gave a worldly shrug. 'She's tired now because of our Cathy. Daddy says we have to leave her be. He shouts if we make noise.'

'Does he? Ciara, do you remember when you saw Cathy last time? Was it here?'

Ciara nodded but Paula wasn't sure she'd understood. Did time even have a meaning when you were seven years old? Ciara said, 'Mammy shouts at Cathy. She's a liar, Mammy said.'

'How come?'

'One time I was bad and I bitted Niamh, but she did it to me first.'

'Really. Did your mammy shout at Cathy in the house?'

'In there.' The child pointed to the latticed window of the kitchen. 'Then Mammy cried and Daddy came and we had to stay in the family room for hours and hours. Niamh falled asleep.'

From her hiding place, Niamh said something incomprehensible.

Ciara went on, 'Niamh thinks Cathy's coming home. But she's not. Is she? She's away to heaven, and you can't come back, not unless you're Jesus in the cave. I don't know if she'll find us, miss, when we go to the new house. Will she find us, if she comes back?'

New house? Paula was sitting very still, and thinking carefully what to say next, as if the child were some rare skittish bird, when Mairead the FLO appeared at the back door of the house to shepherd the girls in.

'Come on, pets, it's getting cold.' She gave Paula a reproving glance. 'They're too wee to be questioned, Miss Maguire. They can't understand it, poor weans.'

'They said something about moving house. Do you know anything about that?'

Another suspicious look. 'The family were building a new house out in the country — needed more room for all the weans.' Mairead shook her head. 'When they had the five, of course. It's a terrible thing.'

It was. But why, if they were planning to move soon, had Paula smelled fresh paint the first day at the house?

As the girls fluttered off, Paula noted how they stopped at the front door and carefully took their shoes off, Ciara helping her sister. Then, with

184

unusual care in such young children, they slotted them into the rack there, which held neat rows of kids' footwear.

Paula stood for a moment wondering if Cathy, like most girls, had worn the same pair of shoes to school each day. St Bridget's had been strict in her day, so you bought good school shoes, made to last, to fit the rules. To grow into. She called, 'Excuse me? Sorry, do you think I could use the bathroom before I go?'

Mairead looked unsure. 'There's one under the stairs. I'll just give the kids something to eat.'

On her way in, Paula examined the shoe rack. Cathy had been a size five, she remembered. The only pair that seemed like they could have been hers were patent, with heels and a Mary-Jane strap. She wouldn't have been allowed to wear those at St Bridget's, surely. If only they'd been able to find the ones she wore to school.

Inside the house, which was still spotlessly clean, Paula decided she was going to deliberately misunderstand what the FLO had said. She could hear Mairead in the kitchen talking to the children as she crept up the cream-carpeted stairs. A TV was blaring in the front room. She made her way along the upstairs corridor, which was lined with more posed family portraits, all of them dark-haired, all smiling. There was the sound of a flush and a door opened, revealing Angela Carr in a silk dressing-gown. Without the heavy makeup of the first day, her face was lined with grief and worry.

'I'm sorry,' Paula said quickly. 'I was just . . . how are you, Mrs Carr?'

Angela brushed past her, not making eye-contact.

'If you ever want to chat, you know — you can talk to any of us. If there's anything I can do to help.'

Angela paused with her small hand on the ornate handle of another white door.

For a moment she looked up, and Paula saw her eyes were indeed green, a deep and mossy shade that gave nothing away. 'You can't,' she said finally. 'Nobody can help. It's too late.' Then she went inside and closed the door behind her. Paula heard a creaking on the stairs and turned to see Eamonn Carr standing a few steps below her. He was dressed in a suit, tie pulled tight to his neck.

'What are you doing here?' he demanded. 'I was told you were going to talk to the children outside.'

'I — I was just looking for the bathroom.'

He came up a step or two, drawing level with her. 'Leave my wife alone, Miss Maguire. I don't appreciate you trespassing in my home. Please go now.' He brushed past her and went into the room Angela had just entered, sliding round so Paula couldn't see in. She thought for a moment, about that rack of shoes and what the kids said. About the padlock she'd seen on the door of Eamonn's shed. Looking at the closed door, she realised she'd pushed her luck with the Carrs far enough for one day.

18

She still wasn't sure she'd made the right decision. Did the good-quality bottle express how grateful she was for the invite? Or did it say, *here I am with my posh city ways and my dazzling knowledge of wine?* There wasn't time to change it now anyway, because she was on Saoirse's doorstep with the Pinot Noir clanking in her shoulder bag. She swallowed down a jolt of nerves as the hall light went on. It was ridiculous. She'd practically lived at Saoirse's when they were teens, sprawled out in front of *Dawson's Creek* while Saoirse's mammy brought in trays of biscuits and tea. It was stupid to be this nervous going to her new house, meeting her new husband.

A huge man had opened the door, almost filling it, the hair on the backs of his hands and all up the arms exposed by the rolled-up sleeves of his Ireland rugby shirt.

'Hiya, I'm . . . er . . . it's — '

'Paula, is it?' Then he was bending to kiss her cheek and she was flustered, accepting it. Surely no one had done cheek-kissing in Ireland in the nineties. 'Come on in.'

She was holding out the bottle like a votive offering, and there was Saoirse in a striped apron, eyebrows going up behind her glasses. 'Very nice.' Sarcasm, or appreciation? Saoirse had always been a sarky little cow, of course, but never directed at Paula.

'Your house is lovely.' Paula had a general blurred impression of beige carpets and tasteful grey furnishings.

'It's Dave, he's a dab hand at decorating.' Saoirse put her arms round her wide husband, who kissed the top of her dark head. Paula didn't know where to look. Last time she'd seen Saoirse with a boy it had been shifting some farmer called Donal round the back of Ritzy's nightclub. Afterwards, Saoirse had declared she'd rather snog one of Donal's sheep than do that again.

Dave was offering a drink. 'Whatever's going, thanks,' Paula said. 'I'm not fussy.'

'It's true,' said Saoirse, smiling. 'She isn't.'

Paula realised she was sweating. 'Can I do anything to help? Smells lovely.'

'It's all done.' A smell of meat and herbs came out of the kitchen; clearly her friend's culinary skills had moved on from Rice-Krispie buns. Saoirse beckoned her in. 'Why don't you sit down and talk to Dave, and I'll finish it.'

But as Paula was about to move to the hessian sofa, the doorbell rang. No one seemed disconcerted; indeed, Saoirse smiled happily. 'Aidan's on time for once.'

'Wha . . . ' Paula swallowed hard. 'Aidan O'Hara? You invited him?'

'He comes round most weeks,' said Dave, who clearly didn't know the backstory. 'You were all friends back in the day, is that the way of it?' He was moving to get the door.

As it opened, and she heard the rumble of male voices, Paula fixed her former best friend with a look dredged up from the past, the one you used when someone talked to you in class and you got in trouble, or boked on your dad's front path. A look that said, *Saoirse McLoughlin, I am going to kill you stone dead. I will kill you like a dog in the street.*

At least Saoirse had the wisdom to look abashed. 'Come on.' She nudged Paula into the kitchen. 'Come in and give me a hand.'

* * *

'I suppose I shouldn't have done that.' Her friend had her back to Paula, cutting a fresh loaf with a long serrated blade. Paula was leaning against the granite worktop, head reeling.

'Why did you?'

'I think I wanted to show you that when you left, you left all of us — me, Aidan, your dad. And it seemed like you forgot all that, but we were still here, you know.'

'How much did Aidan tell you about us — why it ended?'

Her friend turned, eyes bright as the knife. 'Nothing. We don't talk about you.'

That stung. 'I see.'

Saoirse relented. 'I mean, I think he doesn't like to. But . . . ' She hesitated, wiping the blade gently against her apron. 'When you went, I could tell he was confused. He said you just left, no goodbye, nothing. He said you ended it with him.'

'And you believed him.'

'Yeah, I believed him. Because you did the same to me.'

189

The words dropped into the kitchen, among the sound of the meat crackling in the oven and the men's voices and soft rock from the other room.

'Why did you?' Saoirse's voice was curious, neutral. 'Just up and leave, I mean?'

Paula said nothing. To explain would mean having to tell all the rest, and no one knew about that except her father; and the doctors, of course.

Saoirse went on, 'I remember you and Aidan had that big row at the end of school, when he'd done his first year at DCU, but you'd never tell me what it was over. I mean, you used to tell me everything . . . it was weird. And then you were sick over the summer, of course, but I still don't see why you had to leave for England so soon. I thought we could hang out, have some fun before uni started.'

'You had new friends to make. We were both moving on.'

'But you were my best friend.'

Paula swallowed again, remembering all the times Saoirse had come to the house the summer Paula stayed in with the blinds drawn against the light. How her friend had tried to coax her to concerts and beach trips and discos, and PJ's rumbling voice in the hallway. *She hasn't the strength, pet. She can't get up off the sofa.* And she couldn't, but not for the reason they'd given. Of course, Saoirse would still believe it was glandular fever that had stricken Paula in the summer of her eighteenth year, in that shadowy borderland between school and university.

'I'll just say this,' Paula said quietly. 'I had reasons. I can't tell you — I couldn't — but I had them. And if you were hurt by that, all I can say is how sorry I am.' *But I can't take it back,* she meant.

Saoirse set down the knife, and although her friend now wore her hair in loose waves, and had silver earrings, designer specs, and a wedding ring, Paula could still only see the skinny bird-like girl she'd swapped her sandwiches with for years. 'I'm sorry I brought him here. I didn't realise till I saw your face — well. I thought you were OK with him.'

'I was. I am.' She tried to smile. 'Dave seems lovely.'

Saoirse's face softened. 'Ah, he is that. Come in and we'll get you a drink.'

★   ★   ★

Aidan had brought a pack of imported beer, and to Paula's surprise there were still four left. Perhaps, as Pat said, he had changed his ways. 'Hiya,' she said forcedly, gulping red wine. Saoirse was drinking the same and the men had beer. She put on a smile. They were chatting about work, traffic, Gaelic football. Aidan supported Down, Dave the neighbouring county of Armagh, and there was some good-natured banter, while Saoirse slipped in and out of the kitchen. When she came back in she was carrying a great side of beef, steaming with herbs.

Aidan clapped Dave on the shoulder. 'You're a lucky man, fella.'

Saoirse was flushed from the praise and Paula felt a stab of — what? Wishing she'd learned to cook instead of jogging to crime scenes at dawn, staring at sociopaths across prison interview rooms?

Dinner was nice. She'd wanted to ask Saoirse and Dave how they met, what they were like together, but felt ashamed that she didn't know these things. Once, she'd known everything about Saoirse, what mark she got in history, when she had her period, which of her brothers she hated the most. Everything. Now she didn't even know the man her friend shared her life with.

But Saoirse perhaps sensed this. 'You won't know how me and Dave met, will you, Paula?'

'No.' She gulped more wine to cover the taste of shame.

'You remember I wrote to you about my foundation course? You do all these rotations, see, when you're training to be a doctor.'

'Mmm.' The many letters sent by Saoirse, never answered.

'Well, I was in A&E for a time — Jesus, that's tough, I'm telling you. No fear of gruesome stuff now. And this fella here comes in, and as you can probably tell from the cut of him, Paula, he's into the GAA.'

A Gaelic football player then, not rugby. She should have realised.

'And he's his shoulder shattered across, blood pouring down his face, but clamouring to get back to some stupid game.'

'It was the Ulster Youth Final,' said Dave

192

peaceably. It was hard to imagine him streaming with blood. He took up the story. 'There I was, Paula, all battered and blue, and some wee besom of a doctor poking me full of needles, eating the head off me. 'I'll sedate you', says she, 'if you move a feckin' muscle.' Nice talk for a doctor, eh?'

'Don't tell Mammy,' Saoirse laughed. They passed the baton of the story between them. 'I read him the riot act, basically, sitting his arse down till I was finished — and the next day don't I walk into a case conference and who's sitting there, a bandage round his head. 'Oh,' they goes, 'this is Mr Garvin, the hospital's social worker.' Well, I was scundered.'

Scundered. Paula hadn't heard that word in years.

'Lucky for her I like a woman who can stitch me up like a jersey,' said Dave, moving over to kiss his wife, who flushed again. Paula met Aidan's eyes briefly and looked away. She wondered in that moment was he seeing anyone. Surely he'd have brought his girlfriend, if he had one.

Aidan was chewing. 'So, Saoirse, I see you got in the paper for being first on the scene with the wee Carr girl's body.'

Paula flinched, but the other two went back to eating their beef. 'Yes. Unusual case, the water aspect. Very hard to tell how long she'd been in for.' Then Saoirse saw Paula's face and laughed. 'We're a bit of a cabal here. Journalist, social worker, old ghoul like me — it takes a lot to shock us.'

'And do you — do you talk about work?'

They glanced round at each other. Saoirse answered cautiously. 'Not the really confidential stuff. But often it helps, you know, if you have a problem you can't solve.' Was that a hint?

'I was hoping Saoirse and Dave might shed some light on our current conundrum,' said Aidan, raising his eyebrows at Paula across the table. She felt annoyed. Wasn't it for her to ask Saoirse, if she wanted help?

Saoirse set her plate aside as if she'd been waiting for the chance to speak. 'I read the autopsy report on Cathy. The way I see it, what's significant is that blade. It was something very sharp, very long. Not a street knife.' She reached out and lifted the blade they'd used to carve the beef, wicked shiny. 'These are a set we got for a wedding present. They had to be ordered special from Dublin. Mammy thought we were mad — course, she thought a list was the height of rudeness anyway.' She rolled her eyes at Dave, and Paula realised she'd never even sent them a wedding gift. What was wrong with her? But she'd been young, thoughtless, thinking only how to get away, how to survive.

'So you're saying someone owned a dear knife,' Aidan was saying.

'Right. It's not some gurrier. It's someone with money, I think.'

Dave coughed politely. 'I'd not say this if there was . . . but, well, we had no files on the Carrs. No suspicion of anything.'

Paula wondered did they have any files at all on middle-class families.

'But it's weird — ' Saoirse stopped herself. 'You didn't make it public that Cathy was . . . ' She looked significantly at Paula, who shook her head. Of course they hadn't put out that the girl had been pregnant.

'They told her dad, when he identified her, but that's all.' She wondered again how Eamonn Carr would have reacted to that news. Had he told his wife, who seemed to have such a fragile hold on the world?

Aidan was frowning between them, puzzled. Saoirse seemed to think about it, and then said, 'We're all friends, Paula. He'd not tell anyone.'

'But — '

'Cathy was pregnant, Aidan. Two months'.'

There was an odd movement from Dave, and Saoirse put her hand on his arm.

Aidan's face was a picture. 'Jesus, Mary, and Joseph. That puts a different light on things.'

'Dave'll tell you this, but round here teen pregnancy's about as low as you get. And for girls like Cathy . . . ' Catholic girls, Saoirse meant. Wealthy, controlled. Never allowed out.

'Everyone said she'd no boyfriend,' said Paula, when she'd got over the shock of breaking confidentiality. It was Saoirse, sensible Saoirse. She must have a reason. 'There's the obvious random abductor theory, but there was no element of sexual assault in her death. And the way she was wrapped up so carefully, almost like protecting her . . . well, my theory was that someone killed her to hide the pregnancy. It wasn't sex at all. It was damage control.'

'Are you thinking — ' Aidan broke off. None

of them wanted to say what they were all
thinking. 'Am I right?' he continued heavily.
'Would this be the time to bring up our friend
Eamonn Carr?'

'Poor wean,' said Dave, suddenly running big
hands over his face. 'God, the poor wean.' Did
he mean Cathy, or the child she'd never had time
to grow, or both? His voice broke.

Saoirse stood up quickly. 'We'll start the
dishes. Why don't you two discuss it.' And she
shut the kitchen door on her and Dave.

Paula looked askance at Aidan, who shrugged.
'Will we go, Maguire? I can drop you home and
tell you what I've found out on the way.'

She looked pointedly at his beer bottle.

'Only the two,' he said virtuously. 'Come on,
the taxis in this town'll rob you blind.'

'Should we not — '

'It's best to leave them. Honest, it is.'

'OK.' Reluctantly, Paula found her coat,
casting curious looks at the kitchen.

Outside, she hesitated before opening the door
to his battered Clio.

'In you get, Maguire, it'd chill you tonight.'
Inside smelled the same. Tobacco, and mint, and
his sweet aftershave. When she was eighteen it
had been the most exciting smell in the world.
Aidan hadn't switched on the engine. 'I was
telling you about Eamonn Carr.'

'Oh yes.' That was safer, the Carrs, the
present. 'Well, what's he been up to? Apart from
trying to turf the travellers out so he can put up
some tatty old MDF flats.'

'Turns out he's got a fancy woman.'

Her jaw sagged. 'No! Mr Family Man Moral Majority?'

'It's a well-kept secret, as you can guess. Luckily you're talking to Ballyterrin's finest investigative journalist.'

'Its only one, more like.'

'Maybe. Well, according to my source, Eamonn Carr never totally finished with his first girlfriend. She's a beautician in town.'

'No way! Where?'

'You know that place down on Flood Street?'

She nodded. To Dye For. In this context, the name made her shudder.

'Supposedly he goes there all the time, tells the missus he's at the Town Hall.'

'Jesus.' Angela Carr, bereft of her first-born, cheated on. That poor woman.

'You need any waxing done, Maguire?'

'*What?*'

'The beauticians.' He gave her an innocent look. 'I was thinking we'd pay the fancy woman a visit.'

'Maybe. You know what else is on Flood Street, don't you?'

'I do.' The Mission, where Cathy and Louise and Majella had all gone, stood across the street from the HQ of Eamonn's girlfriend.

'And what did Ballyterrin's finest mind discover about *that*?'

'Enough to make your red hair stand on end, Maguire. You heard of an outfit called ESCAPE?'

'No.' She didn't appreciate the reference to her hair colour.

197

'Have a look when you can. It's an anti-cult outfit in the South. Did you know there's over two hundred suspected cults in Ireland? Everyone from the Mormons to mad Druid types. I printed you out this.' He fished out a thick wodge of paper from his back seat, under a layer of boxes from the Abrakebabra takeaway. There was a coffee ring on the front.

'What is this?' She took it gingerly.

'All the dirt on the Mission. Some bedtime reading.' He caught her eye just for a moment, then turned his key in the ignition. As he did it, she heard the clink of his wrist.

'Still wearing it then.'

As the engine turned over he cleared his throat, looking at the watch she'd given him for his nineteenth birthday. And then thrown at him, several months later. The watch had been fine, but them . . . not so much.

'It works, doesn't it,' he said gruffly. 'We better go or PJ'll skin me alive.'

★ ★ ★

PJ was still up when Paula opened the front door, *The Late Late Show* on quietly in the background. 'That was young Aidan's car, was it?'

'Yeah.' She hung up her coat. 'Saoirse invited him. I didn't know.'

'And how's wee Saoirse?'

Paula decided not to mention Dave's crying. 'Grand, I think. Her husband's nice.'

'Aye, so Pat says.'

198

'Was she here today, Pat?' In the kitchen Paula could see clean dishes and a Tupperware box of buns.

'She does be in most days.' PJ kept his eyes fixed on the screen.

Paula felt a wash of guilt. She'd come back to look after him — hadn't she? — but what could she do? He was so stubborn, and she was racing round town like an eejit trying to connect the dots on a puzzle that made no sense.

'Is there nothing I can do to help, Daddy?'

'You could make a wee cup of tea before bed. Load of old rubbish, this.' He stumped up to switch off the TV, purchased in the days before remotes, and she put her arm out to help, then drew it back. Tea she could do. She'd make the best damn cup of tea in Ireland.

★ ★ ★

'These are nice.' They sat at the kitchen table with mugs of tea and Pat's caramel shortbread.

'She's a dab hand with the baking, is Patricia.'

'It's good of her to help you.'

'Aye, she's a good woman. She'd give you the shirt off her back.'

'And John was the same, wasn't he? I don't remember him all that well.'

'A great man. Brave as can be.'

'Wonder where they got Aidan from,' she laughed. Why was she bringing him up?

PJ gulped his tea and eyed her. 'As you know, Paula, I'd have been the first to tell you what a useless eejit Aidan was — '

199

'And you were.'

'I was indeed. But that's a long time back. You never know, he might surprise you.'

'Hmm.'

PJ looked at her over the top of the *Irish News*. 'Make us another pot there, like a good girl.'

★ ★ ★

Paula decided not to take up Aidan's suggestion of bedtime reading. She had enough horrors filling her head — a dead child, murky weeds twisting in her hair, another girl hanging by her neck in her father's garage. And Majella, where was she? Despite repeated searches and posters and appeals, they were no closer to knowing.

She thought again of Cathy's autopsy report. It was always the way in cases. The body had its own mute tale to tell. Forensics and the pathologists would produce the clues, and she would try to write the story. Who had this person been? Who could do something like that — stab a child in the neck and put her in the canal? The question was usually rhetorical, as if the asker was afraid to know the answer. But Paula actually had to. Someone had done it, because there was the body, an immovable fact.

Think, Maguire. She liked to draw diagrams before she wrote her reports, to tease out all the facts before setting them down in black and white. Switching on the Anglepoise lamp, still adorned with the ghosts of stickers from *Just Seventeen* magazines, she felt in the drawers for a pen, taking out a dried-up biro. And there was the hardbacked notebook — her diary. It was almost a physical shock to see it. Why had this one not been burned with the others, in the metal bin in the back garden, the summer before she left? When PJ came home that day he'd just stared at the heap of charred paper. Said nothing, while Paula wept and rocked herself.

This had survived because she'd still been using it when everything happened. Only the first third was filled. She read the first line: *I don't think I can live without him.*

Paula tore the page out, crumpling it in her fist. She flipped hastily through to the blank sheets and wrote *Cathy* in the middle, scrawling a circle round the girl. Then she drew a line and wrote *Family*. Eamonn, strict behind the doors of the perfect home. Fingers in all kinds of juicy pies, including trying to buy up the land where the travellers squatted. The wife, almost catatonic with shock. Was it grief, or had he crushed the life out of her?

Paula went to chew the pen, then stopped herself, thinking of ten-year-old saliva. Next she wrote *Friends*. That bland group of teens, skinny, skirts rolled up, eyes cast down. What did they know? The teacher said Cathy had been crying in school, marks slipping. What was going on in her head?

She wrote *Mission*. They said they hadn't seen Cathy — a lie? If so, how could she prove it? Cathy had gone every Friday evening, or so her parents thought. But that Friday she hadn't, had never made it home from school. Where had she gone after her friend saw her walking out of the school gate? Picked up by Ken from the centre of town, then — possibly — picked up by someone else on the road. A silver car that may or may not have existed. All the leads seemed to curve back on themselves.

Paula drew two more lines, one for Louise, who'd gone to the Mission and also died. Had she left a suicide note? Then Majella Ward. She'd gone there, her sister said. Had she secrets too — a boyfriend, maybe? Paula drew a dotted line and wrote *Katie Brooking*. This was one other girl who had definitely been to the Mission. What did Katie know?

Rachel. Alice. She wrote their names and stared at them. In 1985, both girls had left their homes and never come back, slipping down between the cracks of the known, becoming *the lost*. The ones you knew had to be somewhere, maybe standing right behind you, glimpsed from the corner of an eye, a faint breath felt on your neck. The ones you could never quite get hold of. Were the police even on the right track? There'd been no leads at all in those cases, nothing to link them to the present day or even to each other, except that all the girls had gone from the Ballyterrin area and none of them had left any trace. Runaways, you usually found them fast, washed up quickly by the shallow tides of crime and poverty, hunger, and cold. But here there'd been nothing. Nothing at all. And Annie Miller, hanging in the woods, that blank spot in the investigation — had she been involved, or was her death nothing more than unfortunate timing?

Paula stared at the page for a long time. There was Cathy and there was Majella. At first sight, two girls were gone. What did it make you think? A serial-killer, some kind of monster preying on young girls. But Cathy was dead, so why hadn't they found Majella? The only link between them was the line that led to the word Mission. Paula hesitated, then drew one from Eamonn Carr to Majella. He wanted to clear the land she lived on. Had they ever met?

Through the floor Paula heard her father cough and turn over, uncomfortable in his sleep. So much for minding him, he hardly let her do a thing. She sighed and put the light out, hoping for no more dreams of the dead.

19

Aidan's handwriting was no better than it had been at seven, when he used to scribble on her Ladybird books while their parents played Old Maid downstairs. Back in the office after a weekend of uneasy thoughts, Paula squinted at what he'd scrawled on the stack of print-outs. What did it say? *Who owns them?* What did that even mean?

What he'd given her was mostly dry and technical, the kind of humanless prose she hadn't the mind to trawl through. The gist of it seemed to be that the Mission was part of a big American church group, who also owned radio stations, a children's publisher, and a chain of something called *Tiny Seeds*. Aidan had scribbled across this — *anti-abortion*. She Googled, once her computer had whirred to life, and found the website. The pictures showed worried-looking women and girls, babies with crumpled rose-petal faces. There was also a tab saying *For Prospective Parents*. It was a private adoption agency. She clicked on the section marked *Fees. Our babies are unique and priceless. If you would like to make your family complete, please contact us to discuss our compensation schedule.* Compensation? Of course, the adoption laws were a lot looser in America.

Aidan had drawn a heavy arrow round to the

next page, a print-out of a story from the *Irish Times*. He'd scribbled: *this crowd sold all their buildings off to the American lot.*

Calls for a Tribunal into Safe Harbour scandal, Paula read. Heart racing at the familiar name, she scanned the page rapidly.

Between 1920 and as late as 1995, thousands of Irish girls and women were being robbed of their children. While their mothers were incarcerated in Safe Harbour homes, where abuse was rife, the babies were taken, given new names, and shipped off to new lives in America. Often no records were kept, and Irish law still has no provision to let adoptees find out their birth identity. 'Baby flights' to the US were common, taking dozens of infants at a time to be placed through right-wing adoption agencies.

But what made Safe Harbour so much more shocking was that its perpetrators — nuns and priests sworn to serve God — were charging adoptive families as much as £30,000 per child. This blood money went straight to the coffers of US pro-life groups and the Catholic Church. Meanwhile the inmates of the homes, brutalised and forced to work off the 'debts' incurred by their stay, have never received justice for this gross human rights violation.

Paula exhaled slowly. It wasn't the huge shock it should have been. It was well known in Ireland that the homes for wayward girls had been harsh institutions, and that babies born there had been given up for adoption, often whether the mother wanted it or not. And where was all that money going? She looked at the name of the journalist — Maeve Cooley. The same name cropped up on Aidan's next printout, this one a blog post. *Fears Over Mission*. Aidan had underlined the word 'Mission' three times. The article was from the year before.

The anti-cult group ESCAPE has voiced concerns over a new evangelical Church targeting Ireland. The US-based 'Mission' has opened in five English towns, and is now eyeing Ballyterrin for its first Northern Irish base. Experts fear it is linked to the controversial God's Shepherd Church which flourished in Ireland in the 70s and 80s.

'They are one and the same as far as I'm concerned,' said Paddy Boyle, head of relatives' group ESCAPE, which helps those at risk from cults. 'The same people run it. The same things go on. The Mission is God's Shepherd with a different name.'

The 1980s. An American church group in Ireland, maybe during the year Alice Dunne and Rachel Reilly had gone missing and Annie Miller had taken her own life. Paula started to read faster, a pulse beating in her stomach.

Underneath, Aidan had written: *website targeted by lawyers for the Mission and blog taken down a week later. I know Maeve from*

DCU and she sent it to me.

So, one of his journalism buddies. Paula tried not to let it colour her judgement of Maeve Cooley, who seemed more on the ball than most. Clever. She was probably pretty too. Paula stared at the byline photo from the *Irish Times* article. Yes, definitely pretty, even in black and white an inch square. On impulse, Paula typed in the email address on the bottom of the article and fired off a few lines. *I am working on a case which may involve the Mission . . . I am a friend of Aidan O'Hara . . .*

Was that what she was to him, a friend? Never mind. Her phone rang. She tore her eyes away from the pile of papers. A church group, maybe run by the same people as the Mission, in Ireland in the eighties! God, she hated to admit it, but Aidan had done her proud. As she stood up to take the phone call, she quickly typed another line and pressed 'send' on her email. *Could you by any chance put me in touch with this Paddy Boyle?*

Then she carefully hid the print-outs under the mess on her desk and went out to see who was ringing her.

★　★　★

That bloody hospital again. The sweet smell of bleach. Your feet on squeaky floors. She remembered how the lights had flickered and faded as they brought her in, flat on her back. None of that. That was all gone, and she was a grown up, with an important job, walking to see

207

wee Saoirse McLoughlin, now transformed into a doctor, an expert.

But when she got to the office it seemed to be locked. Paula rattled the metal handle. 'Hello? It's Paula — I came like you said.'

Saoirse's call had said to come right away. Where was she? Paula had just fished out her phone when the door shook in its cheap wooden frame, and Saoirse opened it.

'Christ! What's wrong?'

Saoirse's face was shining with tears. She'd taken off her glasses and behind them the skin was pink and swollen. 'I'm sorry.' She shut the door firmly behind them and wiped her lab-coat sleeve over her face. 'Something's just happened, after I rang, and then you'd already gone, and — '

'Well, Jesus, what is it? It's not Dave?' Paula recalled the odd end to dinner.

'No. Well, sort of.' Saoirse stood for a moment with her arm over her face, like a child. 'Oh, crap. I just got my period, that's all.'

'Oh. And — ' Paula stopped. Of course, they were trying for a baby. They'd have been married for what, five years? The wedding invite Paula had ignored, and would always feel bad about. Yet another stone to sink in the waters of the past.

'We thought, maybe . . . I was a week late. But no.' She wasn't crying now, just shaking her head with a bleak finality. 'I should have known. It was daft to get my hopes up. And Dave — God, he'll be in bits.'

Paula tried to say it delicately. 'Last night, I thought you were having wine.'

Saoirse gave a twisted smile. 'You and your detecting ways. No, it was grape juice. We really thought that this time . . . I shouldn't have told him.'

'How long?' said Paula quietly. She hadn't reached out for her former best friend. They'd never been huggy, and she still wasn't sure what they were now.

'Five years.' Saoirse wiped her glasses on her coat. 'We've been trying since the wedding. We wanted loads — a big Catholic brood.' The crooked smile was back again. Saoirse herself was one of six children.

'Oh.'

'Now you'll say I'm young, we've plenty of time.'

'I wasn't going to.'

'Well, everyone else does. Too young for IVF yet. Keep on trying, wink wink. Christ, I want to scream at them sometimes. I am a doctor, I know how these things work.'

'I'm so sorry. That's awful.'

'It is. Poor Dave.'

Poor Saoirse. She watched her friend.

'Well, that's not why you came here. Sorry.' Visibly, Saoirse got herself under control. 'All this is on my mind — obviously. Last night something about it made me uneasy — about Cathy being pregnant, I mean. Then when you went, it came to me what it was. I'm sorry about Dave, by the way. The thought of dead kids doesn't sit well with him now. It's not great for a social worker.'

'S'OK. What did you realise?'

'Well, I remembered it wasn't the first time I'd seen it. Young girl, early stages of pregnancy, St Bridget's uniform. She came up to A&E and I diagnosed her — I tried to offer support but she just got up and sort of nodded, then she went out. I remember because — well, the next time I heard her name it was on the news. She'd died. I don't like to say her name but — '

The air in the room contracted around Paula. 'It's not Louise McCourt?'

Saoirse's swollen face was surprised. 'You know about her?'

★ ★ ★

'Would you stop pacing? You're doing my head in.'

'Sorry.' Paula made a conscious effort to stop walking up and down on the floor tiles of Saoirse's office. On the other side of the door was the constant buzz of A&E, its antiseptic smell. A place of certainties, of flesh and fluid. Not this morass of unanswered questions. 'It was definitely suicide, was it? I mean, no one else was involved?'

Saoirse screwed up her face, trying to remember. 'I went to the inquest. I think they ruled it inconclusive, but you can tell from the knots, you know, and the body position . . . ' She stopped. 'I won't go into it. But you could tell there was no one else behind it. I felt so guilty, that I'd just let her go that day.'

'Was there a note?'

'Hmm. I'm not sure. I'll look into it — I know the family's GP from med school. But if there

210

was, they'd have ruled it suicide, I'd say.'

Paula nodded slowly. 'I wish I knew what all this meant. These two girls, both pregnant . . . what are the chances of that being random?'

'I honestly don't know. We don't see many dead teens; we don't see many dead pregnant women.' Paula watched her friend's face closely as she said this but Saoirse was cool, professional. 'On the other hand, coincidences happen all the time.'

'Yes.' But it pulled at her like the depths of water. Two dead. Two pregnant. Not to mention Majella missing. 'But I just can't believe it is.'

Saoirse took off her glasses and rubbed her eyes. 'All I can tell you is the facts.'

'Right. Thank you. I better be getting back. Thank you for dinner, by the way — I really appreciate it. Even Aidan wasn't so bad.'

'I told you. He's not such a bad bollox, is he.'

'Not entirely.' Before her friend could move Paula stooped and pressed a quick kiss to her cool cheek. She couldn't recall ever doing that before.

'What was that for?'

'Just for you. To say thanks. And that I'm sorry.'

★ ★ ★

Maeve Cooley was a fast worker. Paula had barely sat down at her desk after seeing Saoirse when Avril came over, voice lowered conspiratorially. 'Phone call for you.' A pause. 'I think it's from the *South*.'

211

'Paula?' A husky Dublin voice on the line. 'Howya. Maeve here.'

'Oh! That was quick.'

Maeve laughed; throaty, seductive. 'Paula, I'll cut to the chase. You asked about the Mission. Any chance you can come to Dublin tomorrow?'

It was less than two hours away, with the bypass. 'I suppose I could . . .'

'You were wanting to be in touch with Paddy Boyle. I can go one better — I'll bring you to see him.'

20

'You're sure you want to drive yourself, pet?'

'I'm sure, Dad.' Paula was racing round filling her bag with papers, pens, notebooks. 'I need to get back as soon as I can, and the buses don't go often enough.'

'There's some terrible bad driving down there. And they'd steal your hubcaps as soon as look as you, those Dubliners. They'll charge you a fortune if you damage that hire car.'

'I'll be fine.'

'You could take my Volvo, you know.'

'I'll be *fine*. You make sure and do your physio now. Pat's coming in to look after you.'

PJ grumbled as he spread jam on his third piece of toast. 'Nothing but women fussing round me morning, noon, and night.'

'See you later, Dad.'

'Keep an eye on those hubcaps!'

Soon Paula was taking the car out of town and down the new motorway. As she passed by the old mill on her way out, she could see a tide of flowers and teddy bears, marking out Cathy's last resting-place. The town hadn't forgotten the girl who'd lived, and grown, and died within its borders. If only she could find something in Dublin, anything that would help get the answers.

The traffic in Dublin was indeed fearsome. A shortage of driving examiners and some archaic

213

laws meant that as many as one in six drivers was on the road without a full licence, and it showed. But Paula had ignored PJ's dire prognostications, and after two hours she was parking in an exorbitantly priced multi-storey and exiting onto the banks of the Liffey, sparkling under cold sun.

She'd planned the trip carefully. Told Guy she'd be following up some leads. Dropped hints that she'd have to switch her phone off, interview policy, etc., so don't ring. She tried not to remind herself that this was what had gotten her in trouble in London, going off on her own. But it could be nothing — she'd tell him if she found something. It would be OK.

Maeve Cooley was where she said she'd be, waiting on double yellow lines outside the car park. Inside, the small Polo made Aidan's car look tidy, as the back seat was lost under coats, files, handbags, shopping, and books. Maeve waved Paula in, all the while shouting into her mobile: 'Don't fecking give me that, Jonny, I'm doing my best. No. *No!* You want to know where the story is? Try looking up your hole for a start, it might be there. *Jesus.*' She hung up. 'Bloody editor, what a shitehawk. Hello, Paula, welcome to my skip on wheels.'

Paula was trying to fit her legs in over what appeared to be an animal cage in the passenger footwell, and to ignore the furry rustlings within. 'Thanks for this, Maeve.'

'No bother. And how is young Aidan?' Maeve was squinting at her in the mirror as she reversed out.

'Oh, he's all right. I've only seen him a few times.'

'I'll have to tell all the DCU lot I finally met the famous Paula Maguire.'

'Oh — what?'

Simply, Maeve said, 'He used to talk about you all the time. Every time he'd had a jar — that's pretty often, as you'll probably know — it was all Paula this, Paula that.'

'Oh.' She'd never told any of her London uni friends about Aidan. Hadn't been able to. She changed the subject. 'Thanks for taking me, it's very good of you.'

'Are you having me on? I've been trying to nail those Holy Joe feckers for years. They're as bad as the Catholics, you know? One word against them and there's lawyers coming out of your arse. So the papers won't touch them now.' Maeve swerved out onto the busy street, causing Paula to inhale sharply and the contents of the cage to emit a low growl. 'I suppose Aidan showed you the numbers involved — these boys are part of a big American business. Plenty of readies in spreading God's holy word.'

'Yeah. I was surprised.'

As they drove, Paula surveyed her driver. Maeve Cooley was indeed beautiful — blonde-haired, full-lipped. She wore torn jeans and her nail polish was chipped, notes scrawled on her hands in smudged ink. As she negotiated Dublin's crammed streets, veering from lane to lane, Maeve explained her theories to Paula, who nodded firmly and tried not to think about dying in a car accident.

'Your article said they had links to the Safe Harbour homes?'

'Yeah, the ones with the baby-selling scandal.' Maeve revved at a traffic-light. 'When Safe Harbour had to close in the nineties, they didn't go away. Just waited a few years, then made all the buildings over to their American counterparts.'

'The Mission's in the old Safe Harbour building in Ballyterrin. I couldn't work out if they'd leased it or if it was just a coincidence.'

'It'll all be secret, with those boys. But it was exactly the same with that God's Shepherd lot — they opened up in old Safe Harbour homes, sometimes even ones that were still running. They were a bad bunch — Paddy'll tell you how bad. But this Mission, it's all just surface happy-clapping and self-esteem. It's the same underneath, same people, same carry-on, same bloody brainwashing. And now the schools are backing it! Jesus.' She made a sharp left turn down a side street. 'It's what they do, get them in young — music, drama. Propaganda, basically.'

Paula frowned. 'There's some big concert in Ballyterrin at Hallowe'en.'

Maeve screeched to a halt. 'I know. That's why you need to talk to Paddy right now.'

★　★　★

The first thing that shocked Paula was that Paddy Boyle was old; much older than she'd imagined. In the overheated sitting room of his small terraced house, he struggled to the door

216

with a metal-framed walker.

'Howya, Paddy.' Maeve seemed unfazed at his decrepitude, or by the stifling smell of boiled food that filled the house. He looked like an old mushroom, Paula thought: face sprouting, clothes in shades of beige and grey.

'This is the wee police girl?' he quavered, sinking back into the armchair.

'Hello, Mr Boyle. I'm Paula. I'm working with the PSNI and Gardaí on a missing persons project.' She knew how most people distrusted the word 'psychologist', and tried where possible not to use it.

The second thing that shocked her was the pictures. They were crowded on small tables, covering the walls, and all along the mantelpiece jostling with pill bottles. All of the same person — a pink-faced, wholesome Irish girl. They went up to what looked like her late teens, then stopped.

'Paddy,' prompted Maeve. 'Would you tell Paula here what happened to Dympna?'

⋆ ⋆ ⋆

Dympna Boyle, the girl in the photos, had been Paddy's only child, his wife Collette having died shortly after the girl's birth. 'She was laughing away, and then she dropped like a stone, her skirts all dripping with blood.' Post-partum haemorrhage, still common in 1960.

'You brought Dympna up all by yourself?' Paula was perched on an uncomfortable chair.

'Aye, I did. I'd a good living as a book-keeper.'

217

He nodded his mushroomy head. 'The nuns said they'd take her for adoption, for all I was still living, but I said no.'

Fair play. Paula knew a bit about how it was for an Irish man to raise a child alone.

'I had the rearing of her myself. And she was a good girl, my Dympna, a good, quiet wee thing. After her schooling she started working at a department store. I'd be on at her to go out and have a bit of life, but she never wanted to leave me, God love her. A shy wee thing. Never any fellas round her nor nothing, for all she was pretty.'

Maeve was nodding along. 'Tell her what happened in 1978.'

Paddy's story had a well-worn air, that allowed Paula to slot him into her mental register of victims. He was the type who grew hard round whatever it was that had wounded them, polished it smooth with re-telling.

'She comes home one day and says, 'Da, I'm away to church group the night. These people come round to the door this morning and they seemed awful nice, so I'll go down and see what's what'.'

'And was it — '

'The God's Shepherd crowd, aye. They were all over Ireland by then. Seemed like a Proddy church to me, but I let her tear away. Well, Dympna took to it, and she was there all the hours God sent, making new friends. I was happy, pet, you see. No harm in it, I thought. This goes on about a month, then one day the phone rings and it's her boss at the shop. Where would she send Dympna's back pay? Turned out she's never been back to work since the first day she was at that church. 'We have to give up material things,' she says, when I ask her. 'I'm sick of selling tights to rich ould women.' That's about as fierce as my Dympna ever got since the day she was born. Then she up and says, 'I'm going away, Daddy. They want to send me on mission work. To Liverpool.' Glowing, she was.'

'That's what they do,' said Maeve. 'They go on to other cities and set up groups there. Like a virus or something.'

'Next thing she says is, can she get her money out. Her post office money — you know, from her Communion and that. I says, 'Dympna, that's for a rainy day.' And she shouts at me! My Dympna! 'It's pouring now, Daddy,' she says, 'The Church needs the money. It's for God.' They took every penny she had so she could go and be a missionary, and they get her to make a Will that says when I die, Dympna gives them this house.'

'You fell out with her?' Paula leaned in to listen.

'Aye, we had words. I wish to God I could take them back now. And off she went, and I never saw her for five years. She was eighteen the day she left.'

'Then what happened?'

Paddy paused to cough wetly into a cotton hankie, which he then pushed up his sleeve. Paula winced; she was finding the airless room increasingly oppressive.

'She turns up on my doorstop, out of the blue,

219

bold as brass. A wreck, she was. White as a sheet and her belly out to here.'

'She was *pregnant*?'

'Oh aye. Six months' gone. Well, it was a shock. Couldn't get a word of sense out of her. She'd hardly sit, wouldn't look at a body straight in the eye, not a word about the wean's father. 'Stay here and I'll mind you,' I says, but she says, 'No, I can't.' I says, 'Of course you can, pet, it's not the Dark Ages, you can come home any time you want.' But she just shakes her head. And her hands on her belly, fit to break your heart. 'He'll find me,' she says. 'He'll take her away anyway. I can't keep her.''

'He?'

'That's all she said. *'He'll find me.* He says I've to give the baby up and that's that.''

Paula glanced at Maeve, who wore a *see what I mean?* expression. 'And she left?'

'She went the same day, and then next I hear, four months on, she's dead. Hanging off a tree, they said, like Judas Iscariot.'

He spoke so matter-of-factly Paula blinked. 'And the baby?'

'Took me a whole crowd of lawyers to find out. I was onto my Senator, in the papers, on the radio. Eventually they says Dympna wanted her wean adopted to America, and I could whistle for all the chance I had of seeing it. Wouldn't even say was it a boy or a girl. She thought it was a girl. Gave her some comfort, anyway.'

What an awful story. Paddy told it in flat, practised tones, as if it was the only thing his life rested on. Probably it was.

'But you didn't stop there, did you, Paddy?' Maeve encouraged.

'Well, people heard me on the radio and that. So I start getting all these letters, So and So else's wean getting caught up with this God's Shepherd crowd, and the next thing you know, they've gone and their money with them. And you'd hardly credit how many of the girls were like my Dympna — expecting, and then the wean vanished and the girl never came back.'

'Paddy was the one helped get God's Shepherd kicked out of Ireland,' said Maeve. 'He looked in the accounts and saw all the deposits they got off rich Yanks desperate for kids.'

'You proved they were selling the babies?' Paula asked Paddy.

'Aye. The ould book-keeping came in handy for once. We couldn't prove the girls didn't want to give the weans up, of course, but why'd my Dympna cry otherwise? Why'd she take her life, God forgive her? Anyway, we got them put out in the end. Tax evasion, like Al Capone.'

Paula looked at the picture of the girl with the seventies haircut, and the pretty pink and white face. Another one dead. Another one pregnant. No more answers.

* * *

'So, what do you reckon to Paddy? He's a character, isn't he.'

Paula's head swam as Maeve backed the car out into traffic. 'And that's all true, is it?'

'Oh yeah. They buried Dympna in Liverpool

221

— never even told Paddy about the funeral, the bastards. He's got a bee in his bonnet, but it's all true. And his ESCAPE charity's pretty big now — Dympna wasn't the only one. It's always the same story. Girl went off with the Church, gets pregnant, gives the baby up, then like as not she either kills herself or she's never seen again.'

'And you think the Mission — '

'It's the same people, for sure. Or as near as makes no difference.'

'The man Dympna talked about — you've an idea who that was?'

Maeve gave Paula a look out of sharp blue eyes. 'You ever hear the name Ron Almeira?'

Paula shook her head. 'No.'

'Hoke out that file in the back there.'

Paula rummaged round in the mess while Maeve ducked from lane to lane, and came up with a fraying manila file. 'This one?'

'That's the one. See that photo?'

The file contained a black and white shot of a fifty-ish man, plump and genial, a big aw-shucks grin on his face, rings on fat fingers. Paula turned over the flyer and read: *Pastor Ron Almeira, God's Shepherd Baptist Church.* Then contact details. *In God's Footsteps.*

'He does preaching tours,' said Maeve, disgusted. 'Faith healing, speaking in tongues, all that shite.'

'So how does he fit in with all this?'

'That man set up God's Shepherd in Ireland. And he was back and forward here all through the seventies and eighties. Until he skipped out for good, just when they were *this* close to nailing him on child abuse charges. Course, we've a bit of a backlog of those here. He's currently on trial for rape in the States, though he'll probably get away with it, yet again.'

'Christ. Maeve, do you know — was there a God's Shepherd group in Ballyterrin, in the eighties?'

Maeve screwed up her face. 'There was a whole load of them, but yeah, I think there was. How come?'

Paula stared down at the picture. Who did this man remind her of? She couldn't see past his plump cheeks and executive suit. 'I just wondered if he . . . ' She stopped, hearing the angry buzz of her phone in her bag. She took it out, looked at the text. 'Thanks a million, Maeve, you've been brilliant. But I think you better drop me at the car park. I have to get back.'

* * *

Running through the multi-storey, Paula dialled the unit. 'You really found it?'

She could hear the excitement in Guy's voice. 'Twelve-inch blade, like we thought — blood-stains on the handle. Picked up by a dog-walker.'

Dog-walkers made most of the grisly finds in police work. 'Where?'

'This is the interesting part. Dockside, in the bushes.'

'Bloody hell.' Near where the travellers lived. 'Are you going down there? You think they might know something about Majella?'

223

'We'll have to go house-to-house . . . I mean, caravan-to-caravan. But it's not straightforward. They're already furious at all the police attention down there.'

'I can imagine.' She remembered the last time they'd gone, the looks on people's faces, the banging and shouting.

'We're having the briefing now. Can you get back?'

She was juggling the car keys with the phone and trying to be quiet. 'I'm in the middle of something. Give me an hour or so?'

'I'll keep you posted.' He rang off, and Paula got in the car and did her best to speed through the Dublin traffic. How could the knife just be under a bush all the time since Cathy's death, undiscovered? She'd been so sure, her gut feelings about Ed Lazarus and Eamonn Carr screaming inside her. Had it deafened her to something else, something more important?

Paula had driven out of Dublin as fast as she could, but it was still an hour and a half before she was nearing Ballyterrin. Her phone was ringing again and she risked an illegal answering. After all, she wasn't meant to be anywhere that required driving. She saw the office number and spoke quickly. 'I'll be down in ten minutes. Just finishing up.'

'Where are you?' It was Gerard Monaghan, his voice cold.

'I'm just leaving.'

'The boss tried ringing you back. Got a foreign ringtone.'

Shit, she hadn't heard it. 'I said I was on my way — '

'You're in the South, aren't you? You'll be for the high jump,' he said with satisfaction. 'Get your arse down to that caravan site. We're going in.'

★　★　★

Paula raced through Ballyterrin, down towards the docks, where the wind blew sharp and icy. She parked her car where Guy had the last time. When she opened the door she heard the shouting drift across the wasteground. It sounded like a full-scale riot. Shivering in the damp air, she started walking. After a few steps she was cursing her heeled boots. She'd anticipated driving today, and had been trying to impress the unknown beauty, Maeve Cooley. Eejit.

As she trekked over the empty ground, the mass in the distance became a familiar scene, one seen on countless news bulletins over the years. A police-issue Land Rover, surrounded by youths, shouting, throwing stones. The calling of voices on the wind. There was Guy's car, in the distance. There was another car, inside the compound. Surrounded.

She started to run, tripping over stones and mud, until she came to Guy, parked up near the gates of the camp. He was crouching behind his BMW in his good suit, and Bob Hamilton was inside talking on his police radio, shouting breathless over the wind.

'*Request Tactical Support Unit attend imme-diately!*' His face bulged, frightened, behind the glass.

'It got out of hand,' Guy said, giving her a quick grim look.

She was panting. 'What happened?'

'We were just going to ask questions. Gerard drove the jeep in, and I left mine here — you know.'

She understood; to keep it safe. And it meant he'd escaped being surrounded too.

'And where — Christ, Gerard's not in there?' But now she could make out a figure inside the car, between the swarming bodies of traveller kids. As she watched, one got hoisted onto the roof and began jumping up and down, to jeers and cat-calls. They were perhaps thirty metres away. 'Where's the fucking back-up?' she exclaimed. Then: 'Sorry.'

'Sergeant Hamilton has radioed.' Guy stood up, and they huddled by the car to look out, a thin piercing rain making them shiver.

'Should we not — '

'It isn't safe. We have to stay back.' Unlike the PSNI officers, Guy and Paula had no guns. Old Bob could barely outrun a shopping trolley.

'Shit.' She strained to see Gerard in the car, and realised Guy beside her was radiating tension from every muscle. She followed his eyes and saw them — a group of men emerging from the caravans, armed with baseball bats. Iron bars.

Guy tapped on the car window; Bob unwound it an inch.

'Aye? I radioed them, but they said — '

'Sergeant,' Guy said quietly. 'Tell them to fucking get here *now*.'

It all seemed to happen very fast. There was a bright flicker on the edge of the group, and Paula realised something was spinning in the air, fluttering — newspaper? Of course, a home-made petrol bomb. Half of Ireland probably knew how to make one of those. Then it was turning, falling, the kids scattering like rats, and it was hitting the car and exploding into points of light. And then the car was on fire, and she could hear the crackle of it, and she could hear Gerard shout across the empty space, and the clunk of the car door, and then he was stumbling back against the flames, and falling, and she saw the man was on fire. Gerard was burning.

Hands were pushing against her, strong and unyielding. 'No!' She was struggling before she understood.

'Get in the bloody car. Stay there.' Guy was bundling her in, and for once, for some reason, she was obeying. She watched out of rain-stippled windows as Guy ran, in his suit, across the ground, hunching down low. *Army*, she thought in a daze. Definitely ex-Army. A moment's startled look at her and Bob was fumbling with the lock and getting out too, charging in his ill-fitting suit, for God's sake. Like Dixon of Dock Green. Both men were running straight into the throng, the flames. In the distance rose the high squeal of sirens.

21

'Will Gerard be OK?' Paula clasped her hands between her knees.

Guy was pacing behind his desk. 'They said so. He has burns on his hands and neck, but he should be out in a few days.'

She nodded, trying to forget the sounds of her colleague's screams as the fire had taken hold. She couldn't seem to stop shaking. 'And the rest?'

Guy stopped pacing and rested his fists on the plasterboard of the wall, as if he would like to punch it. 'It's a mess. Excuse me — it's a fucking disaster.'

It was indeed a mess. Ever since the brawl that morning, the story had been top of radio news bulletins, and would feature prominently not just on the regional TV news, but even on the national. The images were shattering — riot police on the streets of Ballyterrin, for the first time since the 1996 Drumcree stand-off. Ten traveller men in the cells, countless injuries from stones, batons, and out-of-control flames. On the news, images of babies wailing as their mothers looked horrified from their caravan doors, children scooped out of the dirt by terrified arms. Allegations of racism, police brutality. And the worst thing was, it had all been for no reason.

She shuddered. 'So, it wasn't Cathy's blood on the knife after all.'

He shook his head, exhausted. 'Not even human. Cat, most likely. A prank.'

'OK.' She almost wished he'd bawl her out, get it over with, not make her wait forever in his office for the coming punishment.

Guy looked up. 'Where did you go today, Paula? You weren't doing interviews.'

'No.'

'You lied to me.'

'I had a contact — '

He held up his hand. 'Save it. I must say, Paula, I have some very serious problems with how you're carrying out your work. I knew when I hired you — I mean, your old boss said you had problems with authority, but — '

'Allen? He hated me!'

'Maybe. But maybe he was right, too.'

She said nothing for a moment, resting her eyes on the pictures of his children. 'I'm sorry I didn't tell you. I just felt very strongly that the Mission was the key. And I finished all my reports, like you said.'

'That isn't the point and you know it.' He lowered his voice. 'I realise I've weakened my position by our — well, by what happened between us — but I still have to manage you, and I wish I could explain that we are *this* close to being shut down before we've even got started.'

'But I really think this is the answer! If you'd let me explain — I've found out more about the Mission: they used to operate under a different name in Ireland. I think they were here in Ballyterrin! If we could find out when that was — '

He slammed his palm onto the desk. 'For God's sake, Paula! An officer was nearly burned to death! I've got potential lawsuits as long as my arm, a traveller girl missing, another girl dead, and no bloody clue what's going on. I need you here, not messing about with some mad cult theories.'

'It's not — '

'Listen to me. Cathy was taken from the street, OK? We know that. She was nowhere near the Mission. They all have alibis.'

Paula kept quiet for a few moments. When she spoke, her voice was so soft he must have barely heard.

'Pardon?'

'I said, Katie goes there. I saw her.'

'You — how dare you! How dare you talk about my daughter.'

She got up. Talk about burning bridges; she could feel the scorch from here. 'It isn't my place, but someone has to tell you. Ask her where she really goes, Guy. Ask her if she really has friends.' And she went out without looking back at his furious face.

★ ★ ★

The fall-out from the Dockside incident was considerable. The media loved a good riot — it harked back to the golden years of journalism, when a steady stream of bombs, shootings, and stand-offs had kept the newswheels turning. The next day, all the national papers led with it, and the jerky amateur footage of the petrol bomb was shown again and again on TV and online; the men charging, the clang of sticks on metal, and the flames leaping up from Gerard's car. Local politicians put their spin on it — Gerard was either a hero cop, or the police had been heavy-handed, intimidating a minority group. Either way, they were no further on in the case. The traffic cams and door-to-doors had thrown up nothing new on the mysterious silver car Cathy had possibly got into. The interviews in the traveller camp had also turned up nothing, and there was still no sign of Majella or any lead on who'd killed Cathy.

A gloom sank over the unit, as Avril passed round a get-well card for Gerard, a smiling elephant on the front. Paula couldn't imagine Gerard smiling much. He'd been kept in hospital overnight for mild burns, and was on forced recuperation at home, much to his annoyance.

Guy continued to ignore Paula, addressing her if necessary in a clipped tone that made her toes curl up in annoyance. She wanted desperately to talk to him, to explain that he'd got it wrong, that they had to check out the Mission again. Instead she sat at her desk and watched him from the corner of her eye as he slumped behind the glass of his office, often talking on the phone, exhausted, or pacing, or just staring at the photograph of his dead son. Sometimes, she caught him looking at her too, and both would quickly whisk their eyes away. If that was how he wanted it . . .

Living with her father wasn't appealing either. PJ was the world's worst patient, and when Paula came home he would just give her a look and carry on eating his toast or biscuits or sausage sandwich. She was sure she'd put on at least five pounds since being back in Ballyterrin. Many nights Pat came round too, forcing her to eat ever-more sugary cakes, and equally unhealthily, to think about Aidan. They hadn't spoken since the evening at Saoirse's, and Paula kept remembering Maeve, so beautiful and blonde, and what she'd said. But so what if Aidan used to talk about Paula ten years back — it didn't mean he gave a damn now.

To ease her frustration, the mounds of reports to trawl through, the fact that Cathy and Louise were dead and Majella still missing, Paula turned to research. She wanted to follow up on what Maeve had told her.

It wasn't hard to find information on Ron Almeira, Pastor of the God's Shepherd Church, which had formerly held sway in dozens of Irish towns. She clicked through websites about him, of which there were many. He had devoted fans, scathing haters. The church was based on a charismatic style of worship, and Ron claimed direct visions of God, speaking in tongues, healing the sick. She gazed at a picture of Ron Almeira, this one in colour. Face ruddy with good health. And all this had been going on in Ireland in the seventies and eighties, when the country had no money and no hope. It had blossomed here, in the rich soil of superstition and spirituality. And if Maeve was right, it was happening again.

Paula spent some time trying to find out if,

and when, God's Shepherd had been in Ballyterrin, whether it might have coincided with Alice and Rachel going missing and never being seen again, but she had no luck. Even if she found something, how could she prove that either girl had gone to the church, twenty-five years ago? She jotted down the names of towns that came up. Dublin. Tipperary. Galway. None in the North so far. As for Annie, the girl found hanging, they'd had no luck with her either. The mother had quickly followed her daughter to the grave, heartbroken, and as far as Paula could see, there were some cousins in England and that was it. Fiacra was making enquiries, but Paula held out little hope of ever finding whether the unknowable Annie had been to God's Shepherd. Newspaper archives turned up one old shot, blurred and fuzzy, of a girl with black hair and an easy smile. Nothing more. Some people left so little trace on the world it was as if no one had felt them slipping back out of it.

Around her, the office was still subdued. Gerard and Bob were at the main station; Fiacra was still going over the files on Alice, Rachel and Annie, while Avril cross-referenced everything they found to look for links. So far, with the exception of the Mission for Cathy and Majella, there was nothing. A stifled laugh came from Avril, as Fiacra asked her something, too quiet to hear. As she listened to their murmured chat, Paula remembered.

'Avril?' As casually as she could, she sidled over to the younger woman's desk, passing Fiacra Quinn, who had quickly moved back to his terminal, where he was quite openly playing Solitaire. White headphones hung from his ears, and his desk was littered with plates and cups, the bin stuffed with takeaway cartons. Paula's own was bare of ornament, disappearing under piles of print-outs, and ringed with tea-stains, but Avril's was a paragon of office neatness. She had put up a picture of an elderly couple, in a diamanté frame — her parents? There was also a smaller passport-sized picture of a serious-looking young man, tucked in beside the computer as if Avril didn't want it on display.

Avril was swivelling between her large monitor and a laptop — she'd explained she needed both as most police databases weren't compatible with each other. 'You need me? Only I'm up to my eyes processing all the interviews from the traveller camp.'

'I just wondered if you'd had time to do that chart we talked about. You know, from all the old cases on the database. The ones with the church keyword?'

Avril raised her head, rubbing tired eyes. 'Oh right. I lost track, what with all this riot business.' She reached into the top drawer of her desk — Paula caught a glimpse of neat paperclips, a packet of biscuits — and took out a blue plastic folder. 'I found ten cases with a church or mission keyword, in the fifteen-to-thirty age range, took out a couple where it wasn't relevant. Here they are on a map, and here's the dates of the disappearances.'

'Wow, this is great.' Paula leafed through the

234

neat diagrams. 'Did you get the suicide data too?'

Without looking up, Avril reached into the drawer and drew out another piece of paper. 'That should cover it.'

Paula examined the paper. The numbers were there in dry black type, each hiding some other family's loss and pain, a wound that would never scab over. 'Does it match up?'

Avril shrugged. 'Hard to say. There's obviously more suicides than disappearances.'

Paula was trying to puzzle it out. 'But with each of these disappearances, there's at least one suicide in the same area, same year, same age-group?'

'Yes. I couldn't tell you if there's a link though.' Avril was all numbers and data, she clearly didn't want to get dragged into interpreting it.

'Thanks anyway. Really, I'm very grateful.'

'Thank you.' When she smiled, Avril looked like a different person.

⋆　⋆　⋆

'I'm just not sure.' Guy was frowning at the print-outs. 'It could just be coincidence.'

'Or it could be something else.' Paula sat opposite him.

'You're thinking, what, some kind of serial killer, linked to this church group? What's the name — God's Shepherd?'

'It's not so far-fetched, is it? There's convincing evidence of at least two in Ireland

235

over the years. And the guy who ran it here, he's up on rape charges in the States. He could have been over here in the seventies and eighties. Then there's girls going missing, but he leaves the country before anyone makes the connection.'

Guy shook his head. 'How could the police miss it, if all these girls were being killed?'

'You know how overstretched they were in the Troubles, both sides of the border. They didn't talk to each other, the forces. And in Irish towns — well, girls were always going off to England, or even the States. Like this one, look — Deirdre Murphy. *Known to have male acquaintances*, it says. Girl like that disappears, how hard will they really look? They'll think, Oh, she went off with a fella. Or got pregnant, went to England. Or her family sent her to the Magdalene Laundries and hushed it up. And these are only the reported cases.' She waved them at him. 'There could be more.'

'But someone would have spotted it, if they all went to the same church.'

'Maybe not. I've done some research into cults. Often what they do is disengage the person from their life, bit by bit. The girls might have been told to keep it secret, so the families wouldn't have known they were involved. Like Dympna Boyle — her father had no idea how deep in she was.'

'Hmm.' Guy was still sceptical. 'Going off to have a baby isn't exactly foul play, is it? Who's to say there's even a crime here? And I don't know why you think the suicides are relevant, if we're

236

looking at a serial killer.'

She paused. 'That I don't know. It's just, this on top of what we know about the Mission . . . ' He was looking deeply unconvinced. 'We're meant to be investigating these old cases, is that right? Here's ten with a possible link.' She read out the names, leafing through the papers. 'Deirdre Murphy. Susan O'Neill. Karen Courtney. Bridget Fintan — '

'OK, OK.' Guy held up his hands. 'I get the picture.'

'These cases are all in the South, but if there was a God's Shepherd in Ballyterrin — and I think there might have been — maybe Alice and Rachel went there. It all fits, you see? Cathy and Majella at the Mission now, them in 1985 . . . '

He gave in. 'Fine, have a look. Closest ones first — let me know if you're going haring off to Galway or somewhere. Take Fiacra with you, I think he's getting bored with desk-work.'

'Brilliant! You're great.' She jumped up with a smile, and then it seemed that they both remembered at the same moment all the reasons they were angry with each other. 'I mean, I appreciate it. Thank you.'

22

'So has anyone been to update the families, tell them we're looking into the cases?'

Fiacra shook his head as he started the engine. 'Boss said not to. Didn't want to get their hopes up, like.'

Paula said nothing. Perhaps Guy was right. After twenty-five years, it was easier to tell yourself you'd given up, that there wasn't any chance at all. Much easier.

They were starting their cold-case inquiry with the nearest on the list: Rachel Reilly, who in 1985 had failed to return from a night out at a disco. Rachel's parents were long dead, but a sister still lived on the family farm near Ballyterrin, out in the real borderlands, where the line itself snaked through fields and houses, where it was hard to say which side things came down on. An area of almosts, of shades of grey in more ways than one. They had to cross and re-cross the border several times to get there, and when they did, the road signs suddenly became bilingual and the roads noticeably worse. Undaunted, Fiacra bumped the Gardaí car over the potholes. 'Sort of ran out of the readies before they could finish it,' he said, as Paula braced herself.

'This is all new, is it? Do you not have to drive through Drogheda any more?'

'Oh aye, it's the bypass. They'll do Ballyterrin

one day and all, so it'll be straight from Dublin to Belfast. But the EU money's all dried up.' He rubbed together the fingers of one hand, which he was able to do because he drove with only one arm, elbow draped over the window. Fiacra Quinn was clearly a prime example of what Paula's father, a Belfast native, would call a *culchie*; or if you were feeling less charitable, a bogtrotter. The floor of the car was littered with rubbish, and open CD cases spilled from every orifice. Currently Paula was trying to block her ears to the banging sounds of gangsta rap. It was surreal to hear them parse on guns and hos, when out the car window all you could see was a cow peacefully chewing the cud. Jenny from the flock, more like.

To distract herself from the road, the din, and the litter, she leafed through the case-notes. 'So there was no real investigation into Rachel's disappearance?'

He put on his indicator to turn right. 'Aye, there was, but the parents didn't seem too bothered. She was headstrong, they said, always fighting with her mammy, so they thought she'd run off, and so did the RUC.' He saw her face. 'Not to worry, Doc. We're more up to date now. None of the ould sexism or racism now.'

'Hmm.' Paula looked up as they bounced over a cattle-grid and fields became visible at the side of the lane. 'This must be it.'

They parked the car by the barn, and when they opened the door, the sweet reek of animals was thick in the air.

'Ah, would you whist, Jade?' Mary O'Dowd, née Reilly, jiggled her youngest child up and down. Two more had peeped round the door of the farmhouse kitchen; Mary was well on her way to reproducing the five children she herself had been the youngest of. Rachel, her long-missing sister, had been the eldest.

The baby hiccupped, and Paula tried to bring the conversation back. 'So you said Rachel did have a boyfriend, in fact?'

Mary pushed back her straggly hair with one reddened hand. 'She told me she did, but no one else was meant to know. I remember her putting her lipstick on that night, getting ready. She put a wee bit on me too. She was excited. Then her pals came to get her in their car, and she was out the door, and that was that. I never saw hide nor hair of her again.'

Fiacra was eating his way through a packet of Hob-Nobs. 'You told the police this at the time?'

'I tried, but they never paid me any heed. I was only a wean. Mammy had her mind made up that Rachel went off with a fella, and Daddy just went along with whatever Mammy said.' Mary had been eight when her sister vanished, which made her thirty-three now.

Paula tried to subtly brush dog hairs off her black trousers. That had been a bad, bad idea, going to a farm in good clothes. PJ had raised his eyebrows at her when she clattered downstairs that morning.

She said, 'It says in the file your sister's friends

confirmed Rachel went to the disco with them that night, but they didn't see her after. Do you think she met her boyfriend there, maybe left with him?'

Mary rocked the child back and forward on her arm. 'No. From what she told me, he never liked the dances. A sort of churchy fella, seemed like. Didn't want her going out much.'

'Do you know what church, by any chance?'

'Aye, she'd started going to a kind of prayer-group thing, and Mammy lit out, said she'd to go to Mass like everyone else. I wasn't meant to tell anyone about it. Rachel let on she was doing extra shifts in her job — she worked in the petrol station.'

Paula tried to keep her voice casual. 'You don't remember the name of the group?'

Mary shook her head. 'Not after all this time. It was in town though. Ballyterrin.'

'Hmm. So maybe she left the dance and met the boyfriend somewhere else. Mrs O'Dowd, did you know the boyfriend's name?'

'No, I never did. She wasn't meant to say his name to anyone.'

Paula tapped her notebook. 'So when she went missing, they didn't question this prayer group at all?'

Mary looked puzzled. 'Well, no, she was at the dance when she disappeared. It must have been someone there who took her, I always thought. Everyone else just thought she went off on her own bat, but she never took any of her clothes, or her makeup, not even her wages from the petrol station. I never thought she ran away.'

'I see. Mary? Do you have any pictures of Rachel?'

She hesitated a moment, then nodded. 'Hold on a wee minute.' The baby, grizzling and dribbling, was thrust in Paula's arms.

Paula held the child's sticky face away from her good coat. 'There, there, Mummy'll be back soon.'

'You're a natural so,' said Fiacra, spraying crumbs. The baby promptly started to howl and Paula was glad to exchange her for the mustard-coloured album Mary brought back with her from the next room.

'That's our Rachel.' A laughing girl in eighties stonewashed demin, bright strawberry-blonde hair. Mary nodded to the baby. 'I think this one has a look of her.'

'She's a beautiful girl,' said Fiacra sincerely, and Mary's face softened.

'Aye, she was a good big sister. Wish the kiddies could of met their auntie.' She said it matter-of-factly, long grown used to the routine of sorrow. 'You're looking into it again, then? You might find what happened? Only . . . ' she paused. 'I've sort of buried it now. If you find something . . . you'll let me know, so I can get ready, maybe?'

★ ★ ★

'How come you wanted the photo?' Fiacra lent Paula his hand as they picked their way over the muddy front yard through the drizzle.

'I like to see as many as I can. Get an idea of her.'

He nodded, opening the door. 'Make her real, like.'

'Exactly.'

He started the engine. 'Aye, I do the same myself sometimes. You can get too used to things in this job. We need to remember why we do it.'

She said nothing, but gave him an impressed look as they drove on to the next family, in the continuing rain.

★ ★ ★

'Is this definitely the right place?'

'Aye, I think so. Look, it says it — Boyne Farm.'

'It's not exactly a farm though, is it?' Having driven for some time south of the border, the driveway they were now on was flanked on either side by neat, empty fields, and led up to a large Georgian house, elegant and grey-walled. The family of Alice Dunne weren't farmers, it seemed. More like Anglo-Irish aristocracy. So Rachel Reilly had been a Catholic investigated by the largely Protestant RUC, and Alice Dunne had been that rare thing: an Irish Protestant under the auspices of the Gardaí. Paula wondered if that had made a difference.

The impression of subtle wealth was strengthened when they reached the glossy front door and rang the bell, in the shape of a lion's head. The door opened into a hall lined in rugs and mahogany furniture, a smell of beeswax and expensive dust.

The man who'd answered the door was in his

forties, dressed in a golfing jumper and slacks. 'You must be the police.' His tone was distant.

Paula held out her hand, surreptitiously wiping it on her coat first. 'Hello, I'm Paula Maguire, I'm a psychologist working with the Missing Persons' Review Unit in Ballyterrin. This is Garda Fiacra Quinn, who's seconded to us.'

'Roger Dunne.' Alice's brother, then. He shook her hand perfunctorily. 'I'm very surprised you'd be looking into this again, after so many years. At the time, we found the local Guards to be very unhelpful indeed. They seemed convinced my sister went off with a man, when we explained over and over that wasn't the case.'

Fiacra stared politely into the middle distance. Paula forced a smile. 'It must have been very difficult. Unfortunately, quite a few cases went unsolved during that time, so that's why we've been set up. Even after so long, we can still find new evidence.'

The man had his hand on the handle of another door. 'Obviously, we'll tell you what we can. But please bear in mind that my parents were destroyed by what happened to Alice. Destroyed. Not just by her loss, but by the constant fear that not enough was being done to find her, when maybe she was still . . . Just please be gentle with my mother. My father's been dead for several years. She won't be able to stand much.'

'I promise. Thank you so much for helping us.'

He opened the door through to another lovely room, wood-panelled, a fire flickering in the grate. The carpet was a soft, thick apple-green, and the room was once again lined in pictures of a girl who'd gone out one day and never come home. Alice Dunne had been nineteen when she went missing in 1985, back from her first year at university. A slight, fair girl; the pictures showed her playing tennis, fishing, cuddling up to a variety of large dogs.

'Shut the door, Roger, the fire'll go out.' The quavering voice belonged to the woman on the sofa, a red setter stretched across her lap, its tail flickering lethargically.

Roger duly closed the door, raising his voice. 'The police are here, Mum.'

'Yes, I can see that.'

Paula moved closer, holding out her hand, then lowering it when the woman gave her a baffled look. 'Hello, Mrs Dunne, I'm Paula. Er . . . Dr Paula Maguire.'

'You're a doctor?' Sharp blue eyes narrowed.

'A psychologist.'

'Oh, I thought you meant a proper doctor. Well, sit down, sit down.' Paula sat in an armchair across from Emma Dunne, whose white hair was coiffed from what looked like a recent visit to the hairdresser. She wore a lilac jumper and grey slacks; dog hairs were caught in the nap of the fabric.

'Mrs Dunne. I'm sorry to disturb you like this, and reawaken all these sad memories, but we're going through a backlog of missing persons' cases, so we can prioritise those for re-investigation. Alice's case came up as part of a series of possibly linked disappearances. At

245

this stage, I can't say more than that, but anything you can tell us could potentially be very useful.'

'Linked disappearances.' One hand, laden with heavy gold rings, scratched the dog's silky ear.

'That's right. It's only a theory at the moment.'

Emma Dunne raised her eyes. 'You'll have been to the Reillys then, I imagine. They'd be the nearest.'

★   ★   ★

For a moment, Paula wasn't sure how to react. Fiacra was standing awkwardly behind her; she heard the creak of his uniform as he shifted from foot to foot.

Roger Dunne was annoyed. 'Mum, they don't need to hear about all that.'

'All what?' Paula looked between them, confused.

Emma Dunne kept stroking the dog. 'Get the files, Roger, will you.'

'But Mum — '

'They're in the bottom drawer.'

He sighed heavily, but crossed to the desk she was indicating, and returned to hand Paula a hefty purple box-file, fraying at the edges. On the front had been pasted a strip of masking tape, and the words CASES 1970–1990 were neatly inked on this. With misgivings, she opened the file. It was stuffed with paper, yellowing newsprint, old typed sheets, pages photocopied from reference books. She drew out a clipping, dry and fragile

246

as butterfly wings under glass. The face of a girl stared out at her, smiling: ROSCOMMON GIRL MISSING FOR SIX DAYS. Bridget Fintan, one of those on her list. 'What is all this?' Paula asked.

Roger Dunne sat beside his mother, moving the dog's tail aside with irritation. 'After my sister went missing, as I told you, we were very disappointed in the police response.'

'They tried to say she ran away.' His mother curled her lip. 'She would never have gone off without telling me. Never, ever. Alice had everything to live for — she would have been starting back at Trinity in just a few weeks. She was only nineteen, a beautiful girl, clever, kind. She would never have gone off.'

'OK, Mum. Let me tell her.' The son reached over and patted his mother's gnarled hand, which was resting on the dog's head. 'After a while, my father engaged a private detective to try to trace Alice, if indeed she had gone off. There was no sign of her anywhere and all her friends said the same — she would never have run away. She didn't even have a serious boyfriend. So it was something of a dead end. Then, my mother started to believe that, well . . . '

'She was murdered,' said Emma Dunne calmly. 'She must have been murdered. It was the only explanation.'

Roger went on, 'But there was no body, nowhere to start looking. Alice said she was going out with friends in Ballyterrin that night, and she left about seven, and that was the last we saw of her. I'll never forget. I was fourteen. She

247

came in to say bye before she went, ruffled my hair up, laughed. She was happy.' His mother's hand tightened on his. 'None of her friends had planned to meet her, they said.'

Paula remembered the details — Alice's car had been found the next morning, abandoned at the side of the road. The keys were gone and so was she. Nothing more had ever been found of her. No body, no signs of violence, not so much as a hair from her blonde head.

Mrs Dunne said, 'Then I thought, this kind of man, who'd kill a lovely girl like Alice, it wouldn't have been the first time, would it? So I kept notes. Any other girl who went missing. Any old cases you hadn't solved — I went and looked them up. I went to court hearings, even. Maybe some of the girls did turn up, I don't know, but I noted them all down. And there they are. Can you use it?'

'You want me to take this? Well, it might be helpful, if you didn't mind.' Paula leaned forward. 'Mrs Dunne, I need to ask you something about Alice's hobbies at the time. Did she ever go to a kind of church group, or a youth ministry, anything like that?'

The woman looked puzzled. 'Oh yes, there was one thing, at the start of the summer. She only went the once that we knew of. It was a new church starting up in town, in Ballyterrin.' She looked at Paula with alacrity. 'Is it them then? That American crowd? I saw they got put out of Ireland a few years later, but I never thought — none of her friends said she went there. All those times she used to go out — no one said she was going there. Is it something to do with them?'

'I — we don't know yet. It's just one possible link.'

'And the other cases? The other girls, had they gone there?' Mrs Dunne sat bolt upright.

Paula looked at Fiacra. 'I — some of them, maybe. We aren't sure.'

The woman was quivering. 'It's been over twenty years, Dr Maguire. Alice's father died not knowing. I don't want to die not knowing. Please. I just want to know where my Alice is. I want to know if her bones are at rest.'

Paula swallowed hard. 'We're doing our best, Mrs Dunne. You can be assured we haven't forgotten her, however long it's been. She isn't forgotten. She won't be.'

'Thank you.' Tears were pooling on the woman's lined cheeks.

Roger Dunne got up and put his arm round his mother. 'I think that's enough for today, please. She can't take it.'

'All right. Thank you, and — I'm sorry.' Nodding to Fiacra, Paula slipped out of the beautiful, sad house.

23

'Who d'you reckon'll crack first, him or her?'

Avril said, 'I don't think she could get one over on him. He's tough, the boss.'

Gerard was shaking his head. 'It'll be him. Trust me, she doesn't back down from anyone.'

'Why was she off all that time? Seems weird.' Avril looked curious.

'I heard she was getting divorced. Kicked her husband out, people were saying in the station.'

Fiacra agreed. 'I'd believe it. She puts the fear of God in me, she does.'

'She's got lovely shoes.'

'Christ. What is it with you women and shoes?'

'Shut up, Gerard, I'm trying to hear.'

Paula was pretending not to listen to the others as she sat at her desk, but she was just as agog. Helen Corry had been in Guy's office for over an hour now, and no sound was emanating out from the closed blinds. She had a horrible feeling they might be discussing her, too. Then everyone scrambled back to their seats as the door opened and the two came out, Helen Corry wrapped in a long grey coat with a faux-fur collar. Paula thought it was from Jigsaw, she'd seen one like it in Pat's *Easy Living* magazine.

'Thank you, Inspector,' Corry was saying. 'Do let me know the outcome.'

'Of course, of course. Drive safely now.' Guy handled her out of the door with his usual smoothness, but his jaw was tight. He looked into the main room, where everyone was suddenly typing with great industry. 'Paula. A word?'

★ ★ ★

Paula gaped at Guy as if she hadn't understood what he'd said. 'Nothing?'

'I'm sorry.' He looked impossibly tired. 'It just isn't enough.'

'But — it's all of them! All the girls had something to do with a church group.'

'I know. I know. But like I said, it could just be co — '

'You don't really believe that.'

He bristled at her tone and she forced herself to shut up. 'It's not enough evidence, Paula. Not unless we can prove a link between this God's Shepherd lot and our boys at the Mission. There are other leads to follow up first.' He looked round him at the office, which was overflowing now with files and paper and photographs, all so far going nowhere. 'I need you back on Majella's case full-time. Go over it, see did we miss anything. We're under a lot of fire now since that riot. We need to look harder.' To be seen to look harder, he meant.

'You're really not going to do anything?' She shook her head in disbelief. 'They can just go on with their prayer meetings, or whatever it is they do, while more girls die.'

He ran his hands over his tired face. 'I've told you before, all the Mission staff had alibis for

251

when Cathy vanished. The last anyone saw of her was walking up her own street. We've no proof that this Mission is even linked to the one in the South.'

'But the journalist — '

'Yes, I know what the journalist turned up. I'm talking about evidentiary proof. As for Louise — well, it's obvious no one else was involved in her death. What can I do?'

'But — '

'I know.' He spread his hands. 'I know, Paula. As a theory, it's not implausible. And it's awful, yes. I get it. When I think about those girls, and only in their teens . . . well, I get it, OK? But unless we find more evidence, there's nothing I can do.'

'You told Corry about the Carrs moving house? I smelled fresh paint, I told you.'

'Yes. Yes, I told her. She won't search the family home until we get more. Think of how it'd look.'

'Well — you'll look into Ed Lazarus? I'm sure that isn't his real name, he must have another. And if we can find anything on him, any priors . . . '

'Corry's not keen on this angle at all. And we have to be careful. They have lawyers all over them, these American churches, and if we put a foot wrong and the case collapses, we'll have nothing.'

'We've got nothing anyway.'

'I know. I know, OK?'

Paula thought of the pictures in the box file on her desk, Alice with her fair hair and warm smile, Majella's worn jumper and bright eyes. So many of them gone. She could feel it too, the mood spreading through the team. The slump, the hopelessness. A murder that wasn't solved within weeks wasn't likely to be solved at all. And the idea of never finding out who'd killed Cathy and dumped her body in the dark water . . . Well. She wasn't giving up that easily. If she had to prove a link between the Mission and God's Shepherd, then that's what she'd do. There was another person she could try, even though he hadn't been in touch. She'd swallow her pride and ring him.

As she went out, Guy had his head propped in his hands, as if he couldn't lift it up.

* * *

'What was it you booked in for anyway, Maguire? A full Brazilian, or just a tidy-up?'

'Don't be so bloody cheeky.' Paula glared at Aidan as he parked the Clio behind the To Dye For salon. Over on the desolate end of town, near the train tracks and post office depot, it was clear this wasn't a classy establishment. Across the road, the Mission was shuttered up for the night, but Paula still got out carefully, fearful of being seen.

'I'm only thinking of you. Don't want to catch you in an awkward situation.'

'As if. It's only a manicure.' She regarded her bitten finger-nails. 'Which I could sort of be doing with. Wait until I call you, anyway. I don't want her taking revenge on my cuticles.'

'It'll be grand. You said there was something weird about the family, and she's the best person to ask, I'm telling you.'

'But . . . ' Paula looked across the street to the Mission. That was where she really wanted to be looking, not at other angles. 'Just let me handle it — it's a bit dodgy legally.'

Paula felt oddly nervous as the teenage receptionist urged her to 'take a wee seat' in the beauty salon. Beauty treatments were far enough out of her comfort zone, but confronting the mistress of Eamonn Carr, going against Guy's explicit orders — that was a whole other world of trouble. Flicking through out-of-date magazines, she looked round her. They'd gone for a spa-like atmosphere, with some twigs in a vase and a bowl of smooth round stones, but there was no disguising the cracks in the floor tiles and patches of damp on the wall. So perhaps she shouldn't have been so surprised when the beautician came out and she saw how the woman looked.

'Has a Miss Maguire been in?'

The receptionist nodded. 'It's this wee girl here.'

Paula bristled — she was about twice the receptionist's age — but then she looked at the beautician and her mouth fell open.

The woman was probably in her forties, but looked a decade older. Brassy blonde hair twisted up into hairdressing clips, face lined from smoking, huffing as she walked. Nails chipped pink and hands gnarled — Paula tucked her own under her arms, protectively. For a moment she

254

thought they'd made a mistake, but the woman's badge said it quite clearly: *Rosemary.*

★ ★ ★

Paula had been worried Rosemary Mulvany would see right through her, but luckily the woman barely stopped to draw breath as she ushered her into the inner room. 'Ah now you'd be PJ Maguire's wee girl, would you, I do be talking to Pat O'Hara at times she's a lovely woman she's always telling me Paula this, Paula that, she'd a notion of you for her fella, Aidan is it you call him, and he does be running the paper now — is that right?'

'Eh — yes.' Paula's hands were soaking in a plastic bowl of acetone and she was already regretting the whole thing. 'And what about yourself, Rosemary? Are you from Ballyterrin originally?'

'Oh aye, born and bred. Did my training at the college over there.' Pink tongue poking out from her chapped lips, Rosemary was bending to file Paula's nails with vigorous strokes.

Paula winced; it was like being assaulted with an emery board. 'Now, you're not the Rosemary who's married to a Mick, are you? Pat mentions a lot of people.' She could see Rosemary's left hand was bare.

'Oh no, love, footloose and fancy-free, me.' She gave a tobacco-rattling laugh. 'Never been married, no weans. Just this place.'

'Oh right? Because Pat was telling me you used to step out with someone, who was it

255

now . . . ' Paula trailed off. Outside she could hear voices.

'Excuse me, miss, I have every right to get a pedicure.'

'You can't be going in there! It's ladies only!'

'You can't discriminate by sex, it's Article Something of the Human Rights convention . . . '

Oh Jesus. Aidan, already. She'd told him not to do this. Paula pulled her hands back out of the solution, and met the woman's eyes. Kind, bloodshot. Puzzled. 'I'm sorry, Rosemary.' That was all she had time to say, because at that point Aidan burst in through the bamboo curtains.

'Is this where I can get my legs waxed?'

Rosemary pushed back her stool and stared from Paula to Aidan. She looked at the little receptionist, who was desperately wringing her hands. She sighed. 'Never worry, Aimée. Why don't you go on home early, pet.'

* * *

After the girl had gone, and the spilled manicure solution had been wiped up, Rosemary seemed upset most of all by the fact that Paula had booked her appointment under false pretences. 'I was all excited, love. You've not had a manicure since the day you were born, that's easy to see. I'd have done you some lovely acrylic tips.'

'You're very kind, Rosemary, and really, I'm sorry we did it this way.' Paula was going to kill Aidan for his amateur dramatics. 'We just wanted to ask you some things.'

256

'You want to know about Eamonn, is that it?'
Rosemary looked between them. 'Well, this day
was always coming. Don't know about yousuns,
but I need a wee drink.'

Having filled three glass beakers from the
whiskey bottle stashed in her beauty cabinet,
Rosemary sighed and swilled hers round. 'You'd
hardly credit it now, but I was the belle of the
ball when I met Eamonn Carr. Seventeen years
old. Size six, lovely red hair, I had. Everyone
said, oh, the Carr boy's off to law school, he
won't want some girl who's doing beauty therapy
and working in her mammy's corner shop.'

'But he did?' Paula spoke gently. Aidan kept
quiet, mercifully, nursing his whiskey very
carefully. She watched from the corner of her eye
to see did he drink it.

'Aye, for a time. He was at the university, then
doing his law training down in Dublin, but he
got with me every time he came home. Then one
day he comes back and she's on his arm instead.'

'Angela, you mean.'

Rosemary's face twisted. 'She's lovely-looking.
You've seen her? I was surprised she could show
her face back in the town again, poor girl, but I
knew I was beat. Well, I never set my cap at him
again. But a few years on, didn't he come
knocking on my door. Missed me, he said. All
the usual, she doesn't understand me and she's
so cold and — well, the usual shite.'

Paula listened closely.

'But you go along with it, don't you, love?' She
gave Aidan and Paula a keen glance, but
thankfully didn't ask about their relationship.

Paula wouldn't have known what to tell her. 'So, there you go. Next thing you're over forty and you've no man or weans of your own. But he still comes round, love. That's all I can tell you.'

'Ms Mulvany . . . Rosemary. I'm sorry to have to ask you this, but did you ever see Eamonn's children at all?'

'Oh aye, I saw them round the place with their mammy and that big jeep of hers. Off to ballet, tap, all that.'

'And the oldest?'

'Cathy.' Rosemary nodded. 'She was a pretty wee thing. I can't get over what happened to her, I really can't. Haven't seen him since — well, I wouldn't — but he knows how bad I'm feeling for him. I'm sure he knows that. I left some flowers, over where they found her. A wee teddy bear. God love her.' Her eyes quivered with tears.

'When did you last see Cathy? Do you remember?' Aidan was leaning in. Paula was relieved to see he'd put the glass of whiskey down, untouched, on the side.

Rosemary wiped her eyes. 'Course, love. I saw her at his office. I go in to see him sometimes in the Town Hall, bring him a wee bit of lunch. *She's* always feeding him all that healthy stuff, salad and what-have-you. He's a working man, for God's sake. A sausage bap won't kill him. But that day the wee one was coming out of his office — Cathy. Looked upset. God help me, I just ran out, wasn't sure if she'd know me, or maybe say something to her mammy. You know how it is.'

'And when was this?' Paula asked.

'Well, that was the thing. I remembered after, when it was on the news. It must have been the last day she lived, poor wean.' Rosemary crossed herself.

Paula and Aidan exchanged a quick pulsing glance. 'You mean — you saw her that Friday? When she disappeared?'

'Aye, that'd be it.'

'And you didn't come forward?' Paula's head was swimming with the smell of whiskey and acetone.

'No, come on now, love. I didn't want to make any trouble. How'd I explain what I was doing there? Anyway, she was only seeing her daddy, wasn't she? I heard on the news it was later she disappeared, on her way home.'

'And this was lunchtime?' Please God she remembered the time.

Rosemary thought about it. 'I've appointments through the day usually, so I don't take my lunch till late. Hang on a wee minute.' She got up and rifled through the A4 hard-backed notebook that lay on her counter. 'Friday, Friday . . . Aye, there you go. I'd a one o'clock massage, so it'd have been, what, about half two by the time I went up there and brought his lunch and all, stood in that queue, it does be awful busy now in town, you wouldn't believe it.'

So if Cathy had been at her father's office at half two, why had her friend Anne-Marie apparently seen her leaving school at three? 'Does he know — Eamonn? Does he know you saw Cathy that day?'

Rosemary shook her head. 'I haven't seen him

since, like I say. Did he not tell you himself, that she was down with him?'

Paula and Aidan looked at each other. Aidan lunged forward for the beautician's hand. 'Thank you, Rosemary. You're a godsend, do you know that? I'm sorry me and herself are after bursting in on you. We're just trying to find who did this, you know?'

Rosemary pinked up. 'Ah, now, you're OK. I remember your daddy, son. He was a good man and all.'

Aidan's face gave a brief spasm and he stood up. 'Thanks. Paula, let's go.'

She had to try. 'Rosemary . . . I don't suppose you'd tell this to the police.'

The woman smiled a little, tired, getting old. 'Ah, love. What good would it do? I wouldn't hurt them for the world, Angela and her weans. Not when they've lost the wee girl.'

'OK. Thanks anyway. You've been a big help.'

Outside in the deserted street, they stood in the cold breeze. Seven o'clock, the long winter dark settling in, pools of orange light under street lamps. Paula wrapped her coat round her as Aidan opened the car door. 'So?'

'So what?' He opened her side and she got into the tobacco-smelling interior.

'Jesus, it reeks in here. When are you going to quit?'

He fumbled for his cigarette packet. 'When I've rooted out corruption and scandal at every level of Ballyterrin society.'

'You'll be dead of emphysema by then. So, what are we going to do now?'

He frowned. 'Cathy went to her da's the day she disappeared. He never told the police that?'

'No.'

'Hmm.'

'Exactly. Hmm. But I can't tell Guy, can I? None of this is admissible.'

'No, but she'd never have come forward anyway. At least now you know.'

They sat, looking out at the desolate evening street, the dry breeze that blew rubbish across the train tracks. Aidan flicked the lighter over his Marlboro Red and breathed in. The faintly spicy smell took her back twelve years.

'Who do you like for it, Maguire? The da, or the Mission? What does your gut say?'

She chewed on one nail, slightly regretting the attempted manicure. 'They both seem sort of off. But I don't know how, yet. The father's dodgy, I'm sure of it, and the Mission gives me a very bad feeling, and of course there's all those cases, and the links Maeve dug up, but as to which of them I like for it, I couldn't say.'

'Mm. I wonder if there's even a difference, you know.'

She looked at him sharply. 'What's that mean?'

'Never mind. Just a hunch, or something.'

She sighed. 'Guy — Inspector Brooking — he's told me to focus on Majella. I'm not sure I can go to him with this, Aidan. Not unless we find more, or if we can link the Mission to the ones from the eighties. I can't even prove God's Shepherd were here in 1985. I've found nothing so far.'

'But I could look into it.'

261

'That was my thinking. You are Ballyterrin's premier investigative journalist, after all.' But her heart wasn't in the jibe, and both of them sat, lost in thought.

'I'll see what I can do,' Aidan stubbed out his cigarette in the ashtray. 'You know this fella Carr — it's not just the council he controls.'

She didn't understand. 'Hmm?'

'The paper. How'd you think I got it back on its feet?'

'You mean — ?'

'Aye. I'm in hock to my armpits, to a certain company owned by . . . guess who?'

'Oh.' She watched him fiddle with the keys. 'Be careful, Aidan.'

'Never wanted to be the type that cared about money. Publish and be damned, that's my motto. But — '

'But it's your da's paper. I know. Don't risk it, Aidan. It's not worth it.'

'I don't know about that.' He turned the key in the ignition. 'I'll drop you back.'

Aidan started the car, and turned it round in the street in front of the Mission building. As the headlights swept the gloom, they saw it wasn't entirely deserted. 'Oops, looks like we've disturbed a courting couple.' Aidan turned his head to reverse, but Paula saw the faces in the moment of dazzle. They didn't turn in time to see her or Aidan, but she recognised the pair in each other's arms, faces pressed together against the cold.

The first woman was Maddy Goldberg, the girl from the Mission band, dark hair blowing in the breeze. The second, huddled against the wall, was harder to see, but Paula could tell from the glimpse of pale skin and freckles that it was Sarah Kenny. The teacher who'd noticed Cathy crying, on the last day she was seen alive.

24

Maddy and Sarah. Sarah and Maddy. It made sense, in a way — of course, the teacher had been the one to bring the Mission to the school. Their relationship was unusual in Ballyterrin, perhaps, but they were doing nothing wrong. All the same, something about it made Paula uneasy as she plodded into work the next day. Maybe the idea of the two being close to Cathy, both being privy to her secrets, while hiding a huge secret of their own.

Unable to tell Guy what she'd seen, or what she'd learned from Rosemary, at least without getting into even bigger trouble, Paula did her best to understand the Majella Ward case. She was conscious that, as the girl's family had protested, most of their time and energy had gone on Cathy. If she could link Majella to Eamonn Carr, it might be the break she needed, so she threw herself into learning about this other girl, who despite everything had remained something of an enigma.

Majella had also last been seen leaving school on a Friday, two weeks before Cathy's disappearance. Wanting to get a sense of her, fix her in mind, Paula took advantage of a slack afternoon to drive up to Majella's school. PJ had finally convinced her to take his Volvo, and leave the hire car back. Reluctantly, she'd done it. The costs were starting to spiral and there was no end in sight for this case. It didn't mean she couldn't still leave any time she wanted. Of course it didn't.

Ballyterrin Institute was noticeably more rundown than St Bridget's; there was graffiti on the beige walls and an unappealing seventies' decor in the echoing hallways. The Head was a tall stooped man in a stained red sports jacket, hair thinning on top. His hand when he shook hers was chilled. 'The heating's packed in. I'm Mr Campbell. I'm afraid we can tell you very little about Majella. Her teachers found her a pleasant girl, but unfortunately her parents chose to send her so infrequently, she never got the chance to shine. We see this all the time with the traveller girls. She'd have been married off very soon, in any case.'

They were standing in the lobby of the school, vast and cold, a staircase leading up to higher floors. Someone had put up posters, perhaps in an attempt to add cheer, but they sagged at the corners and flapped in the draught.

'Did no one think it was strange, though, when she didn't turn up for two weeks?' Paula asked.

He saw her face. 'Miss Maguire, you must understand that we have one thousand pupils here. The grammar schools cream off all those with good exam prospects, so we're left with children who have little desire to be here, and will never progress beyond a HND in childcare, or a joiner apprenticeship, if they're lucky. I do what I can for those who want to learn. A pupil who never comes to school, and will be married and likely pregnant by the age of seventeen — well, that pupil is already lost to us.'

She didn't know what to say to that. 'Majella was last seen leaving here?'

'We always have a teacher on home-time duty, in case fights break out. Majella was noted walking out when the bell rang, and as far as I know hasn't been seen since.'

She waited for him to ask if Majella was likely to be in danger. He didn't. 'I see. Thank you for your time, sir.'

'I only hope it helps.' He turned, tired and distracted, to bawl at two teenage boys dashing down the corridor: 'WE DO NOT RUN IN THIS SCHOOL! My office, *now*.'

Paula slipped out. The schoolyard was beginning to fill with children in navy uniforms, streaming out of their classes and down to the gates with the unfocused energy of puppies. In one clump of younger girls, arms crossed tight together over new breasts, she recognised a face.

Theresa Ward recognised Paula, too. 'Miss? Did you find Maj? Did you come to get me?' She detached herself from her cohorts and sidled over.

'No, I'm sorry, Theresa, I'm just asking questions. What about you, anything new? You didn't get hurt in the riot?'

'Naw. Me brother got his finger broke by them peelers.' The girl's uniform was shabby, the navy leaving her pale face wan and washed out, so she looked very young and vulnerable. 'Da's on the booze most nights, Mammy's on the warpath. All me da's brothers and that are looking for Maj, but nobody knows nothing.'

The police knew little more. 'Well, if you think of anything, you can always call me.'

'Miss — Paula? You know that other girl, they found her and she was dead, like?'

'Listen, Theresa — we've still no proof there's any connection to Majella's case. We just have to try not to worry until we know we should.'

Theresa nodded dubiously. 'Somebody stabbed her, it said on the news. In her neck, like. That girl Cathy.'

'Yes. But the best you can do to help your sister is keep your eyes and ears open. Anything you see, or if you just want to chat, you ring me.'

The girl still looked doubtful. 'She's been gone a month now, missus. How could she be gone a month and nobody's seen her, like?'

That was the question Paula didn't want to answer. 'I don't know, Theresa. Let's both just keep looking.'

★ ★ ★

The next day, as is often the way, several things happened at once. First, Paula spotted a familiar name in her inbox when she got into work that morning. It had been so long since she'd received an email from Aidan that it gave her the strangest sense of vertigo. For a moment, she was right back to that day when she was eighteen, when the message had come from him in Dublin — *I did something*. She shook it off, clicking on his name. Why was he emailing her, when she'd been ringing him for days with no

267

response? He was always like this. You'd get close, and you'd think everything was fine, and then you wouldn't hear from him for a month.

Found out Lazarus's real name, it said succinctly. His ma was Irish, ran away from home in the 80s, turned up in Birmingham pregnant. Guess what her name was?

For a moment Paula thought he really wasn't going to tell her, but then she spotted an attachment to the email. It was a scan of an old birth certificate, crumpled and handwritten. *Father's name: unknown.* She glanced down quickly to see the mother's name and there it was: *Rachel Reilly.*

A small noise escaped Paula's lips. Had Rachel really been hiding all that time, not dead at all — pregnant like Dympna Boyle and so many others who'd been to God's Shepherd churches? She remembered what Dympna had said to her father: *He'll take her away.* She fired back an email to Aidan: *Is this for real?*

Aidan must have been at his computer, because a reply quickly popped up. She clicked on it. *True as God, Maguire. I bet you're wondering now who the da was. Remember Maeve's idea about Ron Almeira?*

Of course she did, the American pastor who'd been in Ireland in the seventies and eighties, the founder of God's Shepherd. *Check out this pic. Handy to be sitting on newspaper archives sometimes.*

She opened the attachment and as it loaded, found herself looking at another old newspaper clipping. The date on the top was May 1985.

Two months before Rachel Reilly went missing, three months before Alice Dunne. *Pastor Ron Almeira meets Ballyterrin businessmen. Church group to open in town.* There were lots of men in suits standing round, but her eye was drawn by the one in the middle. His face slowly took shape as the picture cleared. *Come on, damn you.* There he was. For a moment she was confused — what was *he* doing there? He'd hardly have been born in 1985 . . . Then she understood. *Holy Christ, Aidan, what have you found?*

'Avril?' Paula kept her voice steady.

'Mm?' The analyst looked up from her desk.

'You're still looking into the Mission staff, are you, for any prior convictions?'

'Well, I did, but there's nothing coming up. They're all clean.'

'Try the name Ed Reilly. That might throw something up.'

Avril looked curious, but nodded. 'OK.'

'And Avril — if there's nothing there, you could try another name too. Ed Almeira. Try that and see.'

★　★　★

She'd barely had time to let this sink in — Rachel Reilly alive, and possibly the mother of Ed Lazarus — when Fiacra came sloping in, late as usual. Avril made a great show of typing fast and Paula smiled at him distractedly.

He yawned, dumping his sports bag on the desk. 'Hey Paula, guess who rang me back yesterday.'

269

'Who?' Paula was still staring at Aidan's email.
'Annie Miller's cousin, that's who.'

She glanced at him sharply. 'And?'

'Well, not much. She lives in Liverpool now — Fiona's her name. Nice girl, sounds like. A physiotherapist.'

Paula wondered if she should say something about flirting with witnesses. 'How old is she? Does she remember her cousin?'

'Ah, not that well. She was three or four when Annie died, and then her ma — that's Annie's auntie — moved the family to England. But she did say they'd talk about it a lot, and that her ma always said Annie was very holy. Like the kind who'd be licking the altar rails, you know.' He was fiddling with his keyboard, extracting it from under the mess of paper on his desk.

'And did she go to a church group?'

'Well, Fiona didn't know that. Just that Annie'd have been the type. And her ma remembered Annie having a big row with her own ma, the sister, just before she died. Sarah said it would always come up if she wanted to go out to something and her daddy wouldn't let her. Her ma would say, look what happened to our Annie. Let the child live her life, that kind of thing.'

Paula took this in. 'OK. Well, that's sort of useful, I suppose. Thanks.'

'No bother.' Cheerfully, he unwrapped a sausage roll and began cramming it in his mouth. Avril tutted, very quietly.

Paula had thought over this new piece of news for a while, and concluded it told her nothing

270

definite, when her phone rang, and the next thing happened. At first she thought she was hearing a seagull screech down the line. 'Hello?'

'Missus, is that you?'

'Yes, this is Dr Maguire — who's that?'

'Theresa. Theresa Ward, yah know?'

She sat bolt upright at her desk. 'Are you OK, Theresa?'

'Missus, is it all right to be phoning you? Is anyone listening?'

'No, it's just me.' She glanced round the office. Just Avril in one corner, her brow furrowed at the computer, and Fiacra in another one, slumped in his seat, a tinny sound escaping from his headphones.

'You said I was to ring you if I heard anything, aye?'

'And did you?'

Silence from Theresa. 'Missus, you know what a match-maker is?'

'I think so. A lady who comes round when you want to get married?' Sort of a dating service for travellers, Paula thought.

'Aye. Some ould busybody. Well, missus, she came round last night, when Da was in the pub, and she was in talking to Mammy for ages. They sent me out. I mean for Jaysus' sake, I'm not a wean.' Theresa's voice stung with indignation.

'But you heard something?'

'Course I did. Walls is like cardboard. I heard them saying about our Maj.'

Paula frowned. 'Majella? What about her?'

'Who she'd be wed to. And I heard her say — missus, I couldn't hear the lot, but I'd swear

271

blind Mammy said Rathkeale. Me Auntie Jacinta lives in Rathkeale, doesn't she?'

Paula was trying desperately to understand. 'Theresa? Do you mean . . . do you think your mum knows where your sister is?' Silence. 'Theresa?'

'You know before she went, our Maj, the night before she . . . went away.'

'Yes?'

'They were fighting the bit out, her and Mammy. Screaming. Mammy called her a wee slapper. That's not like our Maj, you know, she's a right Holy Joe normally. And Dad wasn't there, and he didn't meet the matchmaker last night neither. But if our Maj was getting wed, Dad would have to be there. You see?'

'I think so. Why didn't you mention this before?'

'Didn't want all me family business in the paper. Never thought it mattered till you said to keep an eye out. And missus, when the matchmaker went, I had a wee look in Mammy's special drawer. She keeps her housekeeping money and that in there, but sure the key's only under the doorstep, we can always get it open.'

'And?'

'The phone was in there. Our Maj's phone.'

'Majella's phone is in your mum's kitchen drawer?'

'Yeah.'

'OK.' Paula took a deep breath. 'Never mind, Theresa, you did the right thing. Do you know where your auntie lives?'

'I only went there one time. It's a big caravan

272

place. Like, it's near Limerick, but not *in* Limerick. Where travellers stay.'

Paula thought hard for a moment. 'Is there somewhere you can go, Theresa? A neighbour, a friend? Just for a few hours?'

'Can't leave the wee ones, I'm minding them.'

It was 11 a.m. on a school day, but Paula let it go. 'Well, stay inside. See if you can lock the door and keep the kids in.'

'Missus? Are you coming to lift Mammy? She's away to Dunnes now for the messages.'

'How long since she went?'

'Dunno, not long.'

'OK. I have to hang up now. You stay with the kids. Listen, Theresa, if we find your sister — if we find Majella because of this — I want you to remember, it was because of you. OK?'

'Ah, away on,' said Theresa, with the world-weary scorn of someone four times her age.

As soon as she put the phone down, Paula went over to Fiacra and tapped on his desk to arouse him from Solitaire. 'Rathkeale. You know it? It's near Limerick, right? Isn't that what they call the traveller capital?'

He looked startled. 'It is. Eh — I went there on my holidays one time.'

'Can you ring the station there? Ask them if they know a big caravan park.'

He was already lifting the phone, such was the force of her voice. 'How come?'

'Because I think we'll find Majella Ward there.'

★ ★ ★

Afterwards, Paula saw it on the news like everyone else. The Gardaí Land Rovers sweeping in, whipping dust in the wind and flapping laundry on lines. It was shown over and over. The large white caravan, bushes tended round its door. The scrum of Guards surrounding. And wrapped in a blanket, led out by a policewoman, was a skinny girl with chestnut hair, visibly weeping and wailing. She looked familiar, even if you'd never met her before. After all, her face had been staring down from *Missing* posters for nearly a month now.

'I can't believe it.' Guy stilled the image on the screen. The team was gathered in the meeting room, watching it on playback.

'So — it was her mother all along?' Avril was clearly stunned by this development, and in fact they all were. What did it mean if you couldn't even trust the grieving parents of the lost?

'It does happen,' said Guy unhappily. 'There was that case in Leeds, of course, where the mother wanted money. This time we're not sure. We think Majella's mum just wanted to get her away from something, but was afraid to tell her husband what she'd done. She did try to put us off investigating.' He paused. 'I suppose that should have been our warning.'

'Will they charge the mother?' Gerard's face was unreadable, still bearing the scars of his trip to the site. Looking for a girl who wasn't even lost.

'We don't know yet. If she can prove she was under duress from her husband, well . . . It won't stick.'

'And why did she want Majella gone?' Paula could guess, but she was trying to behave, not go haring off like a dog after clues.

Guy didn't meet her eyes. 'That's what we need to find out.'

★ ★ ★

Majella Ward was still crying when they brought her into the new police station the next day. After a night in hospital, it had been ascertained that she'd suffered nothing worse than an enforced stay at her aunt's.

Her mother was in the custody suite on the other side of the building, where she also hadn't stopped crying once in four hours. The interviewing officers didn't know what to do with her. 'You tell me, mister, what was I meant to do? She comes to me and says, 'I've a boyfriend, Mammy, and I've had sex with him' — so what choice did I have? Her daddy'd have thrown her out if he knew, and nobody'd marry her once she was ruined. I'd no choice. Her life would've have been over. How was I meant to know he'd get the peelers in? Sure he can't stand the sight of yis normally.' Mrs Ward had a lurid yellowing bruise over one eye.

Helen Corry had been watching through the window when Paula arrived, arms folded, wearing a black suit, face inscrutable. 'You're here to help with the girl, then?'

Paula once again felt awkward in Corry's presence, aware of the scuffs on her suede boots and that her grey jumper had a loose thread in it.

275

'Inspector Brooking wants me to observe.'

'Hmm. Does Inspector Brooking realise we're a police station? As in, we do actually know how to conduct interviews ourselves?'

'I — I think he just wants to understand her state of mind. In case it helps us with other cases, if they're linked maybe.'

Helen Corry gave the same smile again, the one that totally wrong-footed you. 'I'm sure you'll do an excellent job, Paula. After all, we have to use you while we have you. We'll get what we can out of Mammy here. Now, what do you say to helping me prepare for this interview?'

★ ★ ★

'They didn't lock her up or anything?' Paula was now watching Majella through the two-way mirror, as she sat on the sofa of the nice interview room, the one they used for children and the especially vulnerable. Although she was fifteen, Majella was hugging an oversized teddy bear to her chest, rocking slightly. Her hair hung like curtains over her face.

Corry shook her head. 'Seems not. She's grand, except she won't stop crying. Shock, the doctors said.'

'OK. You want me to listen in?' They'd gone over various strategies to get the most from Majella; though Paula still felt nervous suggesting things to the other woman.

'Yes. If you think I'm getting nowhere, give me a shout.' Corry welded on a smile and went in. 'Hello, Majella, how are you feeling?'

276

'OK,' the girl said in a very small voice.

'Good. My name's Helen. I'm here to let you know you're not to worry, we're going to sort all this out.'

No reaction.

'Can you tell me what happened to you, Majella?'

'Mammy took me phone off me, it wasn't fair. Me cousins were standing over me all the time. Never let me out of the caravan.' Her voice was slightly whiny.

'No one recognised you? It was on the news a lot, that you were gone.'

The girl shrugged. Quite probably the whole camp had known, but they looked after their own. She seemed healthy enough, if skinny. In this case, the offence they could possibly charge her mother with — kidnap — meant rather enforced house-arrest. Or caravan-arrest.

'Tell me what happened when you left school that day, on the Friday.'

'I went out, and I was walkin' home, like, and this car came up beside me, and I recognised it was me Auntie Jacinta's car. And Mammy was inside with one of her brothers, me Uncle Danny.'

'So then what happened?'

She bit her nail. 'They said I had to get in and then we went down to Auntie Jacinta's, in the South. Then I just stayed there till yous came.'

Corry changed tack. 'Are you worried about your mum, Majella?'

The girl jerked, then nodded suspiciously.

277

'They've told you she could go to prison?'

She did a sort of twisting shrug and chewed on a hang-nail.

'You must have been cross with her, when she sent you away.'

Majella's eyes flickered. 'She never had to take me phone. She said Daddy'd skin me if she didn't get me away.'

'Skin you why?'

That was when the girl clammed up, like a blank screen coming over her face. 'Dunno.'

Paula waited outside, watching. '*Go easy with her,*' she muttered to herself. They didn't have the facilities for an earpiece, so Corry wouldn't be able to hear her.

Corry went on, 'Your sister said the matchmaker was over the night before you went away.'

A flush came over the girl's face. 'She's nosy.'

'But you didn't want to get married — you already had a boyfriend, is that it?'

More silence.

'Your mum told us you'd lost your virginity,' Corry said as gently as she could, and Paula saw the girl's head go up at the unfairness. 'She said that's why she had to send you away, before it was too late to get you married.'

'Wha-at?' Majella gaped.

'So who was he, your boyfriend?'

Down went the head and the curtains of hair.

'You know you need to tell me. Or else your mum might really go to jail. Kidnap is a very serious crime, but if we can show you were in danger . . . '

'I'm not meant to tell.' Tears were dripping down her pale skin. 'He said I'd get in trouble.'

Outside, Paula closed her eyes for a second. How many times had she heard those exact words from children, young girls? Did they give the abusers a manual or something?

Luckily, Corry was handling her well, speaking reassuringly. 'Majella, you can't get in trouble. You're only fifteen. Whatever's happened isn't your fault. But your mum might go to prison if you don't let me help you.'

The girl sobbed.

'You had a boyfriend?'

She nodded slowly, tears streaking her cheeks. 'He said I wasn't meant to tell.'

'That's OK. Just give me his name.'

'Ed,' she said finally. 'His name's Ed. From the Mission. He was my boyfriend and we did it and I told Mammy and she went mental.' Wobbly lip, more tears. 'Miss, I just want to see him. She wouldn't let me say bye to him! And he had some other girl, and Mammy wouldn't let me see him to get him back. Can I see him, can I?'

'Who was the other girl?'

Majella shook her head. 'I just want to see him.'

'Majella. You have to tell us.'

A fresh burst of tears welled up. The girl covered her face. 'It was that Cathy. Her. He liked her. Now *please*, miss, can I see him?'

The best Corry could manage was a tight-lipped, 'We'll see,' as she struggled to keep her face neutral. Paula saw her look up to the corner of the room, where the video camera had its red light on, to show this interview was indeed being recorded. She wondered if Corry was thinking the same as her: *Got you, you bastard*.

25

The tension coming off the team was palpable. Guy looked round at them. 'I'm sure you don't need reminding how serious this is.'

It was the day after Majella Ward's taped interview, and the girl was now being cared for by Social Services. Her mother was still in custody at the police station, but the charges against her had taken something of a back seat, since Majella had accused the leader of the Mission of what amounted to statutory rape. Paula was back at the unit building, where they were deciding on their next move after all they'd learned.

'Is it enough, sir?' Fiacra was tentative. 'I mean . . . '

'It's enough to get him fired, at least. But you're right, we've only Majella's word that Ed was Cathy's boyfriend too. We're going to have to tread carefully. He had an alibi for the day she disappeared, after all.'

Paula was clenching her hands under the table. Why were they still talking? Wouldn't Ed realise, wouldn't he see on the news that Majella had been found? Was he so arrogant he imagined girls never talked? She was trying to keep her rage under control. What if that smug bastard was leaving town as they spoke?

'Right.' Guy snapped to business. 'Gerard, you go in one car. Myself and Sergeant Hamilton will go on ahead and meet DCI Corry and the Tactical Support team. They'll be taking records, files, anything that might help us bust these guys. We're going to interview Lazarus here, if he'll come quietly — keep him away from the scrum at the main station. It seems increasingly likely there may be some link to Cathy's case.' He didn't meet Paula's eyes. 'Avril's searches have thrown up several convictions for indecent assault relating to an Ed Reilly from Birmingham. We need to confirm it, but it looks like this could be Ed Lazarus's real name, making our missing girl Rachel his mother. As to why he'd come back to Ballyterrin after all that time, we don't know.'

Paula found her voice. 'Can I come?' They all looked at her. 'Please?' She telegraphed the words to Guy: *It was my theory. Please let me come.*

He hesitated. 'OK. Go with Gerard. Come on, it's time.'

Paula saw Gerard's face. Oh well, she wasn't too keen on going with him either. But there was no way she was going to miss this.

★   ★   ★

'Fecking traffic.' Gerard swore as, once again, the Hill Street box junction exacted its dues. Traffic snarled up the main road and the police car sat, fixed. As they waited, Paula looked him over. Muscles tensed in his forearms. His tie worn loose and eyes deep blue. Shame he spoiled it all with a face like a slapped arse.

He caught her gaze. 'I suppose you're pleased with yourself.'

'No more so than usual.'

He turned on her. 'No one else would get away with your carry-on. Going off to Dublin on your own, lying to the boss, upsetting families of victims . . . But all you have to do is make eyes at him and you're like a pig in shite.'

She raised her eyebrows but kept quiet. Gerard slammed into second gear, swearing under his breath. He turned, and she saw the flash of scar tissue under his chin, still red and shiny from the petrol-bomb attack.

'How's your neck?'

He muttered, 'Never mind my neck. It's grand.'

'I'm sorry about what happened down there. It wasn't my fault, you know.'

'Never said it was, did I?'

'You know what I'd love to know, Gerard?'

He glared at her but said nothing.

'I'd love to know what your problem is. You're arsey to Avril, who's a lovely girl, you're horrible to me for no apparent reason — do you not like working with women, is that it?' She said it calmly. The car lunged forward and slammed to a halt at a traffic-light. 'Jesus!' she exclaimed. 'What are you at? Guy'll go spare if you get penalty points.'

He took a deep breath. 'I've no problem with women, Miss Maguire. I've a problem with people doing whatever they like. If we catch the fella who killed this girl, and your antics mean we can't get him behind bars, think what you'd be doing. Not just to all of us, busting our guts here, but to that family. Could you live with yourself if that happened?'

She opened her mouth. Not sure what she was going to say — that she was only thinking of Cathy, that she was only doing what she thought was right. Instead she said, 'You're right, Gerard. I messed up. And I did get in trouble, if that makes you feel better.'

He looked away.

'I bet it makes you feel a bit better. Does it?'

He just shook his head, but his frown had eased a little as they moved forward.

★ ★ ★

The Mission seemed oddly calm when they arrived. Paula wasn't sure what she'd expected — a riot, perhaps, the do-gooders barricading themselves against cops with shields. Instead there were four uniformed PSNI officers taking notes, rifling through files with gloved hands, getting statements from the Mission staff — a collection of tie-dyed young men and women with long hair and subdued, worried expressions. Corry was co-ordinating them, and gave Paula a small nod as she entered. Paula relaxed; the DCI would have been well within her rights to send her home, say she'd no place there.

As they passed into the big hall she saw Guy walk out, followed by Ed Lazarus, who today wore his fair hair loose and shampooed about his face, a white Jesus-like smock over his jeans. He flashed Paula an unfathomable look and she tried to blend into the breeze-block walls.

Ed said clearly, 'Do you normally bring psychologists to police raids, Inspector?'

Guy looked at Paula warningly. 'It's not a raid, Mr Lazarus. You've wisely agreed to come in voluntarily for now.'

'I have.' He held out his sinewy arms. 'I'd gladly go in handcuffs, Inspector. If it could in any way ease the pain of that child's family, I'd go in chains, like Our Lord Jesus Christ Himself.'

'There won't be any need for that. The team will finish taking statements here and we'll have a chat at the unit.'

'Certainly. Always happy to have a 'chat' in the name of law and order.'

Guy ushered him out, leaning in to Paula to hiss, 'Do NOT do anything, you hear? Just watch. I'm so far out on a limb for you, you have no idea.'

She thought about what Gerard had said. 'Cross my heart.'

He gave her a suspicious look and went out, Ed walking with ostentatious, jerky moments, like a freedom-fighter arrested on a protest march.

Paula turned back to the hall, looking in from where she stood in the corridor. Gerard had gone in to talk to the officers, and was pointing at things and nodding as he took notes. There wasn't much for her to do but watch, as Guy had said. That was annoying.

She heard movement behind her. 'Hey there.' A girl with dark plaits and heavy eyebrows was coming out of the office, her arms stacked with files. It was the same girl Paula had seen on her first, fraudulent visit, and then later, illuminated in the headlights of Aidan's car. Paula blushed at the memory. The girl said, 'You look kinda familiar. I've seen you here before?'

'Yes — it's Maddy, is it?' Was it her imagination or was Maddy trying to block her view into the office? Paula shifted but couldn't see past the door.

'Sure is.' Maddy pushed the door shut with one wide hip, clothed in an ethnic print dress. 'Jeez, the cops are all over us today.'

'I know, I'm with them. Paula Maguire. We met before, briefly.'

'Hey, Paula, how are you.' Maddy almost dropped the files as she stuck out her hand to shake Paula's. The nails were bitten close, and Paula noticed a lattice of scars under the flapping sleeve of the girl's dress. She looked away quickly, eyes darting to the darkened window of the office. Was that movement?

'You're not from around here by the sounds of it, Maddy?'

'I'm from the good old U S of A.' Her smile was bright. She had striking eyes, an unusual moss-green flecked with gold. 'Mid-Western girl.'

'And you've ended up in Ireland, isn't that strange.'

In the hall they heard snaps as things were being photographed, the low murmur of voices. 'We go where the Mission sends us, but if I'm honest, I asked to come to Ireland. My roots are

286

here in Ballyterrin too. Bet you didn't guess that.'

'I didn't.' Besides the accent, the girl just *looked* American: solid, clear-skinned, white teeth. 'Your name's Goldberg though, isn't it?' That didn't seem to indicate an Irish heritage.

'Sure, sure.' Maddy seemed not to notice what was going on behind them in the hall. Paula found it very disconcerting, to be the focus of her attention. 'Mom and Dad are Jewish, of course, but I'm Irish. I was adopted from Ireland. Bet you didn't think that was still going on in the eighties, huh?'

Paula stared at her in astonishment, distracted by this bombshell from trying to see into the dark office. 'The eighties. How old are you, Maddy, if you don't mind me — ?'

She answered with alacrity. 'Twenty-five.' Considerably younger than Sarah Kenny, Paula was sure.

Paula could only think of one type of organisation that still sent Irish babies to America in the eighties. And the girl had been born in Ballyterrin, so . . . 'So you . . . ?'

'That's right.' The gold flecks flashed in Maddy Goldberg's eyes as she smiled. 'I was born right here in this building. A Safe Harbour baby. And now I want to find my real mom — that's why I'm here. I used to talk to *her* about it all the time.'

Paula frowned. 'To who, sorry?'

'Cathy. We were close, y'know?'

The girl suddenly seemed to be standing too close. Paula looked round, keen for the solid,

287

grumpy presence of Gerard Monaghan. 'Maddy, we're trying to talk to everyone at the Mission. I wonder, would you mind if we asked you a few questions? At the unit building, perhaps?'

'Sure!' It was delivered again in that odd, off-key tone, as if one of the notes in the song that was Maddy Goldberg was ever so slightly out of tune. As Maddy swung her hips down the corridor, Paula looked back in time to see the office door click shut, a figure darting out and down the corridor to where the leaders had their rooms. Maroon uniform, dark curly hair. Was this the elusive Katie Brooking?

⋆ ⋆ ⋆

Gerard hissed out of his mouth as they looked into the station interview room. 'You're unbelievable, you are. Did he not say you'd just to watch?'

On the other side of the door, Maddy Goldberg sat very still, her hands flat on the table in front of her, eyes half-closed. She'd requested some time to pray before they questioned her.

Paula held up her hands. 'I know, I know! I'm sorry — she just sort of . . . started talking. Honestly, I think she knows something about Cathy. It was as if she wanted to tell me, but I don't know what.'

He grunted. 'You better be right, Maguire. Watch and see what she says.'

She thought it was a good sign he'd dropped the 'Miss'.

Gerard led into the questions, after asking with hyper-politeness if he could tape Maddy's responses. He was keen to point out she wasn't under caution, just 'helping with enquiries'. 'Now, Miss — Goldberg, is it? I understand you spoke with our psychologist, Miss Maguire, at the Mission, and we'd just like to get that on tape if we can. So, how well did you know Cathy Carr?'

'Pretty well. She was like a kid sister to me, you know? We'd talk all the time about her family, school. Some of her friends were giving her a rough time. When she went missing we were all real worried.'

Gerard tapped the table. 'But when we made preliminary enquiries, you didn't come forward to say Cathy had confided in you. Why not?'

Maddy didn't even pause. 'You know, we gotta respect the kids' privacy.'

'Even when they turn up dead in a canal?'

Maddy just shook her head; calm, plaits swinging. 'God took her to Himself. It was part of his plan.'

Even Gerard looked floored by this. 'You're saying you think it was God's plan that Cathy was killed?'

'Everything is His plan.' Her face was still, pious.

Gerard tried again. 'Where were you on the Friday Cathy disappeared, Miss Goldberg?'

She was still smiling. 'Oh, Officer.' Her voice was sweet, like the Homecoming Queen. 'I can't remember that far back, can you? Usually I hang out at the Mission, y'know? We have a team meeting, and we pray. Get ready for the Friday-evening session.'

'Mr Lazarus told us he'd been leading the meeting — can you confirm that?'

'He must have been, if he said it.'

'Were you there yourself, Maddy?'

'I guess. We all go to the meetings.'

Gerard was stern. 'I'm afraid *I guess* isn't good enough, Miss. Were you or weren't you at the meeting that day?'

'Am I under arrest, Officer?'

'I've already said you aren't.'

'Well, then I guess it's OK if I don't answer that.' She smiled. 'It's just the American way. We don't comment without a lawyer. And my lawyer's, like, six thousand miles away.'

Gerard had little choice. 'All right. Will you excuse me a moment, please?' He pushed back his chair and got up. 'The woman's wired to the moon,' he muttered as he filled his coffee cup in the main office. 'Says the wean's like a sister to her, but doesn't turn a hair when someone dumps her in the canal? I'll be checking out her alibi, this Miss Madeleine Goldberg. Suppose we'll have to let her go for now, though.'

Just then Guy came round the corner, his face serious. 'Paula. You need to come here.'

★ ★ ★

Ed Lazarus had been in interview for several hours and still no sign of answers. 'He keeps breaking off to pray,' said Guy, as he and Paula watched through the two-way mirror.

290

'You'd think Bob would like that,' she observed, watching the red-faced policeman on the other side. Bob sat with his pen poised, eyes trained on Ed Lazarus, who was praying out loud. 'Mr Laz . . . Mr Lazarus, I really — ' Paula wondered if she ought to suggest a pray-off. But it was possible even Sideshow Bob might lose this one.

'Lord, I know they're doing their best,' intoned Ed Lazarus. 'Sergeant Hamilton here, he just wants to find who hurt poor Cathy. Inspector Brooking, he wants justice. Help them see, O Lord, that the Mission only wants to bring Your light to the world.'

Guy made an irritated noise in his throat. 'You'd better just watch. He doesn't seem to like you much.'

She winced at the memory of her fake niece. 'No, he wouldn't.'

Guy pushed open the door, saying loudly, 'Amen. That's enough for now, Mr Lazarus. I'm sure you wouldn't want to waste the money of hard-working taxpayers.' Bob got up and made a hasty exit, buttoning the jacket of his suit in relief.

Ed didn't open his eyes. 'O God, help them clear out their temples as You cleared the money-lenders from Your Holy Father's.'

Guy sat down. 'Would it help if I called you Mr Reilly?'

It had the desired effect. Ed lowered his hands and gave Guy a slit-eyed look. 'That isn't my name.'

'Used to be though, didn't it — when you

were convicted of assaulting a minor?' Guy threw a sheet of paper down on the desk, but the man didn't look at it.

'I am a sinner, Inspector. I've atoned for mine by bringing God's word to the people. What have *you* done?' He stared at Guy, and Paula willed her boss not to look away first, but it seemed no one could hold that poison-green gaze for long.

Guy tried again. 'Course, you could have used your dad's name too, couldn't you? Almeira? He is your dad, isn't he? Lead Pastor of the church behind the Mission. Funny, that. And you're following in his footsteps.' Paula watched his face, but Ed didn't even twitch. Had he known? He must have known, surely. 'Ashamed of him, were you? I hear he likes little girls, too.'

Ed didn't react. 'He's a famous man, and I wanted to make it on my own.'

'I see. Like Jesus. Except His mother didn't run away when she got pregnant.'

The man ignored this jibe.

'That is what happened, isn't it? Your mother went to a God's Shepherd church group in the eighties, when she was, what — seventeen? And she got pregnant, and ran away. She's been classed as a Missing Person for nearly thirty years.'

Ed's mouth twisted. 'My mother made her own choices. She wanted to keep me, and the church's policy is not to condone extra-marital sex. We feel children should be given the best start in life, with married, Christian parents.'

'You wish she'd given you away, then?'

He said nothing, closing his eyes again, as if in silent prayer.

'Did you know you still had family here, Ed? Your mother's sister still lives on the farm, with your cousins. Is that why you came back, to find them?'

No answer, but Paula detected a slight tremor in his hands. *Push him, Guy, push harder.* It was a good question. Why had Ed come back?

'Maybe we should ask your mother why she ran away. Find out what was really going on.'

Ed looked up. 'You're welcome to try, Inspector. Of course she's been dead for five years, so I doubt she'd answer. Breast cancer. You'd know that if you had the first idea about me.'

Shit. She watched Guy, willing him not to show he hadn't been aware of this.

'Let's talk about your father then, Mr Reilly. The Pastor. Does he know about you?'

Nothing.

'Mr Reilly? Or do you prefer *Almeira*?'

Ed snapped. 'There's only my mother's word he was even my father. Women lie, Inspector. I've never met the Pastor. Perhaps one day, if I carry on with the Mission, I'll get that honour.'

'Not if he's convicted of rape, you won't. Did you know he was on trial in the States?'

His face was impassive. 'Judge not, lest ye be judged, Inspector.'

Guy laid his hands on the table. 'Do you understand why you're here, Mr Reilly? We've found Majella Ward. Her mother took her away, because Majella was sleeping with an older man. You, she claims.'

Not a flicker on his handsome face. 'Inspector,

293

you have a daughter yourself. I know Katie well. She's very troubled, poor girl. Her brother's death hit her hard.'

Guy's fists clenched, but he sat still.

'Girls lie, don't they? They have so many secrets and problems, all their little dramas.' Ed spread his thin, feminine hands. 'These girls come to us, and they have so little self-esteem. They feel ugly, fat, uncared for. We teach them to love themselves — is it any wonder some of them think they love me, too?' He smiled.

Guy pushed on. 'Did you have a relationship with Majella?'

'Of course. We all have relationships in God's love.'

'I mean a sexual relationship.'

'Ah, Inspector. Back to sex. 'Remove the plank from your own eye first', as the Bible says. You only have the girl's say that I ever went near her.'

'What about Cathy Carr? You dumped Majella for her, I believe.' And Louise, thought Paula. Would he ask about Louise McCourt? There was still no proof she'd been involved with Ed.

No reaction. 'The girl who died? She may have visited the Mission, I don't know. Many girls come to us.'

Guy leaned in. 'We can prove you were with her too, you know. We can get the DNA from her baby, the one that was killed when she died. It'll tell us who fathered the child.' Guy watched him. 'You did know she was pregnant?'

Paula stared at the man's face. Had he known? Was this the person who'd picked Cathy up on that last Friday, the person in the second car? What had happened after that?

Ed gave nothing away. 'It's very sad. That's why the Mission is here, of course, to try to curb these behaviours.'

'Murder, you mean?'

He shook his head slightly, as if offended by the cheap shot. 'Pre-marital sex.'

'That's rich coming from you. You're twenty-five, are you, Mr Lazarus?'

'I am, Inspector. Good detective work.'

'Shame you have to sniff round teenage girls then. The older ones not interested?'

Ed gave a high, girlish laugh. 'Grasping at straws, Guy?'

Guy looked back at the mirror and Paula saw something in his eyes. *Help.* Whatever it was, she didn't stop to think, just picked up a blank sheet of paper from the printer and hurled herself through the door. Even Ed Lazarus looked momentarily thrown, before slipping back into his usual smug mask.

'Sorry, sorry, Inspector, Mr Lazarus.' She caught a flicker of hate in the man's gaze. 'I just wanted to give you this. Notes from Miss Goldberg's interview.' She slid the blank paper across to Guy.

Thank God, Guy had picked up on what she was doing. 'Oh, I see. Well, that's very interesting, isn't it? We'll have to ask Mr Lazarus how it fits with his story.'

Ed's voice was like a knife. 'What do you mean?'

'Nothing, nothing.' Guy folded the paper and

handed it back to Paula. 'Thank you, Dr Maguire.'

Ed glanced between them. 'I think there's been some kind of . . . Look, I'm fond of Madeleine, of course, like a sister, part of God's family, but — I should tell you, she doesn't always tell the truth.'

'Oh?' Paula looked mock-confused. 'But she said the same about you. So who can we believe?'

He snapped, 'I wouldn't believe the person with scars all up their arms, for a start.' He stretched out his hands, as if to prove they didn't shake. 'Maddy's very unstable. Just look at her records — she was sectioned three times in her teens. I told our leaders she shouldn't be working with children, but her parents had put up serious money for her to be let in the programme. Her adoptive parents, I should say. And that's another thing: what kind of person comes all the way across the world to confront some woman who gave her away in the first place — ' He stopped himself. 'Just do your jobs, will you? Ask *her* where she was that Friday. I told you I was with ten other people until late in the evening. They'll all vouch for me. What I didn't see was Maddy at that meeting. She was ill, apparently. She told me she had a doctor's appointment.'

Guy frowned. 'Yet when questioned, you said all the staff were at the meeting.'

'I was trying to protect her. I gathered her appointment was something — delicate.'

Guy looked at Paula. 'So you're saying Maddy's a liar?'

Ed said, 'Of course she is. I don't know what she's said, but it isn't true.'

Paula couldn't stop herself. She said, 'I guess you do prefer little girls then, like Majella says. Or is she a liar too?'

The man's face was smooth as marble, and then suddenly he was out of his chair and she was backing into the corner and he was right in front of her, hands on the wall beside her head. Guy scrambled up and tried to pull him off but Ed didn't move. He watched Paula from those cool eyes, and lifting one hand, passed it in front of her face. In the background, dimly, she heard Bob shouting into the main station: 'Lads, a bit of back-up here!'

'You're damned,' Ed said softly. 'Whatever you do, however many you find, you're damned, Ms Maguire. Because of what's in *here*.' For a second he rested his finger on her chest, between the second and third buttons of her shirt.

Then, with a wrench, Guy had dragged him back to his chair. 'Sit! You'll be in the cells for this.' Paula leaned gasping against the wall, sucking in air as if the man's hand had been made of stone.

Ed Lazarus didn't turn a hair as Guy gripped him in a restraint hold. He just watched Paula with his green eyes. 'Your heart's eaten up, Paula. You think everyone's the same, but it's you who's damned. You can never put the past behind you. You can never get away from it.'

She felt strong arms. 'Come on.' It was Gerard Monaghan, surprisingly gentle, moving her out of the room and shutting the door behind them.

'You all right?' He watched her keenly as she drank down a strong cup of tea.

'Yeah. Yes. I mean, it's happened before.' As part of her doctorate Paula had spent a year working in a high-security mental hospital, a fact she reminded herself of now, as she tried to calm her breathing. She'd been through much worse. So why could she not stop shaking?

'You've had a shock. Sit down.'

She found herself obeying Gerard's gruff order, legs folding under her. Jesus. Those green eyes, staring into hers . . . Nothing in them, no humanity. She felt cold even though the creaky ceiling was spewing out heat.

'Thanks, Gerard. And I'm sorry — I'm sorry I did it again.' Was there any point in apologising when she actually didn't think she could stop being this way?

He shrugged it off. 'It's good you brought her in, the Goldberg girl. She definitely knows something. You should get home, you're in a state.'

She shook her head. 'There's too much to do. We're getting close now.'

They both looked up; Guy was standing over them. 'Are you OK?' His expression was unreadable. 'Gerard's right, Paula,' he went on. 'You should go home. I can't have you around Lazarus after that.'

'You're not going to let him go?'

'We might have to. We don't have much. Even the phone records — the number he gave

Majella doesn't match the one Cathy was calling when she went missing. Likely he's been using pay-as-you-go, then switching sims. Smart bastard. Even if we show he fathered her child, it's no proof he's behind Cathy's disappearance.'

He wanted her out of the way, she understood. She was annoying too many people. 'I can't go home,' she said after a moment. 'I have to do something. Is there nothing to do?'

Guy thought about it. 'Go back to the school and see what you can get from Cathy's friends. There's a good chance Majella Ward isn't the only other girl he slept with. Find out who else.'

'OK. Thank you.' She tried to read his face again, but he was turning away, shoulders stooped with worry.

26

Paula stood at the entrance to the gym, looking in at the girls. 'What are they doing?'

Beside her was Sarah Kenny, the English teacher, her face hidden by the cloud of curly hair that fell over it. 'They're rehearsing a play for the prayer concert in town, on Hallowe'en. Is something wrong, Ms Maguire?'

Paula tried to smooth out the frown that puckered her face. 'It's just . . . I assumed the concert wouldn't be going on, after everything.' She was astonished, if she was honest. A girl who'd gone there had been murdered, another was claiming she'd slept with the leader, and the Mission was still allowed to operate in local schools?

The teacher seemed to choose her words very carefully. 'We did consult with Cathy's family. She'd have played a lead role in the performance, so of course we asked them.'

'And?' She was aware the question was rude, but couldn't help asking.

'They asked for it to go ahead. The Mission was very important to Cathy, they said, and she'd have wanted it to happen, and help other young people who felt . . . lost. There'll be a dedication read out to her before the concert. It would have made her happy.'

'I see. Miss Kenny — do you mind if I ask — it was you who brought the Mission to the school wasn't it?'

The teacher looked surprised. 'I set up the link with them, yes. My little discussion group, it's all girls who've gone there since the start. The inner circle, I call them.'

'And you think it helps them?'

'Of course. It does wonders for their self-esteem. And isn't it better than hanging out round street corners, going about with boys?'

The teacher's face was earnest, watching the girls with pride through the glass of the doors. Sarah Kenny had been Cathy's form teacher, and she was involved with Maddy Goldberg in a way Paula was sure the church wouldn't approve of. Maddy had been close to Cathy, she said. How did it all fit together?

'You think it's a good place, the Mission?' Paula asked. 'Is it judgemental, I mean, if someone can't live up to the high standards they set? If someone has sinned, say?'

Sarah Kenny did not look round. 'We all sin, Miss Maguire. Sometimes, what we need is to know we'll be forgiven.'

'Hmm. Would it be all right if I watched them for a moment, before I go in?'

'Of course. It'll do them good to get used to an audience, before the performance.'

'Thank you.' Once Sarah Kenny had loped away on her flat sensible shoes, Paula surreptitiously took out her phone. Hiding behind the glass doors of the auditorium, she punched in Guy's direct dial. Luckily, he answered right away. 'It's me,' she hissed.

She heard his voice tighten, his usual way of talking to her. 'Why are you whispering?'

301

'I'm in breach of school rules. Listen, I'm up here now, and the teacher says this prayer concert is going ahead!'

'I'm afraid it's true, yes.'

'What? How?' They had the leader in custody, and still this?

'Paula. We had to let him go for now. We couldn't get enough on him. It's his word against Majella's, and she's already said it was consensual, and — well. The PPS aren't too inclined to trust her family at the moment. Statutory rape isn't enough to bring a murder charge. Plus his alibi's rock-solid, we checked.'

Her heart felt leaden. 'So he's going to get away with it. Again.'

'Maybe not. You're at the school, right? Well, see what the girls will tell you. They've got to trust you, Paula. Everything's resting on this. Get them to trust you and you'll find something to hang him with. I'm sure of it.'

She tried again. 'But surely — surely Cathy's family can't want this going ahead? I mean, if there's even a chance he might have been involved in her death — if we can prove he fathered her baby . . . '

Guy's sigh was like a gust of desolate wind down the line. 'Paula. Eamonn Carr was the one who got him out. He came down here half an hour ago, all lawyers blazing. I'm sorry. The family are backing the Mission all the way. Unless you get something off those girls, there's nothing we can do.'

★ ★ ★

On the stage, a figure moved forward into the light. The curtains were closed against the weak October daylight, and the gym was almost transformed. Under Paula's feet were ghostly hoops and swirls that marked out courts, like a dance diagram. Or a crime scene.

'You're here to be judged.' Paula jumped for a second, before realising it wasn't addressed to her. The play had started. 'You haven't lived by God's rules. You've sinned.' The figure on the stage was revealed to be a girl, dressed in a white robe. She spoke clearly and confidently.

'But everyone else was doing it!' Another girl stood in the middle of the stage, also robed. From a distance, hooded, you could only tell them apart by their height. Her voice was more stilted, as if she'd memorised the lines whole.

'If you want to be loved by God, you have to give yourself up to Him. You have to renounce sin.' The first girl thundered the words. 'Do you give yourselves?'

'I give myself.'

'I give myself.'

'I give myself.'

They came forward — seven more girls, bringing the total on stage to nine. The one who had sinned knelt down in front of them and in a circle they surrounded her. Cathy, who would have been the tenth, had been buried under a granite stone in the local graveyard. Paula kept back in the shadows, feeling prickles along her neck. What was she seeing? Amateur dramatics, or something worse?

'We give ourselves.' They spoke perfectly in unison, though there was no teacher leading the chorus. The girls moved in and out in patterns. Each one knelt down in a line, and put back their hoods. The sinner was isolated, alone with her head bowed.

She saw the moment when they saw her. The invisible chain that linked their rise and fall, which almost seemed to glisten in the air, suddenly ruptured. They looked up, frightened to see an observer, and murmurs broke out.

She was standing by the door, and she hit the panel of lights by her head, watching them blink. 'Sorry, girls. I'm afraid I need to talk to you all again.'

★ ★ ★

They sat in a circle. They had all kept on their robes and their pale stage makeup, which made Paula feel a bit freaked out. She wished she had opened the curtains to let in the light, as dark shadows still pooled in every corner. 'So, the play's nearly ready?'

The girl who seemed to be the ringleader said primly, 'We're doing the dress rehearsal soon, miss.'

'And it's for the big prayer concert — that's on Hallowe'en?'

They kept their hands folded, heads down.

'Well, it looked very good from where I was.'

Some glances were exchanged. 'It's not ready yet,' said another girl. Paula recognised her behind the makeup. 'Anne-Marie, is it?' Cathy's best friend. The girl hesitated a moment before nodding.

Paula decided it was time to play hard-ball. 'Girls. This isn't a proper interview today — I'm just here to talk to you. To explain a bit about what's going on. I know Cathy was meant to be in the play, is that right? What part was she going to have?'

The main girl lifted her chin. 'It was a different bit. We took it out.'

'And what was the topic?' No answer. 'I can find out, you know.' Paula focused on Anne-Marie. 'What was it?'

The girl seemed to squirm. 'It was only a short bit. Sort of about peer pressure and bullying and that.'

'And who was Cathy in it?' No answer. 'Girls. You need to tell me.'

The first girl spoke. 'She was the one who was bullied.'

A heavy silence had settled on the group, and Paula felt her chances of getting them to talk were slipping away. 'Listen. Cathy is dead, you know that. We need to find who did it, so they don't hurt anyone else. You understand this? Now I need you to tell me if Cathy was in any kind of trouble. I know she had a boyfriend. Do you know who it was?' Her eyes raked round the group, short girls, tall girls, spotty girls. None as pretty as Cathy had been.

'If she did, we didn't know,' said the first girl again. She had bobbed fair hair held back in a clip, cat-like blue eyes. Paula remembered her name now — Siobhan. That was it. 'I don't think any of us knew, miss.'

'Maybe she'd a secret boyfriend,' ventured Anne-Marie. Siobhan looked at her and she dropped her head.

Paula groped in the depths of her brain for some inspiration. 'Look — I know you don't want to get in trouble. I remember what that's like. But your friend is dead. Somebody killed her. She'll never get to go to her formal, or get married, or have a baby, or — ' She broke off. One of the girls had started to cry, and then another two were scrubbing at their eyes.

Then Anne-Marie was sobbing into her robe, tracks appearing in her white makeup. The girls next to her soothed her, rubbing her shoulders, as girls always seem to know how to do. 'She's upset, miss,' said one reprovingly. 'Her and Cathy were best friends from when they were little.'

Paula tried one last time. 'Girls, tell me about the Mission. Please. Tell me about Ed Lazarus.'

The briefest ripple of a look went round the group, so fast she almost missed it. 'What is it?'

Siobhan once again spoke. 'He's nice, miss. He listens to us. Everyone there is nice.'

A small dark girl piped up, 'They really listen to you, miss. Everything that makes you sad — '

Suddenly they were all speaking at once.

'If you feel fat, or ugly . . . '

'If your teacher's mean to you or your mammy shouts . . . '

'They were so nice to me when my granny died, and I was sad all the time . . . '

'They even talk about boys, so we don't feel so

306

bad and we don't have to do things to make them like us . . . '

'Respect, yeah, they teach us respect . . . '

'Self-esteem . . . '

'All right.' She held up her hands to stop the chorus of voices. 'All right, so you like it at the Mission. But listen, girls: if any of you want to talk — if Ed ever did anything that made you uncomfortable, or if you want to tell me something as a secret . . . you can talk to me. Ring me — reverse the charges if you need to.' She passed out some cards and the girls took them dutifully, giving nothing away with their eyes.

'What if we don't need to talk to you, miss?' The main girl lifted up her cool face to Paula.

'Well then — it's Siobhan, isn't it?'

The girl waited a moment. 'Yes.'

'Well, Siobhan, if you don't, so much the better. But the offer's there.'

'Can we get back to our play now?'

'Yes. Go on.' She sighed at how quickly they got up. 'Hang on a minute there, Siobhan.'

The girl hovered. For fifteen she was graceful, poised. 'Yes, miss?'

'You wouldn't be the Siobhan who has the sleepovers, would you?'

She frowned. 'So do lots of people.'

'You know Katie Brooking?'

'Katie's in my class, yeah.' Her eyes were narrow.

'And she goes to your sleepovers?'

She sniffed. 'Mammy invited her one time. She felt sorry for her 'cos her brother's dead.'

307

'I see. Just one time?'

'Yeah.' The girl's tone was high, defensive. 'We're not *friends*.'

'Well, off you go. Thanks, Siobhan.'

* * *

As Paula left the school, it was four o'clock, shadows gathering around the street lamps. She'd parked her car outside the school gates, and as she walked down the now-deserted street, winter-dark, she was fumbling in her bag for the keys.

In retrospect, PJ would have killed her for ignoring all his rules. Her mind was full of the girls, and how on earth she was going to nail Lazarus if none of them would talk. She wasn't paying attention to her surroundings. She didn't have her keys out and ready to use. She hadn't parked the Volvo under the light — rather it was in a patch of darkness by a damp hedge. That was why she didn't see the figure until it sprang out and was suddenly between her and the car.

'Jesus Christ!' She jumped.

'You take the Lord's name in vain a lot, don't you?'

'What are you doing here?'

'Oh, they let me go. And they really should be more careful down at that station about what they say in front of prisoners. It wasn't too hard to overhear that 'Paula's gone to the school'.'

Breathe, breathe. She tried to slow her heartbeat. 'You aren't a prisoner, are you, seeing as you're here.'

'I'm a suspect though — thanks to you. I could lose my job for this.' Ed Lazarus was so close she could see the dark centre of his eyes. 'My job means everything to me.'

'You must have known it would catch up with you sometime, Ed. You slept with minors. It's a crime.'

He made a sort of impatient gesture, clutching at his head. 'This country and its bureaucracy. Is there no such thing as a second chance any more? Jesus welcomed sinners; He forgave them.'

She made herself speak confidently, while wondering if she could feint round him and get inside the car before he grabbed her. 'That's true, but He also said 'Go, and sin no more'.' Finally a use for all those Scripture classes — arguing with sociopaths. *Thanks, Sister Carmel.* 'Why'd you come back here, Ed? Did you want to find your mother's family? You know, they've no idea what happened to her. All these years, waiting. You should tell them who you are.'

His eyes flashed. 'Everyone wants to know where they come from. I wanted to see it. That's all.'

'And your father?'

His voice had grown higher, almost child-like. 'This is the last place he was. Do you understand that? I know he's somewhere, but this is the last place he was when she knew him. She still loved him. All those years — she'd never go back to her family, never even contact them. He wanted her to give me up, and she wouldn't, but she wouldn't cause him any trouble either. So she just left. She gave all that up for him.'

'That night — she hadn't planned to go?'

'No. She told me — she said he was angry when she told him about me. She was frightened, so she ran away. Left everything, except me. See, she loved him.'

'But Ed — you know he didn't love her back. He was hurting her. Same as you're doing with these girls.'

He laughed, catching at his head again. 'They come to me, do you know that?'

She was perhaps a metre from the car door. 'The girls?'

'Yes. I give them self-esteem, I help them. I make them feel good. You find it hard to believe they'd come to me of their own accord?'

'No, I can believe that. You're a handsome man. And I do remember what it's like to be a teenager.' She could hear the steel in her own voice. 'But these girls, they don't know what they're really offering. It's up to the adult to turn them away, to help them.'

'Of course they know. They know *exactly* what they want.'

Paula tried not to shudder. How many times had she heard those words from abusers, however young or vulnerable their victims? *They wanted it.* Grasping the cold metal of keys in her hand, she pulled them out and made her voice steady. 'I said you were a handsome man, Ed. It's true, but I don't think you've got much else going for you. So you better step away before I use these to scratch your face up.'

He laughed. 'You're so tough, Paula, so good

310

at rooting out everyone else's sins. What about your own?'

'I have sins, of course — we all do. But I haven't changed my name so I can get off scott free and abuse young girls.'

For a moment she was afraid he would lash out, but he moved back, giving her arm a brief spiteful push as he went, like a child might do. 'This isn't over, you know. You've cost me too much.'

'I know it's not over. In fact, I promise you it isn't.'

As soon as he'd stepped back into the shadows she was scrabbling the key into the lock. Missing it. Finding it, fumbling the door open, and inside with her heart racing. *Jesus.* She heard the doors lock behind her and let all her breath out in a rush. As she drove off, she could see his green eyes gleaming in the darkness.

★ ★ ★

When Paula parked outside her dad's house and saw every light was blazing, a cold pocket settled in her stomach. Opening the front door, she saw Pat sitting on the sofa in the front room. PJ was opposite, patting the edge of the chair as if he didn't know how to comfort the woman beside him. For a moment Paula had the mad idea they knew Ed Lazarus had followed her.

'Dad, what is it, is something wrong?'

PJ gave a brief shake of the head. 'It's all right, pet. Pat's had a wee shock.'

'What's happened?'

Pat wailed. 'Oh Paula, my heart's scalded. It's Aidan. We just got word that fella's getting out of jail. Sean Conlon — you know who he is.'

'I know.' No one had ever been convicted of killing John O'Hara, but everyone in Ballyterrin knew who they suspected. Of the three men who'd most likely shot Aidan's father, one had skipped the country and was believed to be hiding out in South America. One had been convicted of other crimes, got out after just five years under the Good Friday Agreement, and was promptly shot by a Loyalist gang on his way to the dole office. And the third, that was Sean Conlon, who had now served ten years in jail for his part in a post-Agreement shooting that killed two soldiers. 'What happened?'

'Aidan was over for his tea. I made shepherd's pie, his favourite. But then the phone went and it was the police liaison saying that fella Conlon'll be free by next year. Good behaviour.' Pat gave a small sob, mashing a tissue between her hands. 'I've made my peace with it, love, but Aidan . . . he was never right. Him being there when it happened, I suppose.'

Paula cut in. 'Pat. Where is he?'

'He just took off, down the pub no doubt. Oh, love, he's been doing so much better! He was really off the booze and the paper was going so well, and . . . and . . . ' Pat gave way to noisy tears.

Paula met her father's eyes over Pat's head. 'I'll go.' She had barely got in and it was so cold and dark out. 'Never mind, Pat, I'll find him. Don't you worry.'

She waited for them to stop her, but her father just nodded slowly. 'Aye, he always listened to you, pet.'

He did? She was shrugging her coat back on, and as she went out again, PJ had finally managed to touch Pat's hand, and she heard him say something about a nice cup of tea.

27

It was funny how you could know someone, Paula thought, as she restarted the car. Know them in the sense that you'd no idea had they a girlfriend, or what went on in their mind on any given day, but still after twelve years be sure where they'd go when their whole world had been reduced to the bottom of a glass.

True enough, Aidan was slumped over the bar in Flanagan's, the seedy old-man pub where he'd first started drinking at fifteen. His black shirt was rolled up at the arms, eyes half-closed as he nursed an empty bottle of beer.

'Well, Aidan, what's all this?' She was counting the glasses in front of him. He'd had, what, five whiskeys? Not beyond hope, then. 'No more for him,' she said to the barman, who was watching hurling on the TV with a *not-my-problem* air.

Aidan stirred. 'Give us another, Trevor.'

'You better bloody not.'

Trevor, the antiquated owner of the pub, gave Paula a bloodshot look. 'I remember you. It's the wee Maguire girl, is it?'

'I'm not a wee girl now. I could have you shut down.'

He gave a dry chuckle. 'Never bothered you when you were in here at seventeen, drinking lemonade Hooch and all that shite.'

Paula tried not to react to that. 'Please, Trevor. He's in a bad way. He's had a shock. Give me a hand with him, will you.'

Aidan was much bigger than Paula, and not inclined to leave, so even with her and the old barman, it was a struggle to get him out to the car.

'Hey, what's this! Lemme go, Maguire. I wanna nother drink.'

'Well, you can't have one. Come on.' As Aidan sagged briefly, she took advantage of the moment to stow his legs into the footwell of the car, and slam the door. His dark head slumped against the glass. Turning to Trevor, who'd seen it all before, she said, 'If you see him in that state again, would you ever think about not serving him, maybe?'

'It's a free country, love.'

She shot him a look. As a teenager she'd appreciated Trevor's blind eye when it came to dodgily-forged IDs, but as an adult she wished he had more respect for the law.

Aidan sat up with a start when she turned the ignition key. 'Here! Here! What's this, I wanna drink!'

'No chance. I'm taking you home.' She realised she had no idea where his flat was. 'Will I take you to Pat?'

'No, no. Don't wanna see . . . Mammy.' It was a good drunken point. Pat shouldn't have to see her only child like this. She'd been through enough that night.

'Where will we go, then?'

'The paper — haveta do the paper.'

'What?'

'Deadline. S'deadline day . . . '

315

'You mean you've not sent it off yet?' She remembered that Friday had always been the deadline for the main text of the *Gazette*. 'For God's sake, Aidan, you're pissed. You can't do the paper in this state.'

'Da — he never missed an issue in his life, no, he never. You know why he was even there that night they got him? Why *I* was there? Didya ever wonder where me mammy was?'

She was trying to settle him in the seat. 'Put your belt on there. Where Pat was, you mean? I never thought.' But it was a good question. Why had Aidan even been there with his father, so late at night?

'She was in the fucking hospital, losing another wean. All miscarriages, 'cept me. And he was here all the same. Haveta do the paper.'

'It's just a paper,' she said, as gently as she could. 'People can wait another day to find out who won the bloody Classic Car competition.' But on the other hand, it was as good a place as any to take him. She suspected he often slept there anyway. 'Come on, I'll do what I can to help.'

★ ★ ★

The *Gazette* offices gave every sign of being recently abandoned. Aidan's chair was pushed back, his jacket thrown over it, a cigarette crumbling in an ashtray. The computer was on and a cursor blinked on the screen.

'Hmm. You really must be at deadline.'

Aidan seemed to have sobered up considerably

316

during the car ride, during which she'd kept the windows open in case he boked on the interior of her father's car (not for the first time, she'd admit). Had she read somewhere that this was a sign of an alcoholic, that booze barely touched the sides?

Aidan sat down in the chair. 'Was gonna finish up after me tea at Mammy's, but then — '

Paula perched on the desk beside him. 'Listen. I'm sorry about what happened. I know it's — well. I know it's not easy.'

His shoulders were rigid, hands shaking. 'It's just the idea . . . you know, I could be out doing my messages, having a wee jar, and that fella could just come walking in, right as rain, living his life, and my da dead these twenty years and more. How's that fair?'

'It's not.' He wasn't the only one in Northern Ireland who had to share the streets with the person who'd smashed their life to pieces. This was what they sometimes called *the price of peace.*

Aidan squinted at the screen. 'And now I'm letting him down here. Can't even get the bloody paper off to print.'

'No, you're not.' She got down, pushing his chair firmly up to the screen. 'I'm going to stand over you till you do it. Type.'

Aidan pulled the keyboard towards him and tapped out a few strokes. Then he put his head down on the desk and groaned. 'I can't, Maguire, I'm too pissed.' Without opening his eyes, his hand felt along for the half-smoked cigarette, and the other produced a lighter, which he snapped at ineffectively. 'Feck.'

Paula leaned over and plucked the fag from his mouth.

'Hey!'

'No smoking here, it's a workplace. Fecking *type*, will you.'

'Jesus, Maguire, you're not me mammy.'

'No. Your mammy would have her heart broken if she saw you in this state.'

He slumped. 'Can't. Need water . . . '

'Water we can do.' Paula filled a mug from the small sink in the corner, and stood over him while he drank it down. Then, shaking his head like a dog, he started to type, fingers rattling as he squinted at the screen out of one eye.

Paula resumed her seat on the neighbouring desk, moving aside a large manila envelope to make space. 'What's this?'

'S'for you,' he said, sucking on the unlit cigarette. 'Some of what you asked for on Carr and that.'

'Thanks.' She pulled it open and saw the mess of papers inside. 'Hey,' she said after a while of leafing through it. 'This isn't half-bad, what you've found out.'

He cocked his head at her without interrupting his tapping. 'Well, thanks Maguire. Always good to get the approval of a sophisticated ex-pat such as yourself.'

'Ah, here we go. You must be feeling better then, if you're getting the boot in.'

'I'll do.' He tapped on for a while, before stretching and leaning back. 'Think she's done, Maguire. Full to shite with typos, but sure most people round here can't spell.'

'And it's not like anyone reads it.'

'Ha ha.' He looked round at her. 'Will I send it then?'

'What are you on about? Of course, send it. I thought your deadline was nine.' She nodded at the clock, which now said ten to.

'It is. You don't want to see it first?'

'No, there's no time. Go on.'

'All right then.' With a flourish, he pressed the key. 'Gone. *Fait accompli*, Maguire.'

'Don't start speaking French, Aidan. Try mastering English first.'

'Ah, you're full of wit, Maguire.' He stood up and came over to where she sat on an adjoining desk, feet on someone's wheely chair. Suddenly she felt very exposed. She was wearing the same clothes she'd been in all day, black trousers under black knee boots, clingy grey wool jumper over a white shirt. She crossed her arms over her chest. 'What are you looking at?'

'Couldn't have done it without you.'

'Come off it, as if you've never written drunk before. Anyway, it's not the first time I've helped you home pissed.' It had seemed funny when they were teenagers, and drink was new and exciting. But now he was thirty-one, it just made her worry. He was standing in front of her, and he pushed the chair away from her feet and sat down in it, between her legs. She drew them up to her chest; this abrupt re-animation was making her anxious.

'Well, well. Maguire.' He was watching her closely, eyes no longer unfocused. His pupils

319

were very wide, several days of stubble on his face. She could smell the whiskey on his breath.

'What?'

'You know what.'

'I don't.' But she couldn't meet his dark, steady gaze. 'Come on, Aidan. Don't mess me about.'

'I'm not. I'm trying to say — how did I manage without you all these years?'

'Well, that's funny. As I remember, you were the one who dumped me.'

He shook his head sadly. 'Maguire. You know that wasn't the way of it. Come on. I might have made mistakes, but that was never what I wanted. You know that.'

She pushed him away, and got off the desk in a burst of energy, moving to the door. 'Look, I only came here to help Pat. You've her worried sick, that's all.'

'Paula.' He never called her this, and it made her freeze.

'What? What do you want from me?'

He got up and came over to her. They were an inch apart. He didn't touch her. 'Same thing I always wanted.'

'I'm not doing this. You're drunk.'

'I am that. Maybe that's why I can say these things.'

'What things?'

'That maybe I was an eejit back then. Christ, I was all of nineteen — of course I was an eejit, but it doesn't mean I didn't lo — '

'Don't!'

He put up a hand and touched her face; she

flinched. 'I mean, what was I meant to think, Maguire? One day you were here, listening to god-awful music with Saoirse, drinking Peach Schnapps, getting your da to put the frighteners on me . . . then the next thing, no one sees you all summer, PJ's putting me away from the door like a dog, and you won't talk to me, and then you're gone, and I don't see you for twelve years?'

'Stop it!'

'Jesus, I know Ballyterrin's not got much on London, but could you not have dropped us a line once in a while?'

She was shaking. 'That's not fair. You know that's not fair.'

'I don't know anything much, Maguire, and that's the God's honest truth. I never did.'

Paula was leaving. She snatched her bag up from the floor and was storming out, struggling to see the door through the film that suddenly veiled her eyes. 'Just fuck off, will you?'

'That's nice. I try to have an honest conversation for once, and you tell me to — ' He stopped. 'Ah, Jesus, Maguire, don't cry. I never could stand it when you cried.'

'I'm not crying,' she sobbed, and her whole body sagged. Aidan came closer, and then she was weeping into his black shirt. He smelled exactly the same — of mint, and booze, and something else she could never identify, but could have picked out of a darkened room. Paula cried solidly for a minute, everything suddenly crowding in on her — the dead girls, and Ed emerging from the shadows, and the memory of what had happened that summer, the one where she'd lost Aidan for good. She pulled away, wiping her face with her hands. 'I'm sorry. I'm sorry. I'm just stressed, I think.'

He was brushing back her damp hair, cupping her face. She still couldn't look at him. 'You don't have to be sorry, Maguire. It was me who fucked it all up.'

'You did. And you're drunk.'

'That's true. And because I'm drunk, that's why I can do this,' he said, and kissed her.

★ ★ ★

It was some time before Paula disengaged herself and sat up. Somehow they were under his desk, on the floor. She pulled together the open sides of her shirt. 'It's not very comfortable down here.'

'I never noticed.' Aidan's hand was stroking her waist, very softly.

'That's because you're plastered.' And she wasn't. So why did she feel as if she were, as if she might fall over or cry or vomit at any moment? The worst thing was, it had always been this way, and she had only just remembered. Like finding a box hidden at the back of the wardrobe. Back then, whenever they'd touched each other, they'd always been able to let go of the rest, his father and her mother and all of it. That was what had nearly killed her when she lost him. When suddenly there was no way to forget.

She ran her hands over his torso, pale, sinewy.

'What are we at, huh?'

'You want me to draw you a diagram?'

She looked down at her exposed bra, his shirt crumpled on the floor beside them. 'I mean, this is as far as we ever got. It'll be further, in a minute.'

The hand on her waist moved up an inch, grazing her bra strap. 'That sounds promising.'

She tried not to smile. 'For God's sake, do you ever think about consequences?'

'I'm a journalist. We live one day to the next.'

The hand was stroking her shoulder now, sliding under the strap of her bra, and she half-heartedly pushed it away. 'I think, maybe, we should talk about this.'

'What's to talk about?' He pulled her head down to his again, his mouth soft and warm, and for a moment she lost her thread.

'Stop it! I mean, we shouldn't be doing this.'

'Fuck's sake, Maguire, you need to learn some new lines. You're thirty now, not eighteen.'

'I know, but — '

He stopped kissing her neck to glare at her. 'This better not be to do with that fecking Brit cop.'

'Guy?'

'Yes, that's his name,' Aidan muttered. 'Bloody ex-Army, all muscles and stiff upper lip and . . . Are you and him some kind of item, is that it?'

'What? No! He's hardly even speaking to me.' She decided not to mention their brief 'indiscretion', as Guy had termed it. Best put it behind them as a bad mistake.

'Good. Because he doesn't know you like I do.'

'Oh, you know me, do you?'

'Well enough to know you like this . . . '

She gasped

'And this . . . '

'For God's sake.' Paula tugged on his hair and they were both gone again.

★ ★ ★

'What the fuck was that?'

Paula came awake slowly. What? Why was she under a desk? Then she remembered, and was flooded with shame. Aidan was sitting bolt upright beside her. Both of them entirely naked. Paula clutched her shirt to herself, burning red. 'What — '

'Sshhh!' He held out his hand. 'You hear that?'

'What?' All she could hear was her own heart, about to explode with embarrassment. Her mouth felt gritty and her back stiff from lying on the floor. What would Pat and PJ think, both of them out all night? She tried to focus on what Aidan was saying.

'Listen. You can't hear it?'

She could now. It sounded like the noise of a lock being broken off. Male voices.

Aidan was sitting very still. 'Sooner than I thought.'

'What's going on?'

He sighed. 'Maguire, you better get your kecks on. They'll be in any minute.'

She started pulling on her trousers. 'What do

you mean? Who is it?'

He got up, still bollock-naked, and looked out of the window, where it was still dark. 'Bailiffs, I'd say. Quick off the mark, these boys.'

'What are you on about?' She was doing up her shirt, the buttons all wrong. Her head was like a block of wood.

'You told me to send it. I said you could read it first, but you said send.'

'What?'

'The paper.' Seeing her blank face, he sighed. 'Look.' He pressed his mouse and the computer sprang into life. A printer began to whir at the back of the office.

From downstairs came a cracking noise. The voices got louder. Paula looked at what he'd printed off. 'This is — this is what you published this week?'

CATHY'S LAST WALK said the headline. Aidan had traced out Cathy's movements on the last day she'd been seen alive. *Why did she visit her father's office? Why did prominent businessman Carr lie to police?* 'Holy God, Aidan, please say this is a joke.'

'Wouldn't be a very funny one, would it.' Almost regretfully, he was putting his jeans back on.

'But — they'll crucify you! You said he practically owns you!'

'Like I said, they don't waste time. Carr gets an advance copy — he must have sent his heavies right round.'

'Fucking hell, Aidan, I can't believe you did this. You'll lose everything. And the investigation!

Christ, it could all collapse now.' She thought of what Gerard had said, about the guilty walking free. About the girls at the school, too scared to say anything. About the cold white flesh that was buried in the earth. 'Oh my God. I'll get fired. Why in the hell did you do it?'

Topless, Aidan stood in the window. His back was turned to her. 'People need to know the truth. At least Da would have been proud. It's not like I'll get shot for what I write.'

'You might not get shot, but you'll get closed down!'

'Come on, Maguire. Get out while you can. I'm staying.' Just in his jeans, he sat back at the chair and swinging, placed a pencil between his teeth like a cigarette. 'Hide round the corner and you might miss them.'

'But you can't stay here! You don't know what they'll do.' Paula was stumbling to the door, shoving her underwear into her bag in a daze.

He shrugged. 'It doesn't matter.'

She cast one last look back at him, at the door. She could hear the men sweating up the stairs. 'Aidan! Why did you do it? I'm going to be in so much trouble!'

He turned. 'I'm sorry, Maguire. We'll talk. Just not now, OK?'

Paula lunged out the door and hid round the small turn of the corridor that led to the toilet. Peering out, she saw three large men barging through the doors. Two of them had lists on clipboards. The third had a large crowbar. As they elbowed open the door into the *Gazette* office, she heard Aidan say in a camp English accent, 'Ah, good fellows. I've been expecting you.'

Covering her ears as the sounds of smashing started, Paula crept down the stairs with her knickers in her bag and her head exploding in confusion.

28

There weren't many people around in Ballyterrin at six in the morning. Nevertheless, Paula felt deeply embarrassed as she walk-of-shamed it back to the car and drove off home through the murky gloom, brightening to a thin cold dawn. PJ was of course up as she went in. She used to wonder did he have some kind of sixth sense for being there when she most didn't want to get caught. Though she'd never really done anything she needed to hide at eighteen. Back when she still thought letting Aidan undo her bra was a mortal sin.

'Morning, Dad.'

PJ lowered the *Irish News* and fixed her with his beetle-black eyebrows. 'You were out late.'

'Well, I had to get him settled.' She started to take her coat off, then realised her shirt was done up wrong, and put it back on. She saw PJ notice this.

Her father cleared his throat. 'What's the story then?'

'Oh, he'll be all right. I got him before he was too far gone.'

'Mm.'

'How was Pat?' She switched on the kettle, grateful as the hiss filled up the meaningful silence from her father.

'She'll do. Been through worse.' PJ looked

pointedly at his watch. 'You can't have got much sleep, Paula.'

Don't blush don't blush. 'I got a bit. Didn't want to leave him alone.'

'That was very good of you. At least you've no work today.'

'I might go in anyway. I'll sleep an hour or so now.' Paula took her tea and escaped upstairs to her narrow box-room. But it was all too familiar, too strange — lying in that same bed, looking up at the same crack in the ceiling, thinking once again about Aidan's hands on her skin. Except this time, she hadn't made him stop. All in all, Paula's mind wouldn't stop whirring, and after an hour, when the Saturday traffic was already starting to rush in the distance and the birds were beginning to sing, she accepted defeat and got up to get ready for work.

★ ★ ★

The first thing she saw on entering, early, was Guy at his desk. A sudden stab of guilt took her breath away. What was that for? It was nothing to do with him if she slept with Aidan. He'd made it very clear he saw her as nothing more than a liability.

She contemplated sneaking past — Guy had his head in his hands again — but decided that would look suspicious. And she'd nothing to hide, had she? She knocked on the glass door of his office.

'Come in.'

'You're here early.'

He rubbed his hands over his face. 'Paper-work. Maddy Goldberg's been alibi-ed.'

'She has? Who by?' But Paula could guess.

'One of Cathy's teachers said Maddy met her at the school on Friday afternoon. They were going for coffee — they're friends, apparently. Cathy would have been getting out of Crawford's car then, and maybe into the mysterious silver one.'

'If it's who I think, they're a bit more than friends, Guy, I — '

He sounded exhausted. 'It's no crime though, whatever they are. And the Goldberg girl knows the law. We can't touch her until we get something more concrete.'

Paula digested this; another lead gone. 'So what do we . . . ' She saw what was on his desk. A copy of the *Ballyterrin Gazette*, fresh off the press. 'How did you get that? It's not out till Monday.'

'I was sent it.'

'Oh.'

'You'd better sit down,' said Guy.

'I didn't know about this,' she started. 'It was nothing to do with me.'

He frowned. 'I wasn't going to suggest it was. We can't muzzle the press, although it's not exactly good for the investigation. Have you seen it?'

'Er . . . not really.'

'I don't know how he got hold of this. Apparently a 'source' told him Cathy went to visit her father on the day she disappeared. O'Hara's looking at a serious libel suit.'

'That wouldn't stop him.'

'If it's true, it throws our whole timeline out. She didn't go straight home — she must have left school earlier, gone somewhere else before Crawford picked her up.'

'To see Lazarus?' It was bad, what Aidan had done, but at least this way Guy knew the truth.

'I don't know. O'Hara's basically printed everything you were saying — all three girls went to the Mission, the two that are dead, and Majella. Why are we letting it into our schools and so on. All the links with the other church that you dug up, the God's Shepherd lot. But that's not the really damaging thing.'

'No?'

'He's printed the names of the company directors who financed the Mission here in Ballyterrin.'

'And?' She had a feeling she already knew the answer to this.

Guys face was grim. 'Eamonn Carr is one of them. What's that going to look like? The local paper says the dead girl's father is linked with the group that might be behind her death? It's going to destroy any fair trial we might get.'

'Aidan's . . . ' Paula tried to explain. 'He knows all this. He doesn't even care. Did you know Eamonn Carr also basically owns the *Gazette* now? Aidan's got no money. The paper never made a penny for years.'

'But he still did this?'

'That's Aidan.'

'Hmm. I suppose you have to admire that kind of bloody-minded stupidity.'

That was a fair summation, she thought. Then she had a flash of remembering the night before, under the desk, and her stomach was knifed by desire and embarrassment. 'So what happens now?'

'I don't know.' He sat the paper aside. 'That isn't the real problem for us.'

'No?'

'No. This is.' He pulled towards him a large packet of documents. 'I received this last night from Eamonn Carr's legal team.'

Paula stomach sank again, but not with desire this time.

'It's about you, I'm afraid. How you've — let me read it — harassed his children at home, targeted a friend of his who runs a beauty salon, carried out your own side-investigations . . . It goes on. He also says you can't possibly be impartial in a case like this one.'

'I see.'

'Don't you want to know why he says that?'

'I can guess.'

Guy looked at her. 'Paula. I checked through the files.'

'Good for you.' She folded her arms.

'You gave a police statement in 1993.'

'Yes, I suppose I did.'

'You didn't think you needed to tell me? About any of it?'

'What, that I spoke to the police seventeen years ago? Or that my mother's been missing since then?' She shrugged. 'What was I meant to say? 'Yeah, she's gone, we don't know where she is, she may be dead'? I don't have any updates. If

I did, I'd be sure to tell you.'

'I'm sorry. It's just I needed to know this, really.'

'Everyone else knows.' But then he wasn't from around here.

'I think there's a lot everyone knows that I don't.' He paused. 'Will you tell me what happened — just the facts? If you can.'

Oh God, she was so sick of it. She'd promised herself she would never talk about this again. She ticked it off on her fingers, the old old story. The only one she had to tell. 'What do you want to know, Guy? It was 1993, as you've discovered.'

'How old were you?'

'Just thirteen. I came home from school, and unlike every day of my life up to then, my mother wasn't there making me a cup of tea. So I waited. I didn't think to ring the police, because I was thirteen. I had no idea she'd any kind of life except, you know, waiting for me and making me a cup of tea when I came in.'

'Go on.' His voice was low.

'Well, I waited for two hours and she never came back. You know how when you're young, you just sort of think it'll be all right? Like there's no way your parents could ever let you down, so you don't even consider it? I thought if I sat there, she'd come in and we'd have a biscuit and — ' She shook her head. 'Then Dad came in from work and said, 'Where's your ma?' and I said I didn't know, she wasn't here, and I saw his face. That's when I knew — she wasn't going to come walking in. So he called the police — well, he *was* the police — and they came, and that's when I gave the interview. That what you want to know?'

He was looking at her. 'And?'

'And nothing. They never found her, not a trace. When I came in, the door had been left open — which I should have realised was weird. It was open and sort of swinging in the breeze, so they thought someone must have taken her. The IRA, maybe. There was some talk that Mum . . . well, that she had something to do with the Army, helping them in some way. Informing, like. There used to be a barracks outside town. It was a load of rubbish, anyway. Or because of Dad being a Catholic RUC officer, it made her a legitimate target. You know.'

'The IRA? Was she one of those Disappeared, did they think?'

'Most of the Disappeared were taken in the seventies and eighties, and Mum was much later than that. But it had some of the hallmarks of it, yes. And if you remember, things were getting pretty bad again in the early nineties. Someone dead every day. Same year as the Warrington bomb attack.'

'The file said you saw a man near the house?'

'The day before, I came home from school and Mum was at the back door, talking to someone. I saw him walking past the kitchen window on his way out. A man in a sort of hat. I thought it was the milkman, but I should have realised he came in the mornings. That's really all I know. That's the story.'

'So all this time, all these years, you've found out nothing?'

'They found bodies a few times. We went. It wasn't her.' Running down the hospital corridor, time slow and sticky as if her feet were in treacle. Her dad, face in his hands. *It's not her, Paula. It's not her.* 'Can I go now?'

'Paula — '

'What? I've told you all I know.' She was shaking. 'I'm sorry. I'm sorry, Guy — sir. I don't mean to be rude. I just don't talk about it. I mean, what's the point?'

Guy was still staring. 'I can't believe they just stopped looking.'

'Well, they had more things on their mind than some Ballyterrin housewife slipping out and not coming back. They kept interviewing Dad. Over and over. I don't think they looked at anyone else, once they got it in their heads he'd something to do with it. Dug up our back garden looking for bones, all Mum's roses . . . that was a bad day. And they used to make me look at the bodies, in case he lied. But it was never her.'

'Christ. I'm so sorry.'

'So? That's what happened. It's not like I can change it. Do you want me off the case?'

He said nothing for a long time. Then 'I've been very hard on you.' She looked away in exasperation. 'It's just, after what happened . . . '

'The 'indiscretion', as you called it?'

He flushed. 'That makes it sound dreadful. I should tell you — I was afraid, I suppose, that everyone would see the effect you'd had on me.' He was speaking very quietly. She couldn't look at him. 'You know what I mean, Paula?'

'I don't want to talk about it,' she muttered.

'I can't say any more. But please believe me — if I've been too harsh, it was just because I couldn't treat you like I wanted to. You've been right all along, it seems. Even if your methods are a bit . . . off the wall.'

'But?'

'But, if you're right, and it's all to do with the Mission, or even the Carr family — although I wonder now what the difference is . . . ' It was exactly what Aidan had said. How annoying. 'If that's right, I can't jeopardise the investigation.'

'You want me off it.'

'If you could just stay in the background — maybe go through those older cases again. Take a bit of time away?'

Paula gave a brief frustrated scream. 'Christ!' He looked alarmed. 'Oh, I'm fine, don't worry. All this time I've been saying, Look at the Mission, look at Eamonn Carr, and all I hear is, Don't upset people, Paula. He's a pillar of the community, Paula. The suicides aren't connected, Paula.'

'We don't know for sure that they are.'

She gave him a look. 'See? And now you're saying I was right, but I can't work on it any more?'

Guy spoke coolly. 'If you'd stayed within the rules, Eamonn wouldn't have grounds to say any of this. You may notice I'm turning a blind eye to the allegations that you visited witnesses off your own bat. This beauty salon thing, for example.'

He had her there.

'Please, Paula. I certainly don't want to lose your expertise. If you could just — '

'Behave myself.'

'Yes.' He looked embarrassed. 'And if you could also forgive me for how I've been with you. There is a reason for it. And maybe after this, you and I can . . . '

She gave another smothered scream. 'Sorry. It's just — your timing couldn't be any worse if you tried.' She stood up. 'I'm going to go before I chew my own arm off. What do you want me doing then, if anything?'

He looked sheepish. 'Why don't you go home for the rest of the day? Then maybe some of the older cases, you could look into them further.'

Where she couldn't offend anyone, he meant. Because they were all most likely dead. 'Will you reopen them, then? The other ones I found, where they'd mentioned a church group?'

'If you can get together a dossier, I'll pass it on to the Gardaí.'

It felt like a sop. 'Fine. I'll just get my things.'

Paula went to her desk and defiantly swept the entire contents into a large bin bag she found in the kitchen. They couldn't stop her taking her notes, anyway. On her way out, the bulging bag in her arms, she encountered resistance.

'Jesus!'

'Sorry.' She lowered the bag to see Gerard Monaghan's chest level with her nose. 'It's you. Great.'

'What's up with you?' He frowned at her. 'Are you not going the wrong way?'

'Apparently not. Ask him.' She jerked her head at Guy's office, where the occupant was staring fixedly at his computer screen.

'Eh?'

'I'm being 'moved to lighter duties', or whatever the bullshit jargon is.' She didn't even care about swearing any more. 'That's what you wanted, wasn't it? They think I'm a liability too.'

His brow creased. 'That's daft. You've been right the whole time.'

'Well.' She hoped Gerard Monaghan wasn't going to start being nice. Then she really would scream. Or even worse, cry. 'Much use it was to me.'

'Listen,' he hissed out of the side of his mouth. 'This is shite. I'll keep you posted, OK? Keep your phone on.'

'All right.' Her lip was quivering. 'Do me a favour, will you? Say something mean? Just for a minute.'

'Eh?' Total confusion now. 'You're mad, you are.'

'That'll do. Bye, Gerard.'

The traffic was minimal at that hour. A few minutes later she was knocking on her father's door, no hands free to find her key. When PJ hobbled out on his crutches and saw her there with her arms full of bin bag, he raised his eyebrows. 'Back already?'

Paula burst into tears.

'Lord save us,' PJ muttered. 'You better come in and get a drop of tea.'

29

For the rest of the day Paula decided to join her father in Retiredsville. She observed PJ's habits carefully. He rose at six — far too early. She heard his radio going from the early hours, still obsessed with keeping up with the news. This, she knew, was a habit born from years of late-night awakenings and blood-red dawns, coughing and stamping feet in the cold, as yet another body was found. After so long in the RUC, every day that he woke up and someone wasn't dead was a victory for PJ. Every political gaffe story and cat-up-tree novelty item was proof they now lived in a sane society, where murder wasn't a way of life. So PJ arose with the dawn, or before it in winter, and drank his first cup of tea of many with an ear out for death and destruction, as Ballyterrin's dark rooftops took shape in the cold morning light. Since falling from the ladder, he'd taken to making the tea the night before, and supping it from an old Thermos top.

Then he would spend an hour in bed, reviewing matters. What matters these were, Paula had to employ some light snooping to find out. Her father had carried notebooks ever since she could remember — the policeman's tool. She remembered fumbling downstairs as a child, in search of water, and finding him still awake with the TV down low, his feet in white sports

339

socks propped up on the 'pouf', as he stared fixedly at the ruled pages of these small black books. On peeking into his room, Paula had seen hundreds of them in a neat stack by the bed. Was he reviewing all his old work, the forgotten cases?

She didn't like to go any further in. The room was exactly as her mother had left it. Chipboard wardrobe with the flecked mirror reflecting Paula's face in the doorway, patterned seventies carpet underfoot, net curtains on the windows. Margaret Maguire had often moaned about the house's décor, and Paula wondered now would the two-up two-down have been transformed had her mother not vanished that day. Cream carpet, underfloor heating. Yet another question that would never be answered. Another gap.

After his morning review, PJ would get up with much clattering and coughing; usually at this time Paula was still burying her head under her pillow and trying to sleep. He would stump into the small lime-tiled bathroom, lodging his crutch in the bidet while he somehow washed and shaved, his bad leg jutting out like a broken branch. Then he'd shuffle into the bedroom and dress in his tracksuit bottoms and walking fleece, before attempting a manoeuvre close to scaling the north face of Everest in order to get downstairs, where he would hobble between the kitchen and TV all day.

What did he do? She watched him on her first day of enforced leave. Gardening leave, it was sometimes called. Given that the barren patch outside their back door had been dug up by the police in 1993 and left to die, Margaret

340

Maguire's roses shrivelled and black, actual gardening wasn't on the cards. So Paula spread the contents of her purloined bin bag all over the kitchen table. PJ, who had the kettle on and was making toast, lifted an eyebrow.

'I stole the case-notes, Daddy.'

'So I see.' He carried on rinsing out the teapot, his crutch rammed under one elbow.

She looked over the notes. Aidan's print-outs, his scrawly writing all over them. Pictures of Cathy, of Louise. Transcripts of interviews with Majella Ward, Ed Lazarus, and Maddy Goldberg. Her own notes on conversations with the Carr children and parents, Majella Ward's family, and Cathy Carr's so-called friends. The autopsy report on Cathy, and the inquest into Louise's death, ferreted out by Saoirse. Aidan's articles on the unit, and the most recent exposé of Eamonn Carr's links to the Mission. Maeve Cooley's blog. A lot of paper had come from the past few weeks. Felt like a lifetime.

PJ cleared his throat again, hands following the familiar ritual. Warm pot, discard. Two tea bags. Fill pot. Set on hob at mark two. Assemble cups, milk always in first, because that was how Margaret Maguire had insisted.

'Dad?'

'Aye?'

'Will you help me?'

PJ gave her a wry look as he waited the requisite three minutes for the tea to stew. 'Thought you'd never ask.'

★ ★ ★

'This is an awful tangle, pet.'

'I know.'

'You'd want to be organising your case-notes better.'

'I know.'

'Tidy desk, tidy mind — '

'*Dad*! Can you see anything?'

He'd been reading over her papers for the best part of an hour, while she paced the small brown kitchen, gulping down tar-strength tea. 'So this neighbour, this Crawford fella — I know the one, works in the bank — he says he ran her up the road, but she wanted out at the bottom of their street?'

'Yes. I know he sounds guilty as sin, but it checked out; some busybody saw Cathy get out like he said, and besides, he's an alibi.' She didn't feel up to discussing gay escorts with her father just then.

PJ's brow was furrowed. 'Where could she have got to, from one end of the street to the other?'

'Exactly. There was some suggestion that she got in another car, but we couldn't find anything. No one saw, apparently.'

'Well, Paula. It seems to me the main question is: did the poor wee lassie get to her house or not?'

Paula was staring at him.

'Well?' he said. 'Is that not it?'

She spoke slowly. 'I asked her little sisters. They said . . . ' What had they said? She hadn't really taken in her conversation with Niamh and Ciara. They were so small she couldn't imagine

342

they had anything to add, and their sense of time wasn't concrete enough to know what 'last Friday' meant. 'The second wee one. She said something like, 'Mammy shouted at Cathy in the kitchen. Then she told us to wait in the family room.''

'Family room.' PJ snorted at this Americanism but Paula talked over him.

'Cathy had no shoes on when they found her. They take their shoes off before they go inside, the Carr kids. And that house had been painted recently — I remember noticing the smell, when . . . and that knife they found, the one that caused the riot, it had cat's blood on it.'

PJ coughed. 'Had the Carrs a cat?'

'They did when we first visited,' she said slowly. 'But when I went back, the cat was missing.' The poster Ciara had been making. LOST CATT.

PJ coughed again, moving his bad leg to get the blood flowing. 'There you go. There's life in your old dad yet, pet.'

★ ★ ★

Sitting in the house all night was excruciating, like being back at school again, during that terrible blank winter after Margaret Maguire had gone, and Paula and her father had sat rigidly night after night, in front of TV shows they couldn't take in, *ER* and *X-files* and *Frasier*, as if afraid that the moment they decided to go out would be the day she'd come back. *Hello, I'm here, did you not miss me?*

343

After several days of this, sitting at home, sifting through the papers with increasing desperation, one night there was a ring at the bell. Paula and her dad looked at each other, confused. No one ever called round to the Maguires' door. PJ was starting to creak up, so Paula said, 'Sit down, Daddy. I'll get it.'

On the doorstep, huddling against the rain in a red ski jacket, was Saoirse. For a moment Paula just looked at her in astonishment.

Saoirse jiggled her arms around herself. 'Well, are you not going to ask me in? I'm fecking freezing.'

In the kitchen, Paula continued to watch her friend in silence as PJ offered tea, chatted happily. 'It's great to see you, love. The doctoring's all going well?'

'Not too bad. I wouldn't mind getting out of the shift work if I could. You know yourself, Mr Maguire, it's not great when you've a family.'

'You're right there, pet. And how is the fella himself — Dave, is it?'

'Oh, he's grand.'

Paula stood up. 'Dad, would you give us a minute, please?'

After PJ had stumped out, a curious look on his face, Paula went to the hob and wordlessly poured Saoirse's tea from the pot. 'It's weird — you coming to the door. It's almost like no time's gone by.'

Saoirse was sitting at the table, small hands red, still in her coat. She sniffed with cold. 'I thought that the other night, too, you and Aidan being there.'

'It's not like that.' Time *had* gone by, and there was no turning back the clock.

'He's never had a girlfriend — least not that I know,' Saoirse said. 'That girl in Dublin — it was a one-time thing.' Paula's hand tightened on the teapot. 'I think he was just in a bad way at the time. I don't think he meant to do it.'

Paula said nothing, stirring her tea very slowly, and after a moment Saoirse changed the subject. 'That's not why I came, anyway. I found you something.'

'Oh yeah?'

Saoirse put down her mug and felt in the pocket of her over-large jacket. It was so big Paula wondered if it was in fact Dave's. That made her obscurely sad, for some reason, thinking what it would be like to be wrapped all around in someone else's love.

'I managed to dig this up,' Saoirse said. 'Don't tell anyone. Like I said, I know the family's GP, and the mother's been in a bad way. She had this hidden away the whole time, hoping they'd not rule it suicide, so maybe the poor kid wouldn't go to Hell or whatever she believes. Tragic really.'

Saoirse slid a sheet of photocopied paper across the table. It had clearly been duplicated from something held in a poly-pocket — Paula could see the ghostly holes of the perforations. A scrap of paper had been held inside it, lined, as if torn from a notebook. On it was some writing in a curly, childish hand. She squinted at it. *Tell Ed I love him. I'm sorry. I just love him so much.* The last underlined three times, until the pen had torn the paper.

345

She looked up at her friend, glasses steamed up and drops of rain in her dark hair. 'Is this . . . ?'

'Yeah. Louise McCourt's suicide note.'

★ ★ ★

So she had it now, the proof that Louise had been one of Ed's victims, that she had stepped up onto that car hood herself and ended her own life. But there was nothing to say he had killed Cathy. Everyone seemed to have an alibi, as if the girl had walked down her own street and simply vanished, yards from safety.

After Saoirse's visit, Paula was no further on than she'd been, still tormented by the idea that everything she knew wasn't enough. Then, on the local news that night, among the ribbon-cuttings and political scandals, there it was. Paula was half-asleep on the sofa, her phone never far from her elbow. She jiggled and poked at the keys in a way that made her ashamed of herself. Sitting around waiting to see if a man would get in touch. Christ, she wasn't eighteen. So why did everything feel disturbingly familiar? She was beyond furious to once again be waiting for Aidan to ring. He'd said they would talk, hadn't he? So why hadn't he called?

' . . . and in Ballyterrin, a local businessman has hit out against allegations in the local paper . . . '

'Turn it up!' She bolted forward, the TV being too old for a remote, and pressed the button for sound, sinking to her knees in front of the screen, and ignoring PJ's look of surprise.

On the screen were both of them. To see them together made her breathless for a second, with all she knew, all she suspected.

Eamonn Carr was being interviewed outside the Mission building, its pebble-dashed walls in the background. Beside him stood Ed Lazarus, smug in a spotless white smock. Eamonn looked awful — grey and worn, as if he hadn't slept in weeks. He was speaking. 'I'd like to say that the Mission has the full backing of myself and my family. Our daughter Cathy got a tremendous amount from the time she spent there. We totally refute the allegations made in the local press that they had anything to do with her loss. Indeed, we find it quite worrying that the police would focus on an organisation that's doing such good for our town. Someone out there killed our daughter, and we urge the police to continue looking for him, instead of wasting their time harassing the young people here. Thank you.'

The voiceover continued, '*The local paper has since been shut down due to a dispute over finance.*'

There he was, bloody Aidan O'Hara, at the press conference where he'd made such a fuss. Look at him, the bastard, pencil behind his ear, shirt untucked, face unshaven. Why hadn't he rung her?

'*The Ballyterrin Gazette is operated by Aidan O'Hara, son of former Editor John O'Hara, who was shot dead by paramilitaries at the paper's office in 1986.*' There were the library pictures that cropped up from time to time, the grainy eighties footage of blown-out glass, a security tape across the door of the building, an ambulance outside. A scene repeated a thousand times across Northern Ireland.

'*Locals have been vocal in opposition to the closure, and are now raising a collection to keep the paper going for its next issue.*'

The shots were of Ballyterrin now, a bucket being shaken at a street corner — the sign reading *Save the Gazette*. The pert local reporter was asking one man in a beige anorak why he had just thrown in a pound. 'Well, it's important now, isn't it.'

'Do you read the *Gazette*, sir?' The reporter moved the large microphone from her mouth to his.

'Oh aye, never miss it. For the death notices, you know. And there does be good articles from time to time.' Paula nearly laughed at that.

'*And that's the news, now the weather with Kirsty . . .* '

She looked up. PJ was getting painfully to his feet. 'Dad?'

'I've to ring Pat. Not right, her seeing that on her own, is it, John's blood on the steps.'

Paula was ashamed she hadn't thought of that. 'No. You're right.' Because Aidan wouldn't be much comfort; he probably hadn't even seen the news from whatever den of iniquity he'd holed up in. He likely had no idea the people of his hometown were doing their best to save his rubbish rag of a paper, since it meant so much to him.

As PJ hobbled into the hall, her phone beeped

348

and Paula leaped a mile in the air. She was glad her father was out of the room, but he still heard. 'Who's that texting at this hour?'

'It's not that late, Dad. Anyway, it's work.' Her heart slowed as she realised it wasn't Aidan. Of course it wasn't, the bastard.

It *was* work; Gerard, in fact, true to his word. He texted all in one efficient, punctuation-free message: *nothing to report no news cant get any more on mission g*. She sighed and pocketed the phone. 'I'm going up to bed, Dad. See if I can make any headway in the morning.'

'All right. Don't read too late.'

As if she was twelve. 'I won't. Night, Dad.'

Paula's mind raced all night as she tried to sleep in her narrow single bed. The cat. She remembered seeing the homemade poster the little girls had been drawing. A fat ginger scribble and the words LOST CATT . The force had dismissed the knife find as a prank, some sick person messing with animals, but what if . . . Really, she needed to talk to Aidan. He was the only person who could help her draw her thoughts into some kind of order. It was inconvenient, then, that she wasn't speaking to him.

As she thought about it, a wave of anger swamped her so that she had to sit up in bed. How dare he do *that* with her, after all these years, and then not get in touch! It was — it was juvenile, that's what it was. Although of course she wasn't getting in touch with him either.

The orange street light slanted in through glass streaked dark with rain. What time was it?

349

Three, four? She'd barely shut her eyes, tossing and turning, her mind churning up impossible plans. There had to be a way to investigate Carr, even though he'd shut down the paper and got her thrown off the case. This was a man who thought he could do anything, that no one would ever challenge him.

She thought of what Theresa had said. *Mammy'd skin her if she went with fellas.* What if Cathy had told her parents her secret — told them she was pregnant? How would that fit in with the Carrs and their perfect life?

She thought about Cathy. If you were fifteen, and you'd just found out you were pregnant, who would you turn to? How could you tell your parents what had happened, when your father led the local council, and your mother was Angela Carr? Angela who said going out with boys was 'dirty'. Angela who never let her daughter out. Angela who'd been so pale and terrified the last time Paula had seen her, at the house.

Mammy . . .

Paula snapped on her Anglepoise lamp, hoping PJ would actually have relaxed his constant vigilance and gone to sleep. The thing she wanted was somewhere in the vast pile of papers she'd lugged back from the office, she was sure of it. But where?

Shuffling into her old dressing-gown and fluffy slippers — it was always cold in the house — she eased open the door and made it down the stairs by the light from the street, feeling her way along the flocked wallpaper. In the kitchen it was

350

brighter, next door's security lights flickering on in the wind and rain. She shuffled through the papers, which PJ had arranged into a tidier system more to his own liking. It was something Aidan had given her, she was sure of it, in that great dossier of doom. Financial records, blog print-outs. Cathy's school reports — how on earth had he got hold of those? She didn't even want to know. Family pictures, paper snippets . . . There!

She saw the name she wanted, and then suddenly light exploded onto her eyes. 'Christ! You blinded me.'

PJ was standing in the door, leaning heavily on his crutch. Coming out of the cut-off leg of his tracksuit bottoms, the cast was snow-white. She realised how stupid she looked, kneeling on the cold lino tiles in her pyjamas, squinting in the half-dark at bits of scrappy paper.

'Sorry, Dad. I didn't want to wake you.'

He came in. 'You're a grown woman, Paula. You can put the light on if you need to.'

She blushed. 'Sorry.'

'Whatever would you be at down there?'

'I just had an idea.' She turned back to the papers, frustrated as it slipped out of her grasp again, the thought she'd had. 'I remembered something I'd seen.'

'Did you find it?' He was putting the kettle on, as if on auto-pilot.

'I'm not sure. I'll take it back up to bed, sorry.'

In the bedroom she knelt in the pool of light from the Anglepoise. It was so late it was early, but she had to keep searching through it all until her hands closed on a crinkly piece of old newsprint. *Bingo*.

The piece of paper that had driven Paula out of her bed to the cold kitchen was a clipping from the *Ballyterrin Gazette* in its former heyday, when it had actually served up hard news, rather than the car rallies and dog shows Paula liked to make fun of. Twenty-five years ago, in fact. The year before John O'Hara had been shot in front of his young son, dying to protect his right to tell the truth, whether anyone wanted it or not.

Scandal of Case M, it read.

For years in the North we have followed events South of the border, often priding ourselves on our moral superiority. Many cases have come to light in recent years that seem to prove this. Abuse scandals. Cover-ups by the Catholic Church. Pregnant women banned from leaving the country for an abortion by a government more concerned with bowing the knee to men in cassocks than protecting the vulnerable. Many will have been raped, or told that giving birth was likely to kill them, and yet there is no choice at all. We may well have felt smug. That could never happen here, in the more enlightened North. Yet abortion is just as illegal in the North, despite being part of the United Kingdom and subject to the laws and principles of that domain. Unless, of course, you happen to be young and female. And in

Ballyterrin we've just witnessed one of the worst miscarriages of justice this country has ever seen.

When social worker Ann Cleary made a regular visit to one of her cases, she had no idea what would greet her that day. The family had been on her books since their mother died six months before. Although they lived on the notorious Shorelands estate, it appeared the father had been coping well, and the only child, a girl of twelve, had taken over the care of the house. But when Ann Cleary arrived at the door that day, there was no answer. She could hear loud sounds of choking from upstairs. Becoming alarmed, she managed to gain access to the property, and dashing to the bathroom found the twelve year old on the floor, bleeding from multiple cuts to her arms. She called an ambulance and the girl was rushed to hospital. Too inexperienced to know where to cut, her life had not been in danger. But the ordeal wasn't over, as it was discovered that the girl, barely more than a child herself, was several months' pregnant. A tragic story.

Yet due to this country's draconian abortion laws, alienated from the rest of the UK by our moral rectitude, the story didn't end there. According to the girl's father, his daughter had been 'out of control' since her mother's death, and sleeping with many boys in the neighbourhood. Not only will this child now be forced to give birth to her *baby, she will also be sent to the notorious Ballyterrin Safe Harbour home where she will work off her 'debt'. When her baby is born it will be shipped off with hundreds of others to wealthy childless couples in America, who pay through the nose for this vile cargo of Irish blood. Ballyterrin has failed this girl, and it continues to fail hundreds like her, who would rightly think that no one in this whole town cares if they live or die.*

Paula blinked on finishing the article. She'd never realised that John O'Hara had been such a stern prose-writer — she'd only been six when he died. A child. And that other child, the brutalised twelve year old, what had become of her? What was her real name?

There was a paperclip on the cutting, as if something had fallen off in transit. She scrabbled through the papers until she found it. Yes, this had been it. It was only one sheet — a court listing. The case title was *R vs McGreavy, A.* What did the A stand for?

Something was in Paula's corner vision, poking her in the shoulder. Something she remembered, recently, someone saying, *I'm twenty-five . . .* But it was too late, and she was too tired. Perhaps in the morning she'd swallow her pride and call Aidan herself, find out if he knew any more than this.

Paula alternately dozed and tossed for a few hours, before the black outside the window began to lift somewhat, and she heard PJ's familiar cough next door. Must be six, then. Early. But there was another sound . . . She sat bolt upright in bed, as if a tap of cold dread had suddenly been turned on inside her. The phone was ringing, a sharp fractured sound. Phones at this hour, it was always bad news. News to make the heart turn over and the blood still. Next door, through the thin walls, she heard her father wake too. He had a receiver in his room, because of his leg, and almost agonisingly slowly she heard him pick it up. 'Ballyterrin 94362.'

A long silence. Paula felt as if her legs had frozen.

Then, a very slow shuffle. He was coming to her door. Oh God. In a minute, he was going to say something bad — someone else dead, something awful. The door squeaked open and PJ stood there in his pyjamas.

'Dad?'

'You better get up, pet.'

30

It was like her dreams, or her nightmares. The house, artificially lit. Every window bright with light. Like Christmas, but for the worst of reasons. Like the day seventeen years ago, when she'd come home and her life had changed forever. For a moment, Paula couldn't get out of the car. Then she swallowed hard, and parked it outside Guy's house.

Bob Hamilton was in the kitchen, the receiver of the phone held to his ear. 'Aye, I'll hold.' He shook his head at her, grim-faced.

'When did he realise?' she asked quietly.

'He wakes up early most days. Doesn't sleep.'

'And her things? Did she take any things with her?'

'They're up there checking.' Bob's round face was as sombre as she'd ever seen it. 'I'm telling you, Miss Maguire, things is in a bad way. When we found wee Majella safe and sound, seemed like that was that, just an isolated incident, but now . . .'

She didn't need him to spell it out. Now all those fears were back again. What if she'd been wrong all along about Cathy? What if there *was* a serial killer at large after all?

'Can I go up?' she asked. 'I know I'm not meant to be here, but — '

Bob Hamilton gave her a long look. 'Inspector Brooking said you was off the case.'

'Come on, Bo — Sergeant. Maybe I can help. I know I've not been — well, I know you don't agree with some of what I did, but if I could do something, should I not try? *Please.*'

He stood back to let her past. 'Miss Maguire, if you can do anything to find the wee girl safe, I think we'd all be grateful.'

The house was full of officers in the dark green uniform of the PSNI, clumping on the stairs and talking into radios. Upstairs all the lights were blazing against the gloom of dawn, as Helen Corry stood taking notes, looking distinctly cross. Paula saw Gerard Monaghan flipping open notebooks on the desk, maths textbooks, a lever-arch file.

Standing over them, dictating orders, was Guy himself. He caught Paula's eye and paused for just a moment before carrying on: 'Make sure they search the train stations and buses. She knows how to get to Dublin, I'm sure.'

Corry was saying, 'We'll do it. Honestly, Inspector, we do this stuff as standard.'

Gerard asked, 'Sir? Is any of her stuff gone?'

Guy glanced round the room, and for the first time Paula saw he was barely holding it together. His eyes were wild. 'I think so . . . where's her schoolbag? Do you see a schoolbag?' They all looked, as if catching the whiff of crazy in his voice. He clutched his head. 'I'm not thinking straight.'

'Guy,' she said quietly.

'We need to talk to her schoolfriends — let's get an officer over to, oh, what's her name — Siobhan? Is that her friend?'

'*Guy!*' Corry and Gerard looked round, one face with plucked eyebrows raised in surprise, the other creased in annoyance. Finally, Guy himself looked up, and she saw his hands were trembling. 'Will you tell me what happened, please?'

'You aren't meant to be here.'

'I know. But I can help. You know I can.' She walked closer. 'You need to tell me. When did you notice Katie was gone?'

He passed shaky hands over his face. 'I don't know. I woke up — I'm usually awake about six. I saw her door was ajar — that's strange, she normally shuts it tight. She's been going on about getting a lock, but I don't know, I didn't — '

'Guy. Focus.'

'All right, yes, what — so I knocked, and I pushed it open and I could see right away her bed was — she hadn't slept in it. So I checked — I didn't know what things she'd take, or what she had, or . . . Christ. I think — I think some of her clothes are missing, maybe her shoes. God, I don't know!'

'It's OK.' Paula turned to the other two people in the room, who were looking from her to Guy with curiosity. 'Gerard, I think you should leave. Let the DCI and me do the rest.'

'Hang on now, we're in the middle of an investigation,' Gerard started.

'Yeah. And you're here even though she's only gone a few hours, because we all know time is critical.'

Guy was shaking. 'I can't lose her too. I can't.'

'I know. But listen, all we know at the moment is Katie is gone. And just because she's not here, it doesn't mean she'd want men going through her things. Not to mention her dad.'

She heard Gerard muttering something about a 'hard ticket'.

Corry cleared her throat. Even dressed in pre-dawn haste she managed to look poised, leather boots pulled over jeans and a cream scarf wound tight to her throat against the cold. Paula was zipped into a black waterproof jacket, trousers black too, at one with the gloom. Corry said, 'Fellas, I'm sorry — she's right, you have to get out. Come on. It's the girl's bedroom.'

In a strange way Guy seemed to draw strength from what Paula had said, as she'd hoped he would. By talking about Katie in the present tense she was reminding him that, as far as they knew, his daughter was safe and well.

Paula crossed the room in three swift steps, and uncaring of who saw, or however much Gerard scowled, she touched Guy on the arm. He was frozen, rigid. 'We'll get her back,' she murmured. 'I promise. We'll get her back.'

Guy pulled away, but when he spoke again it was in a more normal voice. 'I shouldn't have called everyone out, I'm sorry. It's just I didn't think we could afford to wait until twenty-four hours were up, and . . . ' He tailed off but she knew what he meant. Only a police officer knew how low down the priority a probable runaway would be. For Corry to be here with so many officers, she must believe the urgency was real. Guy said, 'I've got to ring Katie's mother. Come on. Paula's right.' Casting a last look round his daughter's small bedroom, he went out.

Even with the men gone, going through Katie's things felt like a violation. Paula was inexperienced in crime scenes, and looked to Corry for guidance. 'Do I need to wear gloves?'

'It's a bit late now, they were all rifling through her things when I got here.' Corry was patting down the clothes in the wardrobe. Paula looked around them. Posters on the wall, boys she didn't recognise. Who were JLS? Fairy-lights strung up round the mirror, a litter of cheap lipsticks and eyeshadow on the dressing-table. Pictures stuck up of the gap-toothed boy, Jamie. The dead brother. One picture in a frame, of a striking dark-haired woman, her arms round a smaller Katie — Tess Brooking. None of Guy.

'Thanks for letting me be here, Chief Inspector,' she said. 'I couldn't stand not to be, if there's anything I can do, anything at all.'

Corry was running her hands expertly between the wardrobe and the wall. 'You can do your job. Help us get into Katie's head. What would you have taken if you'd gone, when you were that age?'

It had crossed Paula's mind, of course, when she was a teenager. To run, to get out, to flee that dark house with the shadows full of sorrow, but she'd had no choice. Her mother had gone, and there was no way she could also abandon her silent father. In the end, she'd felt the only way out was strapped to an ambulance stretcher.

She pushed the thought away. 'You're thinking she ran off?' But even that wasn't as reassuring as it should have been, the idea of Katie creeping out in the damp dark. Who had she gone to meet, for a start?

There was a short silence from Corry. 'We have to look at every angle. From your research, it's the most likely thing, isn't it?'

That was true. God, she hoped it was true. 'Well, I'd take whatever money I could get my hands on. We should ask Guy if he had any lying around. Parents always think their kids can't find this stuff, but they can.' Paula opened a drawer, a mess of pants and socks, all disordered. She ran her hand in quickly, feeling ashamed — the most common place to hide things, the underwear drawer — and came out with a small box. Durex extra-strong. Unopened.

Ever efficient, Corry was frisking down the bedside table. 'I'd take warm clothes, a rain jacket in this weather. Soft shoes, to sneak out, so he wouldn't hear me.'

Paula raised her eyebrows for a second. 'That's true.' She nodded. 'How did she get out without him hearing?' She knew from experience that policemen fathers did not sleep deeply in their beds. 'If she did run away, she might have planned it in advance, maybe been stockpiling food too. We should ask him if anything like that's gone. What else?' Paula paced round to the side of Katie's bed. A wooden-framed one. Space underneath. She dropped to her knees and put her hand under, feeling dust, plastic storage boxes, and something else. Something small, with hard edges.

'We should check with her friends. See if any

of them knew she wasn't happy.'

'Hmm.' Paula was thinking about that group of girls she'd seen at the school, their passive white faces. 'To be honest with you, Chief Inspector, I'm not sure Katie really had many friends.' She was reaching under the bed to pull out the object she'd touched.

'But Brooking was saying she went to her friend's every weekend. For sleepovers, apparently.'

'Yes, well.' Paula got up, dusting off her knees. In her hand was a rectangular pink box, empty. *Accurate to within two weeks of pregnancy.* 'I think we might be about to find out Katie wasn't always telling the truth.'

★   ★   ★

Downstairs in the lounge, Guy was sitting on the same purple armchair Paula had draped her coat over that night. It seemed a million years ago, when he'd reached for her and they'd needed each other; they'd been able to give the only comfort there was. Gerard was in the kitchen with Bob, making phone calls; she could hear his rough voice rumbling low. She shut the door quietly, leaving just her and Guy in the lounge once again.

'Any luck with Tess?' Even then, in the middle of all that urgency, it was difficult to say his wife's name.

Guy was leaning forward, frowning at his phone. 'There's no answer at the house.'

'Did you try her mobile?'

'No answer.'

'Oh. When did you last — when were you last in touch with Tess?'

He said slowly, 'To be honest, we haven't spoken since she asked for the divorce. We — well, *I* — said some things. She kept talking about going off, getting some head-space, that sort of crap.'

'Has Katie spoken to her?' It dug into Paula, the idea of a mother not knowing her daughter was even missing.

'I don't know. She has her own mobile. She could be talking to anyone, for all I know.' He looked up at Paula. 'You must think I'm a terrible father. It's just — I've been so wrapped up in work, and Katie — she's fifteen. She doesn't talk to me. I don't know how to ask her.'

'I'm sorry, Guy.' She had to tell him. Paula held out the box she'd found and watched Guy's face go very still for a moment.

'Do you think this means — ' he began.

'Yes, I think so. Last time I was here, well, I saw her throwing up. I thought she was just ill.'

Guy sank back down again, his hands trembling. 'I heard her being sick a few times, too. I asked her, and she said she'd picked up a stomach bug — all her friends had it. I was worried about maybe, an eating disorder, something like that, not . . . '

Poor Katie. Too proud to ask for help, to admit that those wonderful sharing friends of hers didn't exist. Because that was the thing, wasn't it? The terrible burden of loneliness, of difference, that left these girls holed up in stuffy rooms, carving the names of boys into their files, and eventually, into their skin. Alone, you were nothing.

Guy looked up with hunted eyes. 'Those other girls, Majella and — what was her name?'

'Louise.'

'Louise. Do you think . . . do you think Katie feels like that?'

Paula chose her words carefully. 'I think Katie's very unhappy, that's true. She was obviously trying to hide her pregnancy, and she hasn't been telling the truth about where she's been or who she's been with. Did you ever check with her friends' parents to see if she was actually there?'

He looked confused. 'No. She's fifteen. I thought — I thought she wouldn't like that. And she was — I think it embarrassed her, having just me, and my job.'

'It's OK. Most parents wouldn't check either. It's just that I spoke to that Siobhan and it didn't seem like she actually was friends with Katie. I'm sorry.'

'So what are you saying? Do you mean she might do something, or somebody could have . . . ' He couldn't say the words.

She fell back on professional jargon. 'In most cases where a teen takes their life, it happens at home. We'll often find they talked about it to their friends.' If they *had* any friends, that was. Paula quailed, but struggled on. 'They might have looked up sites on the internet — does Katie have a computer?'

'Yes, yes, a laptop, but I think she's taken it.'

Paula relaxed a fraction. 'So that's a good sign. If she's taken things it means she's making plans, that she left here of her own accord. The most likely explanation is she's run away.'

He nodded dully. 'But where would she have gone? Who's with her?'

'I'm sorry to have to say this, Guy, but I think we should send officers to the Mission. You know I saw her there.'

'You tried to tell me,' he said slowly. 'I didn't listen.'

'I didn't do it very well, I'm sorry.'

'If she's not there — if Lazarus is gone — they'll rip us apart, the lawyers.' His face was pale, haggard. 'I just don't know what to do. I can't . . . I'm the boss here. I can't do — *things*.' He was looking at her keenly, and she understood what he wanted from her, now when it counted more than anything. 'Lazarus, he'll have an alibi for Katie, I'll bet he will. He always does, somehow. But . . . '

Paula took his hand, where a pulse was beating slow. He looked at hers as if he didn't understand what it was. 'Listen, we'll do what we always do. Check the buses, the trains.'

'It's not enough. If someone has her — if someone's keeping her . . . '

'I know.' Then she said the words she always used, to try to keep hope alive. 'She hasn't just vanished, Guy. She's somewhere. I know she is.'

The question was, was she safe and unhurt in whatever place she'd gone. Or whoever she'd gone with.

'Paula?' He stopped her as she put on her

365

jacket. 'How do you know all this — about girls, about why they . . . about suicide?' His voice cracked on the word.

What was the point in pretending? It was all so long ago, and the stakes were different now. Guy's daughter was in danger.

She said, 'Because when I was eighteen, I tried to kill myself. And I didn't run away first and I didn't take anything with me. So that's how I know.' She turned and went out without looking back at Guy. 'Gerard?' she called. 'Could you come with me downtown, please? I need your help.'

31

'Why'd you need me for?'

'I'll explain when we get there. Will we take my car?'

'That heap of shite Volvo? No way, we'll take the jeep.'

Knowing what she planned to ask of him, Paula wasn't inclined to argue with Gerard. They climbed up into the police Land Rover. It wasn't lunchtime yet, but the streets were filling up as they drove. Hallowe'en was a holiday for the local schools, meaning hordes of children were out in black hats, cloaks, scary masks. The murky day had barely got going yet the light was used up and exhausted. It wouldn't be the easiest time to find a missing girl.

Already up ahead, bright flowers of light rent the sky from time to time as people let off illegal fireworks. Gerard drove in silence for a while, cursing under his breath as small figures ran across the road, girls half-dressed in mini-skirts and devil horns.

'Never had any of this in my day. You'd want to put your coat round them.'

His day had pretty much been her day too, but she said nothing. She was chewing nervously on a flap of skin by her thumbnail, a terrible nausea brewing inside her. All the facts they knew so far flitted through her head, turned upside down and inside out.

'Every year on the force we get calls —
fireworks shoved in doors, eggs on houses. It's as
bad as the Twelfth of July. And the cut of some of
these wee girls, their skirts up their bums . . . '
He trailed off as she gave him a fierce look.
'You've done a load of these cases, aye?'

'A few.'

'You usually find them, the girls?'

She looked out of the window. 'Sometimes. It
certainly looks like Katie left the house of her
own free will. But . . . ' She didn't finish her
sentence. It depended very much on where she
had gone after that. *Think, Maguire.* If you
were fifteen, and you'd no friends at your
strange new school, and your father was
preoccupied and brooding, and your mother
had left, and your brother died, and the only
place you could find comfort was a church
group . . . She shook her head. They had to
find a way to get into the Mission again. The
only problem was everyone was at the square,
waiting to perform their big concert. 'Can you
go any faster?'

'Aye, I'll just mow the kids down, will I?' He
stopped. 'Sorry.'

'S'OK.' She looked out of the window again,
as pops of light illuminated gloomy streets. 'Just
get as close as you can, will you?'

But Gerard for once seemed unable to stop
talking. 'You think we might find her, then, if she
went off by herself?'

'I don't know.'

'It's a terrible thing. The boss . . . at first I was
thinking, you know, who's this English fella

coming over here, telling us what to do. But he's a good manager.'

'I know. He is.'

Gerard was watching her closely. 'You and him, you get on well?'

'I don't know about that.'

'Hmmph.'

Paula dug her nails into her palms. 'For God's sake, Gerard. Just pull up here.'

Parking in a residential street near the centre of Ballyterrin, Paula and Gerard shrugged into their rainproof jackets. Both black, plain, made to blend in. Gerard was nervously fingering his phone. 'I hope there's no trouble tonight. There's going to be a lot of people in that square.'

As Paula and Guy made their way into town, most of the shops were closing up early for the big concert. Posters were plastered on every spare surface, a dove arising in a beam of light. *The Mission Prayer Concert.*

'They shouldn't have posted those up,' Gerard muttered. 'That's against town regulations.'

'Yes, well, I think illegal fly-posting is the least of our worries now.' He mumbled something more but Paula ignored him, saying, 'Just let me talk to them. I know these girls. If you just provide' — muscle, she'd been going to say, but he might take the hump at that — 'if you can provide the official back-up. And, you know, charm them a bit.'

His brow creased. 'Charm them?'

'Yes. We're talking convent-schoolgirls here. Nice friendly young policeman . . . do I have to spell it out?'

'That's not my job. I'm a trained detective, not, not — some gigolo.' Was Gerard blushing? Either way, Paula didn't have time for his coyness.

'Just follow my lead, will you?'

They were now in the heart of Ballyterrin, in its main square, lined with shops, many boarded up since the recession hit. In front of the cathedral, dark and Gothic, a large screen was rising up from the back of a lorry. Inside was all incense-scented gloom. Men in headphones were doing sound-checks and switching on and off blinding lights.

Gerard and Paula made their way down the aisle. Everywhere was pre-show fuss, Mission leaders trailing guitar leads and tambourines, teens in school uniform exclaiming with nerves. The concert was going to take place around the altar, and be beamed out on a screen for the watching crowd. Picking through the chaos, Paula enquired of a pale hippy-looking girl with a clipboard where they might find the pupils of St Bridget's.

'You can't come in here.' The girl had fair plaits and spots along her forehead.

'Why not?' Paula glared at her.

'Performers only.' She tapped a pen off her clipboard.

'Well, are you aware the Mission is on the verge of being busted by the police — *again*? That won't be so good for your standing in the local community. I assume you're holding this event to drum up more business?'

'We're bringing God's word to troubled young people.'

'Sure you are. And we're just wanting to talk to a few of those young people, see exactly why it is they're so troubled.' The girl hesitated, and Paula lost her patience. 'Gerard!'

He stepped forward, pulling himself up to his full height. The girl backed away. 'Miss, we're with the police. Are you aware that this whole affair is breaking about a thousand event regulations? Now's not the best time for a fire inspection, is it?'

The girl's mouth was open.

'Aye, didn't think so. Now let this lady past.'

Paula flashed him a grateful look as they entered the small area of changing rooms behind the altar. The walls were damp and close, a smell of dust and snuffed candles in the air. She could already hear the sound of chanting, and followed it down the narrow corridor.

In a small room hung with robes, which Paula recognised as the sacristy, the nine girls were sitting in a circle on the floor. Siobhan was in the middle, her hands held out over the heads of the others, her eyes shut. A strange humming sound came from her, as if she was vibrating, not even using her mouth. The other girls had their heads bowed, eyes closed in prayer. Paula let the door slam and was pleased to see the guilty expressions as their heads snapped back.

'Sorry to interrupt, girls. DC Monaghan and myself have a few more questions to ask you.'

'We answered your questions,' said Siobhan stiffly.

'We've got more. Gerard?'

She watched their faces as Gerard came in,

371

squeezing his broad shoulders round the plasterboard door. He fixed them with a fierce stare. 'Girls,' he said in a growl. 'Ms Maguire has some questions to ask you, and if you don't help her out, I'll be getting on to your parents. I'm sure nice girls like you wouldn't want to have criminal records at the age of fifteen.'

It was working. Several of the girls were exchanging looks, biting their lips. They hadn't put their makeup on yet but they wore the white robes. Only Siobhan stood firm. 'We have to go on stage soon. We're one of the main acts.'

'Don't worry,' said Paula, sitting down on a plastic chair. 'If you tell me the truth, this won't take long at all.' She looked round at the nine of them, at the expressions ranging from shifty to defensive to scared. 'Girls. You better tell me what you know about Katie Brooking.'

Siobhan wrinkled her nose. 'Katie?'

'Yes. Start talking.' Gerard glared at her but she raised her chin.

'She was new this year so Mammy said I should invite her round. She came to one sleepover and she went to Miss Kenny's group a few times, but she was a bit weird.'

'Weird how?'

One of the other girls piped up — Anne-Marie, Cathy's best friend. 'She was sad all the time. We watched this film and she started crying when a wee kid died in it. We asked her what was wrong but she wouldn't talk to us.'

Perhaps because her brother had died just months before.

'And she never let any of us go to her house. I

372

mean we go to Siobhan's all the time, and mine all the time. It's not fair. She wouldn't say why.'

'Katie's got a massive house. She's just being selfish.'

Or more likely, she couldn't stand for her friends to witness the destruction of her family, how her father barely noticed she was there, and no one remembered to buy her lunch. 'Well, girls,' Paula said. 'You might get to see the inside of the house, after all. Katie went missing this morning.'

★ ★ ★

An hour later, Paula pushed her way out of the room, and once she was a few feet away, banged her fists against the old peeling walls, muffling a scream of frustration in her throat.

Gerard came behind her, treading heavily on the stone floor. 'Bunch of hard-faced Hannahs in there all right.'

'The maddening thing is, I'm sure they must know something. You saw their expressions.'

'You think they were bullying her, Katie?' Gerard was fishing his phone out from his trousers and turning it back on, as they walked out of the cathedral and onto its wide stone steps.

'I'm sure of it. But there's no way I can prove anything if they stick together.'

'And it's no crime, bullying another girl. Else the whole school'd be behind bars.'

She sighed in annoyance, but knew he was right. 'You better get back to the house, see if there's any luck at the bus station or on the trains. Katie may well have gone to Belfast, or Dublin. She wouldn't have needed much cash for that.' If she said it often enough, she might actually start to believe Katie was safe somewhere.

Gerard was holding the phone to his ear. 'Hold on, there's a voicemail.'

'Is it — '

He held out his hand to shush her while he listened, and Paula, who did not enjoy being shushed, tapped her foot in annoyance.

'Well?'

'They checked the Mission but no one's there. Bob says I've to get on over to the main station for a briefing — sounds like they're going to arrest Lazarus, if they can find him. This concert'll be crawling in officers soon.'

'I'll see you later then.'

'What are you going to do?' Gerard looked at her suspiciously.

Paula was peering past him to the other side of the square, where the newspaper building stood, one of the lower windows smashed by the bailiffs into a helix of fractures. 'What am I going to do? Well, Gerard, I guess I'm going to put the investigation at risk again. Sorry.'

'Paula, if you find wee Katie, I'll never bring it up again.'

'I'll believe that when I see it.'

He looked at her a moment, and she wondered had he heard what she'd said to Guy. That was why she never told anyone. Couldn't bear how it made them look at her, like she was

374

weak, like she was vulnerable. Nothing worse. 'Listen — ' He stopped, scratching at the still-healing burn on his neck. 'You wanted to know what was up with me. To be honest, I thought everyone knew. The name Pauric Monaghan mean anything to you?'

For a moment it didn't, then it did. 'Wasn't he — '

'Yeah. My uncle.'

'Oh.' Pauric Monaghan had served twenty years in jail for planting a bomb in an Army barracks in England — except he'd never actually been anywhere near the place. Two decades of appeals had finally released him from high-security prison, a broken and bitter man.

'But . . . ' Paula was struggling to get her head round it. 'You still joined the police, even after what they did?' She remembered now. It had been several corrupt RUC officers and their trumped-up evidence that had condemned the innocent man to years in jail.

Gerard shook his head impatiently. 'I'm no Provo. Uncle Pauric, maybe he didn't do the bombing, but he did other stuff. He wasn't a good man, and I've no time for the IRA. They ruined more people's lives than the police ever did.'

'OK.' She was trying to understand.

He sighed. 'It's what I was trying to say the other day, like. You can't go haring around. Else innocent people get put behind bars, and guilty ones walk free. We have to try to be rational. We have to do it right, you know? We have to be the impartial ones.'

'And you can do that, can you?' With his background, she'd meant. But couldn't someone say the same about her? And clearly, the answer would be: she couldn't.

He shrugged. 'I have to try. You'll be careful?'

'I'm grand. Now go — at least one of us should do the job we're actually paid for.'

Paula watched him go, shoulders pumping ahead towards the parked car. She felt strangely desolate without him. A good man to have on your side, Gerard Monaghan.

'Miss?'

She turned back to the cathedral. A small figure had emerged from the heavy doors onto the steps, shivering in a thin white robe. 'Anne-Marie, you'll catch your death. What is it?'

The girl hesitated. Her skinny arms were wrapped round her in the gathering gloom. 'Miss, will I get in trouble? If there's something I didn't say, when you asked us before?'

'Is there?'

Anne-Marie nodded slowly. Her face twisted and a sob tore out of her. 'I'm sorry, miss! I didn't know! I didn't know she'd get killed!'

32

Paula took the girl back into the cathedral, where it was warmer, into a side pew filled with shadows. With voices lowered, no one could hear them over the din of preparations for the concert, the lights flickering on and off and the sound system booming every few minutes as it was tested. Anne Marie was still sniffing and wiping her face on the sleeve of her robe; Paula wished she was the kind of person who remembered to carry tissues.

'Are you going to tell me the truth now, then?'

The girl nodded shakily. 'I don't know where to start, miss.'

'Start at the beginning, I'd say.'

'OK.' She took a deep breath in. 'Miss Kenny started it.'

'Miss Kenny? Your form teacher?'

'She took us down to the Mission first, a group of us. She's friends with the lady there, the American lady.'

'Maddy, you mean?'

'Yeah. Maddy — we liked her. She was nice to us all, especially Cathy; she was really nice to her. And then Cathy; she . . . You know Ed? The leader?'

'I know Ed.'

'Everybody said he was going out with one of the girls at the Mission, in the year above us. She'd been going there since the summer, since the Mission started.'

'Who was she, Anne-Marie?' Paula asked gently.

Anne-Marie sniffed loudly. 'Louise. Everybody said it was Louise. But then, she didn't come any more. And Ed, he was with this other girl from a different school.' She looked up. Her eyes were miserable. 'Miss, I said I didn't know Majella. But I did know her. We all do. She was at the Mission too. I'm sorry I lied.'

'It's OK. Tell me the rest. What happened with Majella?'

Anne-Marie spoke reluctantly. 'In the summer, he liked Louise. Then Louise — one day she just didn't come, and next thing we heard she was dead. People said that maybe she was going to have a baby.' She bit her lip.

'It's all right. Go on, if you can.'

'One day Ed came in when we were doing Group Talk with Maddy. And he saw Cathy, and he talked to her, and then — he was sort of going out with her. Not Majella any more. He was nice to Cathy all the time instead. Some of the girls were jealous.'

'Siobhan, you mean?'

Anne-Marie wiped a hand over her face again. 'She said Cathy was a slut. That we shouldn't talk to her any more. We weren't very nice to her. We made her not be in the play any more. Then one day, Siobhan, she came into school and she had all this stuff.'

'What stuff?'

'Old papers and stuff. Like newspapers. And she said — she said it was about Cathy's mum.

That she'd been a slut too and they'd sent her away to a home to have a baby, when she was only wee. Siobhan was going to tell Cathy.'

'And where did Siobhan get this stuff?'

'Someone gave it to her.' Anne-Marie stared at her hands with their small bitten nails.

'Who gave it to her? You can tell me.'

'It was the American lady. It was Maddy. She gave it to her.'

Paula took this in. 'And — did Siobhan tell Cathy?'

She nodded shamefacedly. 'At breaktime. We found Cathy in the cloakrooms, and we showed it all to her, and she cried.'

'What day was this? Was it the day she went missing? You lied about what time she left school?'

Another slow nod. 'She was that upset, miss, she ran out. She stayed for afternoon register and then she went, about two o'clock. I think she was going to see *him*. Ed.'

'Why do you say that?'

'Well, she'd nail varnish and makeup and that on. We're not meant to have that at school. But the thing is, miss, I don't think he wanted to see her. He had another girl, we thought. We saw him with her.'

Paula was fairly sure she knew the answer, but she asked, 'Who?'

Another sigh. 'Katie. I think he liked Katie after that.'

Of course he did. Katie, who was now also apparently pregnant, and also missing. 'Anne-Marie, this might sound strange, but do you by any chance know what shoes Cathy had on that day?'

The girl didn't even look puzzled at the question. 'Her fancy ones. Heels. We're not meant to wear those either.'

'Are they patent, with a sort of strap across the front?'

'Yeah. We bought them down in Dunnes one day.' Fresh tears welled up. 'Miss, I never meant to lie. It's just Siobhan, she said we should do it, and — I didn't want her to be mean to me too, miss. I just wish I could tell her how sorry I am — Cathy. She was my best friend. Do you think if I prayed, she'd know?'

Paula patted the girl's cold hand. 'It can't do any harm. Now why don't you go back. Your play's starting soon. And thank you, Anne-Marie. You did the right thing.'

As she watched the girl trail down the aisle, her white robe sagging, Paula was thinking about a pair of shoes. Patent leather, high heels, size five. The ones she'd seen outside the Carrs' house on a rack, where Cathy must have left them when she got home that day. The last day anyone had seen her alive.

The square was even busier now, as dusk closed steadily in. The place thronged with teenagers, the boys scuffling their large shoes in doorways, backs turned protectively; the girls coatless, thin arms goose-bumped, laughter rising high and nervous. You could feel it in the air — it was a night when things would happen.

Paula pushed her way through the crowd, aiming for the opposite end of the square, where the Gazette offices stood on a side street. Her ears echoed with excited chatter, and the large screen was already flickering into life. They'd be starting soon, and then what? Would it be too late to find Katie, wherever she was?

She had reached the street and was hurrying down it, ducking past the groups of kids which still kept coming, when a blur of movement caught her eye. There was a small alley down the back of Dunnes supermarket, the place they unloaded pallets and took out rubbish. She'd always avoided the place because local drunks also used it as a handy toilet. Someone was in there. A gleam of fair hair in the shadows.

'Who's there?' Paula moved into the alley, out of the busier street. Overlooked by bare walls, it was already dark in the corners, the stink of urine strong. Her fingers touched the reassuring shape of her phone, zipped into one jacket pocket. She peered behind a large green bin. 'Is someone there?'

Then she was slamming against the breeze-block wall, all the breath knocked out of her. Ed Lazarus was an inch from her face, his wiry arms holding her shoulders down. Shock made her mind move slowly, and for a moment she took in how terrible he looked — a dirty sweatshirt, hair dark with sweat, several days' beard on his cheeks.

Paula writhed. 'Get the fuck off me!'

The man was panting. 'Listen! Listen, I just want to talk!'

'Let me go!' She tried to scream. 'Help, someone!'

You wouldn't have known to look at him, but he was strong. He put his arm over her throat and leaned in so close she could smell him, a mix of fear and unwashed clothes. 'Shut up, OK? Shut up or I'll hurt you.' His voice was a low hiss.

She couldn't get away. His face was too near; she turned hers to the side. 'What are you doing here? The police are looking for you.'

'I know.' He was breathing hard. 'They came to the Mission. But it's not me. That's what you need to understand.'

Paula made herself look him in the eyes, keep her voice calm. 'Where is she, Ed? Where's Katie?'

'Katie?' He looked puzzled, his hands relaxing their grip on her a fraction.

'Yes, Katie Brooking. She's gone missing, as if you didn't know. You better not have hurt her.'

His green eyes went wide. 'Listen, Paula, you have to listen. I didn't do it. It's not me you want. Katie — I didn't even know she'd gone, I swear — and Cathy — it wasn't me, OK? It wasn't me!'

She struggled but he held her fast; her head banged painfully against the wall. 'I know you've been with them. All those girls.'

His voice grew panicked. 'Listen . . . yes, I was with them. But I didn't kill Cathy. I didn't even see her that day, that Friday. I know she was looking for me, but I wasn't with her, OK? I — '

'You were with Katie.' It all tied up so neatly.

'Yes. OK, you're right, I was. But I never

— I'd never hurt them! I don't know anything, I swear.'

Paula tried to breathe. She fought the urge to push his pale hands off her, his touch unbearable. 'We'll find her, you know. You better tell me where she is. Come on, Ed. If she's not hurt, tell me and we can find her safe. She needs to go home.'

He moved away from her in a sudden impatient gesture, clutching at his head. 'I'm trying to tell you! I don't know where she is! I was with her, yes. And Cathy. All of them. I — I couldn't help it. But I didn't hurt any of them. I'm not like *him*.'

She didn't understand. 'Who?'

He moaned. 'My father. I'm not him. I'd never hurt them.'

Paula's hand moved to the zipper of her coat pocket. Could she get her phone out in time? No, he'd see. She took a deep breath. 'Then who, Ed? Who did it?'

'I — ' he gaped at her. 'I've been trying to think. And then I realised — *she* could have done it. She was gone that day, that Friday. She knew Cathy well. And Katie — she knew all of them.'

Paula was confused. 'Who do you mean, Ed? Who knew them?'

'Maddy, of course.'

Maddy Goldberg. For a moment, Paula stood frozen. 'Listen, Ed — why don't you come with me, we'll go to the station, and you can tell me all this and — '

He laughed, a dry desperate sound. 'You must

think I'm stupid, Paula. You want me to say I did it. Well, I didn't. So you're on your own now.' Then he was gone, flashing round the side of the wall and out into the street. Paula ran after him but his fair head was already disappearing into the crowd. She pulled out her phone, calling Guy's number. Gerard would be well away by now.

'Shit!' Voicemail. She tried Gerard too; no answer. They must be in the briefing at the station, working out how best to catch the man who'd just had his arm over her throat. She spoke urgently into the phone. 'Listen, it's Paula — I've just seen Lazarus. He's in the square. He's here now. You have to send some officers. I'm — ' She didn't know how to explain what she was about to do. 'Call me as soon as you can, OK? Please hurry.'

She slipped the phone back into her pocket, paralysed by indecision. But no, she couldn't go after Lazarus on her own. He was much stronger, and much faster, and she'd never find him in this crowd. Besides, there was somewhere more urgent she needed to be.

★   ★   ★

'Aidan?' From the outside, the newspaper offices looked deserted. On the lower floor, the window was boarded, broken glass sparkling over the ground. As Paula pushed open the door, it stuck on the post that had piled up behind the letter-box. Clearly, no one had been in or out for days. She stooped and picked up one letter, held it to the faint orange light from the square. Pencilled on the envelope: *To keep the Gazette going*. Inside, a crumpled fiver. Another, several pound coins jingling inside.

Slowly, she ascended the silent stairs. 'Aidan?' No answer. The steps were littered in paper, trodden over with footmarks. The bailiffs had taken everything.

'Aidan O'Hara, if you're here, you better get the feck out now.' The building was giving Paula the freaks, only her own voice echoing in the dark corners.

At the top of the stairs, a shadowy figure stooped into view. 'It's yourself, Maguire.'

'Of course it is. Who else'd come and drag your arse out of here?' She went up a few steps more, to where the lights from the street lamps fell over his ravaged face. 'They shut off the power?'

'Aye. Shut off everything.' A half-empty bottle of Jack Daniel's hung from Aidan's hand. His words were slightly slurred.

'Well, aren't you the picture of health and sobriety.'

'What d'you want?'

'Is this where you've been hiding yourself away?'

Aidan was wearing ragged jeans and an old grey T-shirt she recognised from way back. Guns 'n' Roses. He passed his free hand over his unshaven face. 'Nowhere else to go. Lost the flat months ago.'

'Thought that might be it.' She walked up the last few steps.

'You've come to gloat, have you?'

Anger boiled up in her. 'I've come to see if you're OK. Screw you, Aidan. Twelve years and you still can't phone me after? What's the matter with you?'

Aidan raised his head, eyes weary and old. 'In case you didn't notice, they cut off everything round here. That includes the phone lines. And the business mobiles.'

She pushed past him into the devastated office, still determined to be cross. 'You couldn't have got in touch somehow? I mean, Christ, it's been a long time coming, what we did.'

Aidan shut the door with a snap. 'And what the hell's that supposed to mean?'

'You know exactly what I mean.' Inside, the office was a wreck. Footprints in ink all over the floorboards. Only two cheap plywood desks remaining, pulled out at strange acute angles. The floor littered with old front pages, scattered pens. It looked as if everything of any value had been hauled out the door, down to the last paperclip. The electrical sockets stood empty and dusty. 'They took your computer?'

'They practically took me underpants, Maguire.' Aidan sat down by a sleeping bag placed on a mound of old papers, where he appeared to have been squatting for several days. Another empty bottle of JD rolled on the floor beside him.

'When did you last eat?'

He lowered himself down heavily. 'Who needs food when you've got my friend Jack?'

'Jesus Christ, Aidan. If you'd the sense to walk

downstairs, you'd realise this paper's about more than you.'

He shut his eyes.

'Hello! What do you think this is?' Paula waved the handful of envelopes she'd scooped up from the hallway. 'People are so keen to keep this bloody paper afloat, they're sending their life-savings. God knows why they want to read about the best Irish dancing outfit in town, but apparently they do. It was even on the news. And what are you doing? Nesting in here on the papers like — like a bloody hamster, a child's hamster, and drinking away what few brain-cells you have.'

Aidan said nothing.

'Did you even hear me?'

'I heard you, Maguire. I'd say they heard you in the South. Do carry on with your insightful commentary on my life.'

Then Paula was across the room and beating him about the head with the envelopes. 'People care about you! People bloody want you to carry on telling the truth, and you can't make it further than the floor!'

'Never bothered you the other night.'

'Ah, here we go. Go on then, let's talk about it.'

'Talk about what?' He still hadn't opened his eyes.

'I don't know, about the fact you finally nailed me, after twelve years? Is that what this is about?'

Aidan opened one dark eye a slit. 'This discussion seems familiar, Maguire. Are we suddenly back in 2000?'

'I suppose we are.' Furiously, she paced the room. 'I suppose we never left it, if you want to go there. So, this seems as good a time as any to talk about how you dumped me because I wouldn't put out. That's what it was, wasn't it?'

'I'm not having this conversation.'

'Why not? Don't you think you owe me that, after all these years? You broke my heart, Aidan. And just because I wasn't ready then, it doesn't mean I wouldn't have been . . . I mean, I knew it would be hard, you going to uni a year ahead, but I thought you'd wait for me. And then I have to hear about it in some bloody *email*, that you've shagged some Dublin girl and we're over.'

'Over? Fuck's sake. Did I ever say I wanted it over? I mean, there was that other girl — I fucked up, yes, but Christ, just some girl — you didn't have to cut me off forever. I tried to ring you. PJ wouldn't let me near the place, then you were gone. Saoirse said you did the same to her. What happened to you that summer? Glandular fever, we're meant to believe. Was that really it?'

'It's none of your business what I — '

'Glandular fever so bad you wouldn't see anyone all summer? You even missed your birthday. We had all those plans.'

She was shaking. 'You should have thought of that before you shagged around. I'd have done it, if you'd just waited, if you'd had a shred of common decency, or patience.'

Aidan started up, sitting on his stack of papers. 'For fuck's sake. I never even *wanted* to sleep with you, as you'd see if you'd an ounce of sense in your head.'

She stared at him. 'Well, fuck you too.'

'Wait! I mean, Jesus, Maguire, you were such a *good* girl — do you remember? All your top marks and your wee camogie skirt, going to Mass with your daddy, making his tea . . . and you were so vulnerable. Christ, you might have talked the talk, but after your mammy went you were so broken — '

She flinched. 'Don't you talk about my mother!'

'I just meant . . . you were sort of so pure. I didn't want to be the one to ruin that. You weren't ready. And I was — well, there was me in Dublin, and I was drinking hard then, drinking every day, going down some kind of spiral, and you're back in Ballyterrin in your school uniform. It wasn't right. I was no good for you.'

She fell silent, clenching her fists. 'I'm not that little girl now.'

'Yes, I can see that.' He sounded sad.

'You know what? Go fuck yourself, Aidan. It wasn't just up to you. Maybe I wanted you to be the one. You ever think that? Maybe it was you I wanted. And then, you just ended it, and — ' She fought back the memory, the lights blurring in and out over her head, wondering: *Will I see her again, if this is it?* No fear. Just curiosity, and a terrible deadening peace. 'You said I was the one who vanished. But you'd left months before. I lost you the day you went to Dublin.'

Aidan bowed his head. 'What's the point of all this?' His voice was harsher than she'd ever heard it. 'It's all in the past. It's dead and gone, Maguire.'

She stood quivering. 'Then why the hell are we still fighting about it?'

He looked up, his expression surprisingly soft. 'Because there's no one in this world can annoy me like you can.'

'And you me.'

Suddenly he laughed, and the tension between them fell down like a house of cards. 'Fecked if I know, Maguire.' He fixed her with his dark eyes. 'I wanted to phone you, of course I did. Didn't know what to say. After all this time — It knocked me for six, I won't lie.'

'You could have started with, 'Hello, Paula, how are you feeling? How was your walk of shame?''

'Did your daddy catch you?'

'Of course. It's not easy to give him the slip.'

'As I know to my cost. Well, is he gunning for my guts?'

'I think he's worried about you, to be honest. So's Pat. And so am I.'

His eyes were tired, but gentle. 'Don't be wasting your time on me. I'm fine.'

She looked pointedly at the JD bottle.

'All right, all right. I might have had a wee slip. Gave me a hell of a shock, hearing that fella might be out soon, and then them busting in, taking the lot.' He looked around the office where his father had died, spilling his life's blood to defend the paper. Now it was a shell, ransacked and empty. 'It'd kill my da to see this. Maybe it's just as well he's gone.'

She took a deep breath. 'I'm going to slap you in a minute. Do you not see this?' She waved the envelopes again. 'People want their paper to tell the truth. God knows why, but they want you to carry on what your dad started. That and the car shows, of course.'

He picked up one of the envelopes she'd thrown at him and peered inside. It held a crumpled ten-pound note and had a scrawled message on the front — *For the paperman.*

'Aidan?'

He was quiet, staring at it. 'Aye. I see, Maguire. I'm not a total blind eejit. Even if I do act like one, on occasion.'

'Come on.' She bent a hand out to help him up from the floor, feeling the electricity between them as their skin touched. 'Now's not the time to get drunk and maudlin. I need you. I've a feeling things are about to come to a head.'

He was suddenly alert. 'Something's happened?'

'Another girl's gone.'

'Shit,' he swore. 'But after the traveller girl wasn't missing at all . . . '

'I know, I know, we thought it was over. But now I don't know. I just don't know.'

'Who is it, Maguire? Tell me.'

'It's Guy Brooking's daughter,' she said. 'So you can see, this is no time for sitting round feeling sorry for ourselves. We have to find her.'

'Right. Shit.' He got up, running hands over his face and giving the impression of trying to forcibly pull himself together. 'Where do we start?'

'I thought maybe with this.' She felt in the back pocket of her trousers for the *Gazette*

391

clipping from 1985. John O'Hara's last year on earth. 'Tell me what you know about Angela Carr.'

★   ★   ★

Aidan was pacing in front of her, tapping a chewed pencil off his thigh. Paula was sitting on the one chair the bailiffs had left, a broken-backed one with a wonky leg.

'So explain it to me again,' she said.

'I'm not making much sense, am I?'

'Maybe if you weren't half-cut it'd be easier.' She relented. 'Sorry. Go on.'

'Like I said, it was Dave gave me the idea in the first place — when he said they'd never had any files on the Carrs. Then I started thinking — what if there was something on the parents, before they married? Well, we know all about the fine Eamonn.'

She nodded. Eldest of eight, father shot on the doorstep, the family held together by a strong-willed matriarch who'd managed to salt away what remained of Patsy's ill-gotten gains until Eamonn was old enough to take over, and funnel it into the property empire that had made his fortune.

'So then I thought, What about the ma? This Angela. You said she was a wee bit funny when you met her. And then when we saw the lovely Rosemary, Eamonn's fancy woman, she said something that jarred with me. Did you not notice?'

'No.' It was annoying, how he could recall

392

verbatim large stretches of conversation. He'd used it to her great irritation when they'd gone out in their teens. *But Paula, you said you'd let me undo another button this time.*

'Are you listening?'

'Sorry. What did she say?'

'She said, *and then he came back with her, and I was surprised she could show her face in the town again.*'

'So?'

'So, it says on Angela Carr's file, which you kindly showed me, that she was born in Dublin. Did you notice a Dublin accent when you met her?'

'No, actually.'

'No. She's from Ballyterrin, or I'm an Orangeman. But she's lying about it. I did a bit of digging, and I got hold of Angela Carr's reference for her first job. She was cleaning in a law office in Dublin, and that's where she met Eamonn. Well, the reference came from a Safe Harbour home.'

'How the hell do you find out these things? No, don't tell me. Go on.'

'Safe Harbour homes were notorious for never keeping any records. There's still no law in the South that lets adoptees find out their real names or birth parents. A disgrace.' He went back to his pacing and tapping, in lecture mode. 'So I just searched the archives for any mention of the home in Ballyterrin round that time. And there was Da's article. The case was quite famous at the time, apparently. We were too young, they'd have sent us out of the room if it came on telly. Now, they kept the family's name out of the news, but everyone in the town knew rightly who they were.'

'So what did you do?'

'Usual. High-tech research.'

'Bought some old soak a pint, you mean.'

'Maybe. Would you shut up? The point is, the fella I asked told me the family was called McGreavy. And the girl's name — it was Angela. You know she was pregnant, and they made her have the baby. Sort of a *cause célèbre*. She was twelve at the time, so she'd be thirty-seven now. Angela Carr's thirty-seven, as far as I can work out. That fits with the dates.'

And that meant the child she had been forced to have, who'd been adopted to America, would now be twenty-five. Another link to Safe Harbour. Another girl pregnant, the same year that Rachel Reilly and Alice Dunne had gone missing. What if Angela had also gone to God's Shepherd? Also encountered Ron Almeira?

'Maguire? Are you listening? You've a funny look on your face. Do you think that's a pile of shite or something?'

'No,' she said slowly. 'I'm fairly sure you're right that Angela Carr is Angela McGreavy. It all fits.'

'So?'

'The thing is, I think I know who her child is, too. Her daughter, I should say.'

'But how — ' At that point they were interrupted by a loud burst of sound from the main square, as if hundreds of loudspeakers had been switched on. Light bloomed in the windows

394

and Paula squinted, holding up her hands. A voice filled the room: 'Hello, Ballyterrin!' Screams. Hundreds of screaming girls.

'Listen,' Aidan said, cocking his head. 'The show's starting.'

★　★　★

Paula and Aidan crouched down by the broken window, peering out between the boards. 'You see him there, that Lazarus fella?'

'No. He must be lying low. They'll arrest him if he shows his face again.' Below them in the street passed clumps of teenage girls, threes and fours, twos and fives. No one alone. Dressed in short skirts, despite the chill October night. Witches' hats, devil horns. Blue-tinged skin and high shrieking laughter. 'They'll hardly find him in this crowd. Please God they get him before he hurts anyone else.'

Aidan was staring down at all the scantily-clad girls, a hounded look on his face. 'Mmm. You think maybe he's got her somewhere — wee Katie?'

'He said he didn't.' Paula had her torch switched on, checking the face of each girl. 'I don't know what I think, and that's the truth.'

The windows were shaking with the noise from the cathedral. The concert was already booming out of loudspeakers round the main square. A pale young boy, who Paula vaguely recognised as the guitarist in the band, was talking about the Mission. God's love. Planting a seed in the town. The shops round the square

395

were shuttered, white vans selling burgers and soft drinks out of shockingly bright interiors, steam rising with the smell of onions. Paula glimpsed stalls here and there for local charities, but more selling Mission goods. T-shirts. CDs. Motivational films and books. And everywhere in the square, moving like a dark wave over the sea, were the girls. It looked as if every teenage girl in Ballyterrin had come out. How many were there? Five hundred, maybe? Standing behind silver crash barriers, they filled the square, moving and calling and sighing as one. It was just like being at a rock concert.

'So who is this you reckon we're looking for?'

'Says her name is Madeleine Goldberg. She's one of the Mission staff. She knew Cathy quite well, it seems. She'd an alibi for the Friday, but — I don't know.'

As they hunched down, Aidan squinted over the crowd. Already the street under people's feet was littered with empty paper cups and popcorn holders. 'Well, that's most of the Mission lot up there, if I'm not mistaken.' Indeed, the stage was filling up with young people, clear-skinned, glowing with righteousness. The boys wore billowing white shirts, the girls flowered dresses, hair in braids. Maddy Goldberg was so far nowhere to be seen.

'I was trying for ages to work out what she'd said that bothered me. She made a point of telling me she'd been born in Ballyterrin, then adopted to America. Like she wanted me to know for some reason. I didn't understand, but then we found out about that McGreavy case,

396

and the child she had to give up.'

'How old is this Madeleine?'

'I'll give you three guesses.'

'Right.' He suddenly dropped to the floor, pulling her down by the ankle. 'Get down!'

'Ow! What the hell?'

'Look.' Aidan was whispering now, staring at the screen. 'Switch that thing off.' He fumbled for her torch and turned it off, so that the only source of light came from outside. There in the middle of the screen, stepping up to the altar inside, shaking hands with the band like a sad dad trying to be down with the kids, was local councillor and businessman Eamonn Carr.

It knocked the breath from Paula's lungs. 'Oh God. He's here too? And with Cathy dead. I can't believe it. I can't understand why he's supporting the Mission.'

Aidan shrugged. 'He's invested in them heavily.'

'But that couldn't be enough. There must be something else.' She stared out of the window.

Up on the altar stage, Eamonn was waiting for the applause to die down. His face looked strained and old, his hair greyer than it had been a few weeks ago. But he wore a smart suit, a black tie, and he faced the crowd with a smile on his face.

'Thank you, thank you, everyone. I'm here today because me and my family have suffered a terrible loss. I know you feel it with me, both the town and everybody at the Mission.'

There was a groundswell of murmuring. Behind him on the altar backdrop, a picture was projected. A girl with dark hair, a bright smile. Paula felt the hairs rise on her neck.

'This concert is given in memory of my daughter, Cathy. She loved the Mission, and I know they loved her too. We're all here tonight to give thanks for her life.'

On screen, he turned and muttered something to the side of the altar. There was a reluctant motion, and out of the crowd appeared two familiar, skinny children: Anna and Sean Carr. They were dressed uncomfortably in a frock, and a shirt and tie. An older woman with rigid grey hair also came forward, holding one younger Carr in her arms and leading the other by the hand.

'Who's that?'

Aidan squinted. 'That'd be the redoubtable Imelda Carr. Eamonn's ma.'

The whole family were there, then. Except the mother, Angela. 'Hey, if Eamonn's here, that means he's not at home.'

'Top marks, Maguire. If you ever want a career in investigative journalism . . . ' They were still whispering.

'Shut up! It means Angela's on her own. Listen, someone needs to keep an eye on our friend Eamonn there, and also look for Maddy. She's very striking, a big girl, lots of dark curly hair.' Like Cathy, now that she came to think of it.

'Fat, you mean?'

She swatted him on the arm. 'No. Reckon you can do it?'

'And what'll you be up to, Miss Marple Maguire?'

'I'm going to see Angela again. Maybe this time she'll be able to talk to me.'

After a moment Aidan nodded. 'You're probably right to go yourself. But Maguire, it's maybe not very safe. If you're thinking what I'm thinking about who killed Cathy . . . '

'I don't know, I said. But he knows something, I'm sure of it. There's something not right in that family. And if he's out of the way, I have to try. You see? If Katie's somewhere — if someone has her and I don't try . . . ' She'd already let the girl down enough, she meant. She couldn't live with herself if she didn't try everything.

'Fair enough. But maybe take some kind of weapon with you, just to be on the safe side.'

She looked sceptically round the ransacked room. 'Just open up your gun cupboard there, then.'

'Ah, don't be messing, you know I'm right. Someone killed that wee girl — slit her throat, yes?'

Reluctantly she nodded. 'All right. But do you even have anything?'

'I dunno. Let's look in the cupboard, they didn't go in there.'

The bailiffs had probably been right to ignore the old supply closet set into the back wall of the office. It held an array of filing cabinets, cleaning apparatus, a detritus of old books and tapes the paper had been sent to review. Paula sneezed at the dust.

Aidan poked a mop with his foot. 'Not much here, is there.'

'Wait. What's that?' She plunged into the dark

399

depths of the cupboard and came up with a long flat piece of wood, several inches across and curved at the end, sanded smooth. 'This'll do.' She swung the stick back and forward.

Aidan just stared at her. 'Have you totally lost it? A camogie stick? What in the name of God are you planning to do with a camogie stick?'

She laughed. 'Aidan, did you never see me play?'

'Oh, right enough, I was forgetting. Wasn't there that girl who — '

'Eh, I still say she broke her own nose. You're meant to *hit* the ball, you know?'

'Fair enough.' He looked at her, suddenly serious. 'You take care. Else PJ'll have my guts for garters — that's if he doesn't want to skin me already after the other night.'

Paula's stomach dipped alarmingly at this reference to their under-the-desk antics, but she made herself look away, focus on the task in hand. 'All right. You watch things here, and I'll go to the house. Aidan?' He turned on his way out. 'You be careful too.'

A brief smile. 'Maguire, I never knew you cared.' And he was gone.

33

Paula was soon cursing herself. Why hadn't she insisted on taking her own car earlier? The Volvo, ugly but reliable, was parked up in front of Guy's house, several cul-de-sacs over from the Carrs'. She'd have to walk. Ballyterrin was a small town, but it still took her a good twenty minutes to get up the hill. She was the only one going the other way, as hordes of teens headed to the concert, and parents led smaller children in costumes to see the fireworks show.

Paula, childless and zipped up in a black jacket and trousers, drew curious looks, as parents shepherded their offspring away from her. Not to mention for the camogie stick she had tucked under her arm, trying to be discreet. She didn't blame them. Among all this mock-evil, devils and witches and ghosts, something real and terrifying was abroad. Someone had cut Cathy Carr's throat and put her in the dark waters of the canal — that much they knew, though the rest of the crossword puzzle was full of blanks. But Paula was beginning to have more of an idea who it was. At least, she thought so.

★ ★ ★

The Carrs' ranch-style house looked deserted in the gloom. Evening was closing in fast around Paula, damp mist pressing on her skin like little

401

ghost hands. The penumbra of a street light illuminated the lawn, jets of rain shooting down into the light. Paula huddled deeper into her jacket, shiveringly aware that Ed Lazarus was still out there somewhere. The windows were all dark, curtains open. Was anyone even there?

Remembering her earlier visit, and Eamonn Carr's threats about trespassing, she slipped in the front gate, careful not to jangle it on its lock, and moved round to the pebble-dashed walls of the house.

The rain fell harder as she passed the kitchen, peering in at the clean surfaces and silenced kitchen appliances. A bowl of fruit stood on the table in the dark. On the outside, everything was normal here. But there was no sign of life, of any kind.

Paula reached the glass-panelled kitchen door and put her hand on the knob, heart pounding. It would be locked, surely. There was no one here.

The door clicked open and swung into the dark kitchen. Shouldering her camogie stick and gulping hard, she eased in. The house was silent but for the hum of the fridge. It felt warm, safe. The white cupboards and tiles were scrubbed clean. Paula thought of the mess a neck-wound made. Surely Cathy couldn't have died in here. She started to breathe quickly, realising suddenly where she was and what she was doing. This was madness. She leaned the stick against the sink, careful not to make a noise as she crept forward to the archway that led into the hall, and the family room opposite where they'd interviewed

Eamonn and Angela that day, when Angela had been so strange and withdrawn. Was that why? Was the woman too terrified to speak up, terrified because she knew exactly who had killed her daughter?

'Angela?' Paula's voice was very small in the dark. She cleared her throat. 'Angela?'

A voice behind her. A man's. 'I'm afraid not, Paula.' Then the stick was flying at the side of her head.

* * *

It's surprisingly hard to knock someone out cold. Paula knew this from a case she'd worked on once, a rapist who'd attacked his victims with a hammer. Even with severe head trauma, many had been able to remember facts about their captor. And so it was for her when Eamonn Carr hit her over the head with the camogie stick. There was a blinding flash to the side of her head, and she must have fallen, feeling for a moment weightless. She didn't know if she passed out exactly, but several seconds exploded into darkness. Then she was looking up at his shoes, her head near the underside of the sink. She heard her own breathing, hard in her ear. 'H — how . . . '

'You shouldn't be talking. You might be hurt.' He was down on his hunkers looking at her with what could have been concern. He still wore the suit she'd seen him in on stage, tie askew.

'Hu — ' She couldn't get enough air in her lungs.

'You're wondering how I got here, is that it? I saw your wee boyfriend, the paper fella, sneaking about at the show. No sign of you, so I put two and two together and thought you might be trespassing in my house again.'

She was trying to turn her body, force some air into her, breathe, get her eyes to work. Above her head the cupboard was a slice of white through her vision.

'And here you are. I thought I got you taken off the case. You're a bit of a liability, Miss Maguire.'

'Wh-where . . . '

'You're wondering where Angela is. You think I'm keeping her here, is that it? Well, you might be very smart, but you don't have a notion what's going on.' Eamonn Carr stood up with a sigh, and set down the stick he'd been holding. 'I don't know why you had to keep poking your nose in. A man has a right to protect his family. It's private, what goes on in a family.'

Not if you've killed your daughter. But she couldn't form the words.

'Now.' He looked down at her again and shook his head. 'What are we going to do with you? I suppose your fella knows where you're off to.'

She tried to indicate with her head that Aidan would be in like the SWAT team to save her any minute now.

'We'll have to take care of you, then, won't we.'

Take care of her? Paula tried to get her body to understand the urgency of this, that she really had to try to get up, but her gaze was caught by

404

something that marred the white underside of the cupboard. A splash of something red and dried, as if someone had wiped the place clean and missed that one spot. Blood.

★ ★ ★

'Come on, come on, stop messing. Sit down.'

Had she blanked out for a moment? Paula had a memory of something dark over her head, and of being pulled up off the floor. Now she blinked around her — the smell of wood and damp was all about. Overhead a bare bulb snapped on: they were in Eamonn Carr's shed. She was sitting on an upright chair, and when she tried to move her arms she couldn't. She was tied on with rope.

Eamonn was bent over a workbench, and in some corner of her brain she realised she should be afraid. He turned, and she saw his face under the dim light. Dark shadows carved out lines of grief. In his hand he had a cloth pad, and as he came towards her he held it out in front of him. His other hand caught at her head, pulling up strands of her hair.

She made an inarticulate noise in her throat, trying to find her voice. 'No — no!'

'Hold still, woman, would you.' Irritated, he dabbed with the pad at the cut on her head, the blood slowly seeping down her face. 'Need to clean up that head of yours, it's in a bad way.'

Since she couldn't move her arms, and he was gripping her hair, Paula let him do it, struggling a little from time to time in token protest.

After he'd finished he sat down heavily on the workbench, staring at her. 'You never should have come here. You don't learn, do you?'

It wasn't the first time she'd heard it, but she glared back at him, finally finding her voice. 'You better let me go, Eamonn. You're going to be in a whole world of trouble for this. I'm with the police force — '

'It's your own fault. You never should have let it get to this point.'

'Think about it, Eamonn. You could lose everything. Your business, the kids . . . Angela.'

He brought his hand down on the bench with a smack. 'Don't you dare talk about her!'

Paula jumped, jerking the rope painfully against her wrists. A moment ticked by. Paula wondered about the neighbours — if she could find the breath to scream, would anyone hear? Ken Crawford, with his sad little secret, or the deaf old lady on the other side?

'Where is she, Eamonn?' Her voice was coming in pants. 'Where's Angela? Are you keeping her somewhere?'

Eamonn's reaction was strange. He laughed for a moment, dripping with bitterness. 'Christ. That'd make sense, I suppose.'

'Did it come as a shock to you?' she risked. 'When you found out about her?'

He said nothing for a moment.

'You didn't know — was that it? You didn't know who she was. But other people did, in the town. And you must have suspected there was something in her background.'

Eamonn looked into space for a while before

starting to talk. 'You know, Miss Maguire, when I finally found out the truth, I was sort of happy. Can you believe that? It made sense, all those years . . . I'd even heard about the case — I'd have been coming eighteen then. You're too young to remember, of course?'

But he looked at her anyway, as if expecting an answer.

'Yes,' she said. 'I heard about it, though.'

'Course you did. The whole bloody country heard about it. I mean, wouldn't *you* change your name, if everyone knew that about you? Jesus, it explained so much — the way she was with me, always shying away, why she'd never talk of her past, her family . . . ' He tailed off, staring at the wedding ring on his hand.

Paula leaned closer. The light in the room seemed worn out, the yellow frazzle struggling against the October gloom. 'You weren't angry, then?'

'How could I be? It wasn't her fault, she was only wee . . . ' His voice cracked and he swallowed. 'I suppose I was sad. Yes, sad — you know, that she didn't tell me before, about the wean. That way, maybe we could have . . . ' He fell into silence, looking at the ring again, as it glinted in the dull light.

Paula cleared her throat. 'You decided you had to protect Angela, no matter what, was that it?'

'Yes.'

'No matter who found out.' He was nodding slowly. She paused. 'Eamonn. Tell me when you realised Cathy knew.'

Something flared in his eyes and died. 'I

407

suppose you know about all those papers she had.'

'Yes.' There was no point in lying now. 'Her friends had them. It was the girls who told Cathy — at school, that last day.' Paula tested the ropes on her wrist — no give. The fibres ate into her skin. She leaned forward as much as she could. 'Eamonn, is that why Cathy came to see you, the day she disappeared?' She didn't want to say 'died'. Not yet. She had to play this carefully.

Again his eyes darkened. 'Well, miss, I see you know everything. Or you think you do, anyway.'

'No, not everything.' The rest she was guessing. But she was getting surer.

'I bet you have it all worked out. Yes, Cathy came down to the office, ran out of school early, crying her wee eyes out. She showed me all this stuff she's found out about her mother, these news reports — way before she was born, even. Someone at the Mission knew, she said. Somebody had found out.'

Did Eamonn know about Maddy too? 'You know who it was?'

'No. Maybe that fella Ed, he might know. He came to me after Cathy went missing — he knew I'd seen her last. Seems she was trying to ring him, over and over. Only he didn't want to see her. He'd some other wee girl lined up by then.' Eamonn's voice broke, bitter. 'He ruined her, my Cathy. He broke her. Said he'd tell everyone what he knew, if I — if I didn't support him. He didn't want to go down for it.'

So that explained why Eamonn had supported the Mission. It was as simple and nasty as blackmail. 'And Cathy went to you when she couldn't find Ed?'

'Aye, she was half-hysterical already. I tried to calm her down . . . She ran off anyhow, before I could stop her. That must have been when ould Ken lifted her. But it turned out he'd an alibi.'

Paula gulped. 'What happened to her school-bag? I always wondered.'

Eamonn leaned across his workbench and pushed aside a tarpaulin, the same type that had been wrapped round Cathy. Underneath was a black shoulder-bag with button-badges on it. A yellow smiley face seemed to smirk at Paula and her vision swam, but she carried on as if they were having a normal conversation.

'And her shoes — you hid them, her normal school shoes?' He nodded. She said. 'But she was wearing different ones that day. Heels. They're still in the rack out there. You missed that.'

He frowned, then shook his head. 'Hardly matters now, does it.'

'And then the knife — the blood . . . did you do it?'

Eamonn put his head in his hands. A strangled laugh. 'The poor weans! That bloody ould cat of theirs. Well, you saw through that and all.'

She held her breath. 'Eamonn, the reason you did all this — supported Ed when it turned out he knew something, and killed the cat — it was because . . . Cathy died here, didn't she?'

He said nothing. She couldn't see his face. 'Eamonn? I saw the blood in the kitchen. Cathy went home, didn't she, after she'd been in your office, and she'd threatened to confront Angela;

she had all the evidence . . . and you — you had to protect your wife, didn't you, even if your own daughter . . . ' Paula was watching him very closely.

Eamonn's mouth was open but she never got to hear what he was going to say, because at that point they heard a splintering at the door, and Aidan's voice shouting, 'Maguire! Are you in there?'

★ ★ ★

Eamonn Carr's shed, despite being used as a prison, did not have a sturdy lock, and Aidan was holding a crowbar he'd somehow acquired. Paula made a mental note to ask him where, then wondered how hard she'd been hit on the head. She focused. Aidan was swinging his weapon wildly at Eamonn Carr. 'Get those ropes off her. What the hell are you playing at, man?'

Eamonn was now speaking calmly, but his hands were shaking. 'She was trespassing on my property. I've a right to protect my family.'

'Aye, we know what you've been up to with your family.' The crowbar was trembling as Aidan tried to insert himself between her and the man. 'Wee Cathy comes home one day and then a week later she's in the canal with her throat cut. Even the bloody useless Missing Persons' Unit could work that one out eventually.'

Paula sucked all the air she could into her battered lungs. 'Aidan! *Shut up!*'

Eamonn moved so quickly they hardly saw. He slipped his hand behind him into the workbench, and when it came up he was holding something black and solid. Of course, Paula's dazed mind thought, his father — of course Patsy would have had a few round the place. Then she realised that where he'd got the gun from wasn't what she should be worrying about, but rather the fact that it was pointing at Aidan's head.

34

For a moment, the only sound in the shed was the rain drumming onto the bitumened roof. Paula was twisted painfully in the chair, Aidan frozen between her and Eamonn, who was holding the gun out calmly, in the same manner with which he'd offered a cup of tea not a million years ago. Then the window was lit by a bloom of purple light and a bang which made them all jump — a firework. Eamonn fumbled the gun for a second, and she saw how close to the edge he was. Aidan took advantage of it to grab for the shiny black barrel; Paula squeezed her eyes shut as the men tussled, every cell in her body waiting for the bang, the smell of smoke . . . It didn't come. She opened her eyes. Eamonn had righted himself and was still holding the gun at Aidan's head.

Aidan, now backed into the corner, met her eyes and tentatively lifted his arms. 'All right, no need to lose the head, Eamonn, or mine, ha ha. One of ould Patsy's, is it?'

Eamonn sighed, as if irritated by this reference to his father. 'You're a cheeky fecker, O'Hara. Always were. Loud-mouthed like your own da.'

'And look what happened to him. Patsy know anything about it, you reckon?'

Oh shut up, Aidan, shut up, shut up! Now wasn't the time for this.

Eamonn shut one eye, either mulling things

over or taking aim. 'He got shot in the head, your father.'

'Yeah. Didn't think these things ran in the family, but . . . ' Aidan caught Paula's agonised look and raised his hands higher. 'All right, all right, let's take it easy. I'll put down my offensive weapon if you do the same.' He laid the crowbar against the wall with exaggerated care.

Eamonn held firm for a minute, then lowered the gun, rubbing the arm that held it as if it was heavy. It looked heavy, dull and black. 'I never wanted any of this to happen. You should have let it be. It was all there for you, a suspect, a weapon in the travellers' camp, for the love of God, but you kept poking your noses in. Why couldn't you let it be? Close the case up? Jesus, if you'd any idea how much was let slide in the old days.'

'But it's not the old days,' Paula said, hearing her own voice high and weedy. 'You know it's not. That's all past. Your father died for it, and so did Aidan's. Come on now. Think about your wee girls, and your boy, and let's stop all this.'

Eamonn looked between them, the gun now hanging uselessly at his side. 'I can't.' He sounded almost regretful.

'Course you can. We can sort all this out, we can protect Angela, we can take care of the kids. It'll all be fine. If we can just talk it over . . . ' Her hands were still tied. She was making frantic head-motions to Aidan to try to grab the gun. His eyes were dark, frightened. He shook his head. No. It was too risky in the small space.

She tried again. 'Eamonn, my hands are really

413

hurting like this. Could you let me go, do you think? Imagine if someone had Angela, hurting her like this. I know you want to protect her, but it doesn't have to come out about who she is. No one has to know. Anyway it wasn't her fault, whatever she did. She was only twelve. No one would blame her.'

He was shaking his head. 'You don't understand. You think you know it all, but you don't know the half of it.'

'Well, try me.' She shifted her hands against the coarse ropes, trying to ease the pressure. 'I know you didn't mean to hurt Cathy. She was upset, wasn't she, when she found out about her mother. She was going to expose her, was that it? A teenage girl, fighting with her mum, not understanding who she could hurt — '

'No!' The gun was up again. 'I told you. You don't understand.'

'You just had to protect Angela, so you followed Cathy home when she ran out of your office, and there was a row in the kitchen, and then . . . you never meant to do it, did you?'

'No! For God's sake, do you ever listen?' She flinched as his voice rang out. 'I know you think it was me — that *I* did it to her. My wee Cathy.' He paused for a moment. 'She was my first baby, you know that? I thought, when she came, everything would be all right, all the problems — my da, Angela being so strange sometimes . . . I thought it'd all be OK. She'd be the first Carr not hiding under her bed from the men at the door with guns.'

'Eamonn — '

'*Shut up, will you!* You never stop talking, and everything you say is wrong. I didn't hurt my Cathy. I'd say it was me, if it'd help, I'd do that. But it's too late now. Too late for that.'

Paula stared at him. From day one, when she'd first come to the house, the suspicion had been growing in her like a hard kernel, how his wife had sat on the sofa, catatonic, how she'd flinched when he put his arms round her, how terrified she'd been when Paula tried to talk to her at the house. Then finding the knife at the traveller site — and the missing cat — she'd been sure it was Eamonn. Not Ed Lazarus, although he'd certainly played his part in the destruction of Cathy and other girls in the town. The girl's own father.

Now she looked into Eamonn's eyes and she wasn't sure any more. Why would he lie? He was the one holding the gun. 'Then what . . . '

'Paula,' Aidan interrupted softly, his hands still aloft. 'That's why I came. She was gone, when I went to look for her.'

'Who?'

'Maddy Goldberg. She saw me in the crowd and she ran. I chased her but she got away. She had a car — a silver Polo.'

'Oh my God. Really?'

Eamonn was looking blank. Was this one piece of the puzzle he didn't know?

Paula looked away from the gun's dark muzzle and tried to explain. 'Eamonn, did you ever wonder about the baby — Angela's baby?' She saw his face contract, remembering that Cathy had been his first child, but not his wife's.

'No. She never talked about it until — until Cathy showed me all that stuff.'

'I think Angela's daughter — it was a girl, Eamonn, I'm sorry — well, I think she was trying to find her birth mother. I think she came to find Angela.'

Confusion crumpled his face. 'But I thought . . . it said in the papers the wean went to the States, to be adopted.'

'She did. But she came back to Ireland, to Ballyterrin. I'm fairly sure, anyway. Eamonn, I think she was working at the Mission.'

He made a strangled noise in his throat.

'I think she made friends with Cathy — on purpose, trying to get close to the family. I think it was her who told Cathy's friends about Angela, and gave them the papers. You said you wondered where she got them, didn't you?'

'Oh Christ.' Still holding the gun, he clawed at his head. 'Oh good holy God. That's why — we could have stopped it then. Maybe my Cathy would still be alive.'

This time Aidan interpreted Paula's frantic eye-signals correctly. He moved forward and touched the man on the arm; Eamonn shrugged him off violently, catching Aidan's face with the end of the gun and Paula shut her eyes again, every muscle rigid. But Aidan didn't flinch, even though she saw that the metal had broken the skin of his cheek and blood oozed.

He said, 'I think she went to find Angela, this Maddy girl. She's very unstable, maybe violent — so I'm thinking we should go and find your wife. Where is she, Eamonn? Where's Angela?'

416

The man looked round at them. 'I never wanted any of this to happen.'

'We know. But we need to find Angela now. So if you'd just let Paula there go . . . '

Eamonn swung the gun round, eyes narrowed. 'You have to come with me. I can't just let you walk away, after all this.'

'We'll come,' said Paula quietly. 'We'll find her. Just please, let me go. I can't feel my arms.'

He held the gun trembling in one hand as he felt behind him in the workbench again. For a moment a knife blade flashed green as another firework went off, and they all jumped. Then Eamonn passed it to Aidan. 'Cut her free.'

*   *   *

Outside, the air was damp and clean, spiced with smoke and sulphur. Paula took in deep lungfuls, trying to work some feeling back into her arms. Eamonn still gripped her left elbow, pushing her over the lush wet grass, where her boots left deep, damp footprints. The security light came on, dazzling, illuminating their strange procession. The man with the gun, dressed in a crumpled black suit. Aidan in front, walking backwards so he could watch Paula, still in his old T-shirt and jeans, skin pale in the darkness. And Paula herself, stumbling in the wet as Eamonn pushed her along.

At the gate he let go his grip, training the gun on her. 'Don't move.' With his free hand he reached into his trouser pocket, then threw something at Aidan. The gleam of keys in the air.

'You — drive. I'll say where. Don't try anything. If you're smart — and if you're half the man your da was you'll be doing well — just do what I say. If I have to hurt you, I will.' She imagined Eamonn's father saying the same words to hapless informants, teenage tearaways. That ruthlessness, bred in the bone. But this wasn't the time to think of the past.

'Don't speed,' Eamonn instructed Aidan as they climbed into the car. He sat in the back with Paula, the gun pointed at her. 'We don't want to get picked up by any patrols. Nice and steady. Head out to the bypass and then I'll tell you more.'

It seemed to take forever to drive the black people-carrier through Ballyterrin, the streets crowded with revellers in costume. There was a heavy police presence outside the bars and clubs, and Paula could feel the tension coming off the man, the gun poking into her side. Sometimes Eamonn would let it drop, and she would hold her breath, trying to catch Aidan's eye in the mirror. Then he would remember and grip it firmly, making her gasp and bite her lip. They were nearing the outskirts of town when a shrill noise made them all jump. The gun pushed into Paula's neck, right over where the blood pulsed fast, and she smothered a cry. 'It's my phone. I'm sorry. It's ringing.'

Eamonn withdrew the gun. 'See who it is.'

She fumbled in the pocket of her black jacket. The screen was flashing up Guy's name. 'It's my boss.' Finally, and too late.

'Answer it and tell him you're fine. I don't

418

want them looking for you.'

'I can't!' How could she lie to Guy, at a moment like this?

'You'll have to.' He pressed the metal in harder to her skin and she gulped.

'Hello, Inspector? Is everything OK?' Surely he would hear how hoarse she was, how terrified.

'Oh, there you are.' She could hear the relief in his voice. 'Listen, Katie's been spotted. The woman at the bus station remembered selling her a ticket to Dublin. She paid in fifty-pees, apparently. Must have raided my change pot.'

'She's OK then?'

'She was OK earlier today. Fiacra's at the ferry office now. We think she was going to travel to England, to her mum.'

She tried to keep her voice steady. Eamonn was silent, and she could feel the tension in his arm. In the front, Aidan's eyes were fixed on the road. 'That's great, Guy, really great. I'm sure she'll turn up safe and sound.'

'I hope so. I'm onto the police on the other side. Got a few contacts. The other news is we arrested Lazarus. Found him skulking round the concert in town as you said.'

She closed her eyes. 'Oh. That's good. He give you anything more?'

'Well, he denies having anything to do with Katie, of course, but we won't let him go just yet.' Guy's voice hardened. 'Corry's working on him now. I reckon he's got a lot to tell us about his dad too, and why his mother was so scared she had to run away and hide herself for years.'

'He won't like being in with Corry. He's not a

fan of women in authority, I don't think.' Amazing how normal she could sound, with Eamonn quietly listening, gun gripped tight.

'No. But what I wanted to tell you was we've busted the Goldberg girl's alibi. That teacher at Cathy's school — Sarah Kenny — apparently she had a fit of conscience when she heard Katie was missing too. She admitted she'd lied — it *was* her car, the one we were after. A silver Polo. She lends it to Goldberg sometimes. What we think happened is that Maddy picked Cathy up that Friday afternoon, when she got out of Crawford's car.'

'Oh.' Timing. Wasn't it everything? If only she'd known this a few hours before, things could have been so different. But that was always the way. 'You think she was the killer, then?' She was very aware of Eamonn listening.

'I don't know. I'm not sure what her motive would be, but we've a warrant out for her now — she's to be approached with caution. She's definitely mixed up in it somehow. Where are you, anyway? Gerard said he left you at the cathedral.'

'I'm . . . I was checking out a lead I got from one of the girls. I'll be a few hours.'

'Of course. You should go home. I'm sorry I dragged everyone out. I was just so worried. I started thinking maybe we were wrong about Cathy, maybe there really was a serial killer out there. But hopefully Katie's not in danger. God, I hope so.'

'Yeah.' She swallowed hard, feeling the metal almost choke her.

'See you in the office tomorrow, then? Thank you, Paula. I won't forget this.'

'It's OK.' She bit her tongue, trying desperately to telegraph it. *Help me, Guy, please help me.* 'B-bye then.'

'Bye.' He clicked off, her last lifeline. Eamonn held out his hand, and she put the phone into it without a word.

★ ★ ★

As they got out of town and onto the famous bypass, Eamonn seemed to relax, taking a deep breath. 'O'Hara. Do you know Listowel Road?'

'Aye, I think so. That the wee one up into the hills?'

'Take it.'

Aidan swung off the main road and onto the narrow country road. They passed several large bungalows, curtains open to see the fireworks, but soon the road had narrowed and grass grew down the middle.

'Do I keep going?' The car was now bumping and rocking on the uneven track.

'Keep going until I say.'

They were in deep country now, the sky above pricked full of stars like a night at sea. Eamonn slid down the window — she could see sweat dripping from his forehead — and the night air rolled in, sweet and smoky; the wholesome stink of earth, and wet grass, and cows somewhere not far off. She gulped it in as if it was the best thing she'd ever smelled. Smelling, breathing, that meant you were still alive.

'Here.'

'Here?' Aidan slowed the car suddenly; you could barely see the turn-off. There was a gap in the damp hedge, and a cattle-grid which the car rattled over.

'Pull up there, under the trees.'

The engine died with a splutter and the silence of the countryside was all around them. Paula could hear an owl call, and the soft lowing of cattle in a field nearby. Through the rain, she could make out dark shapes moving under the trees, eyes glowing. They were on a farm of some kind.

'Get out.' Eamonn gestured to her with the gun, and she climbed carefully out, her feet sinking into mud. He clambered after her, the gun slipping in his hand. 'You next, O'Hara.'

Aidan took the keys from the ignition and closed the door with a soft click. He held them out to Eamonn, who said impatiently, 'Never mind that now. The house.'

It rose up before them, ghostly-white, a tarpaulin flapping in the moonlight. This house was half-renovated, unlived-in. Or so it seemed. Below them, fireworks broke the sky over town, flashing green and red and purple in the dark.

Eamonn took Paula's arm again, gesturing to Aidan to go in front of them. 'You walk on. Watch out for anything.'

There was no car anywhere else, so perhaps Maddy hadn't found this place. How would she, anyway? As they rounded the damp, overgrown hill, wet weeds brushing her jeans, Paula suddenly knew where they were. She'd seen it before on the news, the square porch, the barn alongside. 'Is this — '

He jerked her. 'Keep moving.'

Eamonn Carr's family home. That porch in front was the very one in which Patsy Carr, IRA supremo, had been shot dead when he went to answer the door to what he thought was a collection for the church trip to Lourdes. 'You bought it back,' she said softly. 'It's true. You were going to move. Start a new life . . . '

Eamonn looked at her scornfully. 'Just walk, will you. And try to keep your mouth shut, if you can.'

For once she was obeying, and Aidan too was silenced. Paula could hear his heavy breath, and his feet slipping on the wet grass as they laboured up the hill and the house came into view. Eamonn looked between them as if trying to figure out the logistics.

'Stick close together,' he ordered. 'Don't move, I'm warning you. We're going in.'

35

Aidan and Paula bunched up, all arms and legs, while Eamonn went ahead, walking awkwardly backwards so he could keep the gun trained on them. As they reached the front door Paula felt Aidan's chill hand slide into hers. He ran a finger over her chafed wrist and his dark eyes met hers for a second before they both stumbled in after Eamonn. She'd never seen him look so scared, and it sent her into a long spiralling fall of fear. Why had Eamonn brought them here, if not to get rid of them? She gripped Aidan's hand, felt the pulse in the side of his cold wrist.

'Angie?' Eamonn was calling. 'Angie, pet, are you OK?' His voice was different. They'd never heard him speak that way before, as if to a frightened child, or a cherished small animal.

Paula saw several things at once. One, that the door into the house was padlocked shut from the outside. Another, that through the glass window — still sporting new-bought stickers — Angela Carr was sitting on a sofa, in much the same way they'd found her at her own house. She didn't look up at the noise of them outside.

Eamonn was waving the gun at Aidan. 'You. On the key ring, there's one for the padlock. Open it.'

'This wee one?'

'Aye, aye. Open it.' Eamonn wiped his brow with the heel of his hand, and when Aidan had

424

fumbled the door open he pushed in. 'Angie? Are you OK?' He knelt in front of his wife. Paula and Aidan, still holding hands, stood frozen in the doorway. The walls and floor of the room were bare concrete and there was no electricity. Angela was staring into space, her eyes fixed on nothing at all. She was dressed just as beautifully as before, in expensive jeans and a silk jersey, the cuffs of which seemed to have been taped to her arms so she couldn't take it off. A sleeping bag was unrolled on the sofa beside her, and on the floor were packets of food and a Thermos. There was no other furniture. Paula flicked her eyes to Aidan's, desperately. He just shrugged.

Eamonn was pushing back his wife's hair, kissing her tenderly on the forehead. 'Are you all right, love? I'm sorry I couldn't come sooner. It's OK. Tell me you're OK.'

Very slowly, Angela's eyes focused and wandered round the bare room. 'We have visitors, Eamonn,' she stage-whispered.

Eamonn glared at Paula and Aidan. He still held the gun in the crook of his arm, but it was slipping. 'I'm sorry, love. They — well, they found out some things.'

The woman's body tensed, and a shrill cry came out of her.

'No, no, it's OK. They don't know everything.'

Paula moved so her back was braced against the wall, opposite Angela. It would be hard for Eamonn to spin round and shoot from there. She cleared her throat.

'Angela. We just want to help you. You remember that day I came to yours, I said I

425

would help you? And you said — you said no one could.' She fixed her eyes on the wife, trying to block out the husband, who was watching her closely, drawing his gun back into his hand. 'Angela, he's got a gun. But I know he won't hurt you. Just tell me — how long's he been keeping you here? I saw the locks.'

Angela looked confused. 'Eamonn? Who are these visitors?'

'You've met me, Angela. I'm Paula. I was looking for Cathy, only she was never lost, was she? You knew exactly what happened to her. Was it him — did he kill her? She found out who you were — how you got sent to the home, and that your child had come back. Only he couldn't cope with that, could he, not his perfect little wife, damaged like that, the bad press — ' The words kept coming, as if she couldn't stop.

'*Maguire!*' Aidan screamed, ducking.

Eamonn Carr had sprung to his feet, and then he was across the room and pressing the gun to Paula's temple, one hand grasping her round the shoulders. She felt her knees buckle. 'I told you to stop! Why don't you ever listen?' He was trembling.

Aidan looked round him, muttering, 'Oh fuck oh fuck oh fuck.' He stared wildly at Paula. 'Oh Christ, Maguire, just stay still, for once in your life, will you? Eamonn! What do you want, man? You don't want to hurt her.' Then he was lunging for Paula, and Eamonn was raising the gun, his other hand still round Paula's neck, and a bang rang out. She felt the noise inside her nose and teeth, and then it was replaced by another sound: Aidan howling. 'Fucking hell! Ah Jesus, Mary, and St Joseph!'

'*Aidan!*' she choked out. He was falling back against the wall, clutching at his arm. She saw bright beads of blood run down his pale skin.

Eamonn jerked her neck; she couldn't breathe. Her hair was over her face, getting in her eyes and mouth. She was panting. The gun was rock-hard against her head, cold as ice. Aidan was still hissing and howling in the corner. The only person in the room unmoved was Angela Carr. Slowly, she got to her feet, moving like an automaton. She was crossing the room. As if he'd spoken it aloud, Paula saw Aidan, blinded by pain, wonder about grabbing her, threatening her in some way, and not being able to do it. Angela walked up to her husband, who was still half-strangling Paula. She put her hands on either side of his face. Kissed him on the mouth, briefly. Then, as he sagged, she took the gun gently from his hand. Paula dropped to her knees, fighting for breath. Angela held the gun out as if she'd never touched one before, testing its weight.

She hoisted it in both hands and peered down the sight. 'I wish you wouldn't leave this thing lying around, Eamonn. The weans might get hold of it.' Her voice was high, artificial.

Her husband, slumped against the wall, began to cry. 'For God's sake, Angie, we have to stop them. They *know*, Angie. Not everything, but they know.'

She looked at Paula. Her eyes were green and clear, lovely. Like her daughter Cathy's must

427

have been. Like her first-born daughter Madeleine's were. When she spoke again, her voice was lower, harsher. As if the other one was a part she'd been playing all her life. 'You think you know all about me, do you?'

Paula couldn't speak. She could feel the ache in her neck, from where the gun had pressed. She tried to twist her head to see Aidan; he'd fallen silent. Why had he fallen silent?

'Yes, I'm Angela McGreavy. Yes, I got pregnant when I was twelve and they made me have the wean. And they took her away and sold her to America and I had to live in that home until I was eighteen.' She eyed her husband with something like compassion. 'Poor Eamonn, he never knew. Damaged goods you got, wasn't it, pet?'

'No — no.' He was sobbing on the floor. 'I'd not have cared. I loved you.'

'You wanted it all — lovely wife, lovely kids, big car, nice house. So did I. I thought we deserved it, the shite childhoods that we both had. But it was all a lie, wasn't it? I was trash, like *he* always said.' She sighed, looking at the gun in her hand. 'He said he'd never leave me, even after he was gone. And he was right. You believe in ghosts, Paula?'

'N-no.' She was struggling to draw breath into her lungs. Out of the corner of her eye she saw the slow rise and fall of Aidan's chest. Thank God he was still breathing.

Angela laughed. 'They exist, all right. Or haunting does.'

Who did she mean by 'he'? Could it be Ron

428

Almeira again, who'd fathered Ed Lazarus? Had he also been with Angela, back in the eighties, when she was little more than a child? Paula tried again. 'Angela, it wasn't your fault. We can help you.'

'Nobody helped me when I was twelve, did they? And then my Cathy . . . ' She shook her head as if to clear it. 'My Cathy, some fella pawing at her the same way. Still no abortion allowed in this country. I couldn't have her going through that, a baby at her age, or taking her away to England to get rid of it. And she comes in saying, 'I know all about you, it's disgusting, I met this girl at the Mission and she's your daughter, Mammy. Why did you lie to Daddy all this time.''

'Angie!' Eamonn Carr's voice was practically a scream. 'You don't have to do this, we can get rid of them!'

'Ah, pet.' She bent down to him. 'It's too late, do you not see that? I've had my fill of keeping secrets. I know what I did and I'm ready to take my pay.'

Paula said, 'But it wasn't your fault, Angela, you were only little. It was his fault, not yours.'

'Ah, whist, would you, girl. You're a right busybody. I know all that. I'm talking about what I did to my Cathy.'

Silence. The sound of Eamonn's sobs. A harsh wet breath from Aidan. Angela said, 'I don't know what went on in my head that day. I was in the kitchen — I've a lovely kitchen, have you seen it? Like I always wanted as a wean, all white and clean, lovely crockery and all. And in she

429

comes, my Cathy. She knows it all. All that — filth. The filth of the past. She drags it in like shit on her shoes. 'I'll tell Daddy,' she says. 'I'll tell the wee ones — everyone'll know about you. You lied to me. I've a sister and you never said.' And then she tells me she's in trouble too — she's two months' gone. And I'm doing the dishes. And I'm washing this knife, this set of good knives Eamonn was after bringing me from London. They can't go in the dishwasher, and for the life of me I don't know what happened — it wasn't *me* for a moment.'

'Angela. No, please. No,' Eamonn wept.

'Next thing she's there on the floor, blood all coming out of her throat, and she's choking on it, and the weans are in the next room. I tried to stop it, but — well. It was too late. You can't take these things back.'

'It was you,' Paula said quietly. 'You killed Cathy.'

'So you really didn't know.' Angela sighed. 'Ah sure, what odds. I haven't the strength to hide any more. Yes, I killed her. There's not much you could do with me that'd be worse than I've already been through.'

'You think *you've* been through a lot.' A new voice, coming in from the door on a gust of smoke and wind. All four of them turned, Eamonn bent over crying, Aidan barely conscious, Paula frozen, Angela still holding the gun weighed in both hands. In the half-light, Maddy Goldberg's face was ghostly. The sight of her made Paula's breath die in her throat. She'd seen eyes like that before — dark, dead. She'd seen

430

them across interview rooms, behind prison bars. The eyes of someone who would do anything, and often had. Maddy's hand was outstretched. In it, a carving knife.

'It's you,' said Angela, sighing. 'You've come back.'

'That's right.' Maddy's voice shook as much as her hands. 'You can't get rid of me that easily, *Mom*.'

At her feet, Paula felt Eamonn sag even more, a whimper in his throat.

Angela sneered, 'For the love of God, girl, I'm not your mother. You've a mother in America, who loved you and clothed you and fed you all these years.'

'And you — you wanted to rip me out of you, throw me in a bucket of blood. You're sick, you know that? You stabbed your own kid — my sister! — and you wanted to kill me before I was even born.'

Angela was looking down at the gun. 'You'll never understand what I went through. The stage I got to — all I wanted to do was die, and take you with me.'

'I was innocent!'

'There's no such thing, Madeleine. That's what they called you, is it? The fallen woman. That's a feckin' joke.'

Maddy lunged at her mother, the knife in her trembling hand. Angela still held the gun, lolling lightly between her fingers. She didn't flinch as the girl brought the blade to her neck, blubbering out her words.

'You make me sick! What kind of woman

431

wants to murder her baby? Then when she's grown, and she only wants to know her mom, so bad she travels thousands of miles to see her, you send her away again! I tried so hard to meet you — I made friends with Cathy, even got to know her damn teacher at school, everything — all for you! Just so I could get to you! And God, it made me want to puke sometimes, the way Cathy talked: we're moving to a new house in the country, we're all so happy, me and my mom and dad and all the little kiddies . . . She even told me where this place was. That Friday, that was my chance. She rang me. She was in tears — Ed blew her off, of course, it's what he does. So I said I'd pick her up, take her home, talk to you for her. I was hoping you'd be pleased to see me. But you hadn't even thought about me. All you cared about was your other kids. Your *real* kids. You told me to get out in case they saw!' Maddy jerked the blade away. 'And then when I ran off — you killed her! Your own goddamn kid!'

So Maddy had been to the house on the day Cathy died. That explained why she hadn't been at the Mission meeting. Paula knelt on the concrete floor, breathing slowly.

Angela said, 'I told you, I'm no mother of yours. You were lucky I didn't strangle you at birth.'

'Angie,' Eamonn was moaning. 'Why didn't you tell me? Why didn't you say she found you?'

Angela ignored her husband, focused on her first-born daughter. 'Girl, you've your whole life to live. You're twenty-five. Aye, I know your age

432

to the minute. As if I could forget when they cut you out of me. I was only a child.'

'That's no excuse! It wasn't my fault you were messing around with boys so young! I mean, what kind of slut were you? Twelve! And you never put his name down on the birth certificate, so I can't even find who my father is. All these years, I just wanted a kind dad, someone who'd teach me, look after me — what Cathy always had. She had everything! I was the one you gave away, like a piece of garbage.' Maddy was crying hard now.

Angela's voice was cold. 'A father. Aye, that's what a father's meant to do, all right.'

'So why wouldn't you tell me, when I came that day? I just want to know who my dad is! It's like — it's like a piece of me's been missing all my life!' Gesturing with the knife against her tie-dye top, the girl pleaded.

'He's dead.'

'So you do know who he was? Who — '

'He's dead, and when they let me out for his funeral, I spat on his grave. You want to know what a father is? To me, a father's someone who came into my bed every day from when my ma passed away. Sticking his big hands in my knickers. Shoving himself in me. At me day and night, and then when he gets me in trouble, he looks the police in the eye and he says, 'Officers, my daughter's a liar, she's been going round with boys, now will you take her away and lock her up.' '

Everyone in the room held their breath, except for Eamonn, who continued to cry.

Maddy's sobs came fast and uncontrollable. 'No, it's not true! I don't believe it. You're just twisted, you want to make me hate myself more, oh God!'

'Take it or leave it, girl, it doesn't change the truth. Your da was my da. Happens all the time, especially in Ireland. You'd want to have seen how many girls in that home were there because of their das, or their uncles, or their brothers — their grandas, even.' Angela laughed harshly. 'And once they had us locked up, you know what they did to us there, the priests and the do-gooders who ran those places? They took our babies, and got their blood money for them, and they beat us, and they broke us even more.' She looked at her daughter. 'So maybe you'll see why I never wanted to birth you into that.'

Maddy was weeping.

'And maybe I was right, girl. You've not had a very happy life, by the looks of it.'

Gently hoisting the gun under one arm, she put out her other and took the girl's hand. Maddy flinched as Angela rolled up her sleeve, revealing the painful legacy of scars.

'You cut yourself. Aye, I tried to do the same. Much good it did me. Wouldn't it have been better for us all, you and me and him there, and even my Cathy, if that busybody social worker had let me be? Just let me die there, and you with me, in that bathroom?'

Then it was all happening. Maddy made an inarticulate noise deep in her throat, and lunged at her mother. Outside, a distant boom went off, and the room was filled for a second with a brilliant green light. It was followed a second later by another bang, closer, louder, and a flash in the gloom. The gun. When darkness fell again there was a sound of screaming. A woman screaming.

'Angie! Oh Christ, Angie. Oh no, pet, why did you do it, why?' Eamonn was crawling to his wife, who had collapsed on the floor, gurgling blood. He pushed aside the girl, who was shrieking, weeping. The knife fell from her hand, unused. In Angela Carr's hand the gun was still smoking, her eyes opened wide and unseeing at the fireworks, as blood trickled dark from the hole she'd blown in the bottom of her jaw.

Epilogue

One month later
Ballyterrin, November

Paula winced as she put up her hand to knock on Guy's door. Though she'd been discharged from hospital after one night, treated for mild shock and some bruising, her shoulders still ached and the chafing marks on her wrists were visible, if faded. She could still sometimes feel a cold spot on her neck, where the muzzle of the gun had pressed.

Guy was, as usual, frowning down at the pile of paper on his desk. The aftermath of the Cathy Carr/Majella Ward investigation had caused, in the words of Fiacra Quinn, an almighty pile of steaming cowshite.

'There you are.'

'Here I am.'

'You'd better come in.'

She sat down gingerly on the edge of the hard plastic chair. Her time off had been spent recuperating, PJ fussing round her with cups of tea and Pat's buns, the two of them conspiring to keep her from the phone and never out of the house on her own. Eventually Paula had feigned needing tampons while Pat was at her Zumba class, knowing PJ wouldn't offer to go to the chemist for this particular errand. Since she didn't actually need tampons, she'd used the brief alone-time to slip into the office. It was quiet, nobody there but Guy, computers turned off. No one knew quite what was happening, and in the meantime the others had gone back to their own stations.

'You're OK, then?' he asked.

'I'm fine. My arm's a bit stiff, but nothing lasting.' She didn't mention the nightmares. Not a few mornings she'd found herself flung awake, clutched by memories.

His face was grim. 'You were very lucky.'

'I know.'

'And how's O'Hara?'

'OK, I hear. He's meant to do physio on the arm, but I reckon he won't get much beyond lifting pints to his mouth.' Pat had been in her element with Aidan back under her roof. Eamonn's bullet had only grazed his arm, and he too would recover well. He and Paula had avoided each other since that night, as if afraid to rupture the fragile peace of recovery. But she'd have to face him sometime.

Guy said, 'I suppose things could have been a lot worse.'

That was true. After a short autopsy, the body of Angela Carr, formerly Angela McGreavy, was released to her husband for a private funeral. Eamonn had stood down from the council and it was rumoured his businesses would be up for sale soon too. The four surviving children were being cared for by his mother in her smart new bungalow.

The newspapers had a field day, of course: the lurid details of the McGreavy case dug up, the mother who had killed her own daughter, and the girl who hadn't been believed when she said her own father had fathered her child. There were renewed calls to compensate the victims of the Safe Harbour homes in Ireland, and to change the law to allow adoptees to find their birth parents. The Mission had also been quietly shut down, although the lovely Maeve Cooley said it was only a matter of time before it came back in another guise. Ed Lazarus, though banned from working with children, had in the end not been charged with any crimes, since it couldn't be proved he'd forced any of the girls to have sex with him. There was also much thundering in the press about cults and why weren't schools doing more to protect our children, blah blah.

Meanwhile, in the South, an investigation had been opened into the missing girls on Paula's list — minus Rachel Reilly, who had run away from her family, pregnant, and was laid to rest in Birmingham, where her son Ed had recently returned. Paula wasn't sure if he'd contacted the Reilly family at all before he went, but at least they now knew what fate had befallen their sister. A week before, the PSNI had taken in ground-penetrating radar to the site of the old Safe Harbour home, which had also held the Ballyterrin branch of God's Shepherd back in 1985, and later the Mission. Buried under fresh concrete by the back door, they'd uncovered the skeleton of what looked to be a woman in her late teens. Tests were still going on, but it seemed likely this would be prove to be the last resting-place of Alice Dunne, Alice with the beautiful smile who'd gone out one night and never come home. The girl, whoever she was, also appeared to have been several months' pregnant when she died.

The inquiry would rumble on for some time, Paula was sure, and it wasn't at all guaranteed they'd be able to extradite Ron Almeira, even if they could prove Alice's death matched the dates he'd been in Ireland. When the body was found, the unit had been overwhelmed with calls from all over Ireland, families whose daughters had gone to God's Shepherd groups in the seventies and eighties. Many had never been reported missing, thought to have run off, moved to England, or simply lost touch. Now it seemed some would have met a darker fate. There was still a long way to go before the deaths of Angela and Cathy Carr, not to mention Louise McCourt and all the rest, would have any lasting legacy.

'So.' Paula waited to hear her fate. 'You met with the Chief Constable.'

'Yes.' Guy spoke heavily. 'Well, as you can imagine there was fall-out. The Majella case, it caused a lot of problems. But on the other hand, since she wasn't really missing, it wasn't our fault. And we did find her — thanks to the rapport you built with her sister.'

Paula inclined her head, accepting the compliment. It didn't seem to matter much in the wake of what had happened. One found, one more lost. 'And Cathy?' It still hurt to think of the girl they could never have saved, choked by

439

weeds in the bottom of the dark water. Killed by her own desperate mother, another child no one had helped.

'Again, she was never lost either.' He grimaced bleakly. 'Some Missing Persons Unit we turned out to be. In both cases, it was the family who did it.'

'That's usually the way, sadly.'

'I know. I quoted them your research. Depressing reading, but on the other hand it makes the public feel safer, if the most likely person to kill their kids is themselves. Strange, but true.'

'Oh. I see. So — '

'So I presented it all to the authorities, that at least we'd solved the cases, and the ones we didn't even know were cases, and we'd put an end to the Mission's work. That chap you found from the anti-cult group, Paddy Boyle, he holds a lot of sway down South. And the families of all those other missing girls, they've been vocal too. At least we hopefully did what we set out to do — found some answers, after all this time. It looks as if quite a few cases could be solved, in the end.'

She frowned at him suspiciously. 'All this is sounding quite positive.'

'I know.' Guy looked up and she saw how torn he was. 'Paula — they've commissioned us for another two years. Not just that — they want us to officially co-ordinate and advise on all new high-risk cases North and South of the border. It's unprecedented.'

'Oh, but — '

'And I don't know how to feel about it. I mean, Katie running off to London, it showed me how unhappy she was. I'd let my family basically fall apart under my nose.'

Katie had been traced the day after Angela's death to a women's refuge in West London, where her mother Tess had moved after putting the family's house on the market.

'How is she now?'

He shrugged. 'She's as well as can be expected.'

'Will she be coming home?' It was a loaded question, Paula knew. What was going to happen now, to confused Katie, bereaved Tess, and her foundering marriage to Guy? Could they recover from what had happened? Paula had a flash of regret thinking of her night with him — ill-advised, pointless, going nowhere. She'd not even be able to comfort him now.

'I just don't know. We have to talk, Tess and I. There's a lot to go over.' So he didn't know yet if he'd take the job in Ballyterrin. It had held nothing but sorrow for him, so she could understand why he'd leave. He looked at her. 'And you? There's a job here, if you want it. Corry wants you for her team too.'

'Well. I took the job on secondment, as you know — and my dad's better now.'

'But London — do you have much to go back to?'

Paula said nothing to that, thinking of her sparse flat overlooking the sluggish river, long evenings in front of DVDs with just her case-notes, the pull of the tide outside her flat. 'I don't know. I haven't decided.'

'Right. Listen, Paula . . . ' He paused. 'There's something else. I wondered for a long time should I tell you this. I mean, you've had such a rough time of it.'

'I'm OK. What is it?' She braced herself for more awful revelations about the Mission, about Maddy, now sectioned and suicidal again, about the McGreavy family. But nothing prepared her for what he said next.

'As you know, one of the old files we were given was your mother's.'

'Oh.' She blinked. 'There won't be anything there. It was all picked over many times.'

'But that's the thing. This man who's getting out of prison — Sean Conlon — the one who most likely killed John O'Hara, well, he's been hinting he knows other things. He wants protection in exchange for information — he's got some powerful enemies on the outside.'

'Oh.' *No. No. Not this. Not now.*

'I'm sorry, Paula, but it seems he might know something about your mother. Hers was one of the names he mentioned.'

She looked down at what Guy was pushing across the table. An A4 envelope, very slim.

'I didn't know what to do. It's there, if you decide you want to take it further. He hasn't talked yet, but — he might.'

Paula sat looking at the envelope for a long time. Then she got slowly to her feet, slipping it into her bag. 'Thank you, Guy. For everything. And you shouldn't blame yourself, for Cathy, or for any of it.'

He looked up at her, tired, wry. 'Neither should you, Paula.'

★ ★ ★

On the wide elbow of the Thames, boats passed, shrouded in sea-mist. Mournful hoots made it up to the windows of Paula's Docklands flat, as she knelt on the window-seat looking down. A whole sweep of city on the edge of a vast world. The river curling and twisting about it, opening wide and generous to the salt of the sea. She'd lived here in this city, hiding herself among the crowds, for twelve years. Yet still the sea had swept her home, jetsam on a chill northern shore. *Return to Sender.* She'd ended up exactly where she'd come from. Ballyterrin, its ravaged heart, its dark secrets. Home.

Paula scrubbed a patch in the steamed-up window, and gave a last look at the river that had been her companion for so long. For a moment, a wave of something swamped her — sorrow, nausea, fear — and she pressed her face to the cool glass until it passed. Then she picked up her bag from the floor. Inside was the crackle of the brown envelope Guy had given her. Still unopened after a week. Maybe, soon, she'd have the strength to see what it held.

Never enormously homey, the flat had been emptied of its books and files, pots and pans, clothes and toiletries. The shelves and cupboards had the forlorn look of leaving, stray bits of pasta in the larder, the fridge standing open and unlit. A cleaning company would come in the

443

following day, and then the keys would be handed back to the letting agency, and soon there'd be no trace of the life that Paula Maguire of Ballyterrin had lived here.

One thing remained, and she crossed to the fridge door, removing the strawberry-shaped magnet. The photo had curled a little from being out in the air. She smoothed down the sides, then looked for a moment at the image of the smiling red-haired woman. *Where did you go?* The question she hadn't allowed herself to ask for so many years, now wide open and waiting once again. Because, as dozens of families now knew, thanks to her work, it was never really too late. There was always still a terrible hope, long after you'd given up. That maybe, just maybe, you would find what you'd lost. *Hope.* She sometimes thought it was the hardest thing of all.

Paula slipped the photo into the envelope, switched off the last light, and went out.

★ ★ ★

There was just one more thing to do before she caught the Gatwick Express for her flight back to Belfast. The address she'd looked up on Google Maps was a large house in Chiswick, in the flat rolling west of the city, giving way to the fields round Heathrow, where she'd once found another lost girl who wasn't really lost.

There was no real need for the last errand. This girl also had never been missing in the technical sense. But in some ways, Paula saw now, it was easy to be lost in plain sight.

Paula walked from the tube, past stylish restaurants and boutiques, a thin rain spattering on her hair and trench-coat. As usual, she had no umbrella. At the entrance to the street she wanted, the trees wet and green, another wave of nausea hit her, and she bent over, hands on her knees, until it eased. Christ, if this was the after-effects of shock, it was taking a long time to pass.

Walking slowly on, she consulted the map function on her phone and knocked on the door of a large red-brick house. She saw children's play equipment in the garden beyond, a discreet bronze plaque that said this wasn't the private home you might think. There were footsteps, a trill of bells, and the door was opened by a tall woman in a long dress, bangles on her arm. Dark hair curled in a plait, hooded eyes.

She cleared her throat. 'Hello. It's Paula.'

Tess Brooking looked at her for a long moment. 'I suppose you'd better come in.'

★   ★   ★

The house was light and airy, and through one door Paula glimpsed a baby in a cradle, a young skinny girl rocking her. 'You get a lot of women here?'

'It's a place they can come to if they need it. I'm a midwife, so when I wanted somewhere I could go to find peace — this seemed right.'

'Same for Katie?' Paula risked.

Tess frowned over her shoulder as she led

Paula into a back sitting room, full of old mismatched chairs and vases stuffed with wild flowers. A place for women, you could feel it in the air. Like at St Bridget's. 'I've already told the police. Katie wasn't ever missing. She ran away to find me, and as soon as she tracked me down, she was fine.'

'Was she?'

Tess paused for a moment. 'I know not everyone believes in abortion, but our philosophy here is choice. Millions of women don't have the choice, none at all, including those in Northern Ireland.'

'I know that.' Paula wasn't invited to sit, so she stood by the bay window looking out on the lovely, overgrown garden, slick and green with rain.

'Katie's fifteen, she's been through enough already. It was her decision to have it done, and I helped her out.'

'I know.' She faced the woman head-on. 'I'm not here to judge.'

'So, why have you come, if you're not trying to interfere?' Tess crossed her arms.

'I needed to see. I can't explain.' Paula shrugged. 'I need to see she's safe.' To move her from the lost pile to the found. Left to right. To put her in the past.

Tess said nothing, but crossed the room in long strides, bracelets jingling. At the window she pointed out, and at the back of the wet garden Paula could just make out a sort of summerhouse in the trees, and inside it a flash of red anorak and dark hair. Katie Brooking,

446

huddled against the weather. 'She'll be fine, like I said. Now, is that all?'

Paula swallowed. 'Yes. I just wanted to say — how sorry I am. About Jamie.' She saw Tess stiffen. 'And that I didn't protect her. Katie. I should have seen how unhappy she was.'

Tess's voice dropped a few degrees. 'They're my children, Paula. I don't see what it has to do with you.'

'No. Nothing. I just wanted to say it.'

Tess nodded slowly. 'I see what this is. You're feeling guilty, because you slept with my husband.' She saw Paula's face. 'Oh yes, Katie told me all about finding you in the kitchen the next day.'

'I — I thought he was getting divorced. It was only once. We were drinking, and something happened, something very bad, and I suppose we just . . . ' She tailed off. 'I'm sorry. Really, I'm so sorry.' She clamped her mouth shut as another burst of sickness came. 'I'm sorry, Tess, is there a bathroom I can use?'

In the small room to the right of the front door, Paula breathed in the smell of floral soap as she retched into the toilet bowl. Nothing came up; she hadn't eaten all day. A polite notice over the cistern reminded residents not to flush any sanitary towels. She pulled the old-fashioned chain and went back into to the sitting room, wiping her mouth. 'God. Sorry. I'm making such a mess of this.'

Tess laughed shortly. 'Don't bother apologising. Just tell me one thing, then you can leave.'

She braced herself. 'Yes?'

447

'Is it his?' Tess was staring at Paula with those unreadable eyes.

'Is what his?'

Tess twisted her mouth. 'Come on. I think you owe me more than that, Paula.'

'I don't know what you mean.' Fear was creeping up her legs. Suddenly she couldn't breathe. 'Is what his? I don't — '

'Come on. I heard you throw up. You've been sick like that a lot recently?'

'I've been under the weather . . . ' Since the incident with Angela, it was true she'd felt all wrong. But that was to be expected. Wasn't it?

'Is that why you came here? You want to rub my face in it?'

'Listen, I really don't know what you mean. I came to see Katie, that's all.'

Tess made an impatient noise and crossed the room. The woman's slim fingers approached Paula's stomach. She just stood there paralysed, as Tess probed her. 'Well, it's early days, but you could definitely be a few months gone.'

Paula gaped at her. Tess raised her eyebrows. 'Paula, come on now. You're a smart enough girl, I imagine. It didn't occur to you that you might be pregnant?'

The room was swimming. Rain dissolved on the window. 'No. Eh, no, it didn't.'

'But you could be?'

Paula thought of the night with Guy, careful even when sunk with the weight of despair. But things could go wrong, of course, things could fail. Everyone could fail, however hard they tried. And then Aidan, as always full of fire and

448

thunder, no idea of caution, of consequences.

Guy. Aidan.

'I — I — maybe. I don't — '

'And is it Guy's? Is it my husband's?'

Slowly, Paula shook her head. 'I'm sorry,' she said. 'I honestly haven't a clue.'

Acknowledgements

I'd like to thank everyone at Headline for their support and belief in the book, especially Ali Hope, Veronique Norton, and Sam Eades.

Thanks to the staff at Johnson & Alcock and Blake Friedmann literary agencies, especially Oli Munson.

Thanks to everyone who has helped me with bits of research and information, especially Oliver Sindall and Eileen Dorgan for psychological and medical information. At this point writers always say 'and any remaining mistakes are my fault'. In this case it's entirely true — they are definitely my fault and in some places I've deliberately changed how things might function in Ireland. Thanks also to my contacts in the PSNI who didn't want to be named for security reasons, and to my mum and dad for spotting general and medical mistakes. I'm also sorry if I forgot anyone (it's been a while!).

Thanks to everyone who read and commented on early bits of the manuscript, including Mary Flanagan at City Lit and members of the writing class there. Big thanks to Sarah Day, top reader, writer, and friend. Thanks also to everyone at the York Festival of Writing, who were very enthusiastic about the first 3,000 words of this book.

I'm very grateful to anyone who took the time

to review my previous book, in print or online, and the bookshops which have supported me — especially Goldsboro Books in London, No Alibis in Belfast, and Waterstones in Newry. I'd like to pay a big tribute to everyone in the crime world who's helped me, even (especially) if it was just listening to me moan about the book over a drink. Especial thanks to Peter James, Tom Harper, Declan Burke, Michael Ridpath, Will Carver, Stav Sherez, Tom Wood, Erin Kelly, Jake Kerridge, S. J. Bolton, and Elizabeth Haynes (for help with research and being generally very kind).

The town of Ballyterrin is fictional (the name translates roughly as *Border Town*), though it occupies a similar (but not identical) geographical location to my hometown of Newry. Apart from this, similarity to real people or places is unintended — although I might have stolen a few jokes off my dad. The cases in the book are also fictional, but for a chilling true-life account of Ireland's missing people, you could do worse than read *Without Trace: Ireland's Missing* by Barry Cummins.

Finally, thanks to my home crew: Oliver (for general maintenance and always being my first reader), and Eddie the beagle (for chewing through the laptop cable and burying bits of the manuscript in the garden. Not that helpful actually but good company).

If you've enjoyed the book, I'd love to hear from you. Visit my website at http://clairemcgowan.net, or find me wasting time on Twitter, where I am @inkstainsclaire.

We do hope that you have enjoyed reading
this large print book.

Did you know that all of our titles
are available for purchase?

We publish a wide range of high quality
large print books including:
Romances, Mysteries, Classics
General Fiction
Non Fiction and Westerns

Special interest titles available in
large print are:
The Little Oxford Dictionary
Music Book
Song Book
Hymn Book
Service Book

Also available from us courtesy of
Oxford University Press:
Young Readers' Dictionary
(large print edition)
Young Readers' Thesaurus
(large print edition)

For further information or a free
brochure, please contact us at:
Ulverscroft Large Print Books Ltd.,
The Green, Bradgate Road, Anstey,
Leicester, LE7 7FU, England.
Tel: (00 44) 0116 236 4325
Fax: (00 44) 0116 234 0205

PAGANINI'S GHOST

Paul Adam

It's the most exciting concert Cremona has seen in years. The headliner is a brilliant young Russian playing a violin once owned by the 19th century master, Nicolo Paganini. But the triumphal performance is immediately overshadowed by the murder of one of its sponsors. Solving the murder will require a journey into musical history — and to make that journey, Cremona's police chief will require the assistance of Gianni Castiglione, elderly charmer and only mildly larcenous expert in violins.

EYE CONTACT

Fergus McNeill

From the outside, Robert Naysmith is a successful businessman, handsome and charming. But for years he's been playing a deadly game. He doesn't choose his victims. Each is selected at random — the first person to make eye contact after he begins 'the game' will not have long to live. Their fate is sealed. When the body of a young woman is found on Severn Beach, Detective Inspector Harland is assigned the case. It's only when he links it to an unsolved murder in Oxford that the police begin to guess at the awful scale of the crimes. But how do you find a killer who strikes without motive?

A CHRISTMAS GARLAND

Anne Perry

1857: Lieutenant Victor Narraway arrives at a battered military base at Cawnpore just two weeks before Christmas, but no one is celebrating: they have been betrayed. A soldier under arrest for dereliction of duty killed a guard and escaped to join the rebels, taking crucial information that led to the massacre of nine men on patrol. Someone must have helped him, and medical orderly John Tallis is the only man unaccounted for at the time. He is now on trial for his life, and Narraway is commanded to defend him. The British Army needs justice to be carried out in full, and there seems no doubt of Tallis's guilt. But Narraway cannot see any motive for his actions. Will an innocent man hang before Christmas?

BONES ARE FOREVER

Kathy Reichs

When a newborn baby is found wedged in a vanity cabinet in a run-down apartment near Montreal, Dr. Temperance Brennan is called to investigate. There, she discovers the mummified remains of two more babies within the same property. Autopsies reveal that the children had died of unnatural causes, and the hunt is now on for a young mother with a seedy past. The trail leads Tempe to Yellowknife, a desolate diamond-mining town on the edge of the Arctic Circle. Now, she faces more questions, more secrets and more dead bodies. Taking risks and working alone, Tempe refuses to give up until she has discovered why the babies died. But in such a hostile environment, can she avoid being the next victim?